THE CROSSING

THE CROSSING

LAURIE JANEY

Gemsquash Press

ISBN 9798357291981

Edited by Tallulah Lucy, Cat Hellisen and Nerine Dorman.

Typeset in Minion Pro and Trade Gothic by Namkwan Cho.
Cover design by Namkwan Cho.
Cover illustration by Lindsay van Blerk.

All applicable content warnings and further information can be found at www.lauriejaney.com/thecrossing

For Amy.

PART 1

THE ROOTS

CHAPTER 1

Somewhere in the deep forest lay a valuable corpse, and it was Berro's job to find it. He didn't know anything about this dead person, only that they'd arrived, and they needed to be collected and transported, discreetly and respectfully, to the laboratory at field unit 4. He'd been supplied with a set of coordinates. With his slab fixed to the handlebar of his academy-issue monocraft, the digital map pin pulsing pink in the corner of the screen, he left the lamplight of the settlement behind him and plunged into the gathering dusk.

Birds sang sleepily in the branches overhead and glowflies bobbed and glittered in the undergrowth – a gentle summer evening. The forest thrummed with life, but Berro was thinking about death.

He'd seen his mother's body five years ago. She'd looked much the same in death as she had in the months preceding it, only more still. He hadn't touched her, so he didn't know what the dead felt like, though he could imagine it – cold, stiff, inert. He didn't know if the body in the forest would be like hers, a neat, sad package that could be fed ceremoniously into a mulching machine or a hole in the ground. Perhaps it would be more like a corpse from the war – broken, strewn about in public places with limbs at impossible angles, pieces missing, faces contorted in hatred and fear.

He brought up some war images on the slab and shuddered as his eyes flicked between them and the tangled path ahead, gut clenching sickly with the knowledge he might be faced with one of these horrors in the flesh at any moment. Would he be sufficiently desensitised by then? He didn't trust himself to have a dignified reaction, but he'd come prepared in a practical sense, so he was confident he'd complete his task successfully no matter how his mind and stomach behaved. His backpack held all the necessary gear to deal with a war corpse: liquid-proof bags and gloves, a trowel, chemical salts to dissolve any lingering traces, a spare blue uniform in case he soiled his own, and a compact, fold-out trailer to attach to the back of his monocraft for transporting his findings to the field unit. He'd also packed some moist wipes and a tincture for nausea, just in case.

The wickerwood trees drew the shadows of dusk around themselves like blankets and Berro wove between them, racing the last light, forging a path through the scrub. His speed made the air sting his eyes and punch at his ears, hissing in chorus with the mono's engine. For a moment there was another sound too, in the near distance – a single sharp syllable in three-part harmony. It was gone before Berro was sure he'd heard it at all, and the thumping of his heart against his eardrums took over. His mouth was as dry as his eyes were wet.

He flicked aside the awful images on his screen to see the map, his dot closing in rapidly on the coordinates. As he dropped his speed, the roar in his ears dropped with it. The forest inhaled.

Seconds later, the mono broke through into a wide, uncluttered clearing, twilit, the gap in the canopy above revealing the first stars pinging out between dusty ribbons of cloud. In the very centre of the clearing stood a tall mossy rock, its location and positioning so precise and improbable that it must have been placed there by people long ago, for purposes unknown.

And there, right beside this rock, was the corpse.

Except she wasn't a corpse at all.

Berro brought the mono to a sudden, inelegant halt, tripping off the footboard to stand, reeling, his mouth open.

She crouched, shoulders curled inwards, palms flat in the dirt, staring at Berro with eyes so wide the whites of them were clearly visible in the dim light.

Was she a new academy rival, there to thwart his efforts and sabotage his reputation? He swiftly dismissed this idea. This person wasn't from the academy. Her clothes were ridiculous – too tight and too loud – and she had outlandish sparkling ornaments dangling from her earlobes. They were twice as long and three times as shiny as any earrings he'd seen before.

She was not from here.

None of his equipment was useful for dealing with a live person. *A live person.* The immensity of the truth crashed through him like an avalanche: here was a live crosser – the first live crosser in living memory.

Berro approached her as one would a wild animal, cautiously and with an effort to appear as neither predator nor prey.

'Greetings…' he said, hating his deep voice and his big body. He tried to soften his brow, which he knew to be heavy and severe by default, but it was no use. The crosser made a sound like a dying thing and tried to get away from him, stumbling and scrambling around the rock, her braided hair whipping her in the face.

The attempt was pathetic, and Berro caught up to her in a few strides, taking hold of her arm without any effort at all. She was hampered by fear and impractical clothing, her face a mess of snot and tears – and blood too, from a small wound just below her hair-line. She didn't resist him. She sagged in his grip, overcome, and he felt worse than he would've if she'd tried to kick him or bite him or gouge his eyes out with her fingernails.

Maintaining a loose grip on her arm with one large hand, Berro picked the linga from his forehead and transferred it to hers so he could placate her and give her instructions. She flinched as the tiny silver disc touched her skin and became flush with it, glinting in the fading light.

'I'm not going to hurt you,' Berro said. 'Everything is going to be fine. Don't panic.' He cringed at the panic in his own voice. 'What's your name?'

He released his grip on her arm and gnawed his bottom lip, waiting for her to run. She swayed and heaved once, curling forward against a wave of horror, or misery, or simple nausea, but then, to Berro's immense relief, she steadied herself, swallowed and answered his question.

'Kathleen Star Sibanda-Katz.'

The look in her eyes and the sound of her voice were as defeated as her posture. Berro burned with guilt. The crosser's accent was strange and so was her name, if indeed that was her name. She didn't ask for his name in return, but he gave it to her anyway.

'I'm Berrovan. It's an honour to meet you. You— You must be terrified. And confused. But everything's going to be fine. You just need to trust me.'

She said something then in a strange language, a rapid string of sharp noises separated by warped vowels, pitching up at the ends of phrases.

'I can't understand you,' Berro explained. 'You have my…' He pointed at her forehead, and she ran her fingers over the linga, her face betraying fear, bewilderment, disbelief. Her world did not have access to anything like marrowcore tech, that much was clear.

Still, she seemed reasonably civilised and in control of her faculties, and Berro was surprised by this. The barbarity of cultures from other streams was well documented through evidence found on dead crossers in the past: war corpses, mostly, like the ones in the images.

Whatever culture this crosser had fallen out of must have room to accommodate weak, stupidly dressed people. Perhaps she was a member of their ruling elite, torn from her throne by the downtrodden masses and traumatised through a crack in the world.

He needed to keep her quiet and inconspicuous. Removing the garish earrings was the first step. She protested this instruction, but unconvincingly, and removed them herself when Berro pressed the matter. He pulled the spare uniform from his backpack and presented it to her, commanding her to discard her bright top and ridiculous jewel-studded trousers. Her protest against this demand was far more convincing, even though he couldn't understand a word of it. He was startled when her tears brimmed over and, fearing she was going to make too much noise, he raised his hands in surrender and suggested she put the uniform on over her clothes instead.

She nodded, shivering, and did as he said. She wasn't a slender person and the uniform fit snugly around her abdomen and thighs, but it was far too long. Berro rolled up the legs and arms for her while she twitched in fear under his hands. He felt like he was outside of himself, watching the scene – his incompetent clone, bumbling and stupid with anguish, trying to wrest control of a situation for which he was wholly unprepared. He wished he'd read about trauma and theories on cross-stream dislocation en route instead of looking at pictures of mangled bodies. *Stupid, stupid, stupid.*

The blue uniform was an ill-fitting disguise, and her comically bulky white synthetic shoes were bound to draw curious gazes, even at sundown. He didn't rate his chances of convincing her to go barefoot, so after a brief explanation he crouched down again and smeared her shoes with mud. A couple of her tears splashed onto the back of his shaven head as he did so.

'Kathleenstarsibandacats,' Berro said, standing slowly. 'I need to take my linga back for a moment. Please… please don't try to run. Everything will be fine, I promise. But only if you do as I say.' An unintended threat. It was too late to take it back.

The crosser nodded again, cowering, and wiped her eyes. Sufficiently reassured that she wasn't going to scramble away into the jaws of a shadowcat, Berro picked the linga from her forehead and put it back onto his own. He didn't really need it to speak to Undra, given they were both fluent speakers of the same two languages, but he didn't want the crosser to understand the conversation. He slipped his pod from his pocket and brought up Undra's comlink.

'Berrovan,' said Undra, his voice so loud and distinct in the held-breath quietness of the clearing that both Berro and the crosser jumped slightly. 'Is everything all right?'

'Yes, Imparter, better than that, actually,' said Berro. 'The crosser… she's alive.'

There was a pause, and Berro couldn't dodge the stab of disappointment at Undra's lack of an immediate and enthusiastic exclamation at his report.

'Alive,' said Undra, voice breathy with awe. This was, Berro had to admit, more in character than a dramatic gasp or a yell of surprise, and he was gratified by it. 'Bring her to the field unit immediately. And please don't let anyone see her.'

'Of course, Imparter,' said Berro. 'I've put her into an academy uniform. We should be able to get to you without drawing any attention.'

'Good. Excellent,' said Undra, and Berro heard the distinctive scrape of his chair as he pushed it back from his desk before the link terminated.

The crosser's eyes glistened in the gathering gloom, but they weren't wide anymore. She'd narrowed them, and she didn't seem as frightened as she'd been just moments before. Her lips were pressed together and her face set with grim determination – and something else, too. Curiosity.

'You can understand me now?' she said, touching a finger to her bare forehead.

Berro slipped his pod back into his pocket and inclined his head.

'What's your language? What is it called?'

An unexpected question so early in the interrogation. 'Varrea,' said Berro. He wanted to tell her more, about how most of the locals spoke Kastak as a primary language and how he was an exception to the rule… about how nobody ever showed any interest in his language because, with their lingas, they'd only ever interpreted it as their own. About how that made him feel.

It was as if she could sense his desire to speak as she reached out and pointed at his forehead with a brave finger.

'Can you put that magic thing back on my face?' she said. 'I want to know what's going on. And please, call me Kath.'

• • •

With the linga on Kath's forehead, and Kath staring at him in nervous expectation, Berro was briefly lost for words. He felt deeply impressed with the way Kath was handling the situation and, by contrast, utterly ashamed of his own behaviour. Instead of exuding confidence and authority, he was hesitant, awkward, and sweating profusely.

'We don't have time to stand here and get to know each other,' said Berro. 'I'm sorry. I need to get you to the field unit.'

Kath touched a fingertip to the small wound on her head and winced. She said something Berro couldn't understand.

'I'll talk to you while we ride.' He gestured at the mono lying discarded in the dirt. 'But the conversation will be very one-sided until I can get another linga.'

Kath said something else, and Berro sensed it was a question.

'I'll get you everything you need,' he said. 'You don't need to worry about anything. Can we… is it all right if we go now?'

Kath nodded, and Berro nodded back. He swiped his sweaty palms against the legs of his uniform, hefted his backpack onto his front and hauled the fallen mono upright. Kath mounted the mono behind him without prompting. She seemed reluctant to put her arms around his waist, holding tentatively onto the bag straps around his shoulders instead, but he started the vehicle with a small lurch that made her grab onto him properly out of necessity.

He rode at a brisk but controlled speed, not wanting to draw the attention of any evening walkers or tree-climbers. He imagined

Undra growing more and more impatient with each passing minute, muttering about Berro's failure to be the gifted protege he'd hoped for. The thought wrinkled Berro's brow for a moment. He needed to stop thinking this way, stop denting his own confidence. Already it was affecting his performance. Undra knew who he was, and what he was capable of. That was why he'd trusted Berro with this task in the first place. The man was a brilliant imparter, not one to make decisions lightly, and it was disrespectful to indulge in this sort of uncharitable speculation about his private thoughts. He wasn't pacing or muttering. He wasn't a tetchy, petty person. In all likelihood, Undra was sitting perfectly composed behind his desk in the field unit, flicking through articles on his slab with one hand while the other one alternated between lifting a mug of chayberry tea to his lips and thoughtfully stroking his smooth, shapely chin.

Berro kept to the outskirts of the settlement, following narrow unlit paths crowded on both sides by densely tangled undergrowth that reached leafy tendrils across the ground. The settlement's eco-lamps were beginning to glow between the trees as the last of the daylight faded to purplegrey behind the silhouette blackness of the canopy. The mono hummed and whined, stirring the leaves in its wake.

Kath said something in her bizarre language, and Berro remembered his promise of talking while riding.

'That's the Wooden Hill settlement,' said Berro, taking a wild guess at what she wanted to know. 'We need to keep you secret here, at least for a while, or we'll have crowds of people fussing over you, and I'm sure you want that even less than we do. You're a very rare discovery.'

The lamps glowed richly as the darkness settled. Pedestrians and the odd mono moved along the main paths in the distance, shapes blurred, voices indistinct. Insects creaked and chittered in the undergrowth.

'Imparter Undra will have the answers to all your questions,' said

Berro. 'He's the most brilliant academic studying the crossing phenomenon. I'm his primary assistant.'

Several students had applied to assist Undra in this confidential project, two had been selected, and Berro alone had been offered additional responsibilities on condition that he didn't tell the other assistant – or anyone else – about them. A covert hierarchy, with Berro at the top. It was a sweet victory, especially given the other assistant was Ryndel, his academic rival. He couldn't keep the pride out of his voice as he told Kath about this achievement. Not only was Undra a celebrated imparter, but he was also running to be the settlement's council representative, a contest he'd surely win, if not on the basis of his reputation, then certainly through the power of charisma. The man was born to lead, and he was perhaps the only person Berro was eager to follow.

Berro hoped these credentials would put Kath at ease, knowing she was in safe and capable hands. Kath made another questioning sound.

'You're a crosser,' said Berro. 'You've passed from one world into another one. It's a rare thing. And you're alive – that's almost unheard of.' Kath said nothing. What had he hoped for? That she would be pleased? Proud? Excited to have lost everything, and to be in the company of an oversized stranger in an unfamiliar place with no choice in the matter?

'You're following what I'm saying, right? You understand? Poke me if you understand.'

A moment of hesitation, then slim fingertip jabbed him between the ribs, and his answering ticklish twitch caused the mono to lurch and wobble. He quickly regained his driveline and cleared his throat, grateful that Kath couldn't see his face.

'I'm sorry,' he said, stiffly. 'I don't want to overwhelm you right away. As I said, Imparter Undra will explain...'

Kath trembled against his back, and he twisted the handlebar, picking up speed.

Field unit 4 stood in a clearing about a leap away from the main academy grounds. At first glance, it looked like a massive ramshackle storage shed, but further inspection revealed its academy affiliation. The fence around it was not perfunctory. The fenceposts were heavy and close together to keep animals out, and the gate had a pod lock, opening only for approved academy students and imparters. At present, the only two people with access codes for this unit were Undra and Berro.

The structure itself was surrounded by tangled brush and young trees, obscuring the high windows such that passersby might not notice the reinforced greenglass and strong, sealed frames. This was not a shed vulnerable to parasites or infestations. It wasn't a place to store shovels or monocraft parts. Unit 4, like the other nine field units, was a place of research and study. *And secrets.*

Around the back of the building where the ground met the wall, a discreet hatch opened into a large chute. Berro had been instructed to place the body of the deceased crosser into this chute, allowing it to slide into the underground laboratory sprawling below. Luckily for Kath, she'd be entering the unit via the front door instead.

Kath's weight began to push more heavily against Berro's back, and she shook slightly now as she clung onto him. Fatigue, perhaps, or the shock of the crossing catching up with her. She hadn't said a word in some time.

'Are you feeling all right?' Berro asked, and she groaned in response.

He could see the field unit through the trees ahead. Not far, now. The perimeter lamps were off, but soft light spilled out through the greenglass windows. Undra was in there, waiting for him. Berro's heart thumped against his ribs. He was so focussed on his destination and on Kath's silent, heavy presence behind him that he failed to see two figures on the side of the path ahead until one of them stepped out in front of him.

CHAPTER 2

'Berro!'

Virda leapt sideways with an impressive roll across the dirt to avoid being run over. The back end of the mono fishtailed out to the side, and Berro stumbled from the footboard, catching Kath under the arm to keep her from falling into the dirt like a sack of squash.

Virda rushed over to help, spewing apologies, but Berro shooed her away, his shock already giving way to anger. Under the anger was something like despair, and he postponed it by allowing his blood to boil freely.

'This is a *really* bad time,' he hissed, tugging the mono off the path into the thicker darkness between the trees, where Jex stood with his hand over his mouth, eyes big as moons. Kath flinched as Berro removed the silver dot from her forehead and put it back onto his own. Through gritted teeth, he said, 'What are you doing here?'

'Looking for you, obviously,' said Virda, though there was nothing obvious about it. Virda and Jex had other friends besides Berro. Apart from their mutual friends, they also had their tight-knit community of student tree-climbers who met up almost daily to scramble around in the forest canopy and smoke wickerbloom together. Perhaps they'd already finished their climb for the day and needed a new source of entertainment.

Virda had two twigs and a leaf caught in her hair, and Berro itched to pluck them out because they looked stupid, but he didn't want to risk appearing affectionate. He was livid.

'Who is this?' Virda smiled at Kath. The smile faltered immediately. 'Why is she bleeding? Why is her uniform— Berro, what's going on here?'

He wasn't prepared for this. He glanced towards the field unit and then pulled the mono further out of sight, as though Undra might be watching him disapprovingly through a gap in the fenceposts. 'This is Kath. I'm taking her to meet Imparter Undra.'

'Is she… a crosser?' said Jex, and Virda took an audible breath. It wasn't quite a gasp, but near enough.

'Oh, gods, she *is* a crosser, isn't she?'

'Nobody's meant to know.'

Virda and Jex gawped at Kath, who leaned back heavily against a tree before sliding down onto her backside and letting out a small sob. Her face looked wrong, puffier and blotchier than Berro remembered. Virda dropped down to one knee in front of her and lifted a tentative hand, but couldn't seem to decide where to place it, so she pulled it away instead and rounded on Berro with a face like thunder.

'Berro, you can't take her to Undra. She's ill. She needs the infirmary.'

Berro pinched his nose between thumb and forefinger. 'I have strict instructions to bring her to the field unit. You need to leave now and pretend you never saw me.'

'Likely,' said Jex, with a humourless laugh. He dragged his fingers through his pale, shaggy hair and glanced sidelong at Virda. She was back on her feet and stood stiff and taut, thrumming with potential energy, ready to snap into unpredictable action.

'We'll help you get her to the infirma—'

'*No*,' said Berro, and scrubbed his knuckles across his face. 'No. She can't go to the infirmary. Nobody can know she's here.'

'Why not?' said Virda. 'And it's too late anyway. We've seen her.'

Her mouth formed a straight line, her eyebrows met in the middle, and Berro knew he was in trouble.

'Virda, *please*. Please don't do this now.'

Kath's face dropped between her knees and her hands went over her ears to block out their incomprehensible bickering. She winced, as if each utterance was a projectile aimed straight at her head.

Virda ploughed on. 'Does Undra have a bed in the field unit for her to rest on? Something clean for her to wear that actually fits? A bit of frigram soup in a beaker? Of course he doesn't. I bet he doesn't even eat soup. I bet he survives on laxatives and the blind adoration of students like you.'

'Virda—'

'She has a point, Berro,' said Jex, 'even if she's being a waspik about it. Just tell Undra the crosser was unwell, so you took her to the infirmary.'

Berro's face slackened. He shook his head. 'Jex, you have absolutely no idea how this works.'

Jex gave an exaggerated shrug, palms up, carefree, and Berro wanted to grab him by the shoulders and shake his short, wiry little body until he stopped being so casual, so dismissive of important things he didn't understand.

Virda crouched beside the crosser again. 'You're wasting time, Berro,' she said. 'I think she's about to pass out.'

'No, *you're* wasting time,' Berro snapped, stepping decisively between them and helping Kath to her feet with gentle urgency. 'Undra is more qualified than anyone else to care for her, and I'm taking her to the field unit, and that's the end of it. If you tell anyone about what you've seen, I'll just… Please don't. Please. I'll explain everything as soon as I can. I'll speak to you later, or in the morning, or— Just please, don't do it.'

Berro guided Kath back onto the mono, in front of him this time, so he could support her. She was shaking hard, and it was more than fear; she was clearly unwell – Virda was right about that. Ignoring the protests of his friends, he brought the mono back to life, one arm securing Kath around her waist and the other gripping the handlebar.

Virda glared. The two twigs in her hair had shifted just enough to resemble a pair of fine horns, and she looked ready to charge Berro with them. 'This has to be a Code violation,' she said, loudly.

'Does the Code even apply to her?' said Jex. 'If she's not Rhetari—'

'Probably not. Maybe she qualifies as an extra-Rhetari resource or something. This is huge, you realise that, Berro?' The last words were all but shouted at Berro's retreating form as he manoeuvred the mono back onto the path, and he cringed at the volume.

'Of course I realise that!' he barked. 'I'll speak to you later.'

Virda let out one of her awfully specific Virda noises – something between a grunt and a growl – and called out, 'I hope you know what you're doing!'

• • •

Berro knew what he was doing. He was doing what Undra told him to, and this was the right course of action.

Virda had assumed correctly that there was no bed in the field unit, but there was a softseat – bed-like enough – and Undra helped Berro to lay the crosser onto it. She was barely able to stand, shaking uncontrollably, her face slick with sweat, her pupils blown. She no longer seemed aware of what was going on around her. Berro placed a cushion under her head and covered her with two thick blankets extracted from a storage cabinet.

'It's environment shock,' said Undra, poking a syringe into a small glass bottle of dark liquid. Berro gently turned Kath's head to the side, moved her thick braids and swabbed the clammy skin of her neck. She didn't flinch as the needle pressed into her skin.

Berro quickly placed an adhesive bandage over the puncture as Undra withdrew the needle.

'How long will it take?'

'Five, ten minutes to stabilise. Then she'll need to sleep it off for a while. She'll be fine. You did well, getting her here so quickly.'

Berro drew a breath, considered his options. He wanted to be trusted and to be worthy of that trust, so he chose honesty. 'Imparter, I was seen.'

'You were seen?' Undra straightened.

'By two of my friends. For some reason they were out looking for me. They saw the crosser.'

'And they knew she was a crosser?'

'Yes. They know what I'm studying, and they were quick to guess. Her uh, *otherness* is quite obvious, up close, and I was right near to the field unit.'

Also, they know I only have a small handful of friends, and it was more likely that the person I was travelling with across the forest had fallen into our world from another reality than that I'd met someone new in a social situation and made a good enough impression for them to consent to a doubled-up ride on a monocraft after dark.

Undra didn't need to know that.

The subtle changes in Undra's face would've gone undetected by almost everyone, but Berro had spent enough time with the man, enough time idolising him and obsessing over his life and work, that he read the changes as though they were painted on with a thick brush. Undra eased himself onto the chair behind his large desk, and Berro took the seat opposite. A pad of ecopaper was open between them, and Berro could see some fascinating scribbles he would've asked about had he not been in a state of shame.

Undra pressed his lips together. His eyes were chips of winter sky beneath the silky flop of his fringe. He maintained a boyish look that, combined with the first streaks of silvery grey hair and smile lines, made him look both approachable and respectable, youthful and wise. Berro could see his disappointment, controlled but clear, in the set of his mouth and brows, and it filled him with misery. He didn't expect Undra to ask for details of the exchange between him and his friends, but he almost wished he would, so he could explain, set the scene, make the imparter understand how unexpected and unavoidable it had been. But Undra knew everything he needed to know, and he knew Berro would disclose any details that were relevant, and Berro, in turn, knew that babbling on and on in an attempt at self-justification would not reflect well on him. He was precise and efficient in his work and in his communication. This was why Undra had selected him.

'I've told them to keep quiet about it, and they will; they're old, trusted friends. I'll go to them right now, to reiterate the importance—'

'Please do, Berrovan. If the whole settlement finds out we have a live crosser, it will be Rheta-wide in hours, distro journalists swarming around the unit.' He shuddered. 'We need to finish this study without fanfare and politics getting in the way. It's better for us if she's a secret for now, and it's better for her too. I'm sure your friends will understand.'

Berro nodded emphatically. 'Yes, Imparter. They will.'

Undra's face softened, and Berro relaxed a little. This wasn't a disaster. He could salvage the situation. Undra was depending on him, and he could – he *would* – prove himself. Again. He cast a look at Kath sleeping soundly on the softseat, face smooth and peaceful now. Her chest rose and fell with deep, even breaths.

'Thank you, Imparter,' Berro said. 'Are there any deliveries you'd like me to collect tomorrow?'

Undra flicked a finger across the screen of his slab. 'Yes, in fact, there is one,' he said. 'Just a small one.'

'I'll collect it first thing,' said Berro. The imparter smiled and tapped his slab, sending over details.

Berro rose to leave but Undra stopped him halfway with a slightly raised hand – 'Oh, one more thing,' – and Berro sank back into the chair.

Undra's eyes were warm, creased in the corners, his lips hitched up to one side in a shrewd, intimate smile. The heat rose in Berro's neck and ears.

'Trust your instincts,' said Undra.

He held Berro's gaze. A breeze rattled the branches against one of the greenglass windows, and Berro sat still for a long moment, trying to read between the lines when there was only one line, and his mind was too messy to make much of it.

'Yes, Imparter,' he said, nodding. He got to his feet, which felt as unsteady as pointed stilts despite their length and breadth and the sturdy academy boots encasing them.

With one last glance at the sleeping crosser, Berro stepped out of the field unit and into the dark, closing the door behind him as carefully as he could. Things had gone better with Undra than he'd thought they would, but still he felt jittery with nerves. Outside the perimeter gate, he took a moment to squeeze his eyes shut, swallow hard against the tightness in his throat, and breathe a few deep, calming breaths.

Despite it being midsummer, there was a chill in the air. Berro's anxious sweat cooled quickly on his skin. He rubbed his arms. Somewhere in the branches overhead, a moontuk pierced the silence with a plaintive wail that terminated in a feathery commotion, followed by a deeper silence than before. A shiver ran the length of Berro's body. With his jaw set and his shoulders high, he stepped onto his mono and set off towards the treehouse. He wasn't looking forward to the conversation he needed to have with Virda, but he was quite ready for the hot tea that would come with it.

• • •

The wickerwood tree stood tall and proud, holding the treehouse in its woody fingers as though offering it up for praise. *Look at what I have here! Isn't it marvellous?*

It wasn't, really. It was a battered old thing, in need of a scrub and a fresh coat of sealant. Blue and yellow lichen bearded the windows, leaf mulch clogged the gutters along the roof edge, and the door handle was tarnished a deep, mottled brown, with streaks of rusty colour staining the weathered wood beneath it. Parts of the warped railing along the balcony looked at risk of coming loose in the next big storm.

Someone had left the balcony lamp on, presumably expecting Berro to arrive, and the shabby details of the treehouse appeared spotlit, more glaringly ugly than they were during the day when the sunlight shifting through the soft leaves gave it a more homely, organic appearance. The treehouse wasn't much, but it was Berro's home away from the academy dormitory, and three of his four friends lived here. With the neighbouring treehouses mostly hidden behind the lush summer foliage of their own trees, the place felt pleasantly isolated, even though it was situated at a junction of busy branch paths through the settlement.

Virda must've heard the approach of his monocraft – her face loomed at the kitchen window. Even from this distance below her, and without any special ability to read the marrow of the world around him, Berro recognised the severity of Virda's mood, and he felt faintly sick at the prospect of having to argue about the crosser. Virda had always been a prickly, combative person, at least as long as Berro had known her, but she didn't often have cause to direct this level of anger at him. The last time she'd been truly infuriated with him was during a political argument about the ethics of Rheta's reformatory system, which Berro should've known to avoid engaging in.

Virda and Jex had grown up together in a commune outside of Wooden Hill, and both spoke of their childhood with nothing but warmth and fondness, apart from that one significant sour note: the removal of one of their so-called commune cousins, Shani, to the reformatory many years ago, for reasons unknown. Since Virda's initial telling of the story, and the ensuing argument with Berro, she'd never brought it up in conversation again and would quickly change the subject if someone mentioned it, but Berro knew she was still hurt, still angry, still confused about whatever had happened to Shani.

Perhaps this explained her emotional reaction to the crosser, a particular sensitivity to the plight of anyone who'd been removed from their home without any control over the situation. Or maybe it was just another case of Virda getting worked up about a perceived injustice. She always seemed to have her ears pricked and eyes peeled for it, ready to leap to someone's defence – with more anger and energy than necessary – if she believed herself to be on the side of good.

The front door creaked open, and Magrin's cheerful face popped out, her braids wrapped in a colourful headscarf. She grinned at Berro. 'What are you waiting for? Need me to send the lift down?'

The treehouse was fitted with a rickety lift because the steep stairs were unsafe for Magrin with her prosthetic leg. Berro smiled back up at her and shook his head.

He tucked the mono behind the stairs and tramped his way up, feeling the familiar unsettling pull of gravity at his back as he reached the balcony.

'Virda's in a mood,' Magrin murmured as she opened the door wider to admit him. 'Please don't make it worse. The birds can't stand people yelling.'

Berro kicked his boots off into the box behind the door and stepped into the low-lit mingle room separating the treehouse's two bedrooms. A small, open-plan kitchen occupied the front corner to his right and Virda stood there behind the wooden counter, pouring berry tea into four rustic mugs through a wire strainer with a bent handle. Her face was grim. She didn't have a naturally gentle face – all her features were too large and loud, and her wide mouth curled more easily into sneers than smiles. Still, her hazel eyes warmed as Berro greeted her, his own smile and voice infused with as much affection and apology as he could muster.

When she got to the fourth mug, Virda took the strainer away and allowed the tea to pour out with the pulpy bits of chayberry included.

'Grab two of these,' she said, and they ferried the mugs over to the softseat, where Magrin had settled herself beside a rather sleepy-looking Jex. While the rest of them wore their academy colours – Berro in blue, Magrin in red and Virda in green – Jex had shed his own green uniform for a single-piece white sleepsuit with large wooden buttons at the front, none of which were fastened, exposing much more of Jex's body than Berro cared to see. He was attractive, certainly, but Berro wasn't interested in what he had to offer and was always irritated by his love of flagrant nudity.

The string of little lights pinned up against the wall behind Jex's head made his hair look softly golden and his complexion pale and smooth, and the overall impression was of an oversized baby intruding on a meeting of adults.

'Hey, Berro.' He yawned. 'How's the crosser?'

Naturally, inevitably, they'd told Magrin about the encounter, and it was just as inevitable that they'd tell Fessi. Being keenly attuned to the marrow in a way that none of the others were, Fessi would likely figure it out for herself anyway.

'So you've been brought up to date,' Berro said to Magrin, handing her a mug as Jex took the pulpy tea from Virda. Jex, ever contrary, enjoyed having potent berry bits floating in his drink. He described his tea preference as 'chewy', which never failed to enrage Berro.

'Yes,' said Magrin in a hushed, reverent voice. 'What a thing.'

Virda shoved herself onto the softseat at Jex's side. She was bigger than him, and she squashed him quite thoroughly, but he didn't seem to mind.

Berro took one of the chairs opposite, a low table between them, like he was facing a panel of inquiry. 'Have you told Fessi yet?'

'No, but you can't expect us not to!' Virda snapped. A rasping screech came from the direction of Magrin's bedroom, and Magrin flapped her hands at Virda.

'Shhhhh! He doesn't like it!'

'What are you keeping in there?' asked Berro. Magrin sometimes attempted to justify housing a menagerie of creatures in her room as part of her studies at the academy, but most of her supposedly temporary fosters ended up being permanent pets, each with an intricate, custom-made excuse as to why it wouldn't be fair to release them back into the wild. This bird sound was new.

'He's a vollop chick,' said Magrin as Virda pressed her thumbs into her eyes. Berro sensed a fresh history of conflict around this topic and decided to steer clear. He suspected his sympathies would lie with Virda, as it couldn't possibly be a good idea to keep a large, powerful bird of prey cooped up inside a treehouse, even if it was still a juvenile.

'Anyway,' he said. 'No, Virda, I wouldn't expect you keep it from Fessi. That wouldn't be fair. Or practical. But maybe I should tell her myself.'

'So, how is the crosser?' Jex asked again, blowing the steam off his tea, his big blue eyes peering over the mug.

'She's asleep,' said Berro. 'Environment shock, unsurprisingly. Undra inoculated her. She'll be sleeping it off for a while, but she's fine.'

'So, there's a bed in field unit?' asked Virda, quietly this time to avoid the ire of the vollop and its keeper.

'No,' he said. 'But there's a nice big softseat and lots of blankets. It's a temporary solution.'

'Blooming.' Virda narrowed her eyes. 'I have a lot of questions.'

'And I can't answer most of them. It's an important thing that's just happened, and I'm right in the middle of it. You need to trust that I know what I'm doing, and I'll look out for her. For Kath – that's her name. It was a long, strange name, actually, but I can't remember all of it now. She gave me a shortened version to use.'

Magrin's face lit up and she leaned forward. 'She isn't feral?'

Her naked curiosity was far preferable to Virda's faintly hostile suspicion, and Berro was immensely grateful for her presence.

'Not at all,' he said.

Jex chewed his mouthful of tea and swallowed noisily. 'She seemed very normal when we saw her.' The mere moments he'd spent in Kath's company, in the dark, without speaking to her, were apparently enough for him to make a valuable judgement worth contributing to the discussion.

'Yes,' said Virda. 'Normal and scared and sick and needing to be cared for, not studied like an interesting stool sample.'

Berro wondered if this was what Virda thought was happening to her cousin Shani, locked up in the reformatory at White Peaks. If so, Shani probably deserved it. People weren't removed to the reformatory for nothing. It wasn't a thought he had any intention of ever saying out loud.

Instead, he said, 'We are caring for her, Virda, I promise. I'll be back at the field unit in the morning to find out what happens next.'

'And you'll tell us what Undra says?'

'I'll tell you as much as I can. You know I can't tell you everything.'

'Like how you knew where to find her or what in the hells Undra is actually doing in the field unit.'

'Yes,' said Berro.

It wasn't worth explaining to Virda that even though he knew more about the study than any other student at the academy – most of whom weren't aware of the study at all – he was still profoundly ignorant on the topic. Undra had told him only what he needed to know; the imparter had some special drones he sent out to 'scan for marric anomalies' and he'd come by the coordinates in this way, but Berro knew nothing at all about how the scans worked or how the anomalies manifested. This was a sensitive and important project, bearing the weight of Undra's stellar reputation. Trust had to be earned, and Berro was excited but impatient to earn it.

'I want to know what's going to happen to her once you're done studying her,' said Virda.

Berro shifted in his seat. 'Well, I had an idea.' It was a thought that had been tumbling around in his head since he'd left the field unit. 'What if the crosser stayed here?'

Three silent faces blinked at him.

'Undra knows you saw her, he listened when I told him my friends are trustworthy, there's an empty bed in Magrin's room...'

Magrin wrinkled her nose, Jex's pale eyebrows crept further and further up his forehead, and Virda's mouth pulled pensively to one side. She drained her tea, placed her mug on the table, and brought a hand up to her short, roughly cut hair, twisting the brown strands around her fingers.

'You think Undra would agree to that?' she asked.

'If you thought it was a good idea, I'm sure I could convince him.' Berro shrugged. 'She's a secret for now, but she'll need to integrate eventually. I can't think of a better way to do that than putting her with some locals. I'll get her a slab and a pod, but learning by immersion is far better than reading articles in isolation. She has a whole new world to figure out. And she'll need friends.'

'She'd be all right with my animals?' asked Magrin.

Berro shrugged again. 'She's not feral, like we said. She won't kill them with her bare hands and eat them. And anyway, she could sleep on the softseat if she didn't want to share a room with a vollop.'

'I think it's a good idea,' said Virda.

'Could I think it about it a bit more?' said Magrin, looking slightly fretful.

'Of course,' said Berro. 'There's no rush.'

'Well, I'm up for it,' said Jex. 'Sounds interesting.'

'What does she look like?' asked Magrin, and Berro was relieved to have a straightforward question to answer.

'Uh, she's kind of short, fat, dark brown skin, looks like she might be a bit younger than us, maybe even still a teenager. She has braids similar to yours, Mag, except thicker. She's nice-looking, I guess, but she had the weirdest clothes I've ever seen. All sorts of horrible synthetic sparkly stuff.'

This description seemed to put Magrin more at ease, but not

entirely. Magrin had always been more comfortable around animals than people she didn't know. She was the most quintessentially 'red' student Berro had ever met. She attended her lectures if none of her friends had signed up for them – mostly those pertaining to very specific animal biology – but Virda recorded all their mutual lectures on her pod and sent the files to Magrin so she didn't have to be there in person. Berro had first assumed that difficulties with her leg were the reason why she preferred to study at the treehouse, but she spent too much time out and about on her own in the forest for this idea to hold much water. He felt vaguely guilty for suggesting Magrin accommodate the crosser in her own room, but he was certain Magrin's instinct to look after strays would override her wariness once she met Kath in person.

'Why is she such a big secret anyway?' Magrin asked. 'Why do we have to hide her away?'

A less simple question.

'Because we don't want her mobbed by curious people before she knows how to deal with it, and Undra doesn't want his study trampled by distro journalists and self-proclaimed experts looking to get their names on the publication.'

'I suppose only the great Imparter Undra is worthy of that,' said Virda acidly.

Berro put his mug down on the table hard enough to slop tea onto the wood. He drew a small, folded towel from the breast pocket of his uniform and proceeded to wipe up the mess. 'This is a significant discovery,' he said, his words sounding rehearsed even to his own ears. 'We can't risk letting the public get involved until we've reached some conclusions. And obviously Undra wants priority here; who wouldn't? But that's not the main reason. Kath's safety—'

'Don't be ridiculous,' said Virda. 'Do you think people would tear her apart, just to see if she's put together like we are?'

'No, of course not,' Berro huffed, folding his tiny towel. He extracted a liquid-proof pouch from another pocket and slipped the towel neatly inside before putting it back. 'We just need to be cautious.'

'I don't like that Undra gets to make all the rules.'

'He's the world's foremost expert on the crossing phenomenon, and Kath is a crosser. I think he's the right person to be making the rules. And if I convince him to let her stay here, you'll be more involved in this historic event than anyone other than me. More involved than Ryndel, even. It's a bit of an honour, really.'

'I don't care about Ryndel,' said Virda. 'I care about Kath.'

'And I do too,' said Berro. 'So I'm not sure why we're arguing.'

'Virda loves to argue,' said Jex, and Virda elbowed him in the ribs.

'It's late,' she said. 'Want to sleep on the softseat?'

Berro didn't love sleeping in his uniform, nor did he love the idea of waiting for his turn in the treehouse biocloset, but staying over would mean getting to the station more efficiently for Undra's collection the next morning. Also, he was suddenly tired, bone tired, in a way he hadn't felt in ages.

'That would be good, thank you,' he said, and Virda gave a tight nod.

Magrin retreated to her room and Jex to the other one, and just before Virda followed Jex through the doorway, Berro said, 'Virda. You never told me why you were looking for me. At the field unit.'

Virda huffed. 'We haven't seen you in days, Berro. You've barely texted a word. We thought if we just intercepted you…' A small smile tugged at her mouth. 'Anyway. Sleep well.'

'You too,' said Berro, smiling back at her as she slipped away into the bedroom.

He curled onto the softseat and covered himself with the hand-woven throw draped over it. It had been made, if he remembered correctly, by Virda and Jex's commune parent, a large smiley woman he'd seen only in pictures, who Virda and Jex spoke of with unwavering devotion. He thought of his own mother – small, sharp, brilliant. Dead. His heart burned, and he curled himself smaller.

The seat was barely large enough to accommodate his body, but he was tired enough that it didn't matter.

He watched the shadows of leaves shifting in the moonlight through the front windows and listened to the *crick crick* of night-beetles, the occasional sleepy squeak or squawk from Magrin's room, and the quiet shuffles and murmurs of Virda and Jex, who would be snuggled together like a pair of ursa cubs in a den at the end of winter. The almost imperceptible swaying of the treehouse would've been soothing to anyone familiar with the sensation, but Berro was not one of them. He was used to sleeping on the bottom bunk of a bed five levels under the ground, solid and stable as anything could be. The movement drew him away from the edge of sleep, and his thoughts roamed the darkness.

Despite being surrounded by friends, loneliness gnawed at him, and he closed his eyes against the ache of it, trying to imagine how Kath would feel if she woke to find herself alone in the field unit. A strange room, in a strange forest, in a strange world. Would her determination to survive be stronger than her fear? Would her curiosity be greater than her grief? As much as Berro had loved and lost, he'd never lost everything all at once. And some of what he'd lost, he'd lost by choice. Kath had not been given any choice.

He pulled the throw tighter around himself. It smelled of his friends – the soap they washed with, the tea they spilled, the scented rub Magrin used on her leg to keep the joints supple and the greenskin soft. Berro pressed his face into the folds of the fabric and imagined other worlds, and when at last he slipped away into sleep, he dreamed of them, too.

CHAPTER 3

Fessi sat up in bed, ran her fingers through her hair a few times and settled her slab on a pillow across her knees. In the corner of the dark screen, Virda's name pulsed in time with the gentle chime that had pulled Fessi from sleep.

It was unusually early for a call from Virda. In fact, a call from Virda was unusual at any time. She preferred communicating via text. It wasn't a lack of confidence but a lack of tolerance for the rituals of politeness that voice and video demanded of her. If she called, it meant she wanted Fessi to know something and respond to it *right now*. She couldn't – and wouldn't – wait for a text response. Fessi accepted the comlink.

Virda's face filled three quarters of the screen and Jex's face filled the rest. They too were in bed, lying back against a jumble of mismatched blankets and pillows.

'Gods, how do you look so perfect when you've just woken up?' said Virda, gouging a knuckle into her left eye. Her hair was tangled and wild, and the pink impressions of pillow wrinkles crisscrossed her cheek. Jex mumbled something incoherent, his face tucked against Virda's shoulder.

'Has something happened?' Fessi asked. Something had definitely happened. She couldn't get a marric reading on her friends when they weren't physically near to her, but Virda's face was flushed with eagerness, and there was a bright intensity about her eyes.

'Yes,' said Virda. 'Berro found a live crosser. She's at the field unit now, sleeping off treatment for environment shock. Berro wants her to move into the treehouse with us.'

It was a lot of very big news crammed into very few words. Fessi was surprised, but perhaps not as surprised as Virda expected her to be.

'That explains it,' she said.

'Explains what?'

'I sensed something yesterday. A sudden flowchange in the forest. I knew something had just happened.' She observed the impatient puckering of Virda's chin and abandoned her narrative. 'It's incredible news,' she said. 'Berro must be thrilled. But why does he want her to move into the treehouse?'

'Well,' said Virda. 'They want to keep her identity secret while the project is happening, but she can't live at the field unit, obviously. It's a cack pit. Jex and I, we saw her with Berro in the forest, when he was taking her in. We weren't supposed to know about her, but since we found out anyway, Berro thinks he can make use of us. He came here last night.' Virda rolled her eyes, and Fessi made several confident assumptions about the conversation they'd had in her absence. 'She was young, the crosser,' Virda continued. 'Not feral or anything.'

Fessi took a slow breath and let her eyes flutter closed against the pulse of the world. She wished she could go back to the evening before, to the moment she'd felt the crack in reality. In her sleepy ignorance she'd dismissed it, but now she knew. A person had come through that crack. Not an empty dead thing bearing a jumble of artefacts for imparters and distro pundits to speculate over but never understand with any confidence. No. This was someone they could talk to and learn from directly. Someone with breath in their lungs and thoughts in their brain. Something occurred to Fessi then, an idea so fully formed and obvious in its correctness that she didn't hesitate to share it with Virda.

'The crosser should live here,' she said. 'At the lakehouse.'

Fessi lived with her mother in the house on the island in the middle of Wooden Hill's only lake. Her family had held the role of ecological monitors of the lake resources for many years; nobody else was particularly interested in the job, which was best carried out from their uniquely isolated location. They'd submit reports to the academy twice a year, detailing water quality, flora, fauna, erosion, and any other information they could gather. Fessi's mother, Andish, had been housebound on the island for a decade since the death of her partner. It was a wonderful place to live. More spacious than the treehouse, more practical, far less chaotic. It didn't sway in the wind, either.

The crosser would need to learn vital Rhetari skills before integrating, and the treehouse dwellers were lacking in several important areas. While Virda was the finest tea-maker Fessi had ever met, her skills did not extend to food preparation. Fessi had personally witnessed Jex consume an entire bag of treacle nibs as his main meal of the day, and every meal Magrin had ever prepared in her presence was indistinguishable from the stuff she fed to her menagerie of rescued creatures. This didn't not bode well for either the culinary education or the health of the crosser.

Virda scratched the side of her nose in contemplation, and Jex cracked his sleepy eyes open one at a time.

'Oh hey, Fessi,' he said, and then to Virda, 'Berro still here?'

'No,' said Virda. 'I heard him creep out a few minutes ago. He wanted to tell you about the crosser himself, Fessi, but…'

Fessi smiled. 'What do you think of my idea? The crosser could go outside and explore the island and swim without anyone seeing her. We have two bioclosets. Andish never leaves the island, so she'd always have company.'

'It does sound like a good idea,' said Virda. 'Jex was excited to have her here, but I don't think Magrin's keen on sharing her room. I mean with a person.'

Jex, apparently, had drifted back to sleep, and didn't comment.

'I'll speak to Berro,' said Fessi. Already she'd opened a text box in the corner of her slab. 'Where is he now?'

'On his way to the station to fetch something. So he'll be on his mono for a while. Think he'll be angry with me? For telling you?'

'He won't be surprised,' said Fessi, and Virda's cheeks darkened beneath her sunny freckles. 'Don't worry so much, Virda. He'll forgive you. He always does.'

• • •

The almost-risen sun took the edge off the darkness, and birds began to chirp their morning songs, testing their voices in the crisp air as Berro whipped through the forest on his mono, enjoying the empty pathways and the bracing freshness of pre-dawn. His path out of the settlement eventually merged with another to form a broad lane lined with rustling tinwillows that strobed by, a strip of open sky overhead.

A message from Fessi pinged onto his slab screen.

: Virda told me the exciting news. :

No surprises there. She must've called Fessi as soon as Berro had sneaked out of the treehouse. He activated video, and Fessi's face appeared, framed by her immaculate straight black hair.

'You're up early,' she said.

'So are you,' he replied. 'What are you doing?'

Reeds swayed in a gentle breeze behind her bare shoulders. 'I'm about to swim,' said Fessi. 'But this is more important.'

Berro grinned. 'Well, I'm honoured you think so. I know how much you love swimming.'

'I've had an idea. About your crosser.'

'Tell me more.'

'I don't think it's a good idea for her to stay at the treehouse.

We don't know about her life yet, do we? Her cultural norms. Her anxieties. The treehouse could be disturbing for her. Virda is very intense. Jex walks around naked half the time. Magrin puts up with their relationship in close quarters because she has secret voyeuristic tendencies, but I doubt anyone else could tolerate it for long.' Fessi tilted her head, turned, and shrugged a shoulder towards the little house behind her. 'She could stay with me and Andish instead.'

It was such an unusual place to live that Berro hadn't even considered it for the crosser, but everything on Rheta would be unusual for Kath. He couldn't believe he hadn't thought of it sooner. 'It's a good idea,' he said.

Fessi nodded. She didn't need to be told it was a good idea. She wouldn't have suggested it otherwise. 'I wrote out a list of advantages and disadvantages after I spoke to Virda. The bad outweighs the good for the treehouse. And Virda agrees with me, for what it's worth. I can send you my list. Save you having to think about everything for yourself. I can see you're busy.'

'Thank you,' said Berro. 'I appreciate it.'

'I'd obviously love to be involved in all this. I want to speak to you about it when you have time. I sensed something last night. A flowchange.'

'You sensed the crossing?'

'Yes,' she said. 'It's hard to describe. Will you be at the academy today?'

'Probably not until late. I've lost about a day of reading time already.'

'You can catch up on all that. This is more important. It's history in the making.'

'I know.'

Fessi smiled. 'I'm sending you my list right now, and you can talk to Undra about it. Let me know when you're free.'

Berro's slab pinged as the document arrived.

'I will,' said Berro. 'Enjoy your swim.'

Fessi raised her hand and one of her neat black brows. The

picture on the screen tilted and flipped as she propped her slab up against a tree facing the lake. Just before Berro disconnected, he saw her sleek pale body slip into the dark water, barely rippling the surface.

>>One new document. Fessima Blue > Berrovan Blue
>>CROSSER RELOCATION OPTIONS. ADVANTAGES AND DISADVANTAGES.

Berro kept his pace steady, glancing down at his slab from time to time to read Fessi's list. Each point was accurate and irrefutable.

'There is one biocloset in the treehouse, and it has already proven insufficient for the needs of three inhabitants on numerous occasions. Introducing a fourth permanent inhabitant not only increases the possibility of petty conflict within the treehouse but also threatens the longevity of the biocloset itself.'

In the section on the lakehouse advantages, she'd included something that sent a bolt of sharp guilt through him.

'Any assistance the crosser might provide with gardening or eco-monitoring would be of great benefit to me and Andish. It could also lay the foundation for a future study or work focus for the crosser, who may desire purpose and direction to establish a sense of stability in her new life.'

He hadn't yet considered the crosser's future in such clear terms. Like all crossers, Kath was a person with a fascinating past, but unlike the crossers before her, she had a future too. They had learned so much from corpses, but Kath had infinitely more to offer. They could ask her questions. They could study her language. A tremble of excited pride rushed through Berro as he imagined a recording of Kath's voice inserted into the academic canon: the first interview with a live crosser, conducted by Berrovan of Wooden Hill Academy. *No.* Undra would want to conduct the first interview. Of course he would; he was the imparter running the study. Despite his unique responsibilities, Berro was only an assistant, officially. But perhaps, over time, as Undra witnessed his perspicacity and dedication to the project, he'd become something more. Co-author?

As the first shafts of sunlight felt their way between the trees, Berro's path merged with the Station Path. He filtered smoothly into the traffic streaming in from other parts of the settlement. It was lively for the hour, monos outnumbered by multi-passenger darters, and hovercarts for goods transportation. Summer trading would begin soon at stalls erected along the branch paths in the heart of Wooden Hill, and the trains would already be bringing in imported produce.

The Station Path gradually expanded into a vast open area, loud and frenzied with activity. People and vehicles jostled for parking, vendors called out their offerings of freshly brewed tea and light snacks, and station marshals marched around in their bright pink uniforms trying to keep things orderly.

Morning brightness flooded the area, reflecting sharply off the sides of vehicles. Berro shielded his eyes, pulled into a vacant mono stand, and clipped the handlebar straight into the slot. He made his way towards the raised platform running the length of the hovertube's track within the clearing, a tiny slice of an epic piece of infrastructure that cut the entire way across Western Island, from the desolate Brine Rocks of the far north, down between snow-capped peaks and into the river valleys fanning out to the south, across the open rolling grasslands, through the forest and out to the southernmost settlement of Sea Pebbles before it went through a tunnel beneath the narrow sea and emerged to continue its journey across the mainland of Mass 2.

The station became increasingly chaotic as the tube's arrival time drew near, with rowdy people excited to board, or perhaps excited to meet friends and family coming into the settlement for the summer trade, and marshals on monocrafts barking at people through their mouthpieces.

'Please stand clear of the platform edge!' a marshal shouted in Berro's direction, the volume of the mouthpiece cutting into his ear.

'I'm nowhere near the edge,' Berro grumbled, but took a step back anyway.

A whistling whine signalled the approach of the tube. Leaves fluttered frantically on the trees in the gust of air pushed before the massive vehicle. Berro jolted as it appeared suddenly between the trees. It made a graceful transition between blinding speed and a smooth crawl, then docked at the platform with a powerful hiss. The pulse fields switched off with a pop, and a fug of insects descended on the brushed metal. A patient bird took the opportunity to swoop down out of the trees to grab a few choice specimens, its talons clattering against the tube's curved surface. A nearby tea vendor and a couple of travellers cheered. People seemed in good spirits, and Berro felt his own mood lift, despite his anxiety about the night before and the day ahead.

The tube's passenger segments slid open and the first travellers disembarked, swatting away the insects and wrinkling their faces at the heat. It was always cold in the hovertube. Berro hadn't been on one for years, but he remembered the experience well from the days of visiting his ailing mother at the Grassy Plains infirmary. The one-way, greenglass windows had always made him feel like he was barrelling down an aqueduct. He remembered the taste of the thinly brewed tea they offered to travellers, a taste he still associated with dread, anger, sadness. Virda's masterful tea-brewing skill was a more important bedrock of their friendship than she realised.

The travellers were an eclectic lot – very few academy colours, plenty of clothwraps. All types of people, from the fledgling to the decrepit, had come to Wooden Hill for the summer trade, many burdened with packs full of fresh produce, which would probably be traded for treacle sap, Wooden Hill's coveted primary export, in the form of crystallised drops or jars of liquid.

Berro didn't understand the appeal. He'd grown up eating over-sweetened porridge and wickernuts dipped in the stuff, and by the time he'd left home and moved into the academy, he could barely face another mouthful of anything tainted by a sap derivative.

The travellers bustled and chattered, and Berro held his ground as the crowds flowed around him, linga dots shining on the multitude of foreheads. A passing baby in a backpack bundle reached out to touch Berro's smooth head. He ducked away and ignored the laughter of two nearby teenagers.

Gradually, the crowd of travellers thinned, and the trade workers began emerging, capped and badged, making their way down the platform. Pushers with barrows were already in position. Berro kept his distance. His collection would happen at the end, after all the regular food and supplies had been moved – bags of powdered millbean hauled out, and crates of wickernuts and sap loaded in. Numbers and names were called, slabs scanned, approvals beeped. Barrows hovered back and forth between the tube and the carts. Distilled water, seeds, fruits, grains, and proteins changed hands with beeps and nods. Many of these were special deliveries for the summer trading – delicacies not often available in the forest. Berro watched a station worker offload a pile of massive glossy white snowsquashes and tried to remember their flavour. He hadn't eaten snowsquash since the last time his mother had cooked it for him, around six years ago, before she became too ill. He'd never enjoyed the texture.

After the food, the high-bulk inedibles were moved. Dried leaves, wet-wrapped blocks of mulch, adhesives and compressed wood went into the tube after drums of purified sand, sheets of metal and huge spindles of undyed cloth came out, stacked onto the platform, ready to be taken to Wooden Hill's storage, distribution and manufacturing centre west of the academy. The crowd thinned and the low-bulk trade began. Medicinal bark shavings, feathers, clay crockery and recycled cutlery. And then the crowd thinned even more and, at last, it was time for the controlled substances. Guards armed with paralysers stepped forward to make their presence impossible to ignore.

Almost everyone present for the collection of controlled goods wore academy colours. Chemicals, hazardous biomatter and restricted marrowcore items were handed over in reinforced boxes, and the process involved additional steps that slowed everything down. Trade workers inspected slabs more carefully and beeped them multiple times, asked questions and took facial scans of every collector. For certain substances, they took bloodmarks too: short, thick needles punched into fingertips to register any illness or intoxication that may affect the legitimacy or safety of the trade and to prove absolutely that the collector was who they said they were. Berro winced every time a bloodmarker clicked against someone's finger. The trade workers spoke the relevant details into their slabs to complete the trade records.

'Wooden Hill Academy, Guram, green student on behalf of Imparter Ablin, controlled substance 357, collected.'

'Wooden Hill Infirmary, Disa, red student on behalf of Surgeon Halin, controlled substance 420, collected.'

A couple of voices rose above the rest, angry but indistinct, and Berro saw a guard take a small step forward and tighten his hold on his paralyser. A trade worker's voice rang out, slightly strained: 'Wooden Hill Academy, Viev, green student unconfirmed, controlled substance 799, further permissions required. Trade on hold.'

'What? What *is* this cack? I came all the way out here—'

'Please step back,' said the trade worker, voice wavering. 'Step back!'

People moved closer to witness the altercation. Any form of trouble was a rare enough occurrence to warrant unashamed interest. Berro stayed put. He couldn't see much through the thickening wall of bodies, but he caught the sounds and energised movements of a scuffle, people stepping away as the guards stepped forward. A voice shouted 'Stop!' followed by some incoherent shouting, and then a loud, bright crack of light sent the birds in the nearby trees careening into the air. There was a thud and a collective exclamation from the onlookers as someone fell hard onto the wooden platform.

'Step back!' said another voice, deep and authoritative. 'Step *back*!'

As people scurried away from the conflict, Berro caught a glimpse of a someone in an ill-fitting green uniform lying prone at the feet of a guard.

'Bit excessive,' he heard someone mutter as they passed by.

'Get him up,' barked another guard. Berro saw the trade worker standing on the very edge of the platform, leaning against the side of the tube, eyes wide and arms drawn up, clutching his slab against his chest like a shield. Two guards lifted the fallen man by his arms and ankles and lugged him along the platform towards a security darter idling in a specially marked bay nearby.

The man's head flopped back bonelessly. He had a tanned face, lined, shadowed with black-and-grey stubble – clearly much older than the average academy student. Berro snorted quietly. The response wasn't excessive. Impersonating a student, poorly, in an attempt to seize a controlled substance, deserved a good long stay at the reformatory. His mother would've disagreed, but Berro suspected she'd never actually witnessed any of these pathetic people in action. Best to have them out of the way where they couldn't cause any harm to others or, Berro supposed, to themselves.

Business continued, and the crowd settled down once the impostor's limp form was stowed away in the darter with the two guards standing alongside it, talking conspiratorially into their pods. A trade worker gestured for Berro to come forward. Her brow furrowed as she scanned the permissions document on his slab. Berro wished he knew what he was collecting, but Undra hadn't seen fit to tell him, and the document didn't specify either. He tightened his mouth and narrowed his eyes, hoping to look critical and superior.

'You're collecting this on behalf of…?'

'Imparter Undra. It says so right there.'

As far as imparters went, Undra was one of the best-known in the world – an unlikely choice of cover for someone trying to trick the system. The trade worker flashed her eyes at him, nodded, and beeped his slab, then lifted her own slab for the facial scan. 'You need a bloodmark too,' she said.

Berro's hand shook slightly as he put his thumb against the device. The trade worker smirked.

Thwuck.

Berro bit back a shriek.

'Wooden Hill Academy, Berrovan, blue student on behalf of Imparter Undra, controlled substance 4643, collected.'

The package was a thin black, reinforced rectangular box, sealed and surprisingly heavy. It didn't rattle.

The sun had ripened and the unshaded station was blinding bright. Berro shielded his eyes as he surveyed the scene. Many of the carts and monos had left; most of the remaining people stood at the platform, and the well-trodden clearing appeared vast in its relative emptiness. He took the pod from his pocket and texted Imparter Undra.

: Good morning, Imparter. I've made the collection. :

The reply was almost instant. *: Fantastic! Thank you. Meet me at the field unit as soon as you can. :*

Berro grinned helplessly. *: Absolutely, Imparter. I'll see you soon. :* He pocketed the pod and marched swiftly to his mono, the set of his face and the size of his body making stragglers, lurkers and marshals alike step aside to make way.

• • •

Berro secured the perimeter gate, parked his mono beside the front door of the field unit, and let himself in. A rush of nervous excitement dried his mouth and dampened the palms of his hands.

'Berrovan!' Undra smiled widely, coming around his desk to

take the parcel from Berro's hand. Berro had forgotten he was holding it, his eyes already latched onto the crosser lying on the softseat, apparently still asleep. She was connected with a cannula to a bag of fluids suspended from a pin on the wall. Her chest rose and fell gently beneath the blanket, and her face was slack and peaceful. Finding his hand unoccupied, Berro placed it on his chest and gave a small, respectful bow of greeting to Undra.

'Thank you for collecting this,' said Undra. He sat back down and slipped the parcel unopened into a drawer below his desk. Berro had expected him to open it then and there, and felt a twinge of disappointment.

'It's no problem at all, Imparter,' he said, taking the seat across from Undra, his eyes darting back to Kath. 'The crosser—'

'I'm keeping her sedated and hydrated for now,' said Undra. 'Been monitoring her vitals. She seems well. The fever's broken, so she should be well enough to wake soon.'

'That's good,' said Berro. 'Imparter, I— I've been doing some thinking about where the crosser could stay once she wakes up. After we've interviewed her. Long-term, I mean.'

Undra blinked at him.

'I have a friend, Fessima,' Berro forged on. 'She's a blue student, too. Very interested in the work. She lives at the lakehouse, and she's offered—'

'Was she one of the two who saw you last night?'

'No,' said Berro, and a cold stone of dread dropped into his stomach. 'I had to tell two other people, Imparter. My immediate group of friends is four people. It wouldn't have been practical to try limiting it to just two of them. We're all very close. It was safer to explain to the others rather than risking them getting suspicious and talking to other people.'

'Relax.' Undra chuckled, and Berro swallowed back the rest of his verbal torrent. 'I understand how social networks operate. I told you to trust your instincts, didn't I? Tell me about Fessima. She's a lake monitor?'

Berro exhaled slowly. 'Yes,' he said. 'It's just Fessi and her mother now, living at the lakehouse, and her mother's been housebound for a decade. She's a… a "functional recluse", as Fessi would say. There's no chance of her spreading any rumours.'

'This is quite a rapid expansion of people with inside knowledge of the project.'

'I know, Imparter, and I'm sorry,' said Berro. He felt lightheaded, but he'd rehearsed this the whole way back from the station and he couldn't mess it up now. 'I never meant for any of my friends to find out, but now that they have, I think we can use the situation to our advantage.'

The field unit was not a place to live. It was a workspace, a laboratory fused with an archive and an office, all hard edges and shadowy corners. Berro found it quite fascinating, of course, but to a crosser who didn't have the faintest idea about their research, or indeed the world in which their research was based, it would probably be quite a scary place to stay, especially at night, alone, with the trees scratching on the windows, the alien birdcalls echoing in the darkness, and the metallic horrorscape of the lab kitted out for the dismemberment of crosser corpses sprawling below.

Undra had surely been wracking his brain about where to accommodate the crosser, and now his primary assistant was here to solve the problem before he'd even had to raise it. The academy dorms were out of the question, given how difficult it would be for Kath to keep her identity a secret while surrounded by so many people who'd want to know everything about a new arrival. She needed time to figure things out.

Berro launched into his planned monologue, based on Fessi's list. It was a good list, and Berro delivered the key points with conviction. The lakehouse was perfectly isolated, it would provide the crosser with opportunities for learning and preparing herself for future integration, it was inhabited by people who would be happy to teach her and care for her, and who would cooperate with them should they need to speak with the crosser again after they'd released her from the field unit. He gushed about Fessi's academic record and how she'd read as much of Undra's work as Berro had – that was, all of it.

'Why didn't she apply to be an assistant?' asked Undra.

Berro was slightly taken aback by this question, but he didn't miss a beat in answering it. 'Oh, she's a bit like her mother in some ways. She keeps to herself.'

Undra nodded slowly, his chin resting on the tips of his steepled fingers. 'Yes,' he said after a few quiet moments. 'Yes, I think it's a good plan.'

Berro's stomach unknotted and his shoulders dropped slowly.

'I'd like to speak to Fessima, if you could arrange it,' said Undra, and Berro nodded fervently. 'I'll interview the crosser when she wakes up, but after that, it will be best if we relocate her.'

'When do you think she'll wake up?' Berro looked again at Kath's sleeping form. Her face was slack and still, but her eyes twitched slightly beneath her eyelids. Was she dreaming? Were they good dreams? He hoped they were.

'Tomorrow,' said Undra. 'I'll give her a stimulant injection if she doesn't wake up on her own. All the immunisations should have taken effect by then.'

Despite Berro's blunders and blatant overstepping by involving his entire group of friends and one of their parents in Undra's top-secret study, it had been a good meeting so far, and Undra didn't seem angry with him about any of it – quite the opposite. Berro swallowed against a dry throat and decided to try his luck with one more liberty. 'Imparter, may I be present when Kath wakes up? For the interview?'

'Of course,' said Undra. 'Be back here this time tomorrow, and in the meantime, get some rest.' Undra's expression was genial, the face of a man who would've put a hand on Berro's shoulder and squeezed it fondly had there not been a desk between them. 'You've done very well, Berrovan, but there's a lot of work ahead of us. I need to you sharp and ready.'

For Berro, this was happiness. This was pure, perfect joy. He felt like he was standing on a podium while biodegradable confetti rained down on him. The words '*Please call me Berro*' rose in his throat, but he swallowed them back down. The time for that would come, and if he did things right, perhaps he wouldn't even need to ask for it.

CHAPTER 4

Virda hated post-fundamental Numbers more than any other subject at the academy. It was dry, it was boring, it made her feel stupid, but she'd agreed to record the lecture for Magrin, so she couldn't justify skipping it. She wished she could, though. She hadn't been keeping up with her exercises, and the trajectory of the lessons was more daunting each time. Jex, for all his academic mediocrity, was quite good at Numbers. He had to be – it was a requirement for his Vehicles specialisation. Virda had been forced to shelve her pride and ask him to clarify things for her on more than one occasion. Utter cack.

It didn't help matters that they were running late. Again. The main path through the centre of the settlement, the Trunk, seemed twice as long as normal when you were rushing along it on foot while people sped past riding monos and darters. She and Jex kept having to stop for vehicles filtering in from the branch paths that joined up with the Trunk on both sides. She wanted to snap at Jex, to blame him for taking so long to get ready, for clinging to her like a barkermonkey when she tried to get out of bed on time, for showering long enough to deliver washroom renditions of three of his favourite songs in full at the top of his voice, for getting distracted by the hideous vollop chick Magrin had brought into the kitchen to feed dried ickricks from a jar – but Virda hadn't been particularly efficient either, and the hypocrisy checked her tongue.

The academy stood at the north end of settlement in a vast, grassy clearing on top of the hill that gave the settlement its name. Stupid, Virda always thought, that the hill in Wooden Hill was not wooden at all, being completely devoid of trees.

The academy building was an enormous cylinder topped with a glass dome observatory. It rose ten levels high from the top of the hill, with another five levels below the ground, the upper two subterranean levels accessible via tunnels bored into the hillside. The building was ringed with windows and covered by a carefully cultivated creeper plant that matched the seasonal colour changes of the surrounding forest, presently a rich summer green, rippling in a gentle breeze.

The field crawled with academy staff and students, and Virda and Jex dodged loitering and slow-moving people left and right on their way up the hill to the main entrance. Inside, they raced up the first flight of stairs and slipped into the classroom a couple of minutes late. Virda followed Jex to a pair of open seats at the back of the room next to their friend Kem, the only blue uniform in their tree-climbing group. He wasn't a particularly skilled climber, but he was faster than Disa, more sensible than Jex, more punctual than Gunli, and far less annoying than Tarov. He had a good eye for picking safe, enjoyable trees to climb, and sometimes, if the wickerbloom was strong enough, he'd treat them all to a treetop song. Kem smiled as they took their seats.

Virda propped up her pod on the desk in front of her, using the little hinged clip stand Jex had fashioned for the purpose so she could record the lecture for Magrin. 'I wish someone would do this for me,' she mumbled. 'I don't want to be here.'

'Me neither,' said Kem.

'Is anyone keen on this class? Apart from Ryndel, I mean.'

Ryndel sat in the row just in front of them and swung around at the sound of her name, her long red braid flicking like an angry snake. Her sour face took up a quarter of the frame of Virda's pod screen.

'You're not going to talk through the whole class, are you?' she said in her reedy, nasal voice that perfectly matched her pointy nose and thin, bloodless lips.

'It hasn't even started yet,' said Virda, bristling.

Imparter Brym was up front, writing a series of complicated-looking equations on his slab. A projector displayed his work on the blank wall behind him.

'He's about to,' said Ryndel. 'And you do this every time. You might be here to socialise, but the rest of us have futures we're working towards, so maybe try showing a bit of respect.'

Virda gaped at her.

'*Gods*,' Kem mumbled as Ryndel turned back around. He said it as though she'd been insulting him too, and he had every right to be offended, but she hadn't even been looking at him. Her eyes had locked with Virda's and Virda's alone, and besides, everyone knew Kem had a future in music. It was Virda who didn't have a plan for her life. Ryndel was right about that. Her words had hit their mark, and they hurt.

Numbers, much like every other subject, felt to Virda like a vaguely pointless process of learning for the sake of learning, with no plan of how to put the knowledge into practice. She collected academic credits like a moontuk gathered shiny things for its nest. She didn't know what she wanted to specialise in. The thing she was best at, that she was most passionate and ambitious about, was climbing trees, but she couldn't pursue tree-climbing as a career.

She didn't have a vision of what her life would look like once her time at the academy was over, and this bothered her. It kept her awake at night and occasionally prompted a bout of something almost like grief, in which she'd compare herself to her friends and despair at her failure to make anything of her opportunities. It had been a particularly sore subject after Berro started gloating about his *incredibly important job* with Imparter Undra. Virda had avoided visiting her own commune mother since then, weighed down by a sense of dread that Mama Stitch would interrogate her about her accomplishments and then scold her for the lack of them. As if Mama would ever do any such thing. She wished her climbing accomplishments held the weight that Berro's academic ones did.

Brym had started speaking, and Virda set her pod to record him as he paced back and forth, gesticulating. Every now and then he would ask a question, and the only student who ever offered any answers was Ryndel, who was annoyingly good at everything and unafraid to demonstrate it. Virda wondered if Magrin would roll her eyes every time Ryndel's hand went up in the recording. Probably not. Magrin wasn't petty like that. Virda was, though; she couldn't stand Ryndel – something she and Berro had in common. A dark mood settled over her.

'Can we climb a tree later?' she mumbled in Jex's direction.

Jex shook his head. 'Vehicle training.'

Virda buried her sigh of disappointment under a false cough that made Ryndel shoot a murderous look over her shoulder. Virda cringed instead of scowling at her and immediately regretted the wasted opportunity.

Most levels of the academy contained a ring of rooms, their doors opening into circular areas, the mingles, which were pierced in the centre by the clear glass elevator tube running the length of the building's hollow core. While the main structure of the building and its many rooms were made of smooth, grey stone, the floors and ceilings were lacquered wood studded with ecolamps that gave warmer and more homely feel to the place. To Virda, it was a bit like being inside of a giant tree. Helical staircases twisted up to openings between the levels – an alternative means of getting around the building if the elevator was too crowded. It wasn't particularly crowded after the Numbers class, so Virda took it down to level 5 and found an empty cubicle in the subterranean focussed study room.

Ryndel's words still needled at her, and she sensed the first hum of a headache behind the tight set of her face. She was half glad Jex had vehicle training; it was a good opportunity for her to speak with the only people she knew who didn't know her as Virda, the climber and floundering student. They didn't know her name or her face or her insecurities. They knew her only as an activist, and they respected her for it.

Virda didn't keep secrets from Jex – at least, not entirely. Jex knew she spoke to people on the rhetalink sometimes, but that was all he knew. He didn't know what she spoke about, or why. He didn't know she spoke to the same people every time. He wasn't aware of how Virda's grief and rage at the detainment of their commune cousin had never dissipated but had simply been compressed inside her, growing potent and volatile, waiting for a catalyst, ready to explode at a moment's notice. He didn't know how often Virda thought about Shani, and about Shani's twin sister Kini.

The twins had grown up in the same commune as Virda and Jex, and they'd all been close, a relationship equal parts teasing, playing, and familial affection. Both Kini and Shani had been eager climbers, and had casually mentored Virda and Jex from a very young age. Virda, especially, had always been eager to impress the older girls and determined to succeed even when her arms and legs were barely long enough to reach the right branches and footholds. The twins wanted to be explorers, to venture into no-zones and find relics and study the marrowcore-blighted flora and fauna, and perhaps discover land with the potential for new settlements or research units. They would talk about it all the time and set off on their own missions with rucksacks full of millbean buns and whatever tools they could steal from the commune maintenance cupboard.

They'd been considering their post-fundamental options at the academy when Shani was taken to the reformatory for 'repeated criminal trespassing'. It had been the second most traumatic day of Virda's life. Kini refused to speak about it, and eventually everyone stopped asking her because of the obvious distress it caused. It was assumed and accepted by all who knew them that Shani had done something bad, and only Kini would ever know exactly what it was.

Kini's ambitions changed after Shani was taken away. She first decided to stay on at the commune and become a commune parent herself while she waited for her sister to finish being reformed, but as time passed, and there was no word regarding Shani's release, Kini became withdrawn and ineffective as a guardian, preferring to spend her days taking long, lonely walks rather than interacting with other people. After a few years, she moved away, left the forest and crossed the sea channel to live somewhere out on the plains. Virda hadn't seen Kini in a long time, and only heard about her through the commune guardians, who received brief, vague updates from her every few months.

As for Shani, they never heard from her at all, and every time Virda submitted requests on the rhetalink for permission to visit her at the reformatory or for communication links or for the details of her crimes, she was simply informed that Shani was not interested in communicating, and Virda should respect her cousin's wishes. Shani's crimes, they said, were unique and sensitive in nature, and could not be discussed with anyone outside of the reformatory. They had all the official forms about her admission, but important chunks of information were redacted under some obscure clause of the Code, and everyone seemed to have accepted this and moved on with their lives, trusting in the Code, trusting in the enforcement of it, trusting in the reformatory to do what was right.

Everyone but Virda.

She took out her slab, propped it up on the desk in front of her, and vigorously rubbed her temples for a moment before she tapped her way into the comspace.

>>comspace/locked/reformatory reformation collective
>>2 reformer(s) in comspace
>>reformer treescrat has entered

Treescrat– *: how are we all this afternoon? :*

Burnitdown– *: as ever, scratty :*

Cackfoot– *: livid. denied interaction again. 5th attempt. :*

Treescrat– *: i'm sorry to hear it :*

Treescrat– *: but not surprised :*

Cackfoot– *: you heard back from your latest application? :*

Treescrat– *: no. i didn't apply for interaction though. only information :*

Cackfoot– *: probably way down their priority list then. :*

Burnitdown– *: but more difficult to deny when they get to it, maybe? :*

Treescrat– *: that was my logic, but i'm not sure anymore :*

Cackfoot– *: how long have you been waiting? :*

Treescrat– *: four months :*

Cackfoot– *: cack :*

Burnitdown– *: cack :*

Treescrat– *: >>emote: shrug//sad<< :*

Cackfoot– *: any progress on getting Sarla's boy to join us? :*

Treescrat– *: no, i told you. he's not indifferent to activism, he's hostile to it. we don't talk about this. at all :*

Cackfoot– *: it's so disappointing, honestly. what a legacy to cack all over :*

Treescrat– *: i know, but it's complicated. he's complicated. and i doubt it would help us anyway :*

Cackfoot– *: but we do need numbers. how are we going to convince people that their utopia has a rotten core when we're just four angry nobodies in a private comspace? :*

Burnitdown– *: >>emote: slump//defeated<< :*

Cackfoot– *: scratty, what about the twin? :*

Treescrat– *: no. i've said it a hundred times. she went through enough. she doesn't need to be dragged into this :*

Cackfoot– *: into what? we're essentially an anonymous support group. we're not marching on the reformatory or anything. :*

Burnitdown– *: not yet. :*

Cackfoot– *: >>emote: smile//innocent<< :*

Burnitdown– *: >>emote: smile//devious<< :*

Treescrat– *: i'm barely anonymous. you all know enough about my case and my friends that you could find me if you wanted to :*

Cackfoot– *: do you want us to? :*

Treescrat– *: no :*

Cackfoot– *: well, then we won't. we agreed on this. :*

Burnitdown– *: by the way, scratty, justicenow got correspondence last week. :*

Treescrat– *: really? that's blooming! why didn't you lead with that? correspondence from inside? :*

Burnitdown– *: apparently. i'm sceptical. it was digital. bloodmarked and everything, but to me it seemed off. :*

Treescrat– *: he shared it? :*

Burnitdown– *: yes. it was very holiday-at-sea-pebbles, but it made him happy and i didn't want to upset him. :*

Cackfoot– *: he's a cackwit. :*

Treescrat– *: come on, that's not fair. let's not do that :*

Cackfoot *: i'm sorry but it's true. he thinks it's all an administration problem. like if they get a new secretary, the correspondence will flow. it won't. his brother is dead. :*

Treescrat– *: don't say that :*

Burnitdown– *: stop it, cackfoot. you don't know he's dead. :*

Cackfoot– *: you said it yourself! it seemed off! you're thinking the same thing i am, don't deny it. it's been two decades. no face-to-face, no audio, no video, no handwriting. they're bloodmarking digital messages from a jar of his fluids they have in storage. :*

Treescrat– *: i thought you said this was a support group :*

Burnitdown– *: we can't tolerate this, cackfoot. you have to stop. :*

Cackfoot– *: he's not even in here right now. :*

Burnitdown– *: but we are. it hurts us too. :*

Cackfoot– *: if you really want to burn it down, burnitdown, you need to toughen up, my friend. :*

Burnitdown– *: you're not my friend. :*

Cackfoot– *: >>emote: blink<< :*

>>reformer cackfoot has departed

Treescrat– *: come on :*

Burnitdown– *: sorry scratty. one of those days. :*

>>reformer burnitdown has departed

CHAPTER 5

Berro stooped slightly as he entered the hillside tunnel. He did this out of habit, sometimes even when entrances were tall enough to accommodate his size. Usually, they weren't. He opened the weather door a few paces into the tunnel and closed it behind him, the subterranean quiet and the subtle increase in temperature as soothing as slipping into a pool of warm spring water. The academy wasn't just his place of learning, it was his home, and he loved it.

He emerged from the tunnel into the mingle on level 5, the one just below ground level. It was empty but for a couple of blue students chatting quietly outside the library. In bright white letters, the words 'LEVEL 5: LIBRARY / ARTEFACTS / FOCUSSED STUDY' moved fluidly along a lightstrip around the elevator tube.

Berro pressed a symbol on the glass. The capsule slid down with a sibilant sigh, and a panel on the tube hissed open. He stepped inside, and it closed behind him as he selected number 1 from a strip of softly glowing buttons on the directory of academy levels.

15: Observation dome

14: Grow level B / Laboratories

13: Study / Common area

12: Offices 21–40

11: Offices 1–20
10: Classrooms 21–30
9: Classrooms 11–20
8: Classrooms 1–10
7: Physical Training / Gyms
6: GROUND: Administration / Lecture Halls
5: TUNNELS 2: Library / Artefacts / Focussed study
4: TUNNELS 1: Infirmary / Health consultation
3: Grow level A / Laboratories
2: Kitchens / Ablutions / Laundry
1: BASE: Dormitories

The elevator dropped quietly into the subterranean depths of the building. A few people milled about on level 2, but for the most part, the mingles were quiet and empty, and Berro was glad that nobody halted the elevator to join him on his way down.

At base level, a small cluster of students was waiting to go up, and Berro smiled politely at them as he stepped out. There were three doors on this level, one red, one green, and one blue: the dormitories, available to students who preferred to do their sleeping and their studying in the same building, or simply hadn't managed to find suitable accommodation elsewhere in the settlement.

For Berro, it was the former. Virda, Jex and Magrin had once offered him the spare bed in the treehouse, but he'd firmly declined, and not only because Magrin's room wasn't conducive to sound sleeping. He liked to be early for lectures, to be near to the library, to have his social life on his own terms instead of having his friends around all the time. He appreciated being able to disappear into a crowd sometimes.

Like all three dorms, the blue dorm was a vast room extending beyond the diameter of the rest of the cylindrical academy building, as though the structure had once been a malleable thing dropped from a great height, bulging out at the bottom from the impact to form the shape of an upside-down mushroom before the ground was built up around it. The space was subdivided into corridors and alcoves, each furnished with two double bunk beds and a block of low storage cabinets between them. The blue dorm was almost empty now. Only a few stragglers remained, and most of them were getting ready to head up into daylight.

Berro made his way to alcove 30. The lights were on, and one of his roommates, Kem, was there, sitting on the bottom bunk opposite Berro's, fixing his hair.

'Did you fall asleep in a study cubicle?' he said with a grin.

'No, I stayed at Virda and Jex's. Then I had some errands.' Berro eased his arms from the straps of his backpack and rolled his aching shoulders. 'I need a shower.'

Kem raked his fingers through his mop of orange curls, fluffing them up deliberately. 'I can't smell you, so you're in a better state than Yurek was when he came in last night.'

Yurek had the bunk above Kem's, and though he was normally very quiet and seemed to do more sleeping than studying, he did occasionally go on a late-night bender somewhere in the branch paths and return in the early hours looking thoroughly dishevelled. Ebra, who occupied the bunk above Berro's, was considerate enough, but she snored sometimes and was a bit heavy-footed when she climbed the ladder to reach her bunk. Berro didn't mind, though. He'd heard nightmare tales of terrible academy roommates, and he was grateful for the ones he'd landed up with and the general lack of tension in his alcove. It was a good place to rest his head at the end of a long day. The sound-muffling curtains across the open side of his bunk were enough to safeguard the sanctity of his sleep on the odd occasion of Yurek coming in late or Ebra snoring too loudly.

'Virda and Jex were at Numbers,' said Kem. 'Virda got an earful from Ryndel. That's about all you missed.'

Berro bristled. 'What did Ryndel say?'

'Oh, just some cack about Virda's lack of ambition or something. She wanted to shut her up. You know how Virda is.'

Berro's body clenched with sudden anger, but Kem was checking his own reflection in the blank screen of his slab and didn't seem to notice. He departed moments later with a distracted but friendly wave, leaving Berro alone in the alcove.

Berro pulled his own slab from his backpack and tapped out a message to Fessi, detailing Undra's positive response to her lake-house idea and his desire to speak with her, that day if possible. He sent through Undra's comlink, and Fessi responded immediately with *: Good. Thanks :*

Berro's head throbbed. He resolved to shower, eat, and then spend the rest of the day alone, catching up on reading. Perhaps he'd even indulge in a restorative nap. Undra had told him to get some rest, and Undra knew best.

He was about to clip his slab into the charging port at the head of his bunk when another message blipped onto the screen.

: Berrovan,

I hope you're well. I haven't heard from you in a while, so I suppose you're very busy with your academic work. I'd love to know more about it, when you have the time.

The harvest has been excellent, and I've traded some of the surplus off to a couple heading to Wooden Hill for summer trading. If you happen to eat any remarkable dew beans in the coming weeks, they might be from my farm.

I miss you and I'm proud of you. I hope we can speak soon. Let me know if you need any credits.

Marruvan :

Berro flicked the message away and pressed the corner button on the slab. The screen blanked, and he shoved the slab into its charging port, more roughly than necessary. He didn't like dew beans, he didn't need credits, and he certainly didn't feel like telling his father about his life or his work. Marruvan wouldn't understand most of it anyway. While Berro had spent much of his young life expanding his mind through study, his father had been moving heavy objects or growing starchy things in the dirt at his scrubby little farm on the plains. They had nothing in common, apart from their massive bodies. Berro had inherited his mind from his mother. His mother, who was dead.

His mother, whom his father had failed to save.

CHAPTER 6

The day of Kath's awakening.

From the moment he got out of bed, Berro couldn't stand still, couldn't stop chewing his lip or tapping his foot or picking his nail gloss. Anxious excitement tore through him like fire through a grass field. He had to wrest manual control of his legs to stop himself running full tilt from the alcove, through the dormitory, out into the mingle, up the stairs and into the ablutions on level 2. There was no point in rushing. Undra had told him when to be at the field unit, and he would follow those instructions no matter how desperate he was to race straight there, barefoot, wearing nothing but the clothwrap he'd slept in.

At the ablutions, Berro stripped off his clothes and stuffed them into the chute, where they were sucked into the machine that washed, dried, and spat them out for redistribution in the laundry room. He took a naked walk to the bank of bioclosets, where he spent as little time as possible before his shower. Some people took reading material with them into the biocloset, mistaking it as a place appropriate for relaxation and reflection. Berro couldn't fathom it. The open-plan shower area, however, was somewhere he'd happily spend more of his time, on a normal day. Filtered ground water gushed from the overhead spigots, and Berro cranked his up to full power and high heat, this hissing burn just on the edge of painful yet satisfying, like scratching an itch or pulling a scab. He'd chosen his favourite spot in the shower alongside a bit of vandalism that pleased him, even though its existence was a minor Code-violation. The words *Undra for Council* had been scratched neatly into the wall, and another vandal had added just beneath it, in a far messier hand: *UNDRA FOR DIVINE RULER.*

Berro lathered his body and scalp with herbal gel from a dispenser on the wall and cleaned his teeth with the textured dental paste from another. The scalding water sizzled around him, blinding him with steam. The condensation from this level, which included the kitchens on the opposite side, was channelled up into the humid grow rooms on level 3, where various plants and fungi were cultivated for culinary, medicinal and research purposes. Berro never showered without thinking of the happy, healthy mushrooms above him.

Once clean, dry and wrapped in a towel, he collected a fresh blue uniform from the laundry, dressed quickly and headed to the dining hall, where the early-morning supply of millbean porridge waited for him in a steaming vat. He was the only person present at this hour, apart from the student who had taken the first kitchen shift of the day for extra credits. Berro recognised him as another of Virda and Jex's tree-climbing friends, Tarov. He'd barely spoken to Tarov before, but knew his name and his face and rather a lot about his climbing style and attitude, because Virda took every possible opportunity to complain about him.

Tarov was tall and handsome, with long dark hair and a sharp face that appeared sardonic and superior even in its most neutral state. It was not at all neutral now. He leaned against the counter with a casual arrogance, and Berro greeted him with an involuntary grunt instead of the polite words and smile he'd have offered anyone else. As Berro filled his bowl with porridge, he felt Tarov's eyes on him, bored and entitled. He tried to resist looking up, but failed. Tarov smirked, and Berro cursed himself. To recover a bit of his dignity, he deployed small talk, as though he'd made eye contact intentionally.

'Why would you take this shift? It's horribly early.'

Tarov lifted one shoulder. He wore a clothwrap rather than his green uniform, and Berro could see the edge of a melter scar peeking out from beneath the fabric on his upper arm. 'I'm always up before sunrise,' said Tarov. 'Might as well earn extra credits for it.'

He'd probably spend those credits on wickerbloom and hair oil. Berro had never needed to supplement the basic credits afforded to every Rhetari citizen. He never indulged in pointless luxuries.

He couldn't think of anything else to say.

'I made the porridge extra creamy,' said Tarov. 'I hope you enjoy it.' His voice was extra creamy. There was something about the way he narrowed his eyes that made them more noticeably fervid, hard and bright between the dark sweep of his lashes.

Berro turned away and took a seat at a distant table with his back to the other man and ate as quickly as he could. He much preferred a deserted dining hall to a crowded one, but he wasn't in the mood to be the sole focus of anyone's attention, especially not Tarov's. For some reason, even though Tarov was a green, and even though he was not an academic rival, and even though Berro barely knew him, his good opinion mattered. Perhaps it was because they had mutual friends, and Berro was terminally insecure about his social life.

Virda and Jex's tree climbing collective comprised mostly greens, but Berro's roommate Kem climbed with them too, so the green uniforms obviously weren't a requirement for participation. Not that he'd ever wanted to join in. He didn't feel the need to prove himself in such a physical way.

Berro swallowed another mouthful of porridge. It *was* creamier than usual, but it stuck in his throat like mud.

He wondered if Kath would enjoy millbean porridge. What was she accustomed to eating for her first meal of the day? She seemed healthy enough, with plenty of flesh on her bones and a good set of teeth. She was nothing like the many crossers whose bodies had been found shockingly emaciated and malnourished, who likely wouldn't have lived long even if they had survived the trauma that brought them into this world. Berro added the question about breakfast to the growing list in his head.

What sort of home did you live in? Where did you get those sparkly earrings? Did you have a job in your world? What happened to you, Kath? Why did you cross?

Berro deposited his empty bowl and spoon onto the shelves at the back for steam-washing, bid Tarov farewell with a small nod of calculated nonchalance, and then walked out, pretending not to feel Tarov's gaze following him across the hall.

CHAPTER 7

By the time Berro arrived at the field unit, the crosser was awake. He was annoyed that Undra hadn't told him to come sooner, but the annoyance quickly gave way to nervous anticipation. Two chairs stood near the softseat where Kath was huddled, and Berro eased himself into one, hoping he didn't look as jittery as he felt.

'How are you feeling, Kath?' he asked. Instead of the oversized blue uniform he'd helped her put on over her own clothes, she now wore a comfortable clothwrap. A brand new linga gleamed in the centre of her forehead.

'Better,' she said. 'I feel like I've had the flu.'

'What's the *floo*?' asked Undra, leaning forward.

'A virus?' said Kath, and it sounded like a question rather than the answer to one.

'Ah. Not a terrible virus, I hope.'

'No,' said Kath. 'I mean, it kills old people sometimes. I get it every year, sometimes twice a year.'

'You won't have to worry about that anymore,' said Undra, eyes creasing warmly at the corners. 'I've immunised you against all our viruses. It's not a perfect world, but we have eradicated the plagues.'

Kath didn't seem excited about this information. Instead, her face dropped slightly, and she looked away.

'Kath,' said Berro. 'You understand that we aren't able to send you back.'

She gave a slow nod. 'I keep thinking I'll wake up and this will all…' She waved her hand vaguely, eyes locked onto Berro's. 'I haven't had my feelings yet. They're just sitting here,' she pressed a fist against her stomach, 'like a rock in my gut, waiting for me to accept this situation before it just—' She broke her fist apart, splaying her fingers wide and throwing her hand into the air.

Undra shifted uncomfortably in his seat, and Berro knew it was the first time he'd heard any of this – that she'd waited for Berro to arrive before putting words to any of her thoughts and feelings. He wished she'd stop staring so desperately at him and turn to the imparter instead.

'These are understandable reactions to such a profound event,' said Undra.

Kath dropped her gaze into her lap.

'We'll be here to support you every step of the way,' Undra continued. 'If you need it, we have therapy and medicinal options to help you through the turmoil. And I have no doubt whatsoever you'll find strength you never knew you had.'

He sounded overly formal – stilted, even. His words were reassuring, but something about their delivery didn't quite work. It was strange to hear him falter like this. Undra could command an audience, hold them in rapture, work a crowd with the buttery tones and rolling rhythms of his voice, the sweep of his elegant hands, the twinkle in his eyes. His absolute confidence combined with his humility made him so easy to listen to, so easy to adore. And yet here, face to face with a solitary young woman from another stream of reality, he was out of sorts, unsure of himself.

Berro, desperate to save face on Undra's behalf, nodded enthusiastically at his comments, hoping that his love and respect for the man would prove infectious. He wanted Kath to see Undra as he did, and he felt a strange sense of shame and panic that this hadn't happened automatically.

'Where will I stay?' Kath asked.

'A trusted peer of Berrovan's has offered to house you at her residence on the lake,' said Undra. 'I discussed it with her last night. It sounds like a safe and comfortable place for you to learn about your new world. We'll get you some more clothes and bedding and your own slab for learning and entertainment.'

Kath attempted a smile. 'Thank you,' she said in a brittle voice.

'You'll like Fessi,' said Berro. 'She's a good friend.'

Undra nodded eagerly as though he, too, was a good friend of Fessi's. 'Berro can take you there tonight, if you wouldn't mind answering a few of our questions first. We have so much we'd love to know about you and your world. We don't want to overwhelm you, so if you're not feeling up to it just yet, that's all right.'

'I can answer your questions,' she said. 'Or, I can try.'

'Wonderful,' said Undra, his face breaking into a smile. 'Can we offer you any tea? Or water? Or something to eat?'

'No, thank you,' said Kath. She glanced at Undra, then at Berro and then at her hands clasped tightly in her lap.

'No need to be nervous,' said Undra. His eyes crinkled once more in that way that was both friendly and fatherly. Berro was relieved to see him loosening up and finding his rhythm. 'Just tell us a bit about yourself.'

'Um.' Kath drew her lips to one side and lifted her head to look over Undra's shoulder at the doors behind him, at the ceiling, the high window, and back at her lap. 'Well, I'm from the United Queendom. A city called London.'

'Ah! We've had crossers from worlds with a city called London before. Some of them cross with books and papers on them, you see, and sometimes those texts are very informative. Is your world called Earth?'

'Yes,' said Kath.

Undra pressed his hands together and looked quite excited. 'We've long hypothesised that there's a sizeable cluster of worlds where our planet is known as Earth, and many of those share similar megacities – and a tendency for outgoing crossings – but I don't recall ever reading any sources that referred to a Queendom, so perhaps you're the first crosser from this particular Earth. What is your queen like?'

'Um.'

'Have you met her?'

'No. She's quite young. A bit older than me. She's just a figurehead. She has her say, but the government that runs the place. They pretend to respect her.'

'Hmm.' Undra stroked his chin. 'Tell me more about this government.'

'Well, um, I'm not very knowledgeable about politics. It's not something I'm interested in, really. I mean…'

'Don't worry, this isn't a test,' said Undra.

'Well, the government,' said Kath, 'it's a government. Not the worst one in the world, but they're not the best either. There's a lot of inequality, but they don't do much about it, and the crime is getting worse.'

Undra's face creased. 'Crime. What sort of crime?'

'You know, violence, assault. Theft. I— There was an assault, when I…'

'You crossed into our world during an assault?'

'Yes,' said Kath. The word was barely a whisper. 'A mugging.'

'I'm very sorry to hear it,' said Undra. 'We've discovered that crossing is tied to trauma. It's not that every traumatic event leads to a crossing – crossings are incredibly rare, so of course this wouldn't make any sense – but every crossing is linked to a traumatic event. As far as we know, we haven't had a single person crossing out of our world in a hundred years, but we do have people crossing in from time to time. Most of them, sadly, aren't alive when we find them. That's why you're so special.'

Kath blinked and swallowed. 'Um. Thank you.'

Berro watched Undra's face, but Undra was completely fixated on Kath, as if Berro wasn't even in the room.

'Tell me about your city. Tell me about London.'

London sounded much like a standard pre-war megacity, with a jumble of tall structures packed closely together and heavy traffic between them – too many people, too much noise. Berro couldn't imagine living in such a bustling urban landscape. There was nothing like that left on Rheta. The ruins of most cities were atomised and the land resurfaced for new growth during the reclamation, and the unreclaimed urban areas were no-zones: marrowcore-poisoned wastelands choked by toxic vegetation and overrun by mutated animals. When asked about their technology, it became apparent that Kath's people didn't have access to anything like marrowcore. Their tech was limited and primitive, and their world polluted by the inefficient, unboosted fossil fuels they burned to power everything. They didn't have to contend with catastrophic marrowcore poisoning like Rheta, but the toxic landfills and filthy power stations sounded like no-zones in their own right.

As Kath described her city, her voice grew thicker, and eventually she paused and cleared her throat. 'I will take some of that tea, please, if that's all right.'

'Of course, of course!' said Undra. 'Berrovan will fetch you some.'

So he hadn't forgotten that Berro was present. Kath looked up at Berro as he rose from his seat, and he knew she'd had enough. She wasn't tearful, but she looked like she'd benefit from a good cry. He brewed a mug of tea at the kitchenette, moving everything around as quietly as he could so he didn't miss a word of the interview. Undra asked about the layout of London, the transport infrastructure, the sorts of people you might encounter out and about. Kath gave him what he wanted, but she wasn't relishing the attention.

As Berro pressed the berries, he recalled the earrings Kath had been wearing when he'd found her. He wondered where they were. Undra had locked them away in a storage cabinet, presumably, along with her other possessions. Everything Kath brought with her in the crossing, down to the fibres in the fabric of her clothes and the invisible dirt and pollens trapped in them, were valuable artefacts from another world, and would need to be studied and documented at some stage.

Berro handed the steaming mug of tea to Kath, and she thanked him with a small smile and sipped it. It was clear from the face she pulled that she found it revolting, but drinking it gave her an excuse not to talk so much. Berro could detect a trace of something just bordering on disappointment in the set of Undra's shoulders and the sheen of his eyes. When Kath's responses became mostly monosyllabic, Undra went to his desk and fetched his slab. Berro gave Kath an encouraging smile, hoping he'd be able to relocate her to the lakehouse shortly, but the thought was interrupted by a small gasp from Undra.

'Berrovan,' he said, as Berro swung around to look at him. 'I'd like you to check a location for me, if you don't mind.'

'A location?'

Undra nodded urgently, his hair flopping across his forehead. 'Yes. I've sent the coordinates to you.'

Berro stood – and hesitated. Kath was pressing her lips together like someone holding back an opinion.

'Don't worry,' Undra laughed. 'I won't eat her!'

Berro didn't want to go crashing through the forest in search of a dead crosser now. He wanted to spend this time with the crosser who was alive – the crosser who had just woken and was saying things that no one else on Rheta had heard before. Her words were more valuable than anything a dead body could give them.

'I'll be back as soon as I can,' he said.

'Be thorough,' said Undra. 'Who knows, we might have another survivor on our hands.'

But what were the chances of two live crossers arriving within days of one another? Negligible. Non-existent. Kath's face lit up with an astonished and ignorant hope, and Berro wished more than anything that the imparter hadn't said those words.

• • •

Blip blip blip.

The location was at least half an hour away, at the recommended mono speed. Berro pushed it slightly. There were good pathways for most of the distance; only the last stretch required him to manoeuvre his vehicle through and around uncut masses of vegetation and trees with low branches and roots sticking up like ancient knees and elbows, perfect for breaking the ankles of lost walkers.

Berro tried to focus his mind on the task at hand but couldn't quite dismiss his frustration at being ejected from the interview with Kath. Of course, Undra couldn't help it if another crossing was happening right at that moment. An unlucky coincidence. Berro still didn't have a clue how the process of 'detecting marric anomalies' actually worked. What were the drones scanning for? He looked up at the canopy, half expecting to see a silent drone hovering there, watching him, but there was nothing.

Blip blip blip.

He arrived. Or at least he was as close as he could get to the coordinates without crawling into the shadowy maw of a great, thorny bush. It grew around the bases of several trees, and the entire arrangement was choked in a thick snarl of vines. Berro parked the mono and stood staring at this colossus as he pondered his options.

'Hello?' He dropped his backpack onto the ground. The forest swallowed his words and gave nothing back. He'd have to go in.

On hands and knees, he crept into an unsettling gap in the foliage. He was confronted immediately by thorny obstacles and contorted himself to slide like a giant blue gastropod along the mucky, mulchy ground. His uniform snagged once, twice, three times on a tangle of large thorns, the third pull piercing the fabric to prick savagely at the skin of his lower back. He yelped in surprise.

Something moved ahead of him. It was dark under the cover of so much vegetation, but Berro was certain that the darkness congealed just then, and shifted to the left.

'H… hello?'

He stared, unblinking, his eyes as wide as they could go, trying to interpret the shadows ahead of him. An unpleasant musky smell filled the close space. Berro's heart thumped against the ground. At a sudden sharp rustling of leaves, an icy dread lanced through him. He tried to call out again, but his throat was solid and his mouth dry.

He slid himself slowly backwards, the same thorns snagging at his uniform again. The ground was loose where he pressed his hands against it. He felt for something to grab onto, something to push against, found a branch, gripped it, jerked in surprise as a thorn sank into the soft fleshy skin at the joint of his thumb.

And then, again, there was a movement, a rustling just ahead. A low sound lifted every hair on Berro's body. The fangs of a shadowcat appeared in the dark, gleaming so white they seemed to emit a milky light. Berro scrambled backwards, grazing his head along twigs and branches, thorns raking at him like talons. He didn't feel them, didn't hear the tearing of his uniform – there was nothing but the pummelling of his prey-heart and the burning scream of his breath.

He fought his way out of the bush and kept moving towards his mono without even taking the time to get to his feet, limbs flailing and scrabbling at anything and everything to get away from the beast in the shadows. It materialised at the entrance of the bush, one of its back legs poised on a low branch, its head low to peer out at him, fangs bared, eyes blazing, the deep, otherworldly rumble of its growl seeming to come from everywhere at once, as though Berro was surrounded by them.

The animal didn't advance, and Berro kept his eyes on its face as he hauled his backpack onto one shoulder and himself onto the mono, and brought it to life with an unnecessary roar. The creature did not retreat into its leafy hollow. It was Berro who had to leave. He turned the mono wildly and took off at speed, twisting around the obstacles with skill enhanced by pure terror. The forest expanded and contracted with the pulsing of his heart as if he were inside the heart, blood slapping against his eardrums. He maintained his pace for as long as he could and then veered to the side of the path and stepped off the mono, hands on his knees, head down, eyes closed, breathing, breathing, breathing.

He had never seen a shadowcat in the forest before, only in pictures, and he'd never had his blood rush around his body like a hot broth boiled by primal fear. He had been scared when his mother was dying, but that was different; that was a slow, heavy dread – everything thickened, sour and sluggish.

If there had been any crosser at the location, the body would be a meal for the shadow cat, and he was not equipped to fight the animal for it. But there was no crosser. He couldn't have explained why, but he was certain of it.

• • •

'You're sure?' asked Undra.

'Yes,' said Berro. 'No crosser. Just an angry shadowcat.'

Kath sat very still in a chair beside Undra's desk. She stared at Berro with wide eyes and a slack jaw, and Berro was keenly aware of how awful he must look, with his filthy uniform in tatters and his hands smeared with blood.

Undra blew out a long breath. 'I'm so sorry, Berro. That must've been terrifying. You should go to the infirmary.'

'No need,' said Berro. 'It's nothing serious. I'll fix myself up with my own kit.'

Undra smiled with a sort of proud sympathy. 'This is why I chose you,' he said. 'Stoic, resourceful…'

The flattery took some of the sting out of Berro's injuries. He excused himself, taking his backpack into the little washroom at the back of the field unit, where he cleaned and dressed his cuts and scrapes as best he could and traded his ruined uniform for the fresh spare he had with him. When he stepped back out, Undra was chatting quietly with Kath, imparting interesting bits of information about shadowcats, while she nodded politely. Berro cleared his throat.

'Imparter, should I take Kath to the lakehouse now?'

'I'm sure Kath would appreciate that very much,' said Undra. 'I've assured her she won't be encountering any shadowcats while she's there. They can't swim, after all.'

Kath didn't smile. 'Would it be okay if... Can I have my things back? Please?'

'Your things?' said Undra. 'Oh, your— yes, of course,' he said, and rummaged in his desk drawer, bringing out a clear sealed bag that looked ready to submit for testing. The sparkly earrings were visible in among a jumble of other small artefacts. Undra clearly hadn't intended to return Kath's property before she asked for it. 'I'm afraid your clothes will need to be kept for specialist testing. All sorts of interesting things in the fibres, you see. It wouldn't be safe for you to wear them anyway, for now, so—'

'That's fine,' said Kath, taking the bag from him. 'I care more about these. Sentimental value.'

Undra opened his mouth, then closed it. He seemed suddenly remorseful and awkward. It was the first time any of his precious artefacts had held this sort of value to someone living in his own world, and he was unprepared for this reality, which struck Berro as amusing, given that Undra was the world's foremost expert in Realities.

The study of Realities, and reality itself, were two quite separate things.

CHAPTER 8

At the edge of the lake, Fessi stood tall and straight and motionless, eyes closed, one hand resting on the bow of the little boat, and allowed her senses to flow out into the forest like treacle spreading slowly between the trees. The space around her was a swirling three-dimensional canvas painted in marrow, as vivid at twilight as it was in the sunshine. The marrow flowed in the gentle currents of the air, it hummed in the soil, the rocks and the water, and it pulsed strongest of all through the bodies of living creatures and plants. It was everywhere, and it was everything. Like her mother, Fessi had always experienced the world around her in ways that few others could comprehend. They all knew what marrow was, of course – it was the essence of the world around them, and the essence of themselves as well.

Marrow was lifeblood, flaring bright in outbursts of emotion, in the use of technology, in the consumption of intoxicants. When Virda and Jex smoked wickerbloom, Fessi could sense it sparking through their blood. They glowed with it in a way that was almost literal. When she closed her eyes, she could see it. When she blocked her ears, she could hear it. When she pinched her nose shut, she could smell it. Always, always she could feel it. And she knew as soon as she sensed Kath approaching that Kath didn't fit into this world.

Accompanied by Berro's familiar energy – warm, bright, intense and quietly powerful – Kath was a void, a hollow space moving through the marrow as it parted around her like a stream splitting against a rock. She was unlike anyone or anything Fessi had ever encountered. When Fessi focussed, she could read the air that the crosser was breathing in, sense it within her lungs, like a pocket within the void where the known world could enter, but the marrow in that air was separate from the crosser who breathed it.

Fessi tucked her hair behind her ear and kept her face calm and neutral as the void drew nearer. A monocraft appeared over the rise. Berro parked the vehicle next to a tree and helped the crosser to step off before he did. When he spotted Fessi at the water's edge below, he bowed to her.

As they approached, the crosser's eyes darted all over the place, meeting Fessi's for a moment before skittering away again. 'Hello,' said Fessi. 'You must be Kathleen.'

Kath came to a halt a generous step away from her, glanced up briefly and flashed a small, awkward smile. 'Hi,' she said. 'You can call me Kath.'

She was nervous, embarrassed, confused – Fessi knew this only from her posture and her face. She was accustomed to having far more to work with than external signals alone, but there was nothing else to interpret here. It was more than just an absence of the complex marrow that comprised a person; Kath was actively repelling the marrow around her.

Fessi caught Berro's eye, but nothing in his face or his energy suggested he felt anything so deeply unsettling about the crosser's anti-presence, her nothingness. For all Berro's brilliance, his marric sensitivities were practically non-existent. At that moment, she could sense he was distracted by physical pain. He kept shifting and rolling his shoulder; something itched under his uniform.

'Berro, you're hurt,' she said. 'What happened?'

'Believe it or not, I had an encounter with a shadowcat,' he said.

'I got scratched up on some bushes trying to get away from it. Nothing serious.'

'Magrin will be thrilled to hear about that,' said Fessi, just as she sensed Magrin's approach, along with that of Virda and Jex. 'You invited the others?'

'Uh, no,' said Berro. 'I told Virda I'd be bringing Kath to the lakehouse.'

'Virda would consider that an invitation.'

Berro sighed. 'Kath, I'm sorry. I didn't want to overwhelm you with so many people, but they're all really excited about you.'

'It's fine,' said Kath, and twisted one of her braids around her finger in what Fessi read as a nervous habit, though she couldn't be sure. She looked up as the trio appeared at the treeline.

'Perfect timing!' Jex called out, rushing down the bank to meet them. He held his hands out to the crosser, and when she raised an uncertain hand in response, he grasped it in both of his own and squeezed it. 'Lovely to meet you. Again.'

Virda was next to introduce herself, and then Magrin, who substituted her normally affectionate style of greeting for an uncertain touch to Kath's shoulder, accompanied by a wary smile. She too was unsettled by Kath.

'I can only fit four people in my boat,' said Fessi, as Magrin sidled up and curled an arm around her, drawing comfort from the familiar.

'We'll swim,' said Virda, immediately stripping off her uniform. Jex followed, and soon they both wore nothing but their stretchy green underwear. These fitted garments weren't fully opaque, and Fessi noticed Kath averting her gaze. She was from one of *those* worlds, apparently. They'd all studied bits of the literature that had crossed through into Rheta in the possession of various other crossers, mostly from Earth worlds, and several examples indicated strange and often stifling ideas about natural states, from anxieties about bodily functions and nudity, to illogical prejudices around sexual preference, gender and anatomy. They'd need to have a conversation about this at some point.

Once Kath and Magrin were settled in the little rowing boat, Berro helped Fessi push it out onto the water before he hoisted himself in and offered his hand to her. Virda and Jex were already in the water, streaking across the lake towards the island.

The little boat glided along in slightly awkward silence. Fessi slipped the oars smoothly into the water, and the surface rippled and wobbled around them, the afternoon light playing on it in muted spangles of silver. Magrin peered eagerly into the lake's shadowy depths, where the puddoos lurked.

By the time the boat slid up onto the muddy bank of the little island with a gentle *slop*, Jex and Virda were already shivering on the shore. Fessi secured the boat to a mossy post with a length of rope. Magrin stepped out and offered Kath a hand, which she accepted, heaving herself awkwardly out of the boat. One of her feet sank immediately into the watery mud. She pulled it free with a sucking slurp and let out a little burst of embarrassed laughter.

Fessi caught Magrin's eye and noted the shift in her feelings: a gentle smoothing and softening of her marrow, like fresh water stirred into drying ink. She would warm to the crosser, as was her way. It was often remarked that Magrin loved animals more than she loved people, but that didn't mean her love for people was stunted in any way. Fessi had never met anyone with a greater capacity for love than Magrin. She was wary of people in the way others were wary of shadowcats, but it didn't take much to win her over. Kath was alone, stranded, vulnerable, alien – all things that would appeal to Magrin's compassionate nature.

Fessi led everyone towards the small house at the centre of the island along a pathway of fitted stones, worn smooth from years of use. The house stood on a subtle rise covered in patchy grass and small shrubs, with a stand of young trees on one side. A few wooden seats were arranged in a swept area beneath the trees, along with a little table where a tiny bright white bird stood, its tail feathers bobbing as it watched the visitors traipse along the path.

'Oh, it's a wirrit!' said Magrin, pointing. 'I haven't seen one in months.'

'Lots of them here,' said Fessi. 'They nest at the edge of the water.' This was for Kath's benefit more than Magrin's.

Kath paused, watching the bird as it hopped once, twice and then darted into the air and vanished among the reeds. 'Beautiful,' she said, and Fessi wondered what sorts of animals she was accustomed to. Perhaps she rarely saw any at all, if hers was a world where nature had been blighted by unsustainable development. Though Kath unsettled her on a deep level, Fessi was eager to speak with her about these things, and Berro would appreciate any interesting information she could learn from the crosser while they lived together.

The lake house was rectangular, built of the same stone as the pathway, with a roof of dark, lichen-spotted tiles, and a stone chimney rising from the back. Pale steam curled gently out of it – something was cooking on the little stove inside. The freshly lacquered front door opened just before they reached it, and Fessi's mother appeared, a warm smile on her soft, lined face and two fluffy robes draped over her arm. She wore a loose, patterned cloth wrap, her long grey hair piled with messy elegance on top of her head and secured with a wooden clasp.

'Hello!' she said, standing back to let them pass. 'Come inside.'

She passed the robes to Virda and Jex, who wrapped themselves up quickly, grinning and shivering. Fessi kicked off her boots into a receptacle in the entrance hall, and the others followed her example, though without the same practised efficiency.

'Hello, hi, thank you,' Kath mumbled. She nodded and smiled at Fessi's mother, who cocked her head for a moment, a curious expression passing over her features before she took both of Kath's hands in her own and stared into her eyes. Kath stared back.

'Kath,' said the older woman. 'It's wonderful to meet you. My name is Andish.'

She released Kath's hands, and the crosser opened and closed her mouth a few times and then said, 'Thanks for having me.'

While Fessi got everyone settled on a jumble of softseats in the mingle, Andish breezed into the small, open kitchen area to fetch the tea she'd brewed in anticipation of their arrival. She brought over a driftwood tray bearing six mugs and set it on a low table in the centre of the room.

'Won't you be joining us?' asked Fessi.

Andish smiled. 'Oh, no, you go ahead and spend some time with your friends, Fessima. I'll have plenty of time to get to know Kath, won't I?'

Kath looked up at her. She was trying to smile, but Fessi could see the tremor in her lips and the sudden liquid sheen of her eyes. Andish gave Kath a quick squeeze on the shoulder, nodded to the others, and then bowed out of the room, disappearing down a short corridor.

'How do you like your tea, Kath?' asked Virda, who had knelt at the table and was already pouring tea from the steaming metal pot.

Kath wrinkled her nose.

'So you haven't acquired the taste yet.' Virda laughed.

Berro shifted beside her and smoothed his hands along the blue lengths of his uniformed thighs. 'I'd advise you to acquire the taste as soon as possible, if you want to pass as Rhetari,' he said. 'I've never met a Rhetari who doesn't like berry tea.'

Virda shot Berro a sharp look.

'It's quite strong,' said Kath. 'Can it be sweetened?'

'No,' said Virda and Berro, at the same time as Jex said, 'Absolutely!'

Fessi fetched the jar of treacle nibs from the kitchen and fished two out, presenting them to Kath in the palm of her hand. They looked like tiny muddy pebbles, and Fessi wondered how Kath would react to them.

'Mama Stitch sneaks them into her tea all the time,' said Jex, while Virda pretended to vomit.

'Unconscionable,' said Berro.

Kath took the little nibs and dropped them into the mug Virda gave her, where they floated for a few moments before melting away, turning the red liquid an unpleasantly bloody brown. She sipped at it as though testing it for poison, then gave a weak smile.

'Better,' she said, and Jex laughed merrily.

'Are things sweeter where you're from?' he asked.

Kath looked from Jex to Virda and then sidelong at Berro. 'You would probably be horrified by the things I used to eat,' she said. Fessi read shame into the tone of her voice, though she couldn't verify it with a sense of the sick belly heat of the emotion like she normally would. 'There were these little cakes I'd have on the train. Unicorn buns. They had bright wrappers in rainbow colours.'

'What were they like?' asked Fessi, when Jex failed to deliver on the follow-up question.

'Very rich and sweet,' said Kath. 'Refined cornmeal, I think, with purple cream on the inside. The outside was glazed with sweet icing and sprinkles.'

'Sprinkles of what?'

'Mostly sugar, I suppose. Sweetener. Colourful little pieces in the shapes of stars and moons.'

'That sounds too pretty to eat,' said Magrin. She was on a single softseat, one leg drawn up so her chin could rest on her knee while she observed Kath like one would a rare animal they'd never laid eyes upon before.

Kath glanced up at Magrin. Her gaze drifted to Magrin's prosthetic foot, but she didn't comment on it. Instead, she turned to Berro. 'Do you think Imparter Undra will want to interview me again?' she asked.

'Yes. You're a trove of valuable information. I'm not sure any of it would be directly relevant to his current research, though, so it might not happen right away, or he might let someone else interview you instead.'

The hope, the wistfulness in this statement, was so poorly disguised, Fessi didn't need any special sensitivities to pick up on it.

'What exactly is his current research?' asked Kath.

Berro tapped his foot and scratched at the varnish on this thumbnail. 'I can't discuss that, unfortunately. But it's more to do with the crossing process itself and less to do with artefacts of that process.'

'And Kath is an artefact?' said Virda.

Berro grunted and stilled his hands on his knees. 'A very special one.'

'Why—' Kath began, and then paused, her eyes sliding out of focus and her lips moving soundlessly, sorting through something in that inaccessible head of hers. 'Why didn't I know that there were other worlds?' she finally said, and her expression suggested this wasn't quite the question she'd wanted to ask, but it was the best she could come up with in a hurry.

'You're not alone there,' said Berro. 'Most realities, as far as we can tell, aren't aware that they're one of many.' He shifted in his seat, straightening his back and squaring himself to present facts to an audience. 'That's either because no one has ever crossed in or out, or because the crossings are so rare, they get dismissed using more familiar explanations. It seems to be the worlds without marrow that are most resistant to the knowledge. They explain away crossings using their own frameworks of understanding. I'd guess some of those worlds have groups of informed elites who do know about it but haven't allowed the knowledge to reach the general populations.' He shrugged. 'If it's a heavily populated or chaotic world, a missing person or a strange arrival aren't going to draw a lot of attention, I suppose.'

Kath nodded slowly. 'So, marrow… is it magic?'

Berro smiled. 'Of a sort. It's a source of power we can't unravel and explain, but we know how to use it. It's basically inseparable from our science.'

Fessi disagreed with this assertion quite intensely, but there was no point in arguing with Berro about it. Marrow for him was the fuel in his monocraft, the linga on his forehead and the always-active pod device in his pocket. He couldn't sense the living stuff like she did, so she could hardly expect him to understand how very unscientific it could be.

Kath opened her mouth to say something more, but then sipped her tea instead, her eyes gone misty.

'Do you like the Wooden Hill, so far?' asked Jex. 'I mean, I know the circumstances aren't great.'

'It's pretty,' Kath said. 'And you're all very nice. It's useful that you have these dot things.' Her finger grazed over her linga. 'It would be so much harder if we couldn't understand each other.'

'What language do you speak?' asked Virda.

'Anglish,' said Kath. 'And a little bit of Kiswahili, from my mother.'

'Your mother is from somewhere different than you?'

Virda leaned forward in the seat she'd taken beside Jex, and Fessi felt the intensity of her interest, mirrored by everyone else's.

'No,' said Kath, 'but her parents were from Urgwanda. Do you have maps? Like a map of the whole world? I was thinking, I wanted to see what this place looks like.'

'Of course.' They all knew from Realities studies that the topography of other streams was usually similar to theirs, at least in terms of the shapes of the land masses, but it would be better to show this to a newcomer rather than simply telling her. Fessi retrieved a folded, waxed map of Rheta from a wooden shelf beside the front window and spread it over the tea table once Virda had cleared away the pot and stray mugs.

Kath made a small, excited sound.

'Oh,' she said. 'Yes. It's upside down and split in a different place, but it's the same. It's the same… planet.'

Jex hopped up and knelt at the table. He jabbed his finger at their location and said 'Mass 2, Western Island. Also known as "home". What did you call it?'

'Britain,' she replied. 'My city was London.'

'And they speak Anglish there?'

'They speak lots of languages. It's a very global city. But yes, most people in London speak Anglish. Most people in the whole world speak it, actually.'

'Ah, like Kastak,' said Virda. 'Everyone speaks Kastak.'

'Then why do you need these dots?'

Berro bristled where he sat watching over the conversation with a mixture of scholarly interest and social frustration.

'They're partly symbolic,' said Fessi. 'We almost never need them, but they've become a *signifier* of the post-war world. We're all meant to understand stand each other now, and the lingas guarantee it.'

'There have been protests though, once or twice,' said Virda. 'Mostly we don't really think about it, but every decade or so you'll hear of some little protest group springing up, refusing to wear lingas.'

'Is that a crime?' asked Kath.

'A Code-violation? Well, no. Maybe a Cohera violation. It's complicated. It's just not socially acceptable, really, like walking around in public with your genitals out. You can do it if you want to, but you'll face resistance.'

'Why don't they want to wear lingas?'

'Well, the argument goes that the lingas destroy marginal languages. If you speak a minority language and most of the people around you speak something else, your linga will help you to acquire the dominant language. It's designed to do that. It wants to use the translation that requires the least amount of work, so the sooner you assimilate, the better. And then, if you have a child, you're less likely to pass your native language on if you've unconsciously switched to using the dominant language most of the time, and eventually... language death. At least that's the idea. I don't think it happens as much as they say it does. Sure, everyone acquires Kastak if they don't start off with it, but that doesn't mean they lose their other languages.'

'Wow,' said Kath. 'So the linga is helping me acquire Kastak right now?'

'Yes,' said Virda.

'And eventually, I'd be able to take the linga off and actually speak it?'

Virda grinned at Kath's obvious excitement. 'Yes!'

'Well, not necessarily with native fluency,' said Berro. 'I can understand Kastak without a linga now, but I'm not at ease in it.'

Kath touched her forehead again. 'Varrea is the name of your native language, you said.'

Berro nodded, clearly surprised by her statement. 'I wasn't born on Western Island.'

'Where were you born?'

Berro leaned forward to tap a place on the map, just across the sea. Kath let out a surprising bark of laughter at this, and Berro recoiled, offended.

'You're a Franc,' she said. 'You're from Francia.'

'I'm from Grassy Plains,' Berro sniffed. 'The academy here is better, so my parents moved when I was a small child.'

'Are they still here?' asked Kath. Everyone in the room tensed at the question – Fessi sensed it as a sudden freezing of the marrow within and around each of them – which caused Kath to tense physically in turn, her eyes flicking from face to face to figure out what she'd said wrong.

'No, they aren't,' said Berro. 'My mother is dead, and my father returned to Grassy Plains to grow vegetables.'

He said this as though growing vegetables was the absolute lowest form of occupation anyone could pursue. Kath looked cowed and confused; her quiet response of 'I'm sorry' had no effect on Berro's stormy face whatsoever.

'So where was your mother's family from?' asked Jex. His breezy tone prompted a collective exhalation, and the tension ebbed out of the room.

'Here,' said Kath, pointing to a spot in the middle of Mass 1. 'Urgwanda.'

It was Magrin who lit up this time, easing her foot to the floor and leaning forward. 'Oh, have you been there? Does it have any megafauna? There used to be megafauna around there, on Rheta. Before the war.'

Kath looked sad, then. 'I've never been to Urgwanda,' she said. 'But yes, it has big animals. Some, anyway. They're mostly extinct now, or endangered. The ones that are left are in captivity.'

Magrin sat back, and the corners of her smiling mouth tugged downwards. 'Captivity.'

Kath nodded, her gaze drifting back to the map, exploring familiar shapes and unfamiliar names.

'No borders?' she murmured.

'We had borders, once,' said Fessi. 'Borders were part of the problem.'

'Borders always are,' said Kath, voice wobbling.

'What's wrong?' asked Jex, and it was not the right question to ask. Kath forced a smile, but it collapsed with a sob.

'Sorry,' she said. 'I know I should be grateful. Everything could've been— But— My mother— I...' She swallowed. Magrin, who was never able to resist soothing a living thing in distress, got up from her seat and put her hand on Kath's shoulder, having apparently dismissed any misgivings about the crosser. Kath didn't seem particularly comforted, though, and her efforts to hold back tears made her tremble and fidget in place.

'Is there a restroom I could use?'

'Right this way.' Fessi stood quickly and led the crosser around a corner to the biocloset before returning to mingle and announcing that it was time for everyone to leave.

Berro blustered. 'What? Why?'

'She's emotional and overwhelmed, and she doesn't need to deal with so many people right now. You've all made a great first impression, I'm sure, so let's leave it that way rather than wearing her out. You can visit again when she's settled in.'

Berro didn't look happy to have anything crosser-related dictated to him in such a manner by someone who wasn't Imparter Undra, but he seemed to agree with Fessi's assessment, so he stood and helped Magrin to her feet.

'Is it fine if we leave the boat at the far bank?'

'Yes,' said Fessi. 'I'll swim out for it in the morning. Magrin, remind Berro to tell you about the shadowcat.'

'You saw a shadowcat?'

Berro rubbed at the small bandage on his hand. 'I did.'

Virda and Jex shrugged off their robes and hung them up on the hooks near the door, and the other two put on their shoes.

'Tell her we're glad to have met her and we'll see her soon,' said Virda.

'I will,' said Fessi.

Outside, Magrin spotted some uncommon butterfly near the bank and insisted on pursuing it before they left. Virda and Jex followed her, but Berro hung back, thrumming with curiosity.

'You said you felt the crossing,' he said.

'Yes,' said Fessi. 'Andish felt it too. Then Virda told me the news, and I knew that's what we'd sensed. It happened near here, didn't it? South-west of the settlement?'

Berro nodded. 'In a clearing with a big rock in it.'

'Ah, the old Singer spot,' said Fessi. 'They used to dance around that rock, apparently.' Fessi could tell right away that Berro hadn't known about the history of that landmark and was embarrassed.

'What exactly did you sense?' he asked.

'It's hard to explain,' said Fessi. 'Imagine you're in a building, all the doors and windows have been sealed up for a hundred years, and then someone smashes a window and lets in a breeze. Nothing major changes, but lots of little things do. The temperature, the smell, the air quality, the currents. It's almost like that. Something happened in the distance and things got stirred up.'

'Is this why you want her to stay with you?' asked Berro.

Fessi tilted her head, and her hair fell over her eyes. She didn't tuck it back. 'I'm interested in her, yes. But this is the perfect place for her to stay, so it's the right choice regardless of my interests.'

'And your mother—'

'Andish is very excited about it. Don't forget she was a trauma specialist, before. She'll know how to care for Kath.'

'Did you tell Undra about that?'

'Yes,' said Fessi. 'He didn't seem too concerned. It was a quick conversation. I got the impression he only spoke to me out of obligation. He trusts your judgement, Berro. If you think the lakehouse is the best idea, then he agrees with you.'

Berro's marrow practically glowed with joy at this assessment.

Magrin's butterfly had evaded capture and soon enough Fessi's friends were in the boat gliding away across the water. Fessi heard Andish's voice in her mind.

-I'll make some food-

-Good idea.- Fessi thought back. *-I think she'd like the broth and dumplings.-*

-Yes. Warm. Comforting.-

A cool breeze ruffled Fessi's hair, and when it stilled, she closed her eyes for a moment and let her mind roll out over the grass and the earth and the stones, through the walls of the house and into the biocloset where it found the hunched and trembling shape of the void named Kath and enveloped it. Fessi shivered with the thrill of the unknown.

>>comspace/locked/reformatory reformation collective
>>1 reformer(s) in comspace
>>reformer treescrat has entered

Justicenow– *: Scratty! :*

Treescrat– *: hi! just the person i was hoping to find inside :*

Justicenow– *: They told you about my correspondence? :*

Treescrat– *: yes! i'm so happy for you :*

Justicenow– *: Thanks, Scratty. Cackfoot didn't think much of it... :*

Treescrat– *: what did your brother have to say? :*

Justicenow– *: He makes it very clear that he's moving on and doesn't really want to keep in touch with me anymore, but he's very positive about the reformatory. I know that's what makes Cackfoot sceptical about it, but he doesn't know my brother. My brother makes the most of any situation. He's the most relentlessly positive person you'll ever come across :*

Treescrat– *: can i read it? i know it's a code violation but i figured since you showed the others... :*

Justicenow– *: Of course! I'm sure the Cohera value of sharing hope outweighs any Code violations here. I'm sending it through now :*

>>One new document. Justicenow > Treescrat

>>One new document. White Peaks Reformatory > [Redacted]
>>STRICTLY PRIVATE
>>Official correspondence from reformatory patient 551.5M ([Redacted])
>>Bloodmark: confirmed

: [Redacted],

I am sorry it has been so long since my last correspondence. As much as I miss you and everyone outside, I have had my eyes on the future more than the past, so I had not thought to write until I heard that you were eager to hear from me. I am writing now to tell you that all is well. My life at the reformatory is comfortable and fulfilling and I know that the guidance I am receiving here is helping to make me into the person I should have been from the start.

I have discovered an aptitude for gardening and have taken to it with enthusiasm. I have even been doing some biological research on high-altitude crops, which I think will be a valuable contribution to the work they do here. There is a lot of research happening at the reformatory and it is exciting. I feel like I am part of something that is really making a positive difference to the world; who would have thought that?

I have made many friends in here and I have something resembling a family now, which has been helping me a lot with my treatment. I am so thankful for them, and for you, of course, for being such an important part of my old life. I made terrible mistakes in that life, and I know that I hurt you, but I hope you have managed to forgive me and move forward. I hope you have found happiness in yourself and I hope you are not worried about me. Not only am I being reformed and given a chance to atone for my crimes, but I am being given opportunities that I never had on the outside – opportunities I sometimes feel I do not deserve, but for which I am deeply grateful.

If a long time passes between this correspondence and the next, please do not be concerned for me, [Redacted]. Know that it is because I am letting go of the past and building a brighter future in a way that is in both of our best interests.

I love you, brother. Be well!

[Redacted] :

>>End of document

Treescrat– *: he seems very positive :*

Justicenow– *: He always was. Always is. I'm happy for him, even though I'm sad that he doesn't see me as part of his life anymore :*

Treescrat– *: i'm sure it's just easier for him while he's inside. when he gets out, he'll be with you again. he clearly loves you very much :*

Justicenow– *: Thanks, Scratty. I appreciate that :*

Justicenow– *: I have to go. Pot's about to boil over! Be well! :*

Treescrat– *: be well, justice >>emote: smile//wink<< :*

Justicenow– *: >>emote: hug<< :*

>>reformer justicenow has departed
>>reformer cackfoot has entered

Treescrat– *: hey cacks. i'm about to head out for a climb, so i can't chat right now but I just spoke to justice. he showed me the correspondence :*

Cackfoot– *: and what did you make of it? :*

Treescrat– *: you're right. his brother is dead :*

CHAPTER 9

The settlement of Wooden Hill wasn't underground, but in Virda's view, it wasn't entirely above it either. The ground and the canopy were two surfaces, and the settlement existed in the shadowy limbo between them, the trees forming the main architecture of this liminal space.

Virda loved the wickerwood trees. They were astonishingly beautiful, with their thick green leaves that shaded the settlement in summer and blazed through a spectrum of fiery colours in the autumn. They grew the precious buds and blooms she enjoyed smoking with her friends in the canopy, and most importantly, they were inarguably the best trees to climb, with strong and springy branches and bark texture smooth enough to prevent unnecessary grazes but not so smooth as to be slippery. Each broad trunk and branch bore a reliable distribution of knots and bumps that made for ideal grips and footholds. The leaves, when crushed beneath climbing hands or feet, gave off a fresh, pleasant fragrance, unlike the leaves of hackerwood trees, which smelled, in Virda's opinion, like scrattin piss. She knew very well what scrattin piss smelled like, because Magrin had rescued two of these rodents, and kept them in an elaborate pen in her room. It was not a smell-proof room, though Virda had considered obtaining a tube of sealant and trying her hand at making it that way.

It was early afternoon, the sun high and bright, and a crisp breeze rustled the leaves. Virda climbed and climbed and climbed a great wickerwood, Jex scampering along behind her, until the forest was a chasm beneath them, the sky an infinite dome of blue, its streaks of blinding white stretching away forever. From up in the canopy, Virda could imagine what it would be like to soar into the light and look down on the endless, rolling green that shaded their home. Whenever she saw the sky in this way, she understood Jex's desire to become a skycraft pilot.

The canopy was too patchy to traverse in this place, so they had to descend until they reached sturdier branches that stretched out towards other trees. They avoided the ground, always preferring to scramble from one tree to the next via tangled branches, or to leap across small gaps if the risk wasn't too great.

Virda was a better climber than Jex, but what he lacked in skill, he made up for with reckless bravery. His climbing style was loose and wild, like a barkermonkey. He threw his limbs around in a way that looked careless, and scrabbled for footholds, expecting the trees to give them to him. Virda was neater and more efficient, something she'd learned as a child from Kini and Shani. She'd studied their movements, the way they anchored their weight before pushing up to grab onto something, and chose their routes with a confident understanding of the trees they climbed and the limitations of their own bodies.

People could walk underneath Virda as she climbed, without getting showered in leaves and wood chips. She valued stealth and efficiency. Jex, on the other hand, valued speed and fun over everything else.

Tarov, Virda's least favourite member of their climbing collective, had mentioned some trees to the east that he hadn't been able to climb further than halfway. Virda wanted to try them out. Tarov was an average climber at best; he wasn't a monkey like Jex, or a scrattin, like Virda.

Jex stood on a knot of branches in a leafless gap, yelling joyfully at the clouds until nearby birds flapped and scattered into the blue. Virda's heart squeezed with affection for him. He saw her toeing her way across a branch bridge and followed overhead, raining leaves down on her.

They darted and scampered, hand over foot over paw. Jex overtook Virda by vaulting a wide breech off a springy new branch and she overtook him on a vertical section when he tried to scale it by trunk-hugging. She was good at spotting the right branches for an ascent or descent. A split second of analysis and they appeared to her like illuminated staircases. Jex never stopped to think. *He's going to break his face one day because of it.*

'Tarov told me about some tricky trees beyond the boulders,' she called out. 'We should try them.'

'Beyond the boulders? We never go out that far.'

'Burned all your energy already?'

'No,' said Jex, throwing another handful of leaves at her. She always lectured him about conserving his energy. His wild climbing wasn't sustainable over long periods. *So what?* was his usual retort. *It's not a competition. I'm not pacing myself.* He was right, but she always wanted to catch him out, to prove that her way was better than his. He already respected her as a climber, but she wanted more than that. She wanted him to *worship* her as a climber. And she wanted the other climbers to do the same. Tarov and Disa and Kem and Gunli. She wanted greatness, even if she pretended to be indifferent about it. She dreamed about climbing all the time – good dreams, in which the climbers cheered for her, or she rushed up or down a tree to save a life somehow, and bad dreams, in which Tarov streaked ahead of her in a treetop race, or Jex stole her foothold and she fell down, down, down and woke as her skull shattered against a root.

'What else did Tarov say about these trees?' asked Jex.

'He said they've had a bit of rot. Big soggy sections and weak branches. Madifer burrows. But they're worth it because—'

'Madifer burrows?' Jex stopped moving and hung with one hand from a branch in front of Virda, forcing her to stop. 'I'm not climbing a tree with madifer burrows.'

'You climb them all the time without even realising,' she said.

'This is obviously different. If Tarov thought the burrows were worth mentioning, there must be an infestation.'

'Then turn back,' said Virda, with more bite than necessary.

Jex pulled that face of his – mouth wrinkled up under his nose, eyebrows crunched together.

'I'll come,' he said, 'but if any madifers get on me, I'm throwing them at your face.'

They reached Tarov's trees, and Virda could see immediately why he couldn't climb them. Tarov was as slow as Jex was reckless, and these trees had suffered some serious rot. It was dead rot, it wasn't spreading, but it was damp and hadn't healed over yet. You couldn't climb a rotten wickerwood tree slowly. More than a second of your weight on any holding point, and the wood would give way and slough off like mulch. She pictured Tarov carefully curling his fingers over a knot and having it crumble in his hand as he tried to hoist himself up.

Jex laughed. 'I can scale any of those.'

'Let's do it then,' said Virda, and they raced to the forest floor. She hopped and swung down the tiers of branches, and Jex did his usual controlled fall, grabbing twigs roughly and grazing himself on the trunk all the way down. There were about eleven rot-blotched trees and they each picked one and started climbing. The first stretch was easy: healthy young branches, just mature enough to be woody and springy at the same time. They paused when they reached the rot. It was further up than it appeared from the ground, and a fall could be deadly. Virda glared at Jex, daring him to back away from the challenge, but he smiled, defiant. And so they climbed.

The wood was like dried mud. It rubbed away and separated from the trunk in clods. The branches were few and far between, and visibly weakened. Jex kept himself close to the trunk, only using the loose branches when he had to. Wood rot smeared onto his uniform, and his determined expression gave way to disgust. Jex didn't get disgusted very easily, but these trees were worthy of it. At some points, Virda's tree audibly squelched.

They kept moving, inching sideways when up wasn't an option. Virda was faring better than Jex. She already had her hands around a healthy branch above the rot when they heard the unexpected whirr of a monocraft nearby. Perhaps Tarov had told the others about these challenging trees, and now one of them had come to see it for themselves. But none of the climbers they knew would choose to ride through the forest on a mono if they could help it, especially not on a beautiful climbing day like today. Virda felt a tingle of curiosity, and perched herself on a healthy branch, craning forward to watch the mono approach.

Jex, meanwhile, was struggling to clear the rot. His hands slipped, and Virda glanced at him just in time to see a look of mild panic pass over his face. He hugged all his limbs around the rotten trunk to keep from falling. From his side of the tree, he was hidden from the mono, which appeared just then far below, partly obscured by leaves. A slight figure in a red uniform, hair tucked away inside a matching red hat, parked the vehicle up against a tree. Was it Disa? Virda squinted between the shifting leaves. She was about to call out, but something stopped her. The figure was too slim to be Disa. Virda didn't want to give the poor red the fright of their life. And besides, their presence was strange, and Virda was curious. After fiddling with something on the tree trunk – perhaps taking a sample of the bark, which seemed to Virda a very plausible explanation for their presence – the figure walked with purpose into an open area beside a low, mossy tree stump and stooped as though to inspect it.

Virda stole a glance at Jex. He looked extremely miserable, with sweat beading on his brow from the effort of clutching the tree. Like Virda, he was keeping quiet, but Virda suspected this was motivated less by a desire not to startle the red and more to spare himself any humiliation. No climber wanted to be seen in the position he was in. Already his arms trembled. A clump of rotten bark came loose under one of his hands and fell, crumbling noisily to the forest floor. The red stood quickly and was motionless for a long moment. 'Hello?' they called out in a vaguely familiar voice.

The climbers looked at each other again. Jex raised one eyebrow in question. The red turned slowly, but didn't pause in their direction. They were just too far away and too obscured by foliage for a face to be discerned. 'Anyone there?'

Virda opened her mouth, ready to announce herself, but again she hesitated. Something in the red's voice – a subtle, tremulous tension – made her think they didn't want to be seen. Her mind flitted to Shani, banished to the reformatory for the unexplained crime of trespassing. Who had called it in? Was there someone living in Wooden Hill right now who was responsible for Shani's banishment? Had they been lurking up a tree just like she was, watching her cousin go wherever it was she shouldn't have? Perhaps this red was up to something they shouldn't be, but it wasn't Virda's business. And anyway, the moment had passed. It was too late now to call out to the stranger without seeming suspicious herself, so she kept quiet and watched, and Jex, as always, followed her lead. The stranger, satisfied that they were alone, went down onto their haunches beside the tree stump.

Jex whimpered quietly, pulling Virda's attention. A large, furry madifer was walking over his arm. He tried to shake it off, but it changed direction and trundled merrily down his spine. The colour drained from his face. He bit his lip hard, and Virda could tell it was taking every bit of his self-control to keep still and resist his natural reaction to madifers, which was a combination of screaming and flailing.

Jex tried to get one of his hands around his back to smack the madifer away without losing his grip on the tree. He panted, increasingly frantic as the rotten wood began to crumble under his other hand. With one last look at the red, who had moved further away to examine a distant tree trunk, Virda hopped, nimble and quiet, across to Jex's tree and slid down, twisting off a green twig and using it to flick the madifer from his visibly tensed backside. It cartwheeled through the air and landed on a lower branch, righting itself and scurrying away indignantly. With an outstretched hand, Virda finally helped Jex to clear the rot, hauling him up beside her. His pride was in tatters. He prostrated himself along the first sturdy branch he could reach and let out his feelings in a breathy whisper.

'Cacking… pissing… madifers.'

Down below, the figure in red had stepped onto the mono again, and was soon disappearing back towards the settlement.

'What do you think that was all about?' said Virda.

She took her pod from her pocket and checked the map on the rhetalink to see if there were any marked research areas or facilities nearby. There weren't. They were just inside an old Singer burial ground, but barely anyone studied the Singers anymore.

'If they'd just been strolling, I wouldn't think anything of it,' said Jex, 'but that was weird, don't you think?'

'They might've been taking bark samples,' said Virda. 'It's none of our business.'

Whatever the mysterious figure in red had been up to – whether taking samples or stashing restricted substances or leaving messages to fugitives – they didn't appear to be hurting anyone, and Virda wasn't inclined to pursue the matter any further. She'd never allow herself to be responsible for landing someone in the reformatory when they didn't need to be there. In her rarely expressed but deeply held opinion, nobody needed to be there.

She ruffled Jex's hair, and he arched into her touch with a small sigh.

'Let's go home,' she said.

CHAPTER 10

The field unit was where Berro and Undra's work took place, but Undra still retained his office at the academy for his duties as an imparter. It was double the size of most other academy offices, and the other large ones were shared between two imparters, while Undra had this one to himself. He used half the space to store his impressive collection of crossing books and paraphernalia in several rows of shelving units – a private museum and library accessible only to his closest colleagues and collaborators. The other half of the office was subdivided into the desk area where they now sat and a boxy private room behind it, the living quarters. Every imparter had one of these in their office – some preferred to keep other accommodation away from the academy, but Undra didn't bother. He slept in that back room, or at the field unit softseat when it wasn't occupied by a living crosser.

Berro wished he could open that door behind Undra's desk and take a proper look inside. He'd caught a glimpse of it once when Undra had ducked in to fetch something during one of their meetings – the corner of a neatly made bed; another, smaller desk, cluttered with interesting things; natural light streaming in through the window overlooking the academy grounds. With the door to the private room shut, there was no natural light in the office, as Undra had covered the window behind the shelves with thick curtains.

The ecolamps gave the office a subterranean feeling that Berro quite liked. He always had preferred being deep underground to being high above it – another argument in favour of dormitory over treehouse living.

When Undra had first briefed him on the role of primary assistant, he'd encouraged Berro to peruse the collection while he spoke. Berro had risen awkwardly from his seat and shuffled between the shelves, equally desperate to inspect every item and to concentrate on every word Undra was saying.

Jewellery was laid out in a tilted, glass-fronted box, each piece pinned carefully for observation. Shiny things with colourful stones, delicate loops of chain wrought of different metals, chunky carved wooden hoops, a hollow jointed finger made of tarnished silver with a sharp, curved point… Berro remembered his first glimpse of a large sparkling gem set into a bent ring, crushed by some violent act. It looked immensely valuable, and he'd wondered what part it played in the story of the crosser who'd arrived with it. There were bits of clothing, various practical and decorative bags, strange devices with wires, assorted tubes and tiny jars made of glass and metal and plastic, some containing strange pastes and gels. There were loose papers, and there were books. *Yorg-Amoranga – Book of Cyclic Obligations*, small and bound in scaly leather. *Historical Walks: Eidyn*, by various authors. *My Kidneys are My Kidneys*, a tattered and incomprehensible tome by someone named Pira-Pira Chun-Chun. *MadiferMan*, the illustrated adventures of a person in a tight-fitting suit of blue and orange, shooting powerful strings of sticky silk from his wrists. A flimsy pamphlet entitled *Survival Basics*, containing crudely drawn images of inefficient fire-building techniques. The book Undra kept in the most prominent position, propped up on its own stand, was a well-worn copy of *The Pursuit of Knowledge*. It bore the names of several authors from another world, along with the subtitle: '*What there was, what there is, and what there could be*'.

Alongside this book was Berro's favourite discovery in the

collection: a picture of Undra from about a decade ago, when he was still a post-fundamental student, already well known in academic circles, no doubt, but not yet globally respected as he was now. In the picture, he was standing next to the partly obscured body of the Rainbow Woman, arguably the most famous crosser, having apparently been granted access to study her. What was wonderful about the picture wasn't just that it was evidence of Undra having seen the Rainbow Woman in the flesh, but that he looked so young, almost unrecognisable with a short beard, shaggy, shoulder-length hair and an open, laid-back body language that made it incredibly easy to understand how he'd become so popular and well-liked. He was grinning widely and unselfconsciously. Berro imagined the person behind the lens had made a joke, and Undra had just finished laughing at it.

Undra's presentation was different now, neat and tidy, more mature, but Berro recognised this younger Undra beneath the surface. His eyes still sparked with the same energy and brilliance, even if his smiles and his hair were more controlled. Berro had discreetly snapped an image of the picture using his pod and sent it to Virda, thinking she might be amused to see Undra looking like an enthusiastic candidate for their tree-climbing and wicker-smoking collective. She'd later replied with an >>*emote: snort*<<, and Berro had been satisfied with that.

Berro eyed the picture now from where he sat in front of Undra's desk, but it was in shadow, and he couldn't make out any details at that distance. Undra, meanwhile, had been scrutinising his slab for some time.

'I've been tracking irregularities around the glasshouse,' he said. 'You know where that is?'

'Yes, Imparter.'

'Great. I can't be sure yet, but I strongly suspect a crossing is due to happen there. The anomalies have been intensifying. Within the next couple of hours, I think the barrier will be as thin as it was when our live crosser arrived. I'd like you to get there as soon as you can, and be prepared for anything.'

Berro smiled. 'Of course, Imparter. Could you tell me more about the anomalies? I'd love to see the...'

See the *what*? What was Undra measuring? And how? He was so ignorant of the actual workings of Undra's research, he didn't even know how to articulate a question about it, and the thought deflated him in his seat.

'Oh, it's an incomprehensible mess right now,' Undra said, with a dismissive flick his the fingers. 'It's just numbers.'

Berro wanted to see those numbers. He wanted to know what they represented. He wanted to understand, but he didn't want to seem impatient or pushy about it. He stood hurriedly.

'Thank you, Imparter.'

'Thank *you*, Berrovan,' the imparter replied, his smile widening enough to evoke that image of the young, carefree man in the picture.

Berro's heart leapt in his chest.

• • •

In the mingle outside the office, Berro used his height and bulk to jostle through knots of students blocking his way to the elevator, ignoring their sounds of protest. He crammed himself into the capsule, even though this forced an innocent red's face into his armpit. Usually Berro tried not to inconvenience other people with his size, but there were important things at stake just then. Undra had given him a task, and he was determined to complete it quickly and correctly.

He rushed across the field to the bank of monocrafts, and then he was off, speeding away to the field unit to collect his gear. In all probability, there would either be nothing or a dead body at the location Undra had supplied, but this time Berro couldn't stop imagining another live crosser waiting for him at the outskirts of the forest, bewildered and alone.

What if it was someone bigger than him? What if they had teeth filed into points, limbs thick with muscles and scars, armed with some sort of weapon he'd never seen before? Berro was big and strong, but that was more by design than by concerted effort on his part. The time he invested in his body – occasional evening runs along the branch paths, and weekly stretch and strength sessions at the academy gym – was only to maintain his health and keep his mind sharp. He wasn't a fighter.

The coordinates took Berro beyond a few small satellite settlements, including the one where Virda and Jex had been raised, to the glass house, a Singer ruin at the literal edge of the forest where the trees gave way to grasslands – a sparkling, shattered memory of the time before.

He'd never been there, but he knew of it from fundamental history lectures and from the tube rides of his past. It was the furthest Undra had sent him out for a collection – so far out, in fact, that if he hadn't been potentially collecting a body, he'd have caught the hovertube to the next station instead of riding the mono all the way. He hoped the imparter was mistaken and that, like the previous time, there would be no crosser to collect, because lugging a body back to the field unit across such a distance was an exhausting prospect.

Roots and branches and creepers pushed their way through the wreckage of the glass house, as though the forest was pulling the structure in to devour it, crush the metal, and powder the glass in the slow, powerful curl of its woody fists. It hadn't succeeded yet, though. One of the house's great curved sides, the side facing out and protruding from the treeline, was still in relatively good condition. Some of the glass panes were unbroken there, and the filigree metalwork between them not yet fully corroded. It was an intricate design of interlinking shapes – corals, shells, the scales of fish. The glasscrafter must've been highly skilled, as many were when it had been considered an important occupation.

The glass house, Berro remembered, was less commonly known as the 'glass boat'. Something to do with its shape, and the marine themes in the design. Perhaps there was some other significance he couldn't recall. He knew it had been crafted to inspire the power of tongues, that the Singers would have been heard for miles around, wailing in their mysterious non-languages when they gathered at this place. They'd been some sort of cult – widely derided as eccentrics, separatists and lunatics, babbling noise and nonsense in defiance of Kastak's growing linguistic hegemony. As the global tongue's privilege and dominance began to creep its way into law, the Singers were among those whose very existence was taken as a threat to Rhetari unity. When it all came apart, when the supply chains were shut down, when the riots began, when the marrowcore bombs started to fall, and people scattered into the last of Rheta's green spaces, armed and frenzied by propaganda and desperation, the Singers didn't stand a chance. The war wiped them out, as it had so many others.

Berro leaned the mono against a tree and crunched tentatively through a hole in the nearest wall of the glasshouse. The metal filigree around it was a gnarled mess, probably from a blast during the massacres. He stood among the tangle of woody roots and luscious ferns inside and gazed up at the expanse of the high glass roof above. Where the branches of the trees could reach them, the glass panes had been smashed out, but otherwise they were mostly intact, and Berro peered through them at the purpling sky and the gliding clouds and the sinking sun that made the house shine like a beacon on clear evenings. The hovertube track, many leaps away, was still near enough for the passengers to see the house reflect the setting sun in the distance. Everyone would crowd to one side of the tube and watch it, a burning candle flaring up white-hot against the dark curved wall of the forest, until they entered the treeline again and lost sight of it.

Berro couldn't imagine what it must've been like when the Singers set the glasshouse ringing with their voices. The place felt utterly abandoned, the possibility of another live crosser unthinkable in the yawning silence. An odd smell, a sort of chemical tang, ebbed and flowed with the breeze, perhaps from the decaying materials making up the glasshouse or from some strange plant growing at this remote edge of the forest, but finding nothing else noteworthy, Berro picked his way back out and scouted the surrounding area, walking outward in a spiral.

First, he saw the blood.

It was small, dark puddle on the dirt in front of him, and he paused, looking from side to side to find its source.

A drop fell into the puddle from above. Time slipped and slowed. Berro breathed and blinked and looked up into the branches overhead. A broken body hung there, partly obscured by leaves and a jumble of cords and ripped fabric. Its head was hidden inside a strange helmet. Dead, judging by the angle of the neck. One of the legs was missing from halfway up the thigh and a branch had pierced right through the torso. As if that horror wasn't enough, the body also appeared to be burnt on one side. A change in the air wafted the smell in Berro's direction, and he drew one of his hands in front of his face.

He'd prepared for this from the beginning of the project, and now he had to put that preparation to the test. For a few moments, he closed his eyes, willing his heart to slow and his breathing to even out. Then he rolled a pair of gloves onto hands that didn't feel like they belonged to him and started to climb the tree. He didn't have Virda's or Jex's climbing experience, so he hoisted himself up slowly, careful to put his weight only on the thickest branches.

The smell intensified as he neared the body. Bloodflies hummed around it. *It's just a specimen. Just a specimen.*

'Greetings, crosser,' he said when he drew level with his target. 'I'm sorry we had to meet this way. My name is Berrovan, and I'm going to take you to the field unit so we can find out more about you. I hope you don't mind.'

He kept talking as he severed the cords and fabric with his

multitool, breathing hard through his teeth. With precision and care, he untangled the corpse and lifted it from the impaling branch, sending the flies into a frenzy as dark blood oozed over the wood. The crosser was a specimen, *a specimen*, nothing but flesh attached to artefacts from another world… but they had been a person once, and Berro couldn't stop talking. He tried to push from his mind a vision of Kath impaled in a tree. The taste of charred flesh was in his mouth, and his eyes burned.

Using the severed cords, Berro lowered the body to the forest floor. The shredded sheet of shiny fabric billowed and swirled down after it, landing gently over it like a shroud. It was a parachute. The crosser had fallen from the sky. Jex's Vehicles instructor, Imparter Pol, would be interested in the design of the parachute, when eventually they had access to all these findings.

The glasshouse was already ablaze with the reflection of the setting sun by the time Berro had the body covered and fastened into the monocraft trailer. He sprinkled chemical salts over the bloody patches on the forest floor and then looked at the glasshouse, looked through it, wondering what incomprehensible words the Singers might've had for what he'd just seen and done. They had believed in an afterlife, in the significance of the body, in honour after death. Berro didn't believe in these things himself, but he knew from catalogued evidence that many people from other streams of reality did. He'd tried to handle the parachutist with care and respect. He hoped it was enough.

Berro moved his cargo carefully through the outer gate of the field unit, closing it behind him with a comforting click. The perimeter fences muffled the forest ambience, leaving nothing but a hush, the breeze stirring the leaves overhead and the creak of nearby insects, close and conspiratorial. Berro's skin prickled as he considered his cargo. He leaned back against the gate, staring intently at the bodybag, waiting for it to move. But it didn't. Of course it didn't. The crosser was thoroughly dead. After a few deep breaths, Berro heaved the trailer around the unit, lifted the hatch at the back wall, slid the bodybag into the chute, and waited to feel relief. Perhaps it would come, when he got the smell out of his nose. He sent a message to Undra.

: Glasshouse specimen (deceased) has been delivered to the field unit without incident.

Respectfully, Berrovan :

PART 2

THE REACH

SEVEN YEARS AGO

year 215, month 1, day 5

Sarla hummed a sweet, meandering tune as she chopped the dried frigram into fine flakes. The kitchen was fragrant and warm, made cosier by the snow swirling outside. Freshwater snails – defrosted, boiled, and battered in millbean flour – were lined up ready for frying, beside a bowl of chopped root vegetables tossed in wickernut oil and dried herbs. Sarla dusted the frigram into the pot boiling on the stove, then added the root vegetables, careful to scoop every tiny piece from the bowl before setting it aside. She had ample supplies at the research cabin, but she'd been raised to understand and respect the Code rules and Cohera guidance regarding food waste. This food would be enough to last her for three days. She had two small cooling boxes open and ready to fill with the extra portions. A splash of oil into the pan, and then the battered snails were dropped in, one by one. Her stomach grumbled as the rich aroma filled the room.

'Hmm, perfect.'

Sarla had taken to speaking to herself over the past few days. It was lonely in the cabin, and she missed her son and her partner. The nights were so cold without Marruvan. She was there to gather data from a nearby Singer ruin rich with linguistic carvings, and to write up the research in peace and quiet, but she was already tiring of the isolation.

The snails sizzled and browned, and she shook the pan to keep them turning. In the clatter of the frying and the bubbling of the pot, she barely heard the first tentative knock at the front door and disregarded it as one of those random noises – branches in the wind, falling seed pods, a scrattin running along the gutter. The second knock, though, was clear and unmistakable, and Sarla stiffened in sudden fright, spattering droplets of hot oil onto her wrist. She bit back her curse words, carefully switched off the two hot stove tops, and dabbed her wrist with the dishrag draped over her shoulder.

The knocking came again, quieter this time.

Sarla edged towards the door. She'd never had visitors call at this cabin. It was remote, to say the least, tucked away in the forest on the outskirts of the vast unreclaimed city of Osgen, one of the largest no-zones on Rheta. This remoteness, however, seemed less significant than the time and the weather.

Steps away from the door, she decided that if it was someone meaning harm, they probably wouldn't have bothered to knock first. And if they did mean harm, pretending she wasn't there wouldn't achieve much. They'd surely heard her clanking about in the kitchen.

'Hello?' she said.

'Hello,' came a deep voice. 'I'm sorry to trouble you at such an hour, but I'm lost. And I'm cold.'

Sarla hesitated. It could be a ruse to get inside without having to break anything. Under normal circumstances, she'd be less paranoid, but she was alone, and her research was all over her writing table, unfiled.

'Who… who are you?' she asked, annoyed at the fearful catch in her voice.

'My name is Terek. I'm a cartographer. I seem to have lost my campsite. Ironic, I know. I suspect I chose the wrong specialisation.'

Sarla took a deep breath and slid back the bolt, opening the door to reveal a cold-chapped man of medium build wearing a strange thermal monosuit in an unpleasant shade of purple.

'Terek,' she said, stepping aside. 'Do come in. I'll make you some tea.'

'You are very kind,' he said, entering the cabin with a puff of snow at his heels, a violent tremble in his limbs as the steamy heat enveloped him. Sarla closed and bolted the door behind him.

'Have you eaten?' she enquired. He had moved directly in front of the marrowcore heating panel and already a puddle of melted snow grew around his feet. She could see he was trying hard to keep his trembling under control.

'I have not,' he said, pulling off his thermal hood to reveal a head of short-cropped dark hair, receding slightly and greyed around his ears. 'I've been lost for some time... What may I call you?' He turned to look at her, his face dripping with the thaw from his eyebrows and sideburns.

'I'm Sarla,' she said, still cautious, imagining Marruvan's reaction at her allowing this stranger into her cabin, at night, in the middle of one of the worst spells of snow since winter began. He'd commend her generosity, of course, but he'd also shake his head and raise his brows and laugh a little bit, like he always did when she exasperated him – something she found both infuriating and endearing, like so many of his words and ways. 'I've just been putting together some food, and there's plenty to spare. I can dish some up for you when it's done, if you like.'

'That would be most kind of you, thank you,' said Terek, his voice breaking slightly. 'It smells wonderful.'

'Last of the summer snails,' said Sarla. They looked done, so she took the pan from the cooling stove top and replaced it with a pot for tea before turning the heat back on.

'Oh, I couldn't possibly eat the last of your snails...'

He was trying to sound casual about it, to be polite, but she could hear his hunger, his words slightly pained and with a salivary quality.

'There are plenty,' she assured him. 'Honestly, it's no trouble.'

'You have my deepest gratitude, Sarla,' he said. Terribly formal. Appropriate, perhaps, for a cartographer. But what was he wearing? It wasn't appropriate gear for long periods outdoors, and the colour...

As if sensing her questions and her curiosity, Terek coughed uncomfortably and moved closer to the heater again.

The tea water had boiled, and Sarla added the berries, more than she normally would, crushing them until the drink was dark and pulpy, with a heady scent. She decanted it into two mugs and handed one to Terek. His fingers were blue with cold, purple in the nails.

'Thank you, Sarla,' he said, wrapping his hands stiffly around the mug. 'Such a relief, to be out of the cold. I'll repay this kindness as soon as I'm able.'

'It's no problem at all,' she said. 'It's good to have a bit of company.' She immediately regretted saying this. Too familiar, too friendly. She didn't want to let down her guard, particularly not in such strange circumstances, but she couldn't help acknowledging the truth of her words. It was *good to have company.*

When the broth was ready, she ladled it into two large bowls, dropping a few snails on top of each. She placed the food on the low table between two soft seats. Terek hesitated beside one of the seats.

'I'm afraid I'm still rather wet...'

'Not to worry,' said Sarla. 'Tuck in.'

He sat and immediately began spooning the broth between his chapped lips with an almost frantic urgency. Sarla watched, wide-eyed. His meal was almost finished before he realised Sarla was staring at him, having eaten nothing herself.

'My apologies,' he said, resting his spoon in the bowl for the first time since picking it up. 'I'm a bit hungrier than I thought I was. Or perhaps it's just the... the quality of this cooking.'

Sarla surveyed him silently while he shifted uncomfortably in the beam of her gaze.

'You're not really a cartographer, are you?' said Sarla, marvelling at her own bravery. If she was right, then this could all go terribly wrong.

Terek sniffed. He said nothing and lifted the spoon again, holding a perfect cube of snow squash in small lake of green frigram broth.

'I am a cartographer,' he said. 'At least, I was.'

Sarla waited. There was more to this story. Terek put the spoon into his mouth, chewed slowly, swallowed with apparent difficulty.

'I'm afraid I haven't been entirely honest with you, Sarla, but I

don't want to upset you. If I'd told you the truth at the doorstep, you probably wouldn't have let me in.'

'And if I hadn't let you in, what would you have done?' she asked.

'I would've begged, to begin with,' he said. 'And if that had failed, I'd have turned away and sought another saviour. Though it's safe to say it's unlikely I'd have found one.'

'And if you failed to find one, what would happen?'

'I'd die, I suppose.'

Terek began eating again. Sarla's food remained untouched.

'So, if I'd turned you away, I'd have sent you to your death, but you wouldn't have forced your way into my house to prevent that. Why not?'

Terek's food was finished, and he looked forlorn as he stared into the empty bowl. Sarla slid her own bowl across the table towards him. He cocked his head at her, questioning.

'Eat,' she said. 'I can see you're still hungry.'

His eyes gleamed, and he sniffed heavily, giving a curt nod and starting on the second bowl of broth and snails.

'This is the best meal I've ever had,' he said thickly, through a mouthful.

It didn't sound like hyperbole, and he didn't seem the sort to exaggerate.

'It's standard fare,' said Sarla. 'Nothing special.'

She was alarmed by the sudden tears that sprang into Terek's eyes. He blinked them back, apparently hoping she wouldn't notice, and she allowed him to eat in silence until he had his emotions under control again. Once the second bowl was finished, she resumed her interrogation.

'Why did you abandon your vocation, Terek? Cartographers are highly valued. Highly trained.'

'I didn't abandon my vocation,' he said. 'I was, unfortunately, unable to pursue it after certain circumstances were imposed upon me.'

She understood. She kept her face passive, kept her suddenly clammy hands resting on her legs where he couldn't see them shaking. She wasn't sure if she should admit to knowing the truth. Perhaps he already knew that she knew. He had wise eyes, set into his face of indeterminate age. Older than her, she thought, but how much older?

He seemed to be wrestling with decisions of his own, picking absent-mindedly at the edge of the table with a rough, dirty fingernail while gnawing on a tag of skin peeling from his bottom lip. His eyes flashed up at her, and he heaved a great sigh and put his head in his hands.

'I'm not going to hurt you, I promise,' he said, voice muffled and cracked. His broad shoulders shook as he was pummelled by some dark tide of grief. 'I've made you nervous. I am so sorry. I'm eternally grateful for this kindness. I mean every word I say.'

Sarla nodded. 'You've come from the reformatory,' she said at last.

'Yes,' said Terek. 'I escaped.'

'Do they make all the prisoners wear that awful colour?'

Terek dropped his hands and stared incredulously. Sarla kept a straight face for as long as she could, but she couldn't keep her lip from slowly curling up on one side.

Terek laughed. 'Yes,' he said. 'Yes, they do.'

'I'm sure the colour of your thermals was the least of your worries, though.'

He nodded, relieved, laying his hands on the table and laughing some more. 'No, you're right. I'd never actually considered the colour before, but now that you point it out… It is horrible, isn't it?'

'How long were you inside?'

'Ten years,' he said, and then again, as though he could barely believe his own words, 'ten years.'

'You don't have to tell me why,' said Sarla. 'I'm no great supporter of the reformatory system. It's too Code-bent. I've read about it. They don't respect the Cohera. Fewer and fewer do these days…'

Terek smiled openly now. 'I can barely believe my luck. I'm on my last legs, I see a lighted window, and not only does the occupant of the house allow me inside and feed me the best meal of my life, but she's also a reformatory sceptic. I knew it as soon as you called us "prisoners". It's against the reformatory sub-Code, did you know that? If you refer to yourself or anyone else in there as a "prisoner", there are repercussions.'

'It's "patients", isn't it?' said Sarla. 'And what are they treating you for, exactly?'

'In general, or me specifically?'

'Whichever answer you'd prefer to give. I won't pry any further. It's your business, not mine.'

Terek shook his head. 'You took a big risk, letting me into your home. I think the very least I can give you is the truth. Perhaps you don't think I owe it to you, but I disagree, and if anything happens to me once I take leave of your hospitality, at least there'll be one person living who knows my story. If you wish to hear it.'

Sarla nodded. 'I do.'

CHAPTER 11

For weeks after the collection of the dead crosser from the glasshouse, Berro did not sleep well. His dreams writhed with maggots, blind and jellied eyes in peeling faces, dark things awakening, gaping mouths of smashed teeth and swollen tongues. Faces from the war melted into the faces of crossers and the faces of his friends, all dead, dead, dead. He didn't eat well, either. The smell of the charred body lingered over everything. White noise resolved itself into the buzzing of bloodflies, and he felt them walking along his skin. He scratched his arms and ground his teeth until his jaw ached. Each time he showered, he scrubbed himself too hard and too long. He trimmed his nails too short and still filed them further until they hurt. The fresh coat of gloss burned at the raw edges of his fingertips.

He had expected Undra to turn more of his attention to Kath, to alter the direction of the study in light of Kath's miraculous crossing, but this had not happened, and Berro was surprised by the intensity of his own disappointment. When Undra didn't request further interviews with the crosser, Berro offered to visit Kath at the lakehouse and interview her again himself, but Undra's reaction to this idea was so indifferent that Berro had left the meeting with an odd sense of shame at having even suggested it.

It was clear that the crossings themselves were of more interest to Undra than the products of those crossings, and Berro couldn't fathom why. He respected his imparter's focus, but was frustrated by his disinterest in Kath, who had far more to offer than any lifeless corpse ever would or could. She was here *now*, living and learning, with fresh memories of another world.

Berro caught himself wishing that Undra would select another assistant to collect the bodies and assign him instead to documenting Kath's progress and recording her recollections of her own world for the canon of Realities literature. But what if he suggested this to Undra, and Undra brought Ryndel into a primary assistant role? And what if Undra put Ryndel to work studying Kath instead of letting Berro do it? It would make sense to leave the big, strong man in charge of lifting dead weight and hauling it across difficult terrain. Berro couldn't bear the thought of elevating his rival only to have her usurp him. Kath was *his* discovery.

Berro's desire to study Kath was as strong as his desire to avoid another encounter with death and gore. In truth, they were not separate desires; Berro had to admit to himself that one was, at least in part, fuelled by the other.

When Undra sent him out to investigate another location, the dread sat cold and heavy in his gut. He didn't want to find a body. He didn't want to touch a body. He didn't want to hear a body sliding down the chute into the field unit laboratory.

Still, he was Berro, and he would do what he had to do, diligently. He reached the location and walked outwards from the exact coordinates Undra had given him in a large, tight spiral, looking up and down and into the undergrowth with each careful step he took. He didn't find a crosser, nor any trace of one. No blood, no fragments of cloth or flesh, no strange items twisted or crushed in the trauma that forced them between worlds. Not even an angry shadowcat.

Berro was not disappointed, he was relieved. He held his pod in front of his mouth while his eyes swept the area around him. 'Imparter, I'm at the location, but there's nothing here.'

He felt guilty about his relief, and he did everything he could to keep it out of his voice. Undra didn't need to know how much the mangled body in the tree had affected him.

'You're certain? Nothing unusual at all?'

'Nothing,' said Berro. 'It smells a bit strange here, but—'

'A smell?' said Undra. 'What sort of smell?'

'Hard to say. A sort of mineral smell.'

Undra was silent for a few moments.

'Imparter?'

'Did you smell anything like it when you found Kathleen or the crosser by the glasshouse?'

Berro cast his mind back. 'I might've, at the glass house. I remember smelling something, but I'm not sure if it was the same thing. When I found Kathleen alive, I was too surprised to take note of everything else.'

'And did you hear anything?'

'Hear anything? No, I— I'm not sure.'

'Never mind,' said Undra. 'Probably irrelevant. Not every reading is going to yield results, and that's fine. You've done great work, Berrovan. You can head back to the academy, if you like. I'm in my office for a few more hours before late lectures.'

It sounded very much like an invitation to chat, and Berro couldn't help but smile. This was what he wanted. To be Undra's protege, his collaborator. Perhaps, one day, his friend. He'd put up with the horrible work if it meant keeping these privileges for himself.

'Thank you, Imparter,' he said, as Undra ended the call.

Undra's tone had been supportive and encouraging, but Berro felt guilty, even though he had no reason whatsoever to feel that way. He stood beside his monocraft, breathing in the strange tang of the air, his eyes still roving over the scene as the light faded. Why did these crossings so often happen in the evening?

As the sun slipped down, a shaft of golden light broke through the clouds and trees, and for a moment Berro saw something glint on a tree trunk, so briefly he might've imagined it. He tramped through a low tangle of undergrowth to inspect the tree. It wasn't difficult to find the source of the reflection – a small, pointed, dark purple crystal, forced into a fissure in the bark. A trickle of fresh sap ran from the wound in the wood.

Berro took a cloth from one of his pockets and used it to wiggle the crystal free. It was perfectly symmetrical, certainly cut using some sort of machine, and a fine silver line, like a metal filament, ran through the middle of it. He sealed it into a small bag and put it in his breast pocket. It wasn't a crosser, but it was something, and maybe Undra would be intrigued by it. *Well spotted, Berrovan!* he'd say, and give his assistant a warm look, eyes twinkling, lips curved into a half smile. *Well spotted, indeed!*

But that was not what happened when Berro, finally seated in Undra's office on the eleventh floor at the academy, took the bag from his pocket and removed the crystal, carefully opening the cloth and lifting it between his fingers to show it to the imparter. It felt cool and strange against his fingertips.

'Hmm,' said Undra, tapping the table. Berro placed the crystal in front of him. 'Curious.'

But Undra didn't look curious. In fact, he didn't even seem to be looking at the crystal so much as gazing right through it and thinking about something else entirely. Berro had a mind to lift the crystal again and draw Undra's attention to its symmetry, but Undra reached out and wrapped it in the cloth, slipped it quickly back into the bag Berro had brought it in and put the bag into his desk drawer. 'I'll run some tests on it and see what I can find out. It might be nothing.'

It might be nothing.

It might be nothing.

I might be nothing.

Nothing nothing nothing…

On his way across the mingle as he headed for the elevator, bitter with disappointment, Berro stumbled, lurched forward, caught himself with a hand thrown out against an obstacle, a person, who cried out and turned around with a shout. Everything dipped and spun around him.

Where was he going again? He couldn't quite remember. The air was unusually fragrant, treacly. He felt like he'd smoked a strong wicker all on his own. But he never smoked wicker – low tolerance, bad reactions. While Jex became a more enhanced version of himself under the influence of wickerbloom, and Virda more relaxed, Berro found that it just made him bewildered and nauseous. But he hadn't smoked or ingested any wicker and he couldn't fathom why he felt so... so...

I might be nothing, he thought or said again, the words painted slowly across his brain by the hand of a skilled pre-war inksmith. His stomach was a water-filled pit and his heart a jumping stone. He walked, more carefully now, ignoring the protests of blurry people, placing one disembodied foot in front of the other while trying to contain a vague tide of panic that surged and retreated inside him. And outside him, too. Its shadowy hands darted out from the milling crowds. What was happening?

A couple of people exited the elevator before he stepped into it, and he had the impression that they were staring at him, that they'd stopped to watch his descent, but when he turned around, they were heading away, a set of green backs, disappearing. Where were they going? A night climb, a night walk, a gathering of friends in a treehouse, with tea. With tea? With tincture. With brew. With that strong-smelling stuff Undra used to sanitise the lab. Corpses sitting on a softseat, smiling, dead. Berro shuddered.

His mind tumbled and glided, unmoored.

And then the elevator moved, its lights glowing around him – such lights! Berro felt a rush of nausea and stopped the elevator at the ablutions. He bolted into a biocloset and knelt before the receptacle, head spinning. But nothing happened. He rested his cheek against the side of the cubicle and closed his eyes. The darkness behind his eyelids swam with strange patterns, purpleblack and living green. His hands burned like they'd been stung by a swarm of waspiks, and he pressed them to the cool surface of the receptacle to soothe them.

Two students entered the ablutions, talking and giggling. Berro heard their words but couldn't seem to connect the words with any meanings. He wondered if he should write down what they said so he could review it later when his mind was clear. No. Why? This was not important. Why was he sitting on the floor in a biocloset? He opened his eyes and immediately the nausea rose again. He tipped himself forward and vomited neatly into the gaping mouth of the receptacle and then slumped back again, spent.

'You all right in there?' said one of the students, giggling suspended.

'You all right in there…' Berro mumbled, then comprehended, then responded, 'I am now, thank you.'

The purging of his stomach, the cool, crisp air and the scent of anti-bacterial cleanser had sobered him a bit, and he managed to reach his dormitory without further incident.

No one was in the alcove. Berro sat on the edge of his bunk and held his head in his hands. He must've flaked out in an upright position, because when he opened his eyes again, people were milling about in the corridors, and Kem stood in front of him, face full of concern.

'Berro,' he said. 'What's the matter?'

Berro shook his head, and it throbbed. 'Just tired.'

'Want me to turn this light off? I'm heading out for a sunset climb. I'll try to be quiet when I get back in.'

Kem, the ideal roommate. Berro smiled weakly and rubbed his hands, which still felt itchy and strange. 'Sure. Thanks. I think I'll sleep through anything, though.'

'Even Ebra and Yurek coming back in?' Kem laughed.

Berro nodded and yawned.

He didn't care if they woke him. He didn't really care about anything except for getting his feet off the ground, so that's what he did. He didn't hear Kem leave the alcove. As soon as he was horizontal, Berro fell immediately into oblivion.

• • •

Virda spotted Tarov first, his back against a tree trunk, one leg extended and one bent, an arm resting on the bent knee and a smouldering wicker dangling between his long fingers. His hair was twisted into a knot on top of his head, and he wore a dark clothwrap that he'd left pooled around his waist, his tanned, toned torso exposed for anyone who cared to look at it. Virda did not care to look at it. In fact, she made a special effort not to.

'Hey, Virda. Jex.' He gave the slightest of nods as they approached, then put the wicker between his lips.

Kem and Gunli sat beneath a nearby ecolamp playing a dice game on patch of cleared ground. Kem, who wore a pale clothwrap with a pattern of orange triangles the exact colour of his hair, raised his hand and smiled at the two latecomers.

Gunli whipped their whiteblonde head around to see who it was. 'Greetings!' they called, ever the performer. Gunli's climbing style was much like their personality: jovial, entertaining and totally uncompetitive. 'Can we get in the trees now? I can't win at this stupid game.'

'You can't win at climbing either,' Tarov drawled, letting two jets of smoke pour from his nostrils.

'Oh, is this a competition?' Gunli laughed, scooping up the dice and tossing them down with a clatter. 'You're going to lose your edge if you keep smoking so much, Tarov, my love.'

'It doesn't affect my climbing at all,' said Tarov. He flicked the wicker butt onto the ground and hopped to his feet to crush it into the soil. 'Makes it more fun.'

'Got some for me?' Jex raised an eyebrow.

'Afraid not,' said Tarov. 'Disa might. Where is she, anyway? Even later than you two.' He rolled the top half of his cloth wrap and tucked it into the waist band so there weren't any loose bits to flap around and catch on branches.

Kem scooped up the dice and blew the dirt off them. 'Let's quit while I'm ahead,' he said, putting them into a pocket.

Disa arrived still wearing her red academy uniform. The only other person in uniform was Gunli, who wore their green uniform everywhere, claiming it brought out the colour of their eyes.

'Hello, climbers!' said Disa, with a small wave. 'Sorry I'm late. I stopped for some wicker—'

Jex punched the air, and Disa smiled, her tongue poking from the side of her mouth, one eye winking. 'I'll roll you one at the top.'

'Excellent.'

Virda and Tarov reached the top first. Tarov did his best to look casual about it, as if he hadn't been trying to beat her, but Virda saw how rapidly his naked chest rose and fell, and there was a thin scratch along his back that he probably would've avoided if he hadn't been racing.

They were up at the very apex of the canopy on a natural platform of intertwined branches. The climbers had helped it along over the years by bending new branches into the weave, and the platform now was like the cupped palms of tendinous woody hands, softened with leaves, strong and secure enough to hold a small group. Virda fitted herself into her favourite spot, where the curve of the tangled branches supported her head and back without any knotty protrusions. Above them, the sky exploded with colour in all directions, giddying in its boldness and brightness in contrast with the shadowy greens and browns of the world below. Purple clouds streaked diagonally across the display, like the trails of massive, high-altitude vehicles in days gone by. Tarov perched himself on the edge of the platform, letting his feet dangle down into the abyss.

Kem arrived next, hoisting Jex up behind him, followed by Disa. She threw herself down beside Virda, pushed her dark curls away from her face, and set about rolling a batch of wickers. Gunli emerged onto the platform a full five minutes after everyone else had settled down, streaked with sap and smiling broadly.

'Would you look at that!' Gunli said, putting hands on hips and staring up at the sky with their mouth hanging open. 'Blooming glorious, that is.'

'Blooming glorious,' said Jex, as Disa handed him a short, neat wicker. He lit it on the quick flame of her flinter and then lay back, one arm behind his head.

'One day, I'll be flying up there,' he said, more to himself than to anyone else.

Virda nudged his foot with her own. 'Will you take me around the world?'

'Of course,' he said. 'I've already asked Pol if I can take a passenger for my first proper flight in the Vollop.'

'Really?'

'It's completely safe. You stand more chance of dying under a falling tree branch than flying in a Vollop. That's what Pol said. My request is under consideration.'

'*Really?*' Virda sat forward. Disa offered her a wicker, but she waved it away, smiling. 'And you'd take me?'

'Who else would I take?' Jex laughed.

'Me!' said Gunli. 'I can't imagine a better flying companion than me, but you seem to have made up your mind.'

Tarov glowered at Jex, took a drag on his wicker and then passed it on to Kem. 'You've got your vocation sorted out then?' he said, with unconvincing indifference.

'Well, I hope so,' said Jex. 'It's the only thing I'm good at, other than climbing.'

Tarov snorted, as if to say, *You're not that good at climbing.*

'I wish I knew what to do,' said Virda. 'I'll just have to stay at the academy forever. Be a researcher.'

'Not a bad idea,' said Jex. He flicked a bit of ash from the end of his wicker. 'You could do data gathering that involves climbing. The hard-to-reach stuff. You're the best climber in Wooden Hill.'

Virda felt a blush spread across her cheeks. She hid how affected she was behind a dry smirk that she pointed in Tarov's direction. 'Hear that, Tarov? *The best*.'

Tarov pretended to be engrossed in a conversation between Kem and Disa about their plans for their performance at the autumn festival later in the year.

A flock of moontuks erupted out of the canopy some distance away, lining up their silhouettes and striking out across the sunset sky, their calls echoing in the expanse. Virda watched them until they became tiny flecks that dissolved into the haze at the horizon.

'Actually, I will have a wicker, if there's still one going,' she said. Disa took one from behind her ear and passed it along, giving Virda her customary wink, the tip of her tongue poking out the corner of her mouth. 'Enjoy,' she said, and tossed her the flinter.

Virda drew the cool smoke deep into her lungs. The marrow swelled within her. It was a strange sensation – one that many weren't partial to – certain senses dulling as others became exquisitely heightened. It wasn't addictive, though some who enjoyed it made a bad habit of it, Tarov and Jex being prime examples. Jex would have to cut down when he started flying skycrafts regularly.

Everyone experienced the effects of wickerbloom differently. For Virda, the concentrated marrow enhanced something that was already there within her all the time. When she closed her eyes, she felt she was closing them against a warm light, even if it was dark. It was a glow inside, but sometimes it felt like it was everywhere, depending on the quality of the wicker. The blooms were readily available to anyone, especially climbers in the springtime, but they couldn't be smoked right off the tree. They needed to be carefully picked, to have all the undesirable bits plucked away and then to be slowly and carefully dried until pleasantly smokable – not too weak and dusty, nor too strong and wet. Disa's wicker was mediocre this time, but good enough. Virda let herself melt into the sky, and the tops of the trees undulated like the waves of a dark ocean as far as the eye could see.

'We climbed your trees the other day,' said Jex. 'The ones with the rot.'

'Oh?' said Tarov. 'How did that go?'

Jex shook his head. 'It was horrible. Madifers everywhere.' He shuddered, and Tarov laughed, but not unkindly. 'We saw someone out there, which was kind of weird,' Jex added.

'Another climber?' asked Gunli.

'No, a red, down on the ground. Seemed to be looking for something. Maybe mushrooms.'

'All the way out there?' said Disa. 'Must be some very special mushrooms.'

'Probably some other pointless red research,' said Tarov.

Disa pulled a face at him. 'Fall out of a tree, greenie.'

'You're outnumbered,' said Tarov. 'What's your focus anyway? Doubt it's more interesting than mushrooms.'

'Moss and lichen,' said Disa, and everyone laughed. She rolled her eyes and pointed up at a lone vollop, wheeling through the darkening sky. 'They eat things that eat things that eat lichen. Did you know that? No lichen, no vollops.'

'Except for the vehicle version,' said Jex.

'Inspired by the real raptors, no doubt,' said Disa. 'Beautiful things.'

'Beautiful things,' said Jex, but Virda thought they weren't referring to the same thing.

'You know those rotten trees you were just talking about,' Disa said, gesticulating lazily. 'I was the one who told Tarov about them. It was a black rot. Bad stuff, spreads really fast if the weather is warm enough and can totally cack up an ecosystem if you don't stop it. I was on the team that contained it. You know how we did it?'

'Let me guess,' said Jex. 'Lichen.'

'Lichen!' said Disa triumphantly, raising her wicker in victory. 'Well, a bioengineered lichen-based salve. Completely neutralised the disease. Those trees will take a while to come right, but the rot's not spreading anymore.'

'I'm impressed,' said Jex.

'You should be,' Disa replied around a yawn. 'You absolutely should be.'

They lapsed into peaceful silence, shifting and stretching occasionally against the curves and bumps of their platform as they basked in the treetop ambience and sent streams of smoke into the sky. Virda nudged her foot rhythmically against Jex's. It was the sort of thing they often did – playing with each other's fingers, drawing patterns along each other's arms, pressing their shoulders together – a constant physical reminder of their loyalty.

'Your friend Berro was looking a little unwell this evening,' said Kem, rekindling the dying embers of conversation as the wickerbloom threatened to put them all to sleep. Tarov turned sharply towards him, and Virda was surprised to see a look of genuine concern etched into his face for a moment before it melted away into the usual studied indifference.

'Berro?' Virda tracked the vollop's lonely path across the sky. 'What's wrong with him?'

'No idea,' said Kem. 'I saw him in the dorm earlier, and he looked awful. Ashen, you could say. Kind of trembling and sweaty. He told me he was fine, but I don't think he'd tell me if he wasn't. He's a stoic sort, isn't he?'

'Food poisoning?' said Jex, doubtfully. 'No, I can't imagine Berro getting food poisoning. He probably eats the same things every day and he's so… healthy.'

'Maybe Big Boy Blue was getting stuck into some illicit substances on the sly,' said Tarov. 'Fits the symptoms.'

'Have you actually met Berro?' said Kem. 'I share a dorm with him. Believe me. There's no chance of that.'

Tarov scowled.

'Kem is right,' said Virda, and after a moment in which she and Jex simultaneously imagined Berro dabbling in drugs, they both erupted with laughter that made Tarov scowl even harder, as if they were laughing at him.

The laughter petered out into another stretch of comfortable silence, and then Kem started to sing. His voice was gentle and smooth, and Virda luxuriated in it, syncing her breath with the rhythm of the melody. It wasn't long before Disa was stubbing out her wicker and joining Kem with a pleasing harmony that sent shivers of pleasure along Virda's spine.

'I could just listen to you forever,' said Gunli, voice slurred with smoke and sleep. 'Forever and ever and *ever…*' Gunli rested their head against Kem's thigh, and Kem absently stroked their hair, eliciting a sound that was both a sigh and a purr.

Jex placed his own head on Virda's thigh, hoping for similar treatment, and Virda couldn't deny him; she never could. She combed her fingers through his shaggy blond hair, gently teasing out the tangles.

She rubbed the warm shell of his ear between her fingertips and remembered when their relationship had first become physical. It had seemed faintly taboo at first, even though they weren't related by blood, and had always known this fact. Indeed, they looked nothing alike and had come into the commune at different times, and their closeness had been a choice, a natural compatibility between them from an early age rather than an effort by Mama Stitch to raise them as siblings – but they'd tumbled through childhood together in ways that seemed similar to blood siblings around them, and so it took them longer to acknowledge the truth of their feelings, and accept the validity of them, than it would've had they met under different circumstances.

Or perhaps, Virda thought, perhaps they never would've developed the bond they had now if it wasn't for their shared childhood under the watchful eye of Mama Stitch and the commune family.

Jex fell asleep under her gentle ministrations, his head heavy against her thigh. She stroked her fingers into his hair, avoiding the ridge of scar tissue that ran from the top of his head to the space behind his ear. She let her thumb trail across his flushed cheek, traced the line of his jaw and the curve of his bottom lip. His golden eyelashes fluttered slightly, but he didn't wake.

'He is very beautiful,' said Disa, and Virda realised that the singing had stopped. Gunli was asleep, Kem and Tarov were chatting quietly, watching the last gasp of the sunset, and Disa was leaning towards her, elbows on knees and chin on hands, watching as she touched Jex's sleeping face.

'He is, isn't he?' Virda replied. 'I think I'll keep him.'

'As if he'd let you do anything else.'

'I nearly lost him once,' said Virda. 'I won't let it happen again.'

Disa reached out and squeezed Virda's knee. 'You know that wasn't your fault, right Virda? Sometimes these things just happen.'

'I know,' said Virda. 'It doesn't matter whose fault it was. It won't happen again.'

From the corner of her eye, she could see Disa's mouth opening to say something else, but the words never came. Instead, Disa squeezed her knee again and retreated slightly, recognising the thorny line of discussion for what it was.

'We should think about heading down,' she said. 'A third of us are asleep already.'

Virda never could fathom how Jex managed to descend trees so effectively when he was half asleep and intensely mellowed by wickerbloom, but he always did, slithering down and yawning as he grabbed at the branches with lazy hands and sagged against the trunk whenever he paused to rub his eyes or scratch his head.

Most of the summer trade stalls along the branch paths were closed for the night, but a few were still lamplit, with traders in the process of packing away their produce.

'Last bun?' said an old woman as they passed her table. She held out a rustic plate with a single, perfect millbean bun on it.

Virda hesitated, with Jex leaning heavily against her.

'I don't need credits,' said the woman. 'I just need to get rid of it. Been eating them all day. It's stuffed with treacle roosberries.'

The word 'treacle' drew Jex out of his walking slumber. 'Treacle roosberries?' he said. 'That sounds blooming.'

The old woman beamed at him as he took the proffered bun with gratitude. He ate it messily as they walked, several times he attempting to feed a berry to Virda as they stumbled along, but she resisted his clumsy efforts with good humour. Her brief exchange with Disa about the accident had flared the protectiveness inside her, and for the entire walk home, she was fixated on making sure Jex didn't trip and fall while he was distracted by his sticky bun. By the time she got him back to the treehouse where Magrin was already snoring in the other room, Virda was wide awake. To her relief, Jex remained intact and unscathed, though covered in treacle and crumbs.

She led him to the bedroom as quietly as she could so as not to disturb Magrin's infuriatingly vocal young vollop, who had recently taken to commenting loudly on any noise he heard in the treehouse at night with a piercing screech that only Magrin could sleep through. As soon as they got into their room and Virda closed the door behind them, Jex launched himself into the bed, dirty boots and all.

She sighed. 'Jex… clean your teeth first.'

'Why? It'll ruin the treacle berry flavour. You don't want to miss out on that.'

He writhed around under the cover, ejecting items of clothing one by one from beneath it. A boot, another boot, a food- and tree-stained clothwrap, an undergarment. They dropped onto the floor beside the bed, and Jex peered at Virda over the edge of the cover, eyes bright.

'Do you want me to congratulate you for undressing yourself even though you're a full-grown Rhetari man who knows how to pilot a skycraft?'

'No, I want you to get in here and snuggle me,' he said. 'The bed's cold.'

She slipped under the cover with him and immediately his arms were around her and his face tucked into her shoulder. She could smell the berries on his breath.

'Are you all right?' he murmured. She tended to forget that behind his guileless smile and interminable silliness was a perceptive and caring person who knew her better than anyone in the world ever had, or ever would.

'I'm fine,' said Virda, closing her eyes and tangling her fingers with his. 'You're fine, so I'm fine.'

CHAPTER 12

Fessi was torn from sleep as a gust of wind ripped open an unfastened bedroom window and sucked the curtain out, knocking over an empty vase and a box of trinkets on the sill. The weather had turned overnight, and now in the dull light of early morning it screamed through the forest and churned the lake outside. She and Kath scrambled towards the commotion, and Kath reeled in the flailing curtain while Fessi heaved the window shut, fastening it securely against the elements that buffeted the lakehouse and fought to get inside like an army of angry ghosts.

'I'm very glad I'm not in a treehouse right now,' Fessi breathed, rubbing the sleep from her eyes. She stared out at the lake, dark and choppy beneath the stone-grey sky. Reeds and grasses flailed and flattened themselves along the water's edge. A wirrit clung valiantly to one reed stalk, white feathers rippling as it swung wildly from side to side.

Kath settled back on her mattress. 'I hadn't thought of that. They must be getting thrown around up there.'

Heart still pounding from the rude awakening, Fessi righted the vase and placed the trinkets carefully back into their box one by one. A small painted fish that her late father had carved from a dried wickernut, a grass bracelet made by Andish, a glossy black feather from one of Magrin's birds, the wonky handle from a tea mug of Virda's that had fallen to its doom from the kitchen counter at the treehouse, a paper skycraft made by Jex, a strip of blue cloth from the uniform Berro had once torn from his own body to tie around Jex's bleeding head, clean now, but still stained with memories. Once you'd kept an object in a special box for a long time, it started to feel important enough to warrant the special box.

'Most treehouses are designed to handle the swaying,' she said, 'but you can still feel it. I find it a bit sickening.'

'Like being on a boat?'

'For some reason I don't have the same problem with boats. But I've never liked treehouses. I'm used to having my feet on the ground. Or in the water.' She left the curtains open to let in the dun light and climbed back into bed, leaning against the wall and drawing her knees up to her chin. She sensed a flicker of warmth, something like gratitude or contentment or a feeling of safety, and looked curiously at Kath, but there was nothing there, just the usual void. It must've been Andish waking in the other room. She extended her reach and felt her mother stir.

– *Stormy day... Tea will be good.* –

– *Yes,* – thought Fessi. – *Tea will be good.* –

'Andish is going to make tea,' she said, and Kath smiled. She was already beginning to react without surprise to Fessi's prophetic statements, just as Fessi was beginning to grow accustomed to Kath's lack of marric presence. The void wasn't threatening – it simply wasn't anything at all, and there was plenty to be gleaned from Kath just by observing her body language and paying attention to her tone of voice. She was, after all, a whole person, even if the patterns and rhythms of her interior world were out of reach.

'I'll help,' said Kath.

Andish and Kath were taking to each other, and Fessi was glad of it.

She followed Kath into the kitchen as Andish emerged from her room bundled in a thick clothwrap. Her greying hair was drawn up into a loose knot at the back of her head, and she smelled of herbs, the homemade concoction she inhaled to help her sleep peacefully, to keep the dreams at bay.

'Windy morning, daughters,' she said, nodding warmly at them. Again, something almost imperceptible tickled at Fessi's senses, like a flicker of sunshine through a brief gap in the clouds.

'Morning,' said Kath, filling the pot with water and setting it on the boil. Fessi turned her senses to Andish but didn't find anything out of the ordinary. Perhaps it was the wind, stirring everything up, the noise and the movement scrambling signals in the marrow. The kitchen window rattled in its frame, and a low note moaned through a gap, gusting the steam away from the pot.

While Kath pressed the berries, Andish and Fessi set about preparing breakfast: crisp nuggets made from a northern grain and treacle, served in bowls of amberroot water.

Kath laughed when Fessi pushed a serving towards her. 'It looks just like something I used to eat in the morning, before. Probably a lot healthier, though. You won't want to know what we used instead of this juice.'

'Some sort of animal blood?' Fessi guessed.

'Oh god, no. Just milk. From a… big mammal.'

Fessi grimaced. 'Tell me how it compares,' she said, nudging at the spoon.

Kath took a slightly soggy grain ball into her mouth. She chewed it contemplatively while Fessi and Andish watched.

'It's not bad,' she said. 'The juice is sweeter than I thought. Could still be sweeter, though.'

Andish poured the tea, and Kath took two treacle nibs from the jar. 'I think I'm getting used to your food,' she said, dropping the nibs into her tea. 'I'm already down to two nibs instead of three. Eventually I won't need these at all.'

Fessi traded a small, secret smile with her mother.

After breakfast, Andish went outside to see how the vegetable garden was holding up against the wind, insisting that Kath and Fessi didn't need to come with her. Fessi wasn't due at the academy for a few hours, so they sat together in the mingle to play a game of matching stones. Fessi set the carved board and lacquered box on the low table. The tiny stones inside the box were painted in red, green and blue. While Fessi explained the simple rules of the game, Kath held one stone of each colour in the palm of her hand and rolled them around with a fingertip.

'These are the academy uniform colours,' said Kath. 'What do they mean?'

'Far less than Berro would have you believe,' said Fessi. 'It's based on old Rhetari symbolism. Blue for the mind, green for the body, red for the world. Theoretical, practical, and observational. Very vague, and it's impossible to categorise people and subjects neatly into these groups. It's mostly just for administration these days. The academy has three dormitories, and they need to manage timetables and class sizes, so it's useful to have the student population broken up into groups.'

'And you can choose your colour?'

'Yes,' said Fessi, taking her first turn, but foregoing the optimal choice to give Kath a chance at victory. 'They offer recommendations when you join the academy based on what they know about you, if anything, but it's pretty transparent. If they don't know anything about you, they'll just recommend the colour with the smallest student population. Berro refuses to acknowledge this, of course.'

'Why?'

'Because the blue uniform means a lot to him. His mother wore a blue uniform.'

'What happened to her?' asked Kath. 'He said that she died.' Fessi was surprised at how tangible Kath's emotions seemed just then.

'It's a sore subject for him, so I wouldn't ask him about it. Sarla was a well-respected academic, and Berro… He aspires to be like her. At least in some ways. Just before she got sick, she was involved in some political activism against the reformatory. You've read about the reformatory?'

Kath nodded. 'It's where they put you if you violate the Code in a bad way.'

'Yes,' said Fessi. 'Well, Sarla believed that patients at the reformatory were having medical tests performed on them against their will. She claimed to have an inside source of information about it, but she never revealed their identity, so it's hard to say whether that was true. When she got sick, she… she martyred herself. In protest. She refused treatment because she said the treatment had been developed through unethical testing. And she died.'

'Wow.'

Kath bit her lips and didn't say anything as she took her next turn at the game, but Fessi guessed at some of the questions she was considering asking. It felt wrong, divulging Berro's family history to her without him knowing, so she steered the conversation back to safety.

'The academy colour system is also meant to encourage collaboration,' she said, shifting a row of stones on the board, lining up three blue ones and removing them from the game. 'If you have a strong skill or interest that clearly aligns with one of the colours, and you're spending a lot of time with other likeminded people in the classrooms and the dorm, then you're likely to find common interests and foster productive relationships. I'm quoting the academy guidebook here.'

'Okay,' said Kath, 'but what if way too many students choose the same colour? Can they force students into a group they didn't choose?'

'They could, I suppose, but they've never had to before, as far as I'm aware. There always seems to be a natural balance. And anyway, the classrooms and dormitories are never full to capacity. There's plenty of space for groups that are bigger than average size.'

'And if you change your mind about what you're interested in? Would you move to a different group?'

'It's almost unheard of to switch, mostly because it's pointless. Plenty of people aren't sure what they're interested in or good at when they start out. Or they don't know which colour their interests align with. I mean, take Berro for example. I'd never say it to him, but I think his focus on the crossing phenomenon is quite a red subject, and the actual work he does with Undra is very green. But he insists that it's all blue, through and through, because it's so unknown and everything's new and, of course, Undra is a blue.' She sighed. 'Does it matter? I don't think it does.'

Kath moved a few stones on the board. She was already losing terribly and didn't seem particularly focussed on what she was doing, inadvertently breaking the rules, but not to her own advantage. She looked lost in thought, and Fessi didn't interrupt her contemplations to criticise her gameplay.

'I think I'd choose red, like Magrin,' said Kath, finally.

Fessi was pleased to hear this. If Kath was looking forward into her future on Rheta, then perhaps she was coming to terms with her new reality. 'What makes you choose red?'

'Well, I don't have body skills.' Kath smiled, gesturing at herself as though she had some critical defect clearly apparent to a casual observer, but which Fessi couldn't identify. 'I like the idea of learning about the world. This one's all unknown to me. I've never seen trees like these. I've never breathed air as good as your air. I used to regret studying literature instead of botany, back in my other life. I'd sit in a lecture with some old man droning on about some boring book, and I'd be thinking about my friend Jessika, doing plant stuff in the greenhouse. I was jealous. Maybe this is my second chance.'

Kath was prone to melancholy smiles that squeezed at Fessi's heart even though she couldn't feel the emotion behind them. The fondness and longing were clear enough from the sparkle in Kath's eyes, the angle of her brows and the tight-pressed curve of her lips.

They returned to the game and lapsed into a silence made comfortable by the ceaseless rushing of the wind. Fessi won, but not by much.

CHAPTER 13

Berro woke, mouth dry, limbs stiff, and brain throbbing behind his eyes. It took immense effort to move his body from its position on top of his bedsheets, where he'd succumbed to profound unconsciousness, and he couldn't stifle the loud groan that grated its way out of his throat as he heaved his leg over the edge of the bed. He felt wooden.

Ebra's round face appeared above him, upside down, her eyes bleary and her fluffy hair mattered and sleep-squashed.

'Gods, Berro, you look terrible,' she said, and Berro heard Kem stifle a snort of laughter from the other bunk. 'What were you smoking yesterday?'

'I don't smoke,' said Berro, his voice gritty as if he'd smoked something particularly harsh, and a lot of it. Ebra looked suitably sceptical.

'You did seem pretty rough last night,' said Kem. Berro couldn't remember what interaction he'd had with Kem before he'd fallen asleep. His memories were muddled, dream-like impressions. He tried to sort through them as he pushed himself upright. Beneath the shifting current of his confusion was a very solid sense of sadness and disappointment, and he tracked his recollections back through the previous day to find the source.

Ah, yes. A failed collection. Undra, unimpressed. Berro had found something interesting, and the imparter had dismissed it.

'Berro?' said Kem, and Berro looked up to find his roommate staring worriedly at him. Ebra still had her face dangling over the edge of the bunk and was observing Berro from above with lazy interest. Yurek, it appeared, was sleeping soundly through it all.

'I'm fine,' said Berro. 'Probably something I ate.'

Kem looked unconvinced by this but said nothing. Despite it being hours too early for lectures, he was already in his uniform, his red hair combed and gathered on one side of his head in a neat braid.

'Going somewhere?' Berro asked, hoping to turn the conversation away from himself.

'Climbing again,' said Kem. 'Tarov suggested a sunrise scramble.'

'With the group?'

'No,' said Kem. 'Just me, Tarov and Disa.'

'I'm sure Jex is grateful,' said Berro. 'He's not a morning person.'

'Virda would drag him out if we asked them,' said Kem, and Berro half-smiled. She would indeed, even though she'd be grumpy as a wet shadowcat about the whole idea. She was hardly more of a morning person than Jex was, the two of them being very partial to lounging about in bed together whenever they could get away with it, but Virda hated to miss out things, and she'd overcome any reluctance with a mug of strong tea and a determined attitude. Berro was oddly pleased to learn that Virda and Jex weren't always included in the climbing sessions with the others.

'You should climb with us sometime, Berro,' said Kem.

Berro shook his head, which thudded painfully. 'I weigh about three times more than you. I'm sure the trees wouldn't appreciate it.'

'You're underestimating the mighty wickerwoods,' said Kem. 'Think about it.'

He winked as he left the room, and a confusing surge of happiness and nausea rushed through Berro. He'd never climb with Kem and the others, but it felt nice to be invited anyway. Virda and Jex had never thought to invite him, perhaps because they knew him better than Kem did. He was fussy and stubborn. He didn't enjoy smoking wickerbloom or discussing frivolous topics for hours on end. He knew the trees could hold his weight, and he was confident he'd be a perfectly capable climber if he made the effort, but he had no desire to. He just wasn't interested in anyone admiring his strength or applauding him for it. And surely that was what the climbing collective was all about. For them, climbing wasn't just exercise to keep the body healthy and the mind sharp, it was competitive. It was part of their identity. If he had to do something physical, he'd rather swim in the lake with Fessi than haul himself around in the trees like an oversized barkermonkey with Virda and Jex. Still…

'You should go to the infirmary,' said Ebra, pulling Berro from his thoughts. 'You really don't look well, sitting there like a bloated corpse.'

'Go back to sleep, Ebra,' said Berro.

'You're the one who woke me up with all your groaning,' she said. 'Go to the infirmary. You're not my favourite person in the world, but you're usually a pretty good roommate, and if you die they might replace you with someone who farts a lot. It's not worth the risk.'

Berro briefly considered going to the infirmary as Ebra had demanded, but by the time he emerged from the shower he felt much better and decided not to bother. His delirious episode must've been triggered by anxiety. It wouldn't be the first time his mental state had affected him physically, and he didn't need some patronising medical advisor to tell him he should reduce his workload or start infusing his tea with foul-tasting tinctures that, in Berro's experience, made you feel dull and stupid, rather than calm and collected as advertised.

The only effective method Berro had ever found for combatting anxiety was educational distraction, so he browsed early-morning classes on his slab while he ate his breakfast. Undra was giving one of his introductory Realities lectures for new students, and though Berro had heard these lectures too many times to count, and could probably dictate every detail of them from memory, he thought it might be worth attending anyway. After yesterday's disappointing meeting, he was eager to demonstrate his loyalty and commitment to the project, even when it didn't yield the results – the *crossings* – that Undra wanted.

Just then, a text message appeared in the corner of Berro's slab and he felt the corresponding vibration from the pod in his breast pocket. It was Undra.

: How are you this morning, Berrovan? You didn't seem very well yesterday. I was worried about you. :

Berro's heart clenched. It was sort of text message one might expect from a close friend, not from the foremost Realities expert on the planet. The proof of Undra's esteem for Berro was right there in front of him, gratifying and undeniable.

Berro considered their last meeting, trying to remember how he'd felt at the time. His sudden anxious illness had kicked in only after he'd left Undra's office. Hadn't it? But Undra, being as observant as he was, must've seen the signs before Berro himself had been aware of them.

: Good morning, Imparter. I'm well, thank you. I think it was a bit of anxiety, but a good night's sleep has put me right. Thanks for your concern, and apologies if I didn't seem myself at yesterday's meeting. :

Undra's response came moments later.

: Not at all. I thought you looked a little pale, and I'm glad to hear you're feeling better this morning. I hope I'm not causing any of these anxieties, but please do let me know if I am! :

Berro smiled to himself, now resolved to show his face at Undra's lecture in the interests of keeping this goodwill flowing and proving to his mentor that whatever had brought him low the day before was now well and truly overcome a mere twelve hours later. He was ready for more responsibilities – eager, even.

: Thank you, Imparter. Nothing at all to worry about. :

He dawdled in the dining room until it was time to head up to the class. With his mind on Undra, force of habit led Berro to directly the elevator to the eleventh floor where Undra's office was located, rather than the tenth floor where the lecture would be taking place. He realised his error only when the elevator opened and he found himself facing the office door.

A couple of other students were waiting to enter the elevator on this level, so Berro stepped out to take the flight of stairs down to the classroom. He stopped in his tracks when Undra's door opened and a young woman stepped out. It was Ryndel.

Though Berro had been quietly competing against her for years in academics, they'd barely spoken to one another in all the time they'd been enrolled at the academy. Now that they were both involved in the crossing project – albeit in vastly different capacities – their lack of interaction had taken on a vaguely hostile character. Their eyes would often meet across the room as their hands shot into the air to offer answers to questions. He'd see her name high up alongside his own on lists of grading points whenever he dug into the achievement records on the academy rhetalink. The fact that he'd trumped her for the position of primary assistant to Undra was thrilling.

As much as he didn't enjoy the physical experience of venturing out into the forest to collect corpses, the level of responsibility and esteem associated with his task was well worth it, and Berro quietly enjoyed the idea of Ryndel assisting Undra with mundane, trivial tasks like text-referencing and tea-making. Is that what she was doing for him right now? She had a determined look on her pale, pretty face, and she was marching towards the elevator, an elongated black box tucked under her arm. Berro jolted at the sight of the box. It was the same shape and size as the restricted-substance parcel he'd collected for Undra from the station. He'd never been told what was inside that parcel.

As she approached, Ryndel's eyes flicked in Berro's direction and her face blanched, her freckles standing out like flecks of dark blood. She flicked her braided hair over her shoulder, looked away from Berro as though she hadn't seen him, and stepped into the elevator with the other students just before it closed.

Berro loved to watch Undra perform, and to ride the undulations of his audience's emotions. Many of them would be hearing Undra speak in person for the first time: new students, visiting students, previously lazy but recently intrigued students. It would be, as always, a sea of unblinking eyes and open mouths. It had taken a single Realities lecture for Berro to reach a decision about his academic focus, and he knew he was not alone in his awe of Imparter Undra. What he was alone in was his unique access to and relationship with the man, and thinking about this gave him a reliable flush of pleasure.

Berro had sat at the front the first few times he'd attended Undra's introductory lectures, but now he sat at the back instead, so he could watch the audience and the performer, who was already at the lectern, organising his notes and projections. Just before he dimmed the lights, Undra caught Berro's eyes at the back and a smile ghosted across his face as darkness fell. The space filled with the sounds of people shifting around in their seats and whispering excitedly. A gentle spotlamp came on. Undra stepped into the light, commanding dead silence without having to ask for it.

'Good afternoon!' he said, smiling broadly. His academy blues brought out the brightness of his eyes, even at a distance. A few voices responded indistinctly, but most seemed content to pretend they didn't exist in the darkness.

'You're here because you're interested in the phenomenon we call "crossing". It's something we all learn about at an early age. Although it's an uncommon occurrence, it's common knowledge, something so widely known and so easily spoken of that it runs the risk of becoming mundane, just another dull fact of Rhetari life. There is nothing dull about crossing. Crossing is the least mundane topic in existence – at least in *our* existence. The implications of people falling into our world from other worlds are enormous, infinite, almost beyond comprehension. *Other worlds!*'

He took his slab from the lectern and tapped it, summoning an image onto the projector screen – the academy in winter, the grass lush and the trees bare, the vines wrapped around the building nothing more than a fuzz of fine, tangled twigs. He tapped to another image. The northern fields blanketed in endless white snow.

'Winter,' said Undra. 'These are the scenes you'll see in the northern hemisphere on Rheta in the second half of each year. You'll be putting on your thermal undersuits and your snow boots. One would reasonably assume that the seasons would be the same or similar for any and all possible realities occupying the same planet as ours. But then we discover *this*. Do look away now if you're sensitive to images of death.' He tapped the slab.

The next picture was of a dead man, naked except for a small cloth fastened in front of his genitals by a ragged cord around his waist with what appeared to be a drinking pouch attached to it.

'This specimen was found in the field I showed you before. He crossed near to a farmhouse and was recovered before the weather could do too much damage. What do you notice?'

Undra waited patiently through several moments of tense silence before some brave soul volunteered to break it: 'He's tanned.'

'Yes,' said Undra. 'We can see from the paleness underneath his garment that this is a suntan, not his natural complexion. In fact, he looks a bit sunburnt. See the redness on his nose and cheeks. The flakiness on his shoulders. What else?'

'The garment?' someone said, and Undra inclined his head.

'He's not dressed for winter. When he was discovered, the water in his drinking pouch wasn't even frozen. He was dead before he arrived, but he didn't die of cold. No evidence of frostbite. No blueness around the mouth or at the fingertips. So here we have evidence of a parallel reality in which, perhaps, the climate isn't the same as ours. We tend to think of the streams as occupying the same physical reality, but this isn't necessarily the case.

'And if it isn't the case, why not? We can only postulate, but so much about this phenomenon is unknowable. Were there always multiple realities or did something trigger a fracture in some original, singular reality? Assuming this is the case – and most people, myself included, do – how long ago did this fracture happen? How long have these realities had to develop along their own unique paths? What caused their differences? Natural randomisation? The actions of people? What could cause one reality to be so hot that a person might wear a loin cloth and walk around with a drinking pouch and a dangerous sunburn, while another reality in the same geological space is covered in snow? We have more questions than answers, but it's these questions that make crossing so fascinating, and such an important field of study.

'This specimen was thoroughly scrutinised and found to have various ailments that indicate exposure to heavy pollutants – pollutants different to the ones that wreaked such havoc in our world before, during and after the war... more on that later. In certain situations, and if sustained over a long enough period, pollution such as this can cause extremes in climate change – a possible explanation for the burnt and unclothed state of this crosser. He's known as the Sun Man. The cause of his death is unconfirmed, but the effects of the pollution and the extremes in temperature he must've been enduring when he crossed are almost certainly contributing factors. More difficult to look at is the crosser known as the War

Man. Again, sensitive students might consider looking away from this one.'

Undra changed the image. Berro had seen it many times before, but this time was different. Where once the gore had seemed abstract and unreal, now he felt like he was standing beside the body. His insides contracted and the air stuck in his lungs. He heard the inhalation of the other students and gripped the sides of his seat, racked with a sudden sick feeling.

War Man was dressed in strange, heavy-looking clothes made from dark material patterned with interlocking shapes in greens and browns. It was a complicated outfit, featuring buckles and badges and pockets and straps. He wore a helmet and a pair of heavy boots… or at least it would've been a pair if he'd had both of his feet. His left thigh ended in mess of crushed flesh and bloody ribbons of fabric. Most of his filthy face was disfigured by shards of shrapnel poking out of his skin. The left side of his uniform was pocked and bloodied and his left hand curled into a blackened claw, some of the bones visible through the web of charred flesh.

War Man looked very much like the crosser Berro had collected near the glasshouse, and as he stared at the image, he remembered the smell, the flies, the dark blood dripping.

The silence thickened in the lecture room. Everyone waited for Undra to speak. He gave them a few moments more to process the horror and then broke the silence with his smooth, reassuring voice of knowledge and wisdom.

'He's dressed for combat. Heavy gear, coloured for camouflage in the bush, indicating a natural environment that is, at least in some ways, similar to our own. Combat is what killed him, as you might have guessed. The value of War Man is the insight he gives us into the nature of war and combat in other realities; the weaponry, the strategy, the consequences. The context of the war we can only guess at, but it does seem as though people will find reasons to kill each other no matter what reality they live in.'

Some light and slightly desperate laughter rippled through the audience. The shock had been neutralised, but Berro still reeled, his horror gradually giving way to shame at his loss of control. His mind jumped back again and again to the memory of the glass-house crosser and then, quite suddenly, to Kath, crouching in the clearing with blood on her face.

Undra changed the image again.

'Rainbow Woman,' he said. 'My personal favourite.'

She was elderly, shrivelled, wearing an elaborate dress made of strips of different colour fabrics knotted and braided around each other with strings of tiny lights woven in. Her arms were loaded from wrist to elbow with bracelets and coiled strings of colourful beads, her face was painted in stripes of bright green and purple, and she had dyed feathers knotted into her hair. The tips of her hair were coloured with a clumpy blue powder, some of which had stained the pale skin of her shoulders.

'Wonderful, isn't she?' said Undra. And there *was* wonder is his voice – enough of it that everyone seemed to forget they were looking at a corpse. Students chattered with quiet excitement and a few even giggled. The Rainbow Woman's face was quite comical, her mouth stretched into a broad grin, revealing a silver tooth with a gap alongside it. Her eyes were creased closed as if she'd died of laughter.

'She died of drugs,' said Undra. His words landed heavily and crushed the excited atmosphere beneath them. 'The cause of her death is all we know for sure about the Rainbow Woman. We can only guess at the rest. Was it an accident? A recreational overdose? Was it administered to her? Is the outfit related to the cause of death? I suspect so; the drug was a strong hallucinogen, and these colours would've been quite something to behold under its influence. Perhaps she was part of a ritual. Perhaps she intended to die. It's not the worst way to go, I suppose. She certainly died happier than War Man.

'Even when we can only guess at the context of a crossing, there's always a great deal we can learn about the world the crosser came from. From the composition of the fabric, the beads, the dyes and the technology behind those strings of lights, we can build up a picture of the world's state of development, its resources, its methods of production. We learn about her world from the drugs she took, from the contents of her stomach, from the traces on her skin, from the dirt under her fingernails. We look for new ideas, we look for parallels with our world, we look for divergences and we begin to understand the infinite possibilities of existence.'

Berro stared at the Rainbow Woman, but felt none of the fascination, none of the wonder he'd felt at previous viewings of the image. He remembered the picture in Undra's office, of the imparter as a younger man, standing beside the Rainbow Woman, smiling. Then he imagined the Rainbow Woman alive and terrified, cowering in the clearing where he'd found Kath that night. What would she have thought or felt, if she'd been happily hallucinating and then suddenly found herself somewhere she couldn't explain, and a big man in blue coming towards her? He felt hatefully sick, and was glad when Undra switched the projection to text: '*REALITIES – Branches of Study*'.

'The field of Realities is a broad collection of studies that overlap with each other and with other fields in various ways,' said Undra. 'Should you choose to pursue Realities as the focus of your academic career or as your productive focus after graduating from the academy, you'll need to decide which area of study you're most interested in. A popular focus is on the crossers themselves – trying to learn about other realities by studying physical evidence from strange worlds; the bodies, the artefacts, the chemical details. You could spend your life analysing the examples we have of other-world literature, or you could study the skin cells of crossers in a laboratory. There are many ways to specialise within this field.

'Another popular broad focus is on understanding the process of crossing, trying to figure out how rifts form and why. We know that trauma plays a critical role in triggering crossings, but there's still plenty we don't know about the particulars of this process.'

Berro's mind wandered back to Kath, to her crossing and her trauma. His stomach tightened uncomfortably, and only when he steered his thoughts to her new situation, safe and comfortable in the lakehouse with Fessi, did the tension abate. He reached down and pulled his slab from his backpack, opened the note function and stretched it over most of the screen, but kept the chat open in the corner, where he tapped out a message to Fessi, allowing Undra's voice to melt away into meaningless cadences.

Berro– : *At the risk of being annoying and needy, are you free for a walk and talk today? :*

Fessi– : *I am. I'll be at the academy in about an hour. Does that work for you? :*

Berro– : *Yes. Perfect. Meet at the entrance? Could use some fresh air. :*

Undra's voice came back into focus. He was talking about something Berro didn't recall from previous introductory lectures.

'…so much to know. I mentioned before that the pollution responsible in part for causing the demise of our dear Sun Man was different to the pollution from our war. On Rheta, we have marrow and its concentrated form in marrowcore, something we've always taken for granted, and it was only through the study of Realities that we discovered this power is not an inherent part of all worlds. Many – in fact, probably most – realities seem to contain no marrow at all.

'We tend to speak of the war as a time in which we devastated Rheta, but really we only devastated ourselves. Our technology didn't kill the natural world, it empowered it in chaotic ways that we couldn't survive. The rivers became toxic for us to drink, but they teemed with life, with fish and plants we couldn't eat. We didn't kill Rheta – we empowered Rheta to kill us. In Sun Man's world, the by-products of their marrow-free technology degraded their natural world until it couldn't support them anymore. Each of our civilisations made mistakes, but the outcomes were not the same. We were able to recover. I have my doubts whether the same could be said of Sun Man's world.

'Our initial reaction to this might very well be a sort of smug pride, or relief at our good fortune, but I would caution against this dismissive, superior attitude. A lot of our innovations, a lot of our progress, was essentially handed to us by the discovery of marrowcore, a discovery which isn't much of an achievement in itself. Rheta, as we know, is absolutely full of the stuff. It's been said that marrow is simply science we don't understand yet. I think this is true. Rheta is powered by marrow, which is to say – it's powered by ignorance.

'We didn't have to work for our advances. We didn't have to unpick the fabric of the world and figure out how it worked in order to use it. We found ourselves blessed with powerful technology without ever earning the right to wield it. We became masters of Rheta, even though we're ignorant and undeserving of that power. We deserved our war.'

Berro sensed a few people shifting in their seats. He wondered where Undra was going with this sermon.

'In worlds without marrow, they have knowledge we can barely hope to understand. In some worlds, like the world of Sun Man, they failed to use their knowledge properly, and they destroyed themselves. A tragedy. A worthy but failed experiment. But there are many worlds, infinite worlds, more worlds than we can comprehend, and in at least some of those worlds, the power of marrow-free knowledge has surely succeeded, and the people are thriving with it – deservedly so. More deservedly than us, puttering along in our marrowcore-powered vehicles, barely innovating because we're all comfortable and satisfied with our unconditional income of credits we don't even have to work for, all speaking the same language without even thinking about it thanks to our marrowcore translators.'

Here, Undra flicked his forehead with what seemed like disdain rather than respect for the linga, and there was an uptick of tense excitement in the room. He was flirting with controversy, skirting the edges of dangerous ideas, and the young students were enthralled by it.

'We rate ourselves highly because we survived a self-inflicted catastrophe, and we've built something neat and orderly from the wreckage of our old world, but our world now is small, restricted, hamstrung by the fears of another war. To be perfectly frank, it's *boring*. We don't innovate because we don't have to. We don't innovate because we're scared to.

'When you look at these crossers, at these corpses from other worlds, I'd encourage you not to see them as ignorant unfortunates from lesser realities. You don't know what they knew. You don't know what knowledge they might've had to offer us if they'd lived. It's our mission – our duty – in the study of Realities to figure that out as best we can with the limited evidence we have at our disposal. It's not mere curiosity or morbid fascination. It's the pursuit of truth, of knowledge more fundamental, more powerful than marrow.'

Berro agreed with all of this, but couldn't fathom why Undra wasn't making use of Kath, the greatest resource to the field in living memory, to attain some of this enlightenment he was preaching.

It was as though Kath wasn't quite enough for him, and he was looking for something else, something more.

CHAPTER 14

Fessi's hair flicked and fluttered across her face, but she didn't lift a hand to move it away or tuck it behind her ears. She knew the academy and surrounds almost as well as she knew the island on the lake, and she could've walked it easily with her eyes closed. The spiteful wind had driven most of the loitering students into the common area, study rooms and mingles inside, and only a few were outside, either coming or going, faces tight and bags held close against the unseasonable bluster that threatened to catch the broad side of an unsuspecting pedestrian and topple them over for the sake of it. Berro – in tune with the weather – was a stormy presence beside her.

They entered the forest via a narrow footpath that wove indistinctly through the underbrush. The leaves were green and summer-strong, and most held fast to their branches, slapping frantically against each other as the trees creaked and the canopy heaved and rolled overhead, while at ground level it was still and oddly quiet. Ahead, a stream bubbled and chattered, tumbling clear and cold over a jumble of smooth rocks and stones. There hadn't been much rain in recent weeks, leaving the stream shallow and many rocks exposed, dry and dusty above the surface of the water but beautifully slick and dark beneath it. Tinwillows reached out over the stream from its far bank.

There was an open area along the pathway where a couple of fallen trees had been sawed into stout, rough logs and arranged here and there, lashed to the earth by reaching vines. Some were covered in mushrooms and moss, crawling with beetles and pocked with the webby holes of madifer burrows, while others were smooth from constant use as seating by students and walkers from the settlement.

Fessi set herself on one of the logs and crossed her legs underneath her. She finally moved her hair out of her face to fix Berro with a critical stare. 'So, what's going on?'

'Can't you just read my mind instead of me having to find words for everything?' he replied, kicking some leaves and dust into the stream.

'You know that's not how it works.'

She could feel him roiling, hot and cold, bright and dark. The way the marrow pulsed through him was unusual in its vividness. He sat down on another log and hunched over, elbows on knees, a brooding, blue mountain of a man.

'How is Kath?' he asked.

'Kath is well,' said Fessi. 'She's grieving, of course, but she's very brave and determined to make the best of things. I think there might still be a part of her that thinks she can go back one day, even though we've told her otherwise. Maybe by the time she's accepted she's here forever, she'll be comfortable enough not to be unhappy about it.'

'And she's a… a good person?' asked Berro. 'A nice person?'

'Why wouldn't she be? What's this about, Berro?'

'I don't know,' said Berro. He got up from the log and began to pace restlessly back and forth along edge of the stream, glaring at it as though its indifference to his concerns offended him. 'I've just been thinking about crossers, and how unfair it is.'

'Unfair?'

'The crossings,' he said. 'Most of them die, and even if they don't, it's a horrible trauma, isn't it? It would be easier to study them if they deserved it somehow, if it was a consequence of some bad deed, but… it's not. It's just the way things are. Not that I didn't know that before but, I forget sometimes, how unfair things are.'

He closed his eyes for a moment and took a deep breath. Fessi noted how the action utterly failed to calm his marrow. He turned and stalked back to the log, and sat down on it again with such careless force that Fessi could sense the flare of pain across his backside.

'When I found Kath, I thought it would change everything,' said Berro. 'I thought Undra would refocus the project so we could learn from her. But he didn't. We're carrying on, tracking other crossings as if… as if Kath *was* dead.' He picked viciously at corner of his thumbnail until a flake of gloss came loose. 'There was another one,' he said. 'A dead one.'

'Oh,' said Fessi. 'I'm sorry. Was it bad?' She knew it was bad.

Berro nodded and lapsed into silence. A blue dandlefly appeared and danced a single drunken loop around his head, but he seemed not to notice.

'When you say tracking crossings—'

'I don't know how he does it,' Berro cut in, and flinched at the sharpness of his own voice. 'He's detecting marric anomalies somehow. With drones. That's all I know.'

'Something doesn't make sense to me,' said Fessi. 'He says he's detecting marric anomalies, which means he's reading the marrow somehow. I do that all the time. I'm doing it right now. If he's using drones, he must've invented some marric tech. But… he sends you out in advance of the crossings, right? You said that before.'

'Yes. He gets a "reading". He gives me coordinates to check. Sometimes there's nothing there.'

'So he's not detecting the actual moment of the crossing, he's reading some marric anomaly that might precede a crossing.'

'Yes. And?'

'I sensed the moment of Kath's crossing. It was all at once. There was nothing, and then there was something. No prelude to it. I would've woken up sooner if there had been. I don't understand what sort of marric signals he could be reading before the crossing actually happens.'

'Well, I don't know. You'll have to ask Undra that, won't you? But please don't. I'm not meant to be talking to anyone about this.' Berro turned his head slightly and watched a twig as it hurried down the stream, bobbing and turning and dipping under the flow. 'I told you I was ill yesterday,' he said. 'It was a panic attack, I think. A bad one. I lost my mind, falling around, couldn't think clearly. And I woke up with this ridiculous headache.' He rubbed his temples.

'Why didn't you go to the infirmary?'

Berro snorted. 'What if Undra found out and thought I was unstable?'

'What if you are unstable?'

Berro turned his face to Fessi, lips quirked up and ready to laugh at her joke, and his face fell when he saw that she was serious. 'Do you think I'm unstable?'

'I don't know,' said Fessi, and felt how the bluntness of her response stung him. He'd always said he respected her honesty, which was more rational and carefully presented than Virda's cutting brand of truth-telling, but she knew right then he wished she'd apply a bit of salve to his wounds instead, like Magrin would. A dimple-cheeked smile and a warm hand on the shoulder, a light squeeze – *You're fine, Berro. You're great. You're as stable as they come.* Fessi thought of her mother, a similarly warm and caring person, who hadn't left the island on the lake in so many years. 'There's no shame in being unstable,' she said.

The water rushing around the rocks masked the sound of footsteps, but Fessi sensed the approaching walkers and looked towards the pathway before they came into sight – three students with steaming tea flasks.

'Come back to the lakehouse with me,' she said to Berro. 'Speak with Kath. Undra might not care about her, but he didn't say you couldn't.'

• • •

They sat in the lakehouse mingle, each holding a steaming mug of tea – Berro's strong and dark, Fessi's light and fresh, and Kath's muddied with treacle nibs, as usual. Outside, rags of grey cloud scurried across the washed-out blue sky, impatient to be elsewhere. Fessi was grateful to be indoors.

On the low table before them, Kath's artefacts lay in a careless jumble. A pair of astonishingly massive sparkly earrings with fine hooks on the end; a smooth white synthetic object, small and curled like a seashell; a stubby wooden writing implement; an almost-empty spray bottle of perfume with some words on it that Fessi's linga translated, quite ridiculously, as 'Fancy So Fancy', and a glossy card with lots of tiny text printed on both sides. Fessi hadn't inspected any of these things before, having thought they might be too personal to ask Kath about just yet, but Kath had fetched them unprompted when she saw Fessi arrive back at the lakehouse with Berro in tow. Curious, Fessi lifted the small white object between two fingers and peered at it.

'That's tech,' said Berro, leaning forward.

'It's for listening to music and things,' said Kath. 'Goes in your ear. I lost the other one though, and the player, in the crossing. I guess they got left behind.'

Fessi inserted the object smoothly into her ear and then took it out again, unsettled by the dead feel of it. She passed it to Berro, who had his hand held out eagerly.

Fessi ran her little finger along the shiny stones in the earrings. 'These are beautiful,' she said.

Kath beamed and picked them up, shook them out with far less care than Fessi would've expected and then hooked them into the tiny holes in her earlobes. She turned her head back and forth and the delicate strings of jewels transformed the wan light into an explosion of tiny rainbows.

'They must be very valuable,' said Berro.

'Oh, no, not really,' Kath laughed. Her voice sparkled like the jewellery. 'They're just crystals. Not diamonds.'

'And what's this?' Fessi said, lifting the card. 'It's got your face on it! Kathleen Star Sibanda-Katz.'

'It's my driver's licence,' said Kath. 'It gives me… it gave me permission to drive Bugzy.'

'Bugzy?'

'My vehicle. Bugzy was just my name for her. A pet name, you know?' said Kath. 'Our vehicles aren't like monos. They're bigger. Enclosed. They have wheels.'

'Rheta used to have vehicles like that. You said "her"?'

'Ah, yeah, it's an Earth-world thing, I guess. Referring to objects as if they're women. And women as if they're objects.' She huffed.

'Did you need to do training before you got this?'

'Yes, and I had to pass two tests, one written and one practical.'

'Jex would love to know about your vehicles, I'm sure,' said Fessi, holding the card close to her eye and tilting it back and forth, mesmerised by the colourful glinting of the strange holographic designs. 'I like this card,' she said. 'What are all these little symbols?'

'Oh, some of them are just official marks, so the authorities know it's not fake. The others mostly don't apply to me. You can keep the card, by the way. Might be worth something one day. I can't stand looking at it anymore.'

Berro frowned and stiffened, but Fessi smiled, tilting the card a few more times before she tucked it into her breast pocket. 'Thank you,' she said. She caught Berro's eye. 'I'll look after it.'

Kath took a deep breath, gathering herself for something, then turned to Berro. 'Does Undra want you to ask me more questions?'

'He… he doesn't *not* want that,' said Berro. He cleared his throat. 'It's me who wants to ask you questions most of all, but I don't know what to ask first.'

'I'll answer anything, as long it's not the same boring stuff Undra asked while we were alone.'

Berro's marrow flared hot. 'What did he ask you?'

'He started out asking me to tell him anything and everything, but after a while I think he got overwhelmed, or bored, and then he asked more specific things. On topics I knew nothing about, mostly, and I could tell he was disappointed. He wanted to know about our technology, our natural resources. Minerals and things like that. He asked me about science and weapons and machines and medicine and… and infrastructure? I didn't have much to say.'

'Hmm,' said Berro. A deep crease formed between his dark brows.

'He was nice, though,' Kath said quickly. 'He was kind.'

Fessi couldn't tell if she meant this or if she'd said it for Berro's benefit.

Berro took a slow sip of tea and his brow softened. 'I guess what I want to know is, how are you? How are you handling everything?' The heat rose in his face, and his marrow thrummed, awkward and eager at once.

'It's a funny sort of sadness,' said Kath. 'My mum, she's not dead. And I'm hanging onto that. It's not enough, but it's something. I have moments where I don't believe it, and I think I might go crazy, like my mind wants to reject all the evidence because it doesn't fit with anything I used to know. But I'm keeping it together, mostly.' She gave a self-conscious trill of laughter and glanced up. Fessi nodded encouragement. 'I've always been quite a… what's the word?' Kath clicked her fingers. 'Pragmatic. A pragmatic person. This whole situation is testing the limits of that, but I think I'm doing all right.'

'You are,' said Fessi, and Kath smiled gratefully.

'It's interesting,' said Berro. 'You seem very sensible, but when I first saw you, and the clothes you were wearing… I'm sorry, but I thought you looked quite ridiculous. The opposite of sensible.'

'Jeans and sneakers?' said Kath, her eyebrows tilting incredulously. 'That's a perfectly practical outfit.'

Berro gestured vaguely at her sparkly earrings, shaking his head.

'I like sparkly things.' Kath shrugged. 'If I'd been on a mountain hike, I would've worn something else, but I was just walking home from college.'

'So sparkly things are standard?'

Kath shrugged again. 'For people who like sparkly things, yes. You'd look good with an earring or two.'

Fessi looked at Berro, imagining a cascade of jewels swinging from his earlobes. Perhaps something smaller, a single blue jewel in each lobe. It might soften his look of interminable seriousness. 'She's right,' she said. 'Andish could pierce your earlobes sometime, if you're interested.'

'No, thank you,' said Berro. 'If I had to get any sort of body modification, I'd get a melter. But I don't want one.'

'A melter?' asked Kath.

'Scarification with a hot brand,' Fessi explained. 'They're not common, but Virda has a few.'

'So does Tarov,' said Berro, and Fessi felt the hot jolt in his marrow that told her he hadn't meant to say this out loud.

'Tarov?' she said.

Berro gave a dismissive, one-shouldered shrug and said, 'One of Virda's friends.'

Fessi knew who Tarov was.

The dark mood was settling over Berro once more, and Fessi guessed he was about to leave them even before he exhaled, patted his hands against his knees and said, 'I need to be heading back.'

He bid a friendly farewell to Kath, with promises to stay in touch and an open invitation for her to contact him whenever she liked, and soon Fessi had him back on the boat, fighting her way against the wind to get him to the far shore. His face was closed and clouded, and he didn't speak.

'Thank you,' he said as he stepped out onto the muddy bank. 'It was a good afternoon. I'm sorry I'm so…' He waved a hand.

'You're fine, Berro. And you're welcome here any time,' said Fessi.

He smiled and turned away, his marrow juddering just out of sync with the world around him.

CHAPTER 15

The treehouse creaked and groaned mournfully as the wind raked through the forest. On the balcony, Virda angled herself so the wind buffeted against her face and tugged the hair away from her eyes instead of into them. The vigorous freshness cleared her head enough that she no longer felt the urge to crawl back into bed with Jex, but not quite enough to feel enthusiastic about the Numbers class they were meant to attend in half an hour.

'We should visit the commune,' said Jex, and Virda jumped, having failed to hear him step out beside her. The wind filled Virda's head and the forest and the entire world with its relentless sibilance, and the accompanying groans of treehouses forced into reluctant motion.

'Now? Today?'

'Yes,' said Jex rubbing his sleepy face with one hand and scratching his stomach with the other. 'Windy weather always makes me homesick.'

Virda smiled, remembering. The wind usually came later in the year, when the air was colder and the trees just starting to lose their leaves. As youngsters the two of them would wrap themselves up in piles of threadbare blankets as the commune bucked and swayed like an old ship at sea. They'd press their faces against the dirty windows and watch the young trees bend in the gale and pretend they were survivors of a new war.

'What about Numbers?' said Virda, pretending she hadn't just been thinking of skipping the class.

'I can't face it today,' said Jex. 'The wind has my brain all scrambled. I'll be useless.'

'As if you ever aren't,' said Virda, even though this wasn't true at all. Jex grabbed her around the middle and made as if to toss her over the edge of the balcony, before she spun around in his grasp, wrapped all four limbs around him and buried her face in his neck. 'Yes, let's go to the commune. Mama Stitch will be thrilled.'

'Gods you're heavy,' said Jex putting her back on her feet. He pushed his hair away from his face, but it flew forward again immediately. 'We're sharing a monocraft. I don't want to bumble along like an old man so you can keep up with me.'

Virda didn't argue. Jex was better at Vehicles than she was. And better at Numbers. She'd give him that, especially since she was better at everything else.

By the time their Numbers class had started, Virda and Jex had fetched a monocraft from the academy and were thrashing between the trees along the narrower paths, heading for the hovertube station. The forest protected them from the full force of the wind, but it roared above them in the canopy, and the speckled sunshine moved wildly so the ground appeared to be boiling. Virda held onto Jex's back and leaned against his turns.

'Is there any other reason why you have this sudden urge to visit the commune?' she asked, lips touching his ear. 'Apart from the weather.'

'Yes,' said Jex. 'I know it's stupid, but I keep thinking… what if I cross tomorrow?'

'Hah!' Virda crowed. 'That's not going to happen.'

'I know that!' said Jex. 'It's just a thought I keep having. If I crossed tomorrow, would I regret my lack of visits to the commune?

The answer is yes. I think I would. And that means I should visit the commune.'

'You know, if you were a crosser, you'd probably be a dead crosser. Most of them are dead.'

'Cack, Virda, I know.'

'I'm just saying,' she said, prodding him in the side.

'My point is, we don't visit the commune often enough.'

'You're not wrong about that,' said Virda. 'Mama is going to lose control when she sees us.'

They parked the mono securely at the station and managed to board a hovertube just as it prepared to disembark. There weren't many travellers at that time of the day, and so they found good seats alongside a greenglass window. They'd only just settled in when the pulse fields switched on with a *whomp* of ear-popping energy, and the tube pulled off with a hiss. It picked up speed, and Virda rested her forehead against the glass to watch the forest stream by in a flicker of tree trunks and a verdant blur that here and there opened up to reveal a hard grey sky. It was cold in the tube, and Jex drew his legs up onto his seat and wrapped his arms around them.

'What are you thinking about?' he asked her.

'About what you said,' Virda mumbled. 'If I crossed tomorrow… if I survived and found myself in a whole new world with a whole new life, what would I regret about *this* life?'

Jex blinked at her over his knees.

'I'd regret failing to get Shani out of the reformatory,' said Virda.

Jex raised both brows. 'You can't regret not doing something that's impossible to do.'

'It's not impossible. It can't be impossible.'

'Look,' said Jex. 'I know it hurts, and I'll never stop being angry about it either, but it's not your burden to carry. You can't let it ruin your life. Shani wouldn't want that. And I'm sure Kini is still trying to get her out.'

'I doubt it,' said Virda. 'Kini's broken. I've tried getting in touch with her, and she reads my messages but almost never responds.

I haven't heard from her in months. I think she's trying to forget about it altogether. Start a new life as if Shani never existed.'

'But they're twins. They were inseparable.'

'All the more reason,' said Virda. 'It must be agony to be reminded about it all the time.'

'Does Kini know you're still traumatised about this after all these years?'

'I'm not traumatised, I'm just angry. And sad. And frustrated. I hate how hard it is to find information. I can't talk to Kini about it, though. She probably *needs* to give up and move on, just to stay sane.'

'Yes.'

Virda chewed at the rough corner of her thumbnail and tasted the tang of blood. A shudder ran through her, and she twisted her hands together in her lap, thumbs clenched into palms.

'Maybe Mama Stitch has heard from Kini,' said Jex.

'Maybe.'

An elderly person pushing a refreshment trolley stopped alongside their seats and offered them tea, which Jex declined but Virda accepted, even though she knew it would be tepid and under-brewed. She needed something to do with her hands.

The commune was in small satellite settlement near a lonely tube station in a younger part of the forest known colloquially as the Twigs, where many of the buildings were constructed on the ground because the trees – mostly hackerwoods and tinwillows – weren't big or strong enough to support treehouses. The few treehouse structures present needed extra support beams, or they'd snap the trunks of their trees in rough winds and come crashing down – an occurrence not unheard of in the Twigs. The commune was a treehouse, and a large one at that, with an angular jumble of support beams, like the dry legs on the shed skin of a madifer. It spanned two trees and was secured by thick, mossy ropes and haphazard planks. A slow leak from the water tank on the patchy roof had stained one side of the structure and stimulated the growth of colourful lichen on the wooden parts. All the windows and doors were ill-fitting, the gaps sealed with putty and the broken panes covered by boards, some of which were painted with smiling portraits to give the impression that the commune residents were standing at the windows, staring out into the forest.

A real face peered out from one of the unbroken windows, and as Virda and Jex approached the commune, it vanished. Moments later, the front door thumped open with a shower of splinters. A shrill voice filled the air, and a massive woman swathed in a colourful clothwrap with a matching colourful turban came rushing towards them. Having rapidly descended the stairs leading down from the balcony that encircled much of the commune, Mama Stitch broke into a lumbering run and caught Virda and Jex in a hug that almost threw the three of them into the dirt.

'Virdi Jexi ohmyprecious – come in, *come in* – oh, it's so wonderfulamazing*fantastic* to see you my precious, precious…'

She herded them up the broad staircase, through the door and into the main, open room of the treehouse, kicking the door shut with the heel of her naked foot behind them. Light streamed through the unboarded windows at the front and left side of the structure, illuminating the cluttered scene within. The walls between the windows were crowded with roughly framed works of art made by commune children over the years, including a collage by Jex, aged nine: it was a tree composed of twigs gummed onto a wooden board and in the tree were two figures made from small scraps of fabric. They didn't have torsos, just arms, legs and heads. One of the heads was topped with a lock of blond hair, gummed carefully onto the fabric. The other figure bore a tuft of hazel hair.

The room was a maze of softseats, large cushions and low tables arranged in an apocalyptic fashion, with several adults and many more children going about their daily business with a comfortingly familiar air of pandemonium.

Virda cast her eyes around for the lanky form of Kini, even

though she knew Kini wasn't on the same landmass as them. Mama Stitch led them over to an unoccupied corner and they dropped themselves onto a collection of cushions.

'Mama,' said Virda. 'How are you?'

'Me? I'm the same as ever.' She laughed, a deep, bouncy, belly laugh that set them laughing along with her, aimlessly, happily. 'It's so good to see you both. I hope nothing is the matter?' Mama Stitch arranged her face into a serious expression that seemed to take a considerable effort for her to achieve. When Virda shook her head and assured her that everything was fine, Mama's face immediately jumped back to its natural state of smiling openness. Her cheeks shone like polished fruit. 'So, you were missing me, and you had to come. Good! You should come every week. But I know you can't. That's fine. I'm not upset. I don't get upset about that. I know my children think about me even when I'm far away. How is the academy?'

'The academy is fine, Mama,' said Jex. 'I'm going to be flying a vollop soon.'

'A vollop!' Mama sounded impressed. 'Which one is a vollop? A big one?'

'Quite big,' said Jex. 'It can fit six people in it. High-altitude, long-distance skycraft.'

'Amazing, my Jexi. Where will you go?'

'I don't know yet,' said Jex. 'It will just be for practice. It's not a job yet, but maybe one day.'

'Oh, they won't find a better flyer than you. If that's what you want for your job, then you will have it! No doubt. It's good, that you already know what you want. I didn't know what I wanted when I was your age. What about you, Virdi? What job are you hoping for?'

Virda shifted on her cushion. 'I don't know what I want yet, Mama,' she said. 'I'm still deciding.'

Mama Stitch reached out a large, squishy hand and stroked Virda's hair. 'There is nothing wrong with still deciding. There is no rush. When you know, you will know. And then you'll come here, and you'll tell me all about it.'

'You know I will,' said Virda.

A deliciously sweet, nutty smell emanated from the open kitchen, and Jex's stomach rumbled loudly. Mama Stitch was on her feet in the blink of an eye. 'Oh!' she said. 'I need to make sure they do the spices properly. You want some, of course you do. I'll bring it. Stay right there!'

She moved at speed towards the kitchen, dodging people and furniture with effortlessness and grace that belied her size and was testament to her long years in the commune. Virda stood and rested her elbows on the nearest windowsill, and Jex nudged her along so he could look out, too. The wind raged through the trees, but the commune only swayed gently. It was far less exciting than Virda remembered from childhood. Despite its flimsy, cobbled-together appearance, the structure was a solid, reliable feat of Rhetari engineering. Perhaps it had been reinforced in the years since they'd lived there. Virda, in the grips of melancholy, mused at how getting older was fraught with this sort of vague disappointment.

They watched the upper branches of the young trees nearby whip and strain in the pull of the wind. The sky glared a bright grey-white, with the dark specks of a few wind-plucked leaves tumbling across it, along with the occasional hapless bird, wheeling in the gale.

'Do you miss it here?' asked Jex.

'Yes,' said Virda, 'but that doesn't mean I'd want to move back.'

'Hmm,' said Jex. 'It always feels like a dream, coming back here. It's how I remember it, but something's different, and I can't put my finger on what it is.'

'Maybe it's you,' said Virda. 'Us.'

She watched a bird rising above the treetops, bobbing up and down, cresting the waves of the wind, oddly persistent in its fight to fly against the gale. Her stomach rumbled, and she thought about the bowl of hot stew she'd soon have in her hands. It always was worth it to make the trip out to the commune, even just for the food. And there was always food – the sort of rich, homely, flavoursome fare that she and Jex rarely bothered to make for themselves. On the occasions that they did put in effort, the results never compared to the contents of the commune stew pot.

Virda's soft, lazy focus sharpened suddenly, and she squinted through the dirty glass. The bird she'd been watching wasn't a bird at all.

'What's that up there?' she asked Jex, pointing.

'It looks like…' Jex shoved Virda aside and squashed his face against the windowpane. '…a drone?'

'What the hell is a drone doing all the way out here in the Twigs?'

They watched as the drone moved slowly away from them, dipping from side to side as it struggled to stay upright.

'What are you two looking at out there?' called Mama Stitch, bustling back into the corner bearing a tray laden with steaming bowls and a heap of millbean buns. Jex lost interest in the drone immediately and set about making himself comfortable in front of the feast.

'There's a drone out there, Mama,' said Virda, lingering at the window against the wishes of her stomach, which gave another anguished rumble.

'A what, Virdi?'

'A drone.' She turned to look at the food. 'A little flying machine.'

'A toy?' asked Mama Stitch, disinterested. She tore open one of the buns, pulled soft, steaming pieces from it and popped them into her mouth.

'No, Mama, not a toy. They're very expensive and strictly regulated.'

Mama Stitch started spooning fragrant stew into the hollow pocket of her millbean bun. 'Maybe it's from the academy,' she said. 'Maybe they're studying something.'

Virda's automatic instinct was to contradict this assertion, but she realised that Mama was probably right. She turned back to the window to find that the drone had disappeared.

It was time for lunch.

Once the food had been devoured, Jex lay back on the cushions, his hands resting comfortably on his belly.

Virda turned to Mama Stitch. 'Have you heard from Kini?' she asked.

'Yes!' said Mama, dimpling. 'Just last week. She's met someone who lives in Grassy Plains. I don't know much more than that, but she seemed pleased about it in her message.'

Jex half-opened one eye. 'A friend?' he asked on a yawn. 'A lover?'

Mama Stitch shrugged. 'She didn't say, but reading between the lines I think maybe both.'

Virda smiled. 'I hope she's happy.'

'She won't be happy until Shani is back,' said Mama Stitch, 'but maybe with this mystery person, she'll find something like happiness to keep her living until then.'

Until when? Virda wondered. How long did Shani need for the system to 'reform' her? What had she done?

'Can I see Shani's things?' said Virda. 'If you still have them.' When Mama Stitch's face creased with concern, she added, 'I'm feeling sentimental today. It would make me feel better.'

'All right, Virdi,' Mama heaved herself up and drifted into one of the back rooms. While Jex dozed, Virda listened the creaking and scraping of ill-fitting drawers and cupboard doors until eventually Mama emerged back into the mingle holding a wooden box. It reminded Virda of a box she'd seen on Fessi's windowsill at the lakehouse – roughly carved and worn with age. Beautiful.

'Is that all there is?' she asked.

'Yes,' said Mama, handing it to her. 'Everything else wasn't personal, and so it was reused after Shani was taken. Perhaps Kini has some other things.'

Virda ran her hands over the lid of the box, tracing the carvings of leaves and vines. She felt Jex's and Mama's eyes on her so she turned away towards the window, pretending to need the light. Jex began to talk to Mama about his flying progress, and Virda opened the box.

The first thing she saw was a string bracelet made from green, red and blue threads twisted together. She remembered it. Kini and Shani had each worn one of these on their left arm. Virda recalled with sudden sharp clarity that Kini only ever wore that one string bracelet and no other adornments, while Shani had preferred to wear several adornments at once. Braided things and beaded things and wooden charms. A few of those were in the box too, and Virda trailed her fingers over them, indistinct shapes with small holes bored through them so they could be strung onto lengths of cord. Virda trembled with the realisation of how much her memories of Shani had faded, turning her into a shadow of her sister rather than the real, whole, unique person she was.

Beneath the bracelet and wooden charms and loose amber beads and painted stones and tangles of thread were some yellowed sheafs of homemade paper, folded neatly to fit into the box. Virda drew them out and unfolded each with sentimental reverence, as though some essence of Shani was pressed between them and might escape and vanish into the marrow if Virda didn't show the proper respect.

There were drawings, sketches of trees, mainly, sometimes with climbers in them. Virda was raw with sadness. The nostalgia winded her, the innocence of the images opening up chasms of feeling and memory she thought time had filled up. There were letters from Kini, written when the twins were very young, rambling and aimless and full of misunderstood words and silly stories masquerading as facts. There were crude maps of the Twigs and fantasy maps of the forest, of Mass 2, of the entirety of Rheta, with features such as 'Treacle Volcano' and 'Lair of the Madifer God' marked with tiny drawings. Virda's eyes burned at the sight of 'Kini and Shani's Marric Castle', located on an island in the middle of the ocean and surrounded by smiling balins.

The final folded page was a rough, incomplete self-portrait, and as Virda unfolded it, a smaller scrap of paper fluttered out. She laid it in the palm of her hand.

from boatwreck, 20 w, 45 s, snail rock, 4 sw, leaning tree, under root

Unlike everything else in the box, these words weren't written in a childish hand. The paper was brighter too, less yellowed, not yet softened by time. Virda's heart lurched. She looked around surreptitiously, certain that every eye in the commune was on her. But they weren't. Jex and Mama Stitch were engrossed in conversation, and she was unwatched.

She read the words and again, slowly this time. Boatwreck? Snail rock? Directions, but to where? Probably nowhere important, and yet… something about the neatness of the writing, the crispness of the paper, the lack of whimsical illustrations like the ones on every other page in the box gave this little artefact a cold seriousness that set Virda's pulse fluttering in her throat. She wanted it to be significant, and she couldn't squash the rising, irrational certainty that it *was*. With stiff fingers, she slipped the paper scrap into her pocket. She put the rest of the items back into the box and eased it shut.

A mug of hot tea and an hour of idle chat later, it was time to head back to Wooden Hill. On their way out of the commune, Virda stopped to look at the art on the wall, including Jex's depiction of the two of them climbing, to which she had contributed a lock of her hair. Further along, she inspected another joint portrait hanging slightly askew, this one an old sketch by Kini, of she and her sister, standing side by side with their arms raised in jubilation. Virda touched the corner of the frame to straighten it.

Shani, what happened to you?

CHAPTER 16

'Field party!' someone bellowed into the crowded mingle. 'Field party this evening!'

Berro had just emerged from a boring, poorly attended Tech lecture, feeling sleepy and disconsolate. The shouting voice jolted him out of his walking snooze, and then a green student stood before him, pushing a piece of soft, stringy paper into his hands. Berro recognised the student as Gunli, one of the climbers. The paper bore a picture of a cross-eyed smiling person raising a mug to a cross-eyed smiling moon with the words *FIELD PARTY* repeating around the edge.

'Handmade paper?' said Berro before Gunli could turn away. The young climber had a pile of paper prints in their hand and fingertips stained with ink.

'Yes!' they said, face lighting up. 'I made it. Wood fibre and leaves. There's a practical class you can take—'

'I took the class a few years ago,' said Berro. 'I just haven't seen this paper in a while.' He rubbed the print between his fingers and nodded. 'Nicely done.'

Gunli beamed. 'You'll come to the field party then?'

'Oh, I don't think so,' said Berro, and felt a twinge of regret as the youngster's face fell. 'Maybe.'

'You should. Disa's bringing in a barrel of moonjuice.'

'What in the hells is moonjuice?' asked Berro, but the eager climber was already dancing away, pressing flyers into people's hands. One of those people was Ryndel, and Berro was startled to see that she was strolling hand-in-hand with a lanky student in a blue uniform, whose face he knew in passing. They stopped to read the flyer together, and Ryndel *smiled* – a real, genuine smile – before looking up into the blue's face and saying something to him. He said something back, his voice, like hers, lost in the chatter of the crowded mingle and then… and then he kissed her. He kissed Ryndel. On the mouth.

Berro couldn't move, couldn't even blink. Ryndel, his academic rival, had a partner. This blue, whose name he didn't even know. They were together. They knew each other, perhaps intimately. She was performing academically at a roughly equal standard to Berro himself, but she was doing other things too. She was maintaining a relationship. She had this whole hidden layer to her life. Had she even been hiding it? It seemed not. Berro simply hadn't noticed, hadn't even considered the possibility.

He turned away in case she caught him staring and felt an ache in his back teeth as he ground them together.

Did *he* have other layers? A surge of panic rose within him, and he broke into a fast march out of the building and onto the field.

Even as a new student, Berro had never had much energy or enthusiasm for the social side of academy life, and now he wondered, not for the first time, but with greater urgency than before, if he'd missed out on important character-building by throwing himself with such single-mindedness into his academic career. He had friends, and he was grateful for that, but he sometimes couldn't stop the cold creeping dread that he lacked experience in all things non-academic and that this made him, in some fundamental way, inferior to others.

He never got intoxicated, never stayed up through the night to watch the sun rise through a haze of wickersmoke, never threw caution to the winds and gambled his emotional stability on romantic or physical relationships. He'd never wanted to. He'd played it safe, stayed guarded, avoided risky frivolities and reaped the rewards of this focus by emerging into post-fundamentals as a respected, successful scholar, chief assistant to none other than Imparter Undra. His choices were sound, his path was clear, and he shouldn't have had any regrets whatsoever.

And yet.

Seeing Ryndel look so unlike herself, so open and happy, so liberated from the pressure of academic expectation, had shaken him, and Berro wondered if he was suffering from profound delusion – that Virda's frequent teasing jokes about his eccentricities were actually indictments of his shortcomings.

He slipped his pod from his breast pocket, took an image of the flyer, and sent it in a group message to Virda, Jex, Magrin, Fessi and Kath, then meandered down the hill, which was scattered with twigs and leaves after the windy spell. He sat down on the grassy slope, half in the shade of the academy building and half in the blinding midday sunlight, tilting his face in and out of the warmth with his eyes closed until his pod pinged with a response from Virda. *: are you going??? :*

He chuckled. *: Unlikely. Thought I'd share it in case someone else was interested. :*

It occurred to him then that Virda and Jex likely knew about the field party already. They were friends with Gunli, who must've advertised the event in other ways more sophisticated than shouting about it and handing out flyers to random people in the mingles. The information was probably all over the social parts of the academy rhetalink, if he'd cared to look. Apart from privately texting his friends, Berro wasn't inclined to use the link for anything that wasn't academic. How much was he missing out on every day? He was gripped again by a stabbing sense of inadequacy just bordering on shame.

Magrin– *: Thanks, Berro. I'll go if you go? :*

Virda– *: jex and i will be there. he's napping right now. recharging. what about you, fessi? :*

Fessi– *: Thanks, but no thanks. I'm doing crafts with Kath this evening. :*

Kath– *: >>emote: smile<<*

Magrin– *: I'd prefer that! Can I join you two? :*

Kath– *: >>emote: smile<< >>emote: smile<< I haven't figured out how to do the combo emotes yet. :*

Fessi– *: Of course you can, Mag! :*

Magrin– *: Sorry Berro :*

Berro– *: No apology necessary. But you'll be missing out on 'moon-juice', apparently. >>emote: blink//nervous<< :*

Magrin– *: What's that? :*

Virda– *: who told you about moonjuice? :*

Berro– *: Your friend Gunli, trying to incentivise party attendance. What is it? :*

Virda– *: disa made wickerbloom tincture, clarified it, put it with some sweet bluemoss she's been cultivating. tastes much better than regular wickerbloom drinks. i tried some from her flask the other day and i can say it's worth attending a field party for. :*

Berro made a disgusted face even though there wasn't anyone there to witness it.

Virda– *: you're making a face, aren't you, berro? :*

Berro exaggerated his expression, took an image of himself, and added it to the chat, setting off a flurry of emotes. Their amusement warmed him.

In truth, he was a little curious about the moonjuice. He hated smoking wicker, and though drinking it didn't sound appealing either, it would mean he could ingest the concentrated marrow without coughing up his lungs. Perhaps if he could physically achieve the gentle high his friends so frequently revelled in, he'd be able to relax and gain something of the experience he was lacking.

A little later in the day, Berro sat down heavily on his bunk and flicked at his charging slab, noticing, with a clenching of his stomach, that there was a new message from his father.

: Berrovan,

I don't want to make unwelcome demands on your time, but it's been months since I heard from you, and I miss you. I know we've had our difficulties, but you're my child and I'll always care about you and want to know what you're doing and how you're feeling, whether it's good or bad or boring. I don't mind. I'd also love to tell you about exciting developments in my own little life, but would rather share that by voice or video than in a text message you might not read or respond to, because I think my heart might break if that happened. Let me know if you'd like to set a time for a friendly conversation.

As always, I love you, I'm proud of you, I hope you're well and please let me know if you need any credits.

Marruvan. :

The message had been sent less than ten minutes ago. His father was probably still sitting on his softseat with the slab in his hands. Before he could overthink it and inevitably stop himself, Berro activated the video call and watched his father's name pulse grey and white in the corner of the screen three times before becoming blue. A bright spot expanded to fill the screen with the image of Marruvan's face.

'Berro!'

His father's voice came loud and clear and bright with surprise, his blue eyes widening and his lips straight and parted, a precursor to a smile he was more than ready to indulge in as soon as Berro gave him permission to do so. Berro smiled and said 'Hello', and he was treated to a view of the entire set of his father's teeth and, thanks to angle at which Marruvan was holding his slab, the depths of his nostrils too.

'It's good to hear from you! Oh, this is really good. How uh… how are you?'

'Good,' he replied, and Marruvan threw his head back and laughed as if Berro had told a great joke.

'I'm glad! I'm so glad. So, what's going on? What are you…?'

Berro had no doubt that the question his father wanted to ask was, 'Is there something wrong?' He never video called. Ever. They'd suffered through the occasional awkward voice conversation in the first few years after Marruvan had moved away, but those soon became unbearable and were replaced by text exchanges, which, in turn, became a rarity. These days, Berro replied to text messages only occasionally, and only to ease the increasingly frantic tone his father would employ after being ignored for an extended period.

'Nothing much,' said Berro. 'I wanted to hear about your exciting developments.' This was true, and Marruvan's face lit up as Berro admitted it. His skin was paler than Berro's, and the sunlight flooding the room in which he sat, on a distinctly shabby softseat draped in handwoven blankets, made him look pastier than Berro remembered. They had the same build, the same strong jaw, the same brow, cheekbones, ears and chin. Berro's warmer complexion, darker hair, brown eyes and slightly upturned nose were from his mother, but everything else about his physical appearance came directly and without modification from his father.

For some time now, Berro had forgotten, or at least not thought about, how much he looked like Marruvan. He'd avoided the discomfort he'd always experienced when looking at his father, the sense that he was staring at a faded version of his future self: a weathered man, a failed man, a man with dirt rubbed so deep into the lines on his hands that it could never be washed away. A warning.

'Well,' said Marruvan, 'I've been travelling. I hadn't travelled since…' He paused and rubbed his nose. Berro felt a shiver run down his back and arms, as though his mother's ghost had just passed through him. By the look on Marruvan's face, the ghost had taken a ride on the rhetalink and drifted through him, too. 'I found someone to manage the farm in my absence – good man, bit of a drifter, looking for a place stay – and I went up to the north sea, got on a boat, took it all the way up to the pole. It was incredible, Berro. I wish you'd been with us. I wish you could've seen what we saw. The icecaps are reforming, you know, and it's so beautiful.'

'We?' said Berro. 'Who's "we"?'

'Uh, myself and the other people on the boat.'

Berro shook his head. 'That's not what you meant. The way you said it. The way you said, "us", "we". You meant someone specific. You didn't travel alone.'

'You always were smart,' said Marruvan fondly. Berro saw no reason to contradict this. It was the truth, after all. 'I didn't travel alone. That's the exciting development, really…'

'You've met someone,' said Berro. It wasn't a question, and the words didn't encompass the full weight of the facts, but he knew what he meant, and Marruvan knew it too, and the way he was nodding and smiling, not nearly awkwardly enough for Berro's liking, confirmed it all.

Marruvan had met someone. He'd formed a new relationship, an intimate one, the first he'd had since Sarla's death, as far as Berro was aware. Something on Berro's face must've betrayed the sudden deep pain in his chest, because Marruvan's smile faltered and he said, 'Berro? You're not upset, are you? It's been years. I'll always love her, and I'll always miss her, but I've been alone, and we only have one little life on this planet, and we have to—'

Berro jabbed at the screen of his slab with a shaking finger and Marruvan's face vanished, along with his voice. The alcove was shockingly silent then, and Berro sensed everyone else in the dormitory lurking outside his alcove, holding their breath, listening to him. He jumped to his feet, scrubbing at his wet eyes with the backs of his hands and peered into the corridor. There was no one there apart from a few distant figures on their way out, oblivious and indifferent, dressed in colourful casualwear for the field party.

Berro's pod blipped, and he guessed it would be Marruvan trying to reconnect, before he remembered he'd put a partial block on his father's messages, which meant he only saw them on his slab and never on his small portable device. He didn't want to receive them in company. He knew from experience that he struggled to conceal his emotions around his friends, and he didn't need them asking him why he was scowling whenever he saw a message from Marruvan on his pod. As it happened, the message was from Jex, who said *: get your boring blue backside up here, berrovan, or i'm going to come down there and piss on your bed !! :*

Berro released a wet cough of laughter and wiped his eyes again. *: Give me five minutes. :*

All around the academy building the field was alive with activity, more people out on the grass at one time than Berro had ever seen, their shadows thrown long by clean-burning fires that crackled and leapt within boxy grates dotted around the open space. An abundance of large cushions and blankets had been dragged together to form cosy little social islands, from which wickersmoke coiled and laughing voices rose into the sky.

At the foot of the hillslope, a range of tables stood illuminated with coils of tiny ecolamps and groaning under the weight of snacks and drinks. The vendors were enjoying a roaring trade. Some of them were students, but others were summer traders who'd moved their business to the academy grounds for the event. A particularly long line had formed at one table, where two people were filling cups from an exceptionally large barrel. Berro made his way down the hill, weaving between the cushion islands and people lounging on the slopes. About halfway down the hill, a hand grabbed at his ankle, and he almost fell on his face.

'Sorry!' said Jex, releasing his grip and grinning up at Berro from where he lay, feet pointing up the slope and head pointing down, a wicker between his lips. He was on the edge of a large blanket occupied by several other people, including Virda, Kem and Gunli, who were engaged in such an animated discussion that none of them had noticed Berro in the ambient darkness. 'I'm glad you made it! I didn't want to have to piss on your bed.'

'Why don't you lie the other way around? Isn't all the blood rushing into your head?'

'It is,' said Jex, taking his wicker between thumb and forefinger. 'I like it.' He reached for Berro's ankle again with his free hand and tugged it lightly. 'You are joining us, right?'

'Yes,' said Berro. 'I need a drink first.'

Jex arched his neck so he could peer upside down to the bottom of the hill. 'Moonjuice?'

'I guess so,' said Berro. 'Can I get you one?'

'Aww, please, yes, that would be...' Jex poked the wicker back into his mouth, freeing up both hands to grab at Berro's ankles and tug him forward into an awkward lower-leg embrace. 'Tell Disa to join us. She can get some plucky fundamental to serve the drinks.'

Berro shook Jex gently from his ankles and made his way down to the long queue at the moonjuice barrel. It was a quick-moving line, and in just a few minutes he was at the front requesting his two cups. Disa grinned at him and took freshly filled cups from the tall, slim person assisting her, who Berro took a moment to recognise as Tarov. He wore an attractively embroidered clothwrap, loose around his legs and shoulders but fitted close at his narrow waist. His eyes snagged on Berro, and Berro could've sworn that a smirk ghosted over Tarov's face before he turned back to the barrel.

In the concentration of ecolamps near the vendors, the moonjuice had a pearly green, almost bioluminescent sheen. Berro inspected it with interest as Disa beeped the credits from his pod.

'This looks incredible,' he said.

'Thanks,' said Disa. She tucked a wayward curl of dark hair into her headband. 'I hope you like the taste too.'

'Is it potent?' asked Berro, immediately wishing he hadn't.

'It can be,' said Disa, 'but I made this batch pretty mild. One cup has about half as many keeshans as a regular wicker. Perfect for a non-smoker.'

She winked, and Berro gritted his teeth slightly. 'Thanks,' he said. 'Jex said I should tell you to join us, by the way. He suggested delegating your drinks distribution duties to a "plucky fundamental". His words.'

Tarov, who was serving moonjuice to a group of very plucky fundamentals right at that moment, laughed loudly at this. 'They'd drink it all,' he said smoothly. 'The barrel will be empty soon anyway. We'll join you then.'

Berro traipsed back up the hill, careful not to spill any of the beautiful liquid. He lowered himself down next to Jex, who was now sitting upright on the blanket, and handed him his moonjuice. He wasn't surprised when Jex downed the entire cup in two gulps and burped fragrantly.

'Gods, you're disgusting,' said Berro, sipping his own drink. It was pleasantly sweet, with a lingering herbal flavour and a smooth, slightly syrupy consistency.

'Nice, isn't it?' said Jex.

'Yes,' said Berro. 'Worth savouring, even, rather than just pouring it down your neck like water. How many've you had?'

Jex shrugged, lowering himself onto his back again, feet pointing downslope this time.

'Berro!' said Virda, clambering over cushions to get closer to him. 'You came!'

'I threatened him,' said Jex.

'He did. But I was going to come anyway.'

Kem raised his cup of moonjuice in greeting. 'Is it boring in the dorm without me?'

Berro raised his own cup and smiled. 'Yes,' he said. 'Too quiet.'

He scanned the scene around him, wondering why he'd felt so resistant to the idea of being there. It was good, it was calm, people seemed pleased to see him. He took a generous gulp of moonjuice and leaned back on his elbows. At the treeline, a group had emerged pushing a large square piece of equipment on a hovertrailer. Gunli jumped up from where they'd been chattering at the other end of the blanket. 'That's the music!' they said, and dashed down the hill.

'Why aren't you making the music, Kem?' asked Virda. Berro knew Kem was a musician, and that he often performed with Disa, but hadn't heard them perform before, as he never attended festivals, and Kem didn't rehearse anything in the dormitory, being the considerate roommate he was.

'I asked if I could help out, but Gun said no. They didn't want a specific point of focus; no stage, no audience… more of an ambient vibe, which makes sense. We're meant to be talking to each other and lazing on the grass, not facing in one direction watching a show. Looks like their technical team was a bit slow on the delivery, though.'

'I'd like to see you perform,' said Berro, and felt his face flame at the admission.

'You've never seen him perform?' asked Jex. 'Isn't he your roommate?'

'I don't give private shows in the blue dorm, you waspik. And Disa's in red dorm anyway. You can come to a rehearsal if you like, Berro. And we'll perform at the autumn festival.'

'Great,' said Berro. He wanted to say more, to show enthusiasm and support, but couldn't think of any words just then, and nobody seemed to expect more words from him anyway. Gentle upbeat synth music started playing across the clearing, and the sound rubbed warmly like a pair of thumbs massaging the tension out of his shoulders. He swallowed the rest of his drink, eased himself down onto his back, and put an arm behind his head. The stars spattered in the purple-black sky above him seemed to jump slightly in time with the music, creating fine squiggles of starlight that bloomed and faded as elegant strips of cloud unspooled across the expanse.

'Gorgeous, isn't it?' said Jex, reaching over to put a newly lit wicker into Berro's gaping mouth. Berro waved it away with a heavy hand and blinked.

'Moonjuice was enough, thanks…'

'Mmm, that last cup was strong,' said Jex. 'Bottom-of-the-barrel potent.'

'You seem fine,' said Berro, letting his head roll in Jex's direction. 'Same as.' His tongue felt thick and sluggish in his mouth.

'Well,' said Jex. 'I'm used to it. You sound a little wicky, though.'

Berro snorted. 'Wicky… Mmm. I feel great.'

He rolled his eyes across the sparkling sky, down the length of the trees ringing the open field, and saw Disa, Tarov and Gunli strolling up the hill towards them.

'You have very attractive friends,' thought Berro, and only when Virda let out a guffaw of laughter did he realise he'd said it out loud.

'We do, don't we?' she said, pinching him playfully. 'Which one catches your eye?' She tickled her fingers along his arm, and he allowed her to do it, for reasons he couldn't fathom.

'Hmm,' he said, enjoying the attention. 'Tarov.'

Jex groaned. 'Please don't tell him that. He thinks enough of himself already.'

'Kem is also nice to look at.' The words were out of Berro's mouth before he remembered that Kem was not on his way up the hill with the others, but sitting just on the other side of Virda, probably listening in on the conversation. He turned quickly, hoping to link a joke to the back of his comment somehow so that Kem wouldn't be too uncomfortable about it, but the redhead appeared not to have heard him. In fact, he was asleep.

Virda chuckled. 'He wouldn't be offended, you know. He'd be flattered. It's no use, though – he's hopelessly in love with Disa.'

'Mmm,' said Berro. 'That's fine. I just said he was nice to look at. I wasn't thinking about a commitment ceremony.'

'You're funny when you're high,' said Jex. He snuggled up against Berro's side, and again Berro found himself indifferent to the physical contact where normally he'd be deeply uncomfortable with it. Disa, Tarov and Gunli flopped down onto their little island of blankets and cushions, and Berro floated along on the meaningless ebb and flow of their conversation while he watched the moon rise to the apex of the sky. The temperature was dropping, and Jex kept snuggling in closer and closer against him. He was bony but warm, and he smelled pleasantly of wickersmoke.

'Don't let him get used to that,' said Virda. 'He won't want to sleep with me anymore.'

'Yes, he will,' said Berro, charmed. He raised the arm on his free side and nodded at the space beneath it.

'Berrovan Blue, are you offering me cuddles?'

'Well, Jex is already helping himself, so it would be unfair not to.'

Virda's face cracked into a wide grin, and she quickly shifted herself into position, curling against Berro's side and pulling his arm around her. She was bigger than Jex, and softer, but still small enough to make Berro hyperaware of his own size in such close comparison, something he usually didn't enjoy.

'Oh gods,' said Virda with a shiver of content. 'You're like a big warm ursa. Can you stay with us through the winter?'

'In your bed? Urgh. I have no interest in knowing what goes on in there.'

Jex was snoring now, and one of his arms had found its way

across Berro's broad chest, fingertips skimming Virda's shoulder. Virda sighed.

'What's wrong?' said Berro.

'Nothing,' she replied. 'This is nice. It's been a difficult couple of days. I'm… I'm tired. And it doesn't help that Magrin's cacking bird has been keeping me awake at night.'

'Did something else happen?'

Virda shook her head. 'It's complicated. We visited the commune, and it brought up some things.'

'Family is difficult,' said Berro. His mind strayed to his father, and he swallowed hard.

'Yes,' said Virda. 'I sometimes feel like I'm crazy, the way I get stuck on things. The way I can't let things go. *You* know what I mean…' She waved a hand around to encompass the vast scope of stubborn disagreements she and Berro had had over the years. 'I can't move on. I can't accept some things the way they are.'

'Is this about your cousin? Shani?'

'Yes,' said Virda, and when nothing else was forthcoming, Berro jostled her lightly with his arm.

'Do you want to talk about it?'

'No, I don't want to talk about it,' said Virda. 'I just want to enjoy being cuddled by an ursa on this rare occasion that he isn't biting everyone's heads off.'

'Do I do that?'

'Not really. A little bit.'

'I'm sorry.'

'Don't be,' said Virda on a stifled yawn. She arched her back with an alarming crunch of vertebrae and stretched both arms up to the sky before settling back down with a sigh that had a distinctly more positive flavour than the last one. 'We like you the way you are, Berro, venomous spines and all.'

'I thought I was a big cuddly ursa, not a toxic sea creature.'

'Maybe you're both,' said Virda.

Berro contemplated this in a carefree way, feeling at once

extremely present, pressed between his friends, and also nebulous, like he was part of the field, part of the sky, floating. He found himself staring at Tarov again, and it didn't occur to him to be furtive about it, because he didn't quite feel like he was visible. He watched Tarov loosen the messy knot of his dark hair and scoop it back up more tightly. It was something he'd obviously done a million times before, and the easy efficiency of it was pleasant to watch. Berro's gaze lingered on the melter on Tarov's upper arm. He couldn't make it out in detail in the semi-dark, but it was shaped like a tree. He wondered how much it had hurt, and briefly imagined Tarov's face clenched in pain as the brand touched his skin. With a small shudder, Berro pushed the image aside and imagined Tarov's face flushed with pleasure instead.

'I wanted to know,' said Virda, startling him even though she spoke in a voice pitched not to carry. He'd assumed she'd fallen asleep. 'Have you ever been with anyone? Physically, I mean.'

Berro went momentarily rigid. She'd caught him staring, and it was as though she'd seen inside his head just then. He was glad it was dark enough to disguise the sudden rush of blood into his face. Under normal circumstances, the introduction of such a topic would've prompted him to get up and leave, but the soothing moonjuice was still flowing languorously through his veins, and he relaxed, deciding he was unfazed by the question, and relishing the peace and power in this unfamiliar brand of indifference.

'No,' said Berro. 'I haven't been with anyone. I've never wanted to.'

'Never?'

Berro shrugged, the movement provoking a small, sleepy sound from Jex, who squirmed against him until his face was squashed into Berro's armpit.

'It's not that I don't find people attractive,' said Berro, with an involuntary glance at Tarov. 'I do, just not in that way. I don't see myself— I can't imagine— I think I'd feel— I don't know.'

Virda's silence was expectant, and Berro could hardly blame

her. His response had been garbled at best. He'd never really taken the time to examine his feelings on the matter and put them into coherent sentences, and coherency was particularly difficult under the influence of moonjuice. The moonjuice certainly had done away with his inhibitions, however, and he wanted to take advantage of that.

'Let me try again,' he said. 'I'm not against the idea of a physical relationship, I just don't want the things most people want. I can't think of a situation that wouldn't make me uncomfortable. Doing what someone else wants would make me uncomfortable. Someone else doing what I want would also make me uncomfortable.'

'Why, is it something weird?'

'No. I don't even know what I want. I mean— I don't want anything. Like that.' A shudder ran the full length of his body.

'Well,' said Virda, 'you're a brilliant and beautiful person, Berro, and if you ever wanted to experiment—'

'Please stop talking now,' said Berro.

'I wasn't offering myself!' Virda blustered, and Berro quaked with sudden laughter. 'I was going to say I'd put in a good word…'

'What are you three up to over there?' said Tarov. The end of a wicker glowed between his lips, and Berro, still warm and light with laughter, took a moment to appreciate his fine features in the moonlight. Would he want a physical relationship with Tarov? Hypothetically, of course. He wasn't sure. Seeing Tarov with fewer clothes on might be nice, and he wouldn't mind seeing that melter up close, and maybe touching it with his fingertips to learn the texture, but he wasn't sure he'd like Tarov to touch him in return.

'Berro?' said Tarov. 'I asked what you're up to.' He watched Berro watching him, and a smile lifted one corner of his lips, his curiously sharp teeth catching the light. He'd asked Berro a question, and Berro was silent and staring at him.

'Why don't you come over here and find out?' Berro said at last, the words tumbling over each other as they burst out of his mouth.

Virda hissed and punched him on the arm, and Jex, who had

just surfaced from oblivion, honked with laughter. Tarov turned away, chuckling.

'I hope everyone's more intoxicated than I am, so they don't remember any of this,' said Berro.

'Oh, we'll remember,' Jex assured him.

They lay in silence for a while, soaking in the music and the starlight until, like the retreating of the tide, the effects of the moonjuice began to pull away, and Berro's mind, clearing now, strayed again to his father. His eyes prickled.

'I spoke to my father earlier,' he said, and felt Virda and Jex tense slightly on either side of him. 'He's replaced my mother.'

'Oh, Berro—' Virda began, but Berro hushed her.

'It's fine. I just miss her. And I felt… I can never explain how I feel about anything,' he huffed, 'but I felt something, and it wasn't good. And I'm grateful for this.'

'For what?' asked Jex.

'For you making me come out here. It's nice to be someone else for a while.'

'You're not someone else,' said Virda. She poked him in the side. 'No matter how much moonjuice you drink. You're still you.'

>>comspace/locked/reformatory reformation collective
>>1 reformer(s) in comspace
>>reformer treescrat has entered

Cackfoot– *: i was just about to give up! it's been so quiet in here. :*

Treescrat– *: sorry, cacks. i haven't had anything new or interesting to say :*

Cackfoot– *: and you're here now because that is no longer the case, and you have something extremely new and interesting that will forever change all of our lives and free our loved ones from the evil clutches of the rhetari reformatory system? :*

Treescrat- *: i'm not sure. maybe. i found something the other day in the place where my cousin grew up. thought it was a clue. thought it might give me some new information about what happened to her, but i don't know what it's referring to. maybe you can help? :*

Cackfoot– *: what was it exactly? :*

Treescrat– *: a little scrap of paper with some of her handwriting on it*
'from boatwreck, 20 w, 45 s, snail rock, 4 sw, leaning tree, under root':

Cackfoot– *: ooh! directions to something? :*

Treescrat– *: that was my guess too. seems obvious enough. but i'm stuck on 'boatwreck' :*

Cackfoot– *: ah. i see. i know we're meant to be anonymous and we said we wouldn't identify you, but obviously we've guessed you live in wooden hill, since you know sarla's son, so i imagine there aren't a whole lot of boats near to you. :*

Treescrat– *: i know of one boat in wooden hill, at our one and only lake, and it's not a wreck. our rivers are too shallow for boats :*

Cackfoot- *: did your cousin ever leave wooden hill? :*

Treescrat- *: i don't think so. i don't know. i wanted to work it out and surprise my best friend with this new information, but it's just a worthless scrap of paper until i know what the starting point is :*

Cackfoot- *: maybe your friend will know. :*

Treescrat- *: maybe. but i doubt it :*

Cackfoot- *: i'm sorry, scratty. i wish i could help. let me know if you figure it out. :*

CHAPTER 17

On the night of the field party, in the quiet cosiness of the lakehouse, Fessi, Magrin and Kath had whittled figurines out of driftwood, created collages from pressed flowers, and made jewellery using glass beads and wire, while Andish swept into the mingle to offer them drinks and comment on their creations. Kath had seemed more relaxed with the smaller group, and Fessi had felt completely at ease about Kath's void-like strangeness for the first time since they'd met.

A week later, having determined that Berro was occupied with his very important work for Undra, and Virda and Jex were climbing in the trees somewhere, Fessi encouraged Magrin to join them again at the lakehouse for an afternoon of fruit juice and idle chat. Magrin announced that she'd be bringing a juvenile vollop along with her.

: I need to release him, much as I don't want to. >>emote: cry<< He needs his independence, and it's safer if I release him away from the branch paths. :

And so Fessi found herself in the boat, ferrying an emotional Magrin who fussed over the frenzied occupant of a large handmade wooden cage all the way to the island.

'I don't normally cage him,' she said. 'I feel awful about it.'

'He's not scared,' Fessi observed. Her sense of the bird was a static fuzz of wild excitement and confusion – there was no fear. 'He trusts you, Magrin. He'll be fine.'

Kath and Andish waited outside the lakehouse, Andish excited to see the animal and Kath looking understandably apprehensive about it. Even in its juvenile form, the vollop was an intimidating species with broad black wings, a thick beak, and piercing, intelligent eyes. The eyes were still quite dark, as were the feathers on its head and chest, but Fessi knew they would age into a stern slate grey.

'Oh, he is beautiful,' said Andish, as she helped Magrin out of the boat with her cage. 'Does he have a name?'

'No,' said Magrin, but the word lilted, somewhere between unsure and dishonest. 'I couldn't name him. I knew he wouldn't stay with me forever, so...'

'You've given him a great start in life,' said Andish, in her soothing way.

'Yes,' said Kath. 'He looks very glossy and well fed.'

Magrin's eyes were shiny as she smiled at them. 'He's eaten his way through more of my credits than I have lately.'

They all gave Magrin her space as she untwisted the piece of wire securing the cage door and placed the cage on the ground. When she opened it and extended her hand to the bird, he clasped onto her wrist and allowed her to lift him out.

There she stood on the bank of the lake with the bird on her arm, her braids curled tight around her head, her face set with determination not to waver in this duty, and she looked quite formidable then: soft, sweet Magrin transformed into a warrior of old with her deadly familiar.

Magrin flicked her wrist, and the bird leapt into the air with a loud cry and wheeled up, up, up, the beat of his wings stirring the air against their faces. They watched in silent awe as he circled the island, calling out several times as though he expected Magrin to join him in the sky, and when eventually he realised she wouldn't, he banked to one side and soared over the lake, disappearing into the shadows of the trees in the distance.

Magrin's cheeks were dry, but she wiped them anyway, and Andish squeezed her shoulder.

'It's a lovely day,' Andish said. 'Perhaps you should bring some drinks outside.'

'I could use a bit of sunshine,' said Magrin. 'I don't get enough of it at the treehouse.' Her voice was level, but her gaze lingered at the edge of the forest where the bird had gone.

The glare of the sun on the surface of the lake made Fessi's skin tingle in anticipation of its warmth and power. Perhaps she'd manage to convince one of them to swim with her later. They traipsed together into the house, and Fessi drifted into the kitchen, where she filled three glass jars with pale pink juice from a jug in the cooling unit. She held up a fourth one as she caught her mother's eye. 'Are you joining us?'

'If you'll have me,' Andish replied.

Before they headed back outside, Magrin stripped down to her underclothes. Her prosthetic leg was exposed in its entirety, and Kath's eyes widened at the sight. The leg was made of a pale green material with a matte finish and darker green joints. As Fessi knew from experience, the material was soft to the touch, mimicking the elastic give of healthy flesh, but without the warmth. The prosthetic began halfway down Magrin's thigh and had the same thick and curvy proportions as her other leg. The foot had fully articulated toes.

'Great, isn't it?' said Magrin. 'It's customised with a few little hidden storage compartments too.' She patted the leg affectionately.

'It's great,' said Kath leaning in slightly to inspect it. 'I noticed the foot before, but I didn't realise… How did you lose your leg?' She cringed. 'Sorry, that's none of my—'

'Oh, I didn't lose a leg,' said Magrin. 'I never had one there to begin with.'

'Yours looks better than any prosthetic I've ever seen,' said Kath. 'There was a man in my apartment building who lost an arm in a factory incident, and he— Well, never mind. I'm sure you don't want to hear about that.'

'I'd love to, actually,' said Magrin.

They settled themselves on the chairs under the trees outside, the sunshine falling across their bodies in leaf-dappled bands. Kath and Andish wore pale clothwraps, while Magrin and Fessi offered up lots of bare skin to the warm light. Kath seemed unable to keep her eyes on either of them, preferring to look at the view or at Andish.

Andish took a sip from her jar and smiled, raising the drink to catch the light. It glowed bright like a pink jewel. 'It's better than I hoped,' she said. 'A fresh batch I pressed this morning.'

Kath sipped her drink, and her tensed-up shoulders sank as she swallowed. 'It's so much nicer than the berry tea,' she said with relief.

Magrin laughed. 'Different berries. Did you grow them yourself, Andish?'

'I did indeed. Round the back. You're welcome to take some home with you, if you like.'

Magrin tipped her glass at Andish and took a long drink from it. 'So good,' she said, smacking her lips. Every few moments, her focus would drift away from the conversation and out over the lake, but Fessi didn't sense any anxiety for the bird. It was more like curiosity, with the softness of hope. 'What are Earth fruits like, Kath?' asked Magrin. 'Any good berries?'

'Earth fruits are rare,' said Kath. 'The fresh ones, anyway. Most of the fruit I ate was frozen or sugared.'

'Did you have a favourite?'

Magrin was warming to the crosser, that much was clear. Despite being from another world, and alien in so many fundamental ways, Kath had a simple straightforwardness to her that made her easy to be around.

'Umm,' said Kath, pondering Magrin's question. 'I liked mango.'

'Mango!' said Magrin. There was apparently nothing similar enough on Rheta for the linga to insert a translation, and the word reached them intact, with all its delightful strangeness. 'What's that?'

'Big smooth fruit with a pit. The flesh is sweet and juicy and kind of stringy. Normally I'd just have the frozen cubes, but I had a fresh one once, and it was amazing. I had to pick the stringy bits out of my teeth for hours.'

'Fascinating,' said Magrin. 'Sometimes these Earthly things sound familiar, and sometimes they're really weird. Mango sounds weird.'

'It's strange, talking about Earth when I've been spending so much time reading about Rheta,' Kath said. 'I have so many questions.'

Delighted, Magrin placed her drink on the ground and pressed her hands together. 'Ask me one,' she said.

'Um,' said Kath. 'Is marrowcore good or bad?'

'Neither. Both. Marrow is like any element, isn't it? Water brings life, but you can also drown in it. Fire brings warmth and energy, but it can also destroy everything,' said Magrin, while Andish nodded beside her. 'With marrow, it's in everything, and strongest in things with living bodies. It's in our blood, our cells. And that's not a problem, because it's the right amount. It's just part of who we are. But outside of living things, it can crystallise into these massive marrowcore deposits. You can mine it out, use it for fuel. You can't live near those deposits. Too intense.'

'Intense?'

'It's toxic in large amounts,' Fessi explained. 'If you breathe in too much of it or eat things too tainted by it, it makes you sick. Mostly mentally. Physically too, but it's the mind that goes first.'

'Hmm.' Kath chewed thoughtfully on her fingernail. 'Is it the same effect as wickerbloom?'

'You've been reading the important stuff.' Magrin grinned. 'The answer is yes, but definitely no. Wicker has a higher concentration of marrow than other plants around here, but it's still well within the acceptable limits. Smoking wicker is nothing like marrowcore poisoning. I've seen what that looks like.'

'You've seen it? When?'

'Oh, just recordings. Everyone's seen them. Fessi can find one for you on the slab later. Quite terrifying. We all get given the case studies, probably to stop the curious ones from wandering into no-zones.' She laughed. 'They do it anyway.'

'They do?'

'Yes. But not for long. You can feel it, fuzzing up your head after ten minutes or so, and it's not pleasant.'

'You've been into a no-zone?' Kath's voice was increasingly high pitched.

'I have to go into them sometimes, for my research. I wear anti-marrow gear for that, though. But most people go into a no-zone without gear at least once. Usually only once, and not far. Just a few steps. Just to know what it's like. It's not very nice, I can tell you. Didn't you ever break the rules as a child?'

Kath nodded her head, then shook it, then smiled. 'Okay. So what about the reclamation?'

'That's a bit different. It's not about the deposits – you can't reclaim that land without mining it all out. Deposits are quite rare, though, easy to avoid, but everyone was marrowcore bombing everyone else during the war, and the bombs polluted the land and the water, massive no-zones all over the place. There's a neutralising powder they pour onto important areas to speed up the reclamation process, but they can't cover the whole planet with it. It's just a matter of waiting until the marrowcore poisoning decays away, and then we can reclaim the land. The time it takes depends on how heavily the place got bombed, and how badly polluted it was in the first place, and a lot of other factors.'

'Some people are worried about the reclamation,' said Andish. 'They think that when most of the land is habitable again, we'll have a population explosion, and the problems will start over and lead to another war.'

'Is that what you think?' asked Kath.

Andish considered this. 'I don't know,' she said. 'The problem was never that there were too many people. It was just that things were unfair. I'd like to think we've learned our lessons, but circumstances can change quickly and people forget...'

'Wilfully, sometimes,' said Fessi.

'Exactly.'

They fell into a relaxed silence punctuated by bird calls and the whirring sound of an insect in the reeds. The warmth made Fessi's eyelids heavy, and she closed them, letting the heat ebb and flow through her with her pulse and her breath.

She could easily have slipped into a dreamy sleep, but Magrin got there first, and her rumbling snore brought Fessi back to the surface. She opened her eyes just in time to see Kath and Andish exchanging smiles of amusement.

'Want to swim?' she asked quietly so as not to wake Magrin.

'Oh, no thank you,' whispered Kath. 'But you go ahead.'

Andish thought, – *I'll keep her company.* – and Fessi nodded.

The water lapped cool and clear around her legs as Fessi waded into the lake, the spangles of sunlight on the ripples so bright she had to squint against them. There wasn't even the hint of a breeze over the water, and the distant wickerwoods and tinwillows stood static. It wasn't particularly hot, but the stillness made it seem so, and the only clouds in the sky were as lazy as everything else, breaking apart and dissolving rather than moving with any purpose across the burnt blue expanse.

Fessi slipped under the water and glided forward, passing through sun-warmed pockets, feeling her way towards a shoal of silver fish just ahead. She released her breath so she could sink deeper into the clear brown depths to watch the fish dart back and forth, glinting in the shafts of sunlight.

The water was her favourite place to be. Submerged in it, her senses were amplified, her ability no longer contained within her body but encompassing the entire expanse of the water, not simply attuned to it in the way she normally was with the world around her, but existing as an extension of her. She could reach far further and sense connections at distances even Andish was sceptical of.

Floating on her back, eyes closed and arms drifting, she drew in a deep lake-fragrant breath through her nose and released it slowly, turning her focus from the island to the outer banks and further, further, sensing the shimmering pulses of activity in the forest beyond, concentrated in the marrow where people were in abundance, at the academy and in the most populated neighbourhoods along the branch paths. If she thought about her friends, pictured their physical attributes, and allowed her feelings associated with them to course through her body, she could sense them individually – the flicker of Virda and Jex, together as always, moving through the trees and, further out, Berro.

He was far enough away that she could barely sense him, and if she tried too hard to focus on him, he disappeared into the white noise of the marrow. As with gazing at distant stars, where looking at it from corner of one's eye often allowed for a clearer perception of it, she had to put focus somewhere near but just short of his actual location to sense him best.

Fessi eased herself into a light trance, her mind drawing an impression of the marrow in textures and colours and lights, a fizzing, flickering, swirling scene, with Berro's familiar spark at the edge of it.

Apart from Andish, Berro was the person she was closest to, whom she knew the most about, whose body language she could read clearly even before she deigned to delve beneath the surface and rifle through his many messy layers.

Berro.

The pulsing of his lifespark in the distant marrow suddenly sped up, and Fessi jerked slightly. Lake water sloshed across her face. She righted herself as quickly as she could and tried to slip back into the trance, but it was lost to her now, everything beyond the lake swirling and scattering. She turned her mind to Magrin and sensed her surfacing from sleep, a gradual awareness building of the sun that was angled now into a bright band across her face.

Fessi swam slowly back to the island. In the distance, a vollop cried out, its call echoing in the stillness.

CHAPTER 18

Blip, blip, blip.

Berro was off once again into the far reaches of the forest, his mono forging paths through the undergrowth in a flurry of newly fallen leaves. The weather had just begun to turn and the leaves with it – already the vivid green of the wickerwoods was flecked with gold, and the tinwillows ripening from silver to pink, the early evening sunlight rich with colour. This vigorous late-summer beauty made it easier for Berro to push back the memories of the dead man in the tree and the shadowcat in the bush. Shadowcats were creatures of the dark and damp, furred and fanged extensions of the shadows, and Berro felt safe in the glimmering golden haze. Death and danger didn't belong here.

Blip, blip, blip.

The forest opened slightly around a gravelly area, where the trees were separated by great slabs of grey rock freckled with lichen. Berro wove between the rocks and trees until he reached a river, small but strong, gushing through a gully. Tinwillows leaned over the river from both sides, their roots jutting out into it like they were cooling their feet. Berro wanted to do the same. The water looked so clean and inviting, playfully flicking drops of sunlight as it burbled and broke over the stones. Diptids danced in the spray and a few leaves twirled their way down into the current. Berro watched one leaf as it rushed downstream and met an obstacle.

It was not a rock or a branch. Beyond it, the water was streaked with red.

The golden beauty of the early evening vanished as though the sun had slipped behind a cloud and dropped the temperature by several degrees. Berro quaked and gulped for a few moments, then stepped carefully along the river's edge and into the water upstream of the body. The water only took him to halfway up his calves, but the flow was strong, and he had to brace himself against it and move carefully and deliberately.

The body was draped over a rock, back breeching the surface of the water and arms drawn out with the pull of the current. Berro shuddered in cold horror. A ribbon of entrails moved like a snake in the water, still attached to the body on one end. Blood swirled around the stones, frothed over small waterfalls. The head, face down, was mostly underwater, and the hair – long, light-brown hair – tugged and fanned like a tuft of fine watergrass, living, but not.

Berro knew he had to turn the body over and remove it from the river, and his stomach twisted with dread. He did it all in a burst of determined action, blanking his mind, scooping and flipping the corpse over into his strong arms with one swift movement, trying to ignore the cold wet deadness of its skin, not looking at it, not looking at it, *not looking at it*, barely even opening his eyes, breathing powerfully through his teeth as he waded back to the river's edge and up onto dry land, where he placed the body carefully on the leafy ground.

Then he looked.

She'd been dissected, deliberately and precisely, from the base of her neck all the way down her abdomen, the cut disappearing into the only piece of clothing she wore, a pair of loose trousers made from bands of slightly shiny black fabric stitched together.

She'd also been cut open from her left side to her right, beneath her breasts. Her skin was peeled back, and things spilled out of her belly, glistening. With most of her blood sucked away into the water, her insides looked too clean, like synthetic parts moulded for study and reference.

Berro tried to imagine that it was all fake, but he couldn't fool himself enough to avoid throwing up. It was violent and shocking in its suddenness. When it was over, he wiped his mouth and breathed slowly, trembling and empty.

He rolled out the body bag and opened it to receive its grisly cargo. A vollop called out from somewhere above, drawn, no doubt, by the smell of flesh. Berro's stomach heaved again, painfully.

'Greetings, crosser,' he said, keeping his voice as level as he could, which wasn't very level at all. It rasped like sand in his throat. 'I'm sorry we had to meet like this.' With his gloved hands, he carefully folded back the flaps of skin, pressing everything carefully into the woman's abdominal cavity. His eyes strayed to her face, which was partly obscured behind strings of wet hair. Her mouth hung open, but he was relieved to see that her visible eye was not. She didn't look peaceful, but she wasn't staring in blank terror either, and Berro tried to imagine what she must've been like when she was alive, before this terrible thing happened to her.

'Your death won't be for nothing. I'm going to take you back to my imparter, and we're going to learn about you and your world. I hope you don't mind.'

Of course she didn't mind – she was dead. She was totally and horribly dead.

Berro lifted her into the body bag and sealed it quickly. He unpacked the trailer, attached it to the mono, and eased her inside. He wasn't quite ready to head back; his hands shook badly, and the nausea rose and fell in surges that gripped at his stomach and made his head throb.

Tentatively, he stepped back down to the river and looked at the rock on which the crosser had been found. The water had already washed it clean. There was no trace of her, just the tinkling chatter of the current, and the leaves swirling along under the speckled shade of the trees. Beautiful.

Berro traced the lines of the rocks, the graceful twists of the tin-willow roots, the vibrant colours of the lichen, the patterns in the bark of the trees… And then he saw something on the trunk of the tree facing him on the opposite bank, something dark and shining.

He waded across the river, the water pulling hard at his legs, begging him to stop resisting, to let it wash him away. The bank on the far side was steeper, and clods of earth came away between the tree's roots and crumbled into the river as he clambered up.

Another crystal, purple-black and perfect, forced into the wood deep enough to draw sap that oozed like old blood down the crevices in the bark. It stuck to the fingers of his glove as he gripped the crystal and wiggled it free. He removed the glove to feel the cold, smooth surface of it. He weighed it in his palm and held it up to the light. It had that same strange filament running through its core.

What are you? What are you for?

• • •

'Stop wrecking the trees, you Earthling!' Virda shouted.

Jex dropped down onto the branch ahead of her amid a shower of leaves. 'You need to stop saying that. We have someone from an Earth world in our circle of friends now.'

'It's an evidence-based insult. Just about every artefact from an Earth world has some mark of environmental breakdown.'

'I'm sure they're not all bad. Kath seems enlightened enough.'

'I never said they were all bad. It only takes a few waspiks to destroy a pantry. Of course I wouldn't say it in front of her. I like her.'

'Do you think she likes us?' Jex sat down on the branch, dangling his legs over either side. A gentle breeze rustled through the leaves, and dots of sunlight darted and flickered over his face.

Virda rested her back against the trunk of the tree. 'I think she likes us as much as it's possible to like people you never should've met, in a place you never should've been, in a situation that never should've happened.'

'It could've been a lot worse for her,' said Jex.

'Of course, but that doesn't make it easy. We can't even imagine what it must be like, losing everything.'

'She gained a whole lot too.'

Virda laughed. 'You think highly of yourself, don't you?'

'I just mean… you know,' Jex swung his legs back and forth, and the branch creaked beneath him. 'Her old world sounds pretty bad, in my opinion. You just used Earthling as an insult, so you kind of agree. Rheta is better than any Earth stream we've ever heard about. I'm happy for her. She's safer here.'

Virda ran a hand along the tree's firm yet soft bark and considered the concept of safety along with the consequences of falling from this height down to the forest floor. 'Safety isn't everything,' she said.

There was a crunch of twigs, a sound that jarred with the gentle sighing of the breeze and the distant chittering of birds. They both looked down. Someone in a blue uniform was heading along the nearby branch path, walking with jerking, uneven steps. As they watched, the person stumbled and threw out an arm to grab onto something, but finding nothing, fell forward and out of view.

Hastened by concern and curiosity, Virda and Jex clambered along their branch, hopping carefully across onto the limb of an adjacent tree and scooting along it until the walker was unobscured by foliage.

'*Berro?*' said Virda, and rushed to descend. Jex followed.

Berro was on all fours, having made no effort to get back to his feet after losing his balance. He didn't seem to notice his friends standing in front of him until Virda placed a hand on his shoulder and he scrambled up, reeling, backing away and leaning heavily against the nearest tree.

'Virda,' he said. '*Virrrda*.' His face looked waxy, his forehead glistened with sweat, and his eyes roamed blearily, struggling to find and focus on his friends.

'Berro, what's happened?'

'Field unit,' he said. 'I went to... I— Undra wasn't there, so, I just left the specimen for him and— I was feeling a bit— I'm going back to the dorm.'

'The dorm? You're going the wrong way,' said Jex. 'Academy's that way.' He pointed. Berro stared at Jex's finger as though wondering what it was and why it was in the air.

'Berro, are you drunk?'

Berro stared blankly between them.

'I'm not drunk,' he said. 'I don't know what's— I feel— Am I sick?' In answer to his own question, he heaved and threw up all over the ground in front of him.

Virda recoiled in disgust, then studied Berro with growing horror. He looked nothing like his usual neat and tidy self, and the unfamiliarity of his chaotic state shook her to the core.

'Let's get you to the infirmary, right now.'

She threaded one of her arms around Berro's massive bicep, and shot a look at Jex, who stepped gingerly over the puddle of sick and took Berro's other arm. Slowly, they headed in the direction of the academy, Berro tripping with each heavy step.

'What were you doing when you started feeling like this?' Virda asked him.

'I— I...' he said, and the words came thick with the threat of another bout of vomiting. 'I was out. Collecting. Research.'

'Collecting?'

'I can't...'

'Did you eat anything?'

'What?' Berro turned his head and Virda was met with dilated pupils, eyes darting about in their sockets, struggling to stay focussed on her face. 'Did I eat...?' He made a sound that started off as a laugh, but quickly transformed into a choking retch. Jex jumped back, releasing Berro's arm just before he threw up again.

'Virda, should we call a medicraft? His hands look weird.'

Jex was right. There were strange dark stains on Berro's palms and fingertips that Virda hadn't noticed before.

'We're nearly there, Jex, take his cacking arm!'

• • •

Berro surfaced in the academy's infirmary. It had been years since he'd spent any time in such a place, and most of those memories were as a visitor, not a patient. He'd always been a healthy, robust sort of person, not prone to illness or clumsy enough to hurt himself. 'Just like your father,' his mother used to say. He remembered her dry, papery hand reaching out for him, meatless, bloodless, the veins like dark roots beneath her skin. He remembered thinking about her blood, imagining the sickness had thickened it into a coppery mud, imagining her heart desperately trying to pump it around her desiccated husk of a body.

His cubicle was clean, wood-panelled, lit with softly glowing ecolamps. A clock on the wall told him it was almost midnight. He couldn't remember when he'd arrived here, or how. Someone had taken the liberty of removing his uniform – it was nowhere to be seen – and putting him into a loose-fitting clothwrap. His hands were each wrapped in a mass of bandages so thick they resembled large bulbs at the ends of his arms. He wiggled his fingers inside their wrappings, just to check that he still had them. They'd been splayed and separated by soft, wet padding. He had no idea why. A tube fed a pale green fluid into the crook of his arm. He stared at the tube, trying to remember.

The woman. The dissected woman in the stream. He'd put her into the body bag. Then there was the crystal. Berro jerked upright, choking on air.

The crystal. Realisation spasmed through him. He'd touched the crystal, and from that moment onwards, he'd felt wrong, weird, *drugged.* And he'd felt it before, the first time he'd handled one of those crystals, only then he didn't have it with him for so long and it only touched his skin briefly. This time…

The heavy, sound-muffling curtain at the side of his cubicle parted, and Surgeon Halin stepped inside. She was a narrow, bony woman with a gap between her front teeth and small, bright eyes like polished gemstones, surrounded by a sea of fine wrinkles.

'Berrovan Blue,' she said in an ominous sing-song voice, clicking her tongue as she consulted her slab. 'I'm glad to see you're awake.' She fixed him with a searching glare. 'I must confess, I'm surprised by this. I know a bit about your reputation – the Imparters talk, you know – so I wouldn't have expected you to be experimenting with restricted intoxicants, especially not a strain so unbelievably potent that—'

'What?' Berro sat up straighter, and the tube pulled at his arm. He flinched.

'I see the effects are still wearing off. I can't emphasise strongly enough how dangerous these substances are. The local wicker-bloom is one thing, but inevitably some thrill-seeker decides it's not good enough and manages to import an overpowered alternative that someone took out of a no-zone or distilled in a cave somewhere, and then I get these students dragged in here, looking absolutely terrible. Though I must say, you were by far the worst I've seen. It was so strong, your hands changed colour! Why on Rheta didn't you at least wear gloves?'

Berro's skin prickled with hot panic, and he clamped his mouth shut against a shout or a gasp or a garbled collection of furious thoughts as the pieces fell into place. Marrowcore. It was marrow-core. Of course it was – those cacking crystals with their mysteriously purplish hue. What else could they have been? He couldn't fathom what they were for, but he knew now what they were, and that they'd poisoned him. Acutely. Thoughts and theories tumbled over one another in Berro's head. His teeth began to chatter.

'Please don't tell anyone,' he gritted out. 'I didn't mean to.'

Halin's face softened. 'I'm a reasonable person, Berrovan, so I'm not going to tell anyone about this, but my silence is conditional. Whatever it was you were handling, I need you to get some marrowcore pouches from storage and responsibly dispose of the rest of it at the waste facility before it gets into the hands of anyone else.' She patted Berro's foot, which protruded from beneath the too-short bed cover, warm inside a fluffy infirmary-issue sock. 'My job is to keep you healthy, not to get you into trouble. I'm sure you've learned your lesson from this experience, and I can't see any reason to inflict further punishment on you. Just remember this when you're voting for your Wooden Hill Rhetari council representative.' She winked. 'I'm running for the position, and I'd appreciate your support, if you think I'm a reasonable candidate. Code and Cohera, working together, you see?'

Berro nodded tightly, and Halin smiled.

'A couple more hours on the drip and any excess marrowcore in your system should be neutralised,' she said. 'I've wrapped up your hands with ointment to draw the discolouration out of your skin. Big purple patches, like flowers! Quite amazing, really, but you can't walk around the academy with your hands looking like that. It would be like wearing a sign on your head announcing to the world that you've been handling restricted substances!'

She laughed at her own joke. Berro did not.

CHAPTER 19

A false dawn of gradually brightening ecolamps and a subtle change in air temperature drew Berro gently out of a deep and dreamless sleep. He lay blank-brained for several long moments, inhaling the unfamiliar scent of the infirmary bedding and staring at the knots and whorls in the wood panels on the ceiling. When his memories slotted themselves back into place, Berro screwed his eyes shut and cursed. Embarrassment and anxiety bubbled within him like a meal prepared by Jex – something over-spiced and under-cooked. At least his hands were unbandaged, and the tube had been removed from his arm. He flexed his fingers and toes and found them functional.

A clean blue uniform had been placed on the table near the bed, along with his pod and other personal effects. It was time to face the world as someone who'd experienced acute marrowcore poisoning by accident – not an achievement he planned to feature on his records. He got up slowly, dressed carefully. His head was clear, but his body felt fragile and tired.

Two messages waited for him on his pod. The first was from Virda, asking if he was feeling better. The second message was from Undra – a simple acknowledgement of Berro's deposit of the dead crosser at the field unit. There was no mention of the crystal, no mention of a meeting, no enquiry as to where he was or why he'd fallen out of communication right after delivering a crosser, which was surely something that warranted immediate attention and discussion.

Berro remembered now the sequence of events before his mind had started shorting from the effects of the marrowcore. He'd entered the field unit perimeter, already feeling unwell, and opened the deposit hatch at the back of the building. He remembered lifting the bodybag and sliding it into the hatch, listening to the woman's remains slide slowly into the receptacle in the underground lab.

He'd felt sick and sad after that, but instead of leaving, he'd gone inside the building and placed the crystal on Undra's desk. He'd torn a sheaf of ecopaper from a notebook and written '*I found this at the site near the crosser. Looks the same as the one I found before. Could be relevant? Berrovan.*' and left the note alongside the crystal. He'd sent Undra a message on his pod, informing him that the crosser (deceased) had been delivered.

He remembered leaving the field unit and feeling suddenly much worse than before, and encountering Virda – and Jex? – on his walk back to the academy, but he couldn't remember much more than that. The details became increasingly hazy until they reached a complete blank, a chunk of lost time.

He responded to Undra's message.

: Greetings Imparter. My apologies for not being in touch sooner. Unfortunately, I had to spend the night in the infirmary. I left another crystal on your desk at FU4 yesterday. Please do not touch it. I think it was the cause of my illness. Are we having a meeting this morning? I am fully recovered now and I'm sure there is a lot for me to catch up on with regards to yesterday's findings. :

A reply from Undra pinged onto his pod moments later.

: Gods, Berrovan, I'm horrified to hear about your night in the infirmary, but glad you're back on your feet! I owe you a series of

apologies. I'm at the field unit if you'd like a meeting. I'll be here for the next few hours, at least, so come by when you're ready! :

Berro made his escape from the infirmary with great haste, successfully avoiding Halin on his way out. It was an abusively loud and sunny morning, and the clearing was dotted with students lounging on the grass, slurping portable breakfasts. The brightness assaulted Berro's eyes after the gentle dimness of the infirmary, and he found himself succumbing to a sudden, intense impatience that caused him to wrench a mono violently away from its stand instead of displaying his normal respect for academy property. A student in the process of parking a mono nearby glanced at him warily, but passed no comment. Berro sped away onto the nearest branch path, relieved when the cool shade enveloped him.

• • •

'Are you ready?' Virda called, over the sound of Jex urinating forcefully into the biocloset receptacle. He'd left the door open since Magrin had departed for a visit to the lakehouse, and he never did Virda the courtesy of shielding her from the full knowledge of his bodily functions. *We're too close to hold in farts around one another*, he always said. *If I don't let it out, I feel like I'm lying to you.*

'You can hear I'm not ready!' Jex called back, and the sound of his pissing intensified.

Virda twisted the front of her hair and pinned it back against her crown. She was itching to get into the trees, having spent all morning on her backside at the academy, fretting about Berro while trying to work on two of the post-fundamental assignments she'd been neglecting.

She'd made some headway on the most interesting assignment – a nutritional comparison of root vegetable samples grown at various distances from restricted zones, using data gathered by the sort of travelling research unit Magrin would probably join after completing her studies and overcoming her moderate fear of strangers – but she'd barely even touched the other one, which was some horribly dry statistics exercise that didn't interest her in the slightest. A problem with having not found a study focus was that she was left tinkering away at various unrelated subjects to fill her activity requirements, and none of it felt like it was leading anywhere. At this rate, she'd end up being a professional post-fundamental student, albeit an average one.

Jex had spent most of his morning at Vehicles, practising his ascensions in a vollop. He'd been enjoying himself so much, he'd allowed his instructor, Imparter Pol, to keep him at it for half an hour longer than what was indicated on the timetable, leaving a very frustrated and increasingly anxious Virda tapping her foot and gritting her teeth as she waited for him to meet her for their afternoon climb. He hadn't thought to tell her that his lesson was running over, and she'd begun to imagine his body being pulled from the flaming wreck of the vollop, the idea becoming more detailed and believable with each passing minute. He was going to have to work extra hard to improve her mood.

She heard him empty the receptacle into the biotank and begin sanitising his hands, humming with a cheerful nonchalance that made her want to stuff him right inside the tank so he could rethink his priorities while submerged in three months' worth of piss and cack. She stepped out onto the balcony to get some air and prevent herself from snapping at Jex. He could be incredibly thoughtless at times, but if she was insistent about ruining his happy mood now, they'd both be grumpy for the rest of the day, and the climb wouldn't be much fun. And she needed it to be fun, to take her mind off Berro.

Berro hadn't replied to her messages, but she'd pinged the infirmary and been told he was 'sleeping it off' – whatever 'it' was – and that there was no cause for concern. Still, it worried her. She'd never seem him that way before, so wretched and out of control.

If it had been anyone else, she would've suspected them of an overdose – an illicit marrowcore tincture or those crushed crystal powders that had ruined so many lives in past generations before they were banned by an amendment to the Code – but it was Berro. Berro would never take that risk. She was anxious to speak with him, to find out where he'd been, or what he'd eaten to end up in such a state.

It was a bright, still day, perfect for flying a vollop and just as perfect for climbing. It was also perfect for path maintenance, as the process required powdering the ground surface with a growth-retarding and binding agent and compacting it with a specialised vehicle before the wind blew it away. That vehicle was presently thumping its way up a path towards their treehouse. Virda tracked its cacophonous approach, watching the dull powder pour in a wide line from a slit in the front of it before being churned up by the treads underneath and finally thumped flat by a massive rotating mechanism at the back. The operator cabin was enclosed by thick greenglass tinted so dark that Virda couldn't see the person inside.

Jex emerged from the treehouse looking excited by the sound of the compactor, and Virda was amused and bewildered when he leaned over the balcony railing and proceeded to wave at it like a small child waving at a hovertube.

'What—'

'It's Imparter Pol,' said Jex. 'I don't know if they can see me, but—'

'Wait, your Vehicles instructor is operating the compactor? Why? That's a student job.'

Jex laughed. 'That's what I said! They told me nobody ever volunteers for it, even after they doubled the extra credits, because it takes so long, and the compactor is really loud and uncomfortable. I offered to do it, but Pol said they'd rather do it themself, unless I wanted the credits.'

'Why?' said Virda, choosing to ignore the fact that Jex had offered to do something for Pol that would've meant cancelling their climb altogether. She had to raise her voice slightly as the compactor drew level with their treehouse. It sounded like a very untalented rogue percussion section of a marching band from Rhetari parades of old.

'Pol said it's one of the only modern vehicles that actually makes contact with the ground while it's moving, so it's the only opportunity they have to experience what it must've been like when all vehicles did that.'

'People never drove around in compactors! Pol sounds ridiculous.'

'Pol *is* ridiculous.' Jex beamed. 'They put all the extra credits into the community bank.'

'Good of them.' Virda said. 'They should run for council.'

'Pol *is* running for council.'

Virda's eyebrows jumped into her hair. 'Imparter Pol? For council?'

She'd been joking when she'd suggested it. She couldn't imagine the serious-faced little person with the hop-like walk and the reedy voice becoming the global representative for their settlement, but then she didn't know very much about them. She'd only encountered Pol at a few fundamental lectures she'd attended with Jex in their early days at the academy, and occasionally passed them in the mingles or on the field. According to Jex, Pol spent most of their time behind the controls of various vehicles and tinkering around at the aircraft hangar north of the academy grounds. Pol was an odd character, but Jex revered them, and that counted for something.

'They're the perfect candidate,' said Jex, and Virda thought she detected a hint of defensiveness. 'Clever, highly skilled, knows more about Wooden Hill than anyone else who lives here. I mean, who else gets to see it from above as often as Pol does? Remember those rotten trees we climbed? The only reason that rot was contained is because Pol noticed the leaf-thinning and discolouration during an aerial lesson and sent Disa and some other reds out there to look at it. Pol cares. I mean look,' Jex waved his hand at the retreating compactor. 'Pol does more for this settlement than anyone.'

The fading sound of the compactor thumped in time with Virda's heartbeat as she contemplated the idea of her very own Jex being closely associated with their council representative. She'd have a potential direct line to power, if she ever needed such a thing…

'Well, they've got my vote,' she said. 'That was a very impassioned speech, Jex. Are you practising for an argument with Berro?'

Jex shrugged. 'Well, obviously he'll be supporting Undra for council. Undra's the favourite. And I know he's got loads to offer too, but it's Pol for me. Have you heard from him? Berro, I mean.'

'No. I can't stop thinking about him. He looked terrible.'

'Maybe he handled something toxic in the lab at the field unit.'

This was a surprisingly rational idea from Jex.

'Huh,' said Virda. 'Maybe. He'd never admit that to us.'

Jex laughed. 'Definitely not.'

'Can we climb now? Pol might be interested in touching the ground, but I really want to be high above it.'

'Me too,' said Jex. 'Let's go.'

• • •

'I feel awful for not checking up on you,' said Undra, peering into Berro's face with obvious concern. The creases at the corners of his eyes looked deeper than normal. He sat with both hands flat on the surface of his desk, a mug of tea forgotten in front of him. 'In truth, when I didn't hear from you later in the day, I assumed the collection had affected you – it *was* quite grisly – and I thought it best to give you some space. I confess, I disregarded the first crystal you found. When I saw the second one on my desk yesterday, I suspected it might be something dangerous, but you'd left such a neat little note. I didn't think you'd touched it.'

'I was stupid to touch it,' said Berro. His shame and regret pressed his shoulders down and inwards. The light through the field unit's high greenglass windows played across the ceiling, and the effect made him feel like he was underwater. 'The first one affected me too, but I didn't make the connection. Halin said it was some of the worst marrowcore poisoning she's seen, and by the sounds of it, it's something she sees fairly often.'

Undra's eyes widened. 'Are you in trouble? Did you tell her—'

'She was very reasonable. Thought I'd been meddling with drugs and let me go with a warning. I didn't contradict her because I didn't want to tell her about the crystals. I wanted to discuss them with you first. Do you think they're relevant to the study? They were both at crossing locations.'

'Hmm,' said Undra. 'I'm not sure. I have my doubts, though. You didn't actually find a crosser the first time you found a crystal. I can't imagine how they'd be related. You'll probably find they're all over the forest, so it's just a coincidence you found them while you were out tracking crossings.'

'Maybe, but…' Berro rubbed his temples. He felt drained and dull, like he hadn't slept at all. He thought about the academy showers, and the dormitory, and his bed. 'What do you think they're for?'

'I don't know,' said Undra. 'But if I had to guess, I'd say they were part of a rather sloppy drug trade happening in the settlement. Someone must've put them there for someone else to collect.' He lifted one shoulder. 'Where there are students, there are drug-Code violations. It's the way of things.' His eyes warmed, and Berro thought he might say something kind or comforting, but instead, he said, 'So, are you ready to inspect yesterday's crosser? I suppose you haven't had much time to think about her. Perhaps for the best. Not a pleasant find.'

'No,' said Berro. 'Not pleasant at all. But it didn't *affect* me. You said you were concerned about that. It's not an issue.'

The last thing he needed was for Undra to start having doubts about his mental fitness for the job at hand. His position meant too much to him, no matter how horrible it was to witness the aftereffects of violence beyond comprehension.

Undra tilted his head, his brows drawing together slightly. 'I'm glad to hear it,' he said. 'We have to be pragmatic about these things, but witnessing something so cruel and gruesome could affect anyone, especially people in a world as peaceful as ours. We aren't accustomed to seeing the results of brutality. There's no shame in admitting to a mental toll. If you ever do need a referral—'

'Thank you, Imparter, but I'm absolutely fine.'

Undra had spared him the ordeal of inspecting the first dead crosser he'd delivered, but Berro didn't want to be spared. He wanted Undra to trust him, even if that trust meant he'd have to spend more time around dead bodies.

Undra observed him carefully for a few moments, then gave a tight nod of his head.

'In that case,' he said, 'shall we go downstairs?'

In the air-conditioned chill of the laboratory, Berro and Undra stared at the woman laid out on the metal table between them. Berro was grateful to Undra for having prepared her; her legs were straight, arms at her sides, eyes closed and mouth held shut with a band of fabric he'd tied around her face. Her hair had been carefully detangled and brushed up so the tips of it dangled over the top end of the table. Undra had removed her intestines into a series of covered trays, and her abdomen was pressed closed and concealed beneath a length of cloth. If she hadn't been quite so pale and still and lacking internal organs, she might've been sleeping.

'First,' said Undra, 'we need to give her a name for the records.'

They'd decided on 'the Parachutist' for the previous crosser, as he was the first one in history to have fallen out of the sky in that manner. Berro stared at the woman's face – a pretty face, symmetrical and slightly pointy at the nose and chin – and could think of nothing but her horrific wounds.

'The Dissected Woman?' Undra suggested, and immediately shuddered. 'No. My apologies. That's terrible.'

'It's difficult to think of anything else,' said Berro. 'She's… very dissected.'

'They opened her up and rummaged around. I hope she was dead before it happened. The river washed away a lot of the evidence, but we should be able to figure it out. Her trousers are interesting.'

Berro was glad for an excuse to look at the woman's strange black strappy trousers rather than her dead face or the trays of her intestines. 'Synthetic material,' said Berro. 'She's not from a primitive world.'

'We'll open her stomach, see if we can find out what her last meal was,' said Undra. 'You can tell a lot about a world from its food.'

'I wonder if she chose her last meal or if someone forced it on her,' Berro mused.

Undra stepped over to the counter at the back of the room and retrieved two sets of gloves and face masks. 'Let's see if she can answer any of these questions for us.'

As Berro slipped on his gloves, his eyes roved over the crosser again. Unlike the Rainbow Woman or the Sun Man or even the Parachutist, death had not etched any expression onto her face. She looked placid, neutral. Hollow.

'The Hollow Woman,' he said.

'Yes,' said Undra before putting his mask over his mouth and nose. 'That will do.'

>>comspace/locked/reformatory reformation collective
>>2 reformer(s) in comspace
>>reformer treescrat has entered

Cackfoot– *: scrats :*

Burnitdown– *: hey scratty :*

Treescrat– *: hello. what's news? :*

Burnitdown– *: >>emote: sigh//sad<< :*

Treescrat– *: what's wrong? :*

Cackfoot– *: it's justicenow :*

Treescrat– *: is he all right? :*

Burnitdown– *: his brother died :*

Treescrat– *: but we already knew that :*

Burnitdown– *: we didn't, actually. we just made various assumptions about the likelihood :*

Cackfoot– *: he got another letter :*

Treescrat– *: wait, they TOLD him his brother died? :*

Cackfoot– *: no. it was a letter like the first one. an admin blunder. chunks of it were identical to the first letter, but with key phrases switched out :*

Burnitdown– *: he didn't share it, but he said it's obvious they're using templates. his brother didn't write either of them. he messaged the admin office demanding* *answers, but he hit a bureaucratic wall immediately and they deflected his questions with cack and nonsense, as always :*

Treescrat– *: gods. poor justice :*

Burnitdown– *: he said to tell you goodbye. he's not coming back to the comspace. said it hurts too much :*

Treescrat– *: >>emote: grief<< :*

Cackfoot– *: so then there were three :*

Treescrat– *: gods :*

Cackfoot– *: there aren't any gods, scrats. at least none who give a cack about people. it's just us :*

RHETARI DISTRO > WOODEN HILL > year 222, month 6, day 28

>>OPINION: STAYING COHERENT ON CODE AND COHERA — Imparter Hebbel of Wooden Hill Academy

According to the official Document of Definitions, currently used by students around the world even though it hasn't been updated in almost five decades, the Code is 'the set of rules established by the first Rhetari council after the war, in order to maintain order and facilitate the stabilising of Rhetari civilisation into a more peaceful and sustainable system'. The Cohera is 'the counterbalance to the Code' that steps in 'when the correct application of the Code is unclear'.

These widely cited definitions are partly responsible for the way we've started to think of Code and Cohera as separate entities, but that was never how they were meant to be understood. Both exist to maintain peace, order, and prosperity for the Rhetari people, working together, not separately.

We tend to tease them apart because it's so much easier to recite Code rules:

'*You may not take the life of another person.*

You may not invade a person's private living space without their permission.

You may not take from the environment more than the environment can regenerate before you take from it again.'

These are simple ideas, but in reality, things are rarely so straightforward that choices can be made, and consequences determined according to a binary system of right and wrong. If that were the case, why would anyone need to specialise in this field? Experts who can defend you against injustice aren't simply learning a list of rules off by heart. They're learning how to interpret context, choices, influences, actions, and reactions. They're looking at what it means to be Rhetari. What harms and what heals. And often, the Code on its own is misleading in that regard.

The first council understood this, and they built the Cohera alongside the Code. The Cohera is an attempt to codify something that, historically, has been too subjective, too variable, too temperamental to pin down. It was only because the war wiped out more than ninety per cent of Rheta's population and forced the survivors into a desperate monoculture that it was even attempted.

Before the war, there was only a superficial consensus on what was ethical. People were oppressed based on language and heritage. Exploitation and poverty were causes and consequences of so much suffering and conflict, and the early Code – the 'Law', as they called it – reinforced those broken systems, entrenching them deeper and deeper until only a major upheaval could undo them. The Cohera exists to temper the new Code and keep it serving us, rather than the other way around.

We are, however, seeing a regressive trend towards a more inflexible mode of thinking, and it's something I strongly believe we need to push back against. The best way to do this is to encourage more people into the field and open these discussions to a wider audience. We want everyone to understand and be invested in the systems that make our society function, or else those systems will stop working…

CHAPTER 20

Virda flicked the distro off her slab screen and groaned. She wanted nothing more than to put her arms around Jex and feel his arms tighten around her, but once again, he was at Vehicles, and she was at the treehouse failing to make any headway on her readings and assignments. Magrin was in her own room spending time with the creatures. She was a great hugger, but Virda couldn't just knock on her bedroom door and demand affection. It would be very out of character, and it would also lead to Magrin asking all sorts of questions Virda didn't want to answer. She couldn't tell Magrin about the comspace when she hadn't even told Jex about it.

The discussions in the Reformatory Reformation Collective were dangerous, and she'd rather not have Jex caught up in anything like that. It was for his own safety. The less he knew, the better, even if she felt guilty keeping it from him. She still hadn't told him about the note she'd found at the commune, either. She was keeping too many things from him these days, and it gnawed at her.

Unable to vent her strange grief on the shoulder of a friend, Virda turned to the only soothing alternative she could think of. Tea.

It was midday and warm outside, with plenty of people on the branch path below the treehouse, laughing and chatting and definitely not thinking about the reformatory in the mountains at

White Peaks. Those mountains would probably be lush and green now in the late summer, at least on the lower slopes, but Virda always thought of White Peaks as a place trapped in eternal winter, frozen and shrouded in snow, the reformatory itself huddled against the rocks, hard-edged and watchful. And inside, was Shani. Or perhaps not.

Justicenow, whoever he was in real life, had come to accept that his brother wasn't in there anymore, at least not in any sense that one could bear thinking about. Virda's heart ached for him, but some other part of her felt a shameful pang of jealousy. He'd never have the justice he wanted for his brother, but he was free now, released from the burden of worry and responsibility that had been hanging over him since his brother had been put inside. Knowing that he was dead, Justicenow could work on overcoming grief, which, no matter how terrible, was surely more realistic than overcoming the reformatory system itself.

Virda pressed the berries thoroughly, strained the tea with care into her favourite mug, allowed it to cool to the perfect temperature – still hot, but not hot enough to scorch the inside of her mouth – and took the drink out onto the balcony, where she sat on the less rickety of the two wooden chairs they kept stacked in the corner under the kitchen window. She sipped the tea like a medicinal tincture, taking unusually little pleasure in its consumption.

A light breeze ruffled the forest, and the trill of birdsong mingled with the chatter of people passing by. It should've been uplifting, but Virda's mood was heavy and dark. Still, the tea scrubbed away some of her tiredness and set her mind scrolling through her friends, trying to figure out which one she would benefit most from seeing, since Jex wasn't available until later. Magrin, Berro, Fessi, Kem, Disa, Tarov, Gunli, Berro, Disa, Magrin, Berro, Fessi, Berro…

Berro.

She pulled her pod from her pocket and flicked out a quick message. *: you free? :*

: No. But I will be a little later. Join me for History? :

: why would i do that? :

: Hebbel's showing some newly decrypted images from before the war. Some local ones too, apparently. They're going to be in her next publication, but that's only releasing next year. It's going to be a popular lecture. :

Oh, well. That did sound interesting, and Virda had just been reading an article by Hebbel on the distro. A sign, perhaps. She was fascinated by the history of their world from before its most recent rebirth. Whenever she read anything about it or saw any picture or video or artefact evidence, she couldn't help feeling as though she was learning about a completely different world in a completely separate stream of reality – something Undra would study, rather than Hebbel. It was difficult to accept that present-day Rheta was about as different from its own past as it was from other worlds.

She replied unambiguously to Berro's message.

: i'll be there. :

• • •

The ground floor mingle heaved with students and a few imparters, and as Virda moved with the surging crowd into the lecture hall, she doubted she'd be able to find a seat. She'd have to stand at the back or in the wings among the crowds of students already gathering there. She cast her eyes across the hall and her gaze was drawn by a large hand, waving. The large hand was connected to Berro's large body, and Virda wondered how she'd failed to spot him immediately. He was conspicuous, seated in a middle row right in the centre – prime viewing position – and he'd shamelessly reserved a seat for her using his backpack. She muttered apologies as she edged her way along the row and slipped into the seat beside her friend, who looked exceptionally pleased with himself.

'Glad you could make it,' said Berro.

Virda nudged him with her elbow. 'Thanks. I needed to get out.'

'Magrin's creatures driving you mad?'

'Something like that.' She tilted her head from side to side, neither a nod nor a shake.

Berro narrowed his eyes at her but didn't press the issue. 'Where's Jex?'

'In the clouds, as always,' said Virda. She knew she sounded bitter. 'Who would've thought our chaotic little Jex would have his life all figured before I do?'

Berro pursed his lips. 'It was a pretty clear path for Jex. He's always been enthusiastic about vehicles, even after—' he broke off with a light shake of his head and continued along a safer path, for which Virda was grateful. 'Jex is not particularly academic. Flying was an obvious choice. It's more difficult for people with broader interests.'

Under normal circumstances, Virda might've read some vague insult into Berro's assessment and leapt to Jex's defence, claiming that his interests were just as broad as anyone else's and his lack of enthusiasm for the written word said nothing of his academic potential, but today Berro's words soothed that sensitive, fretful part of herself that flared up so easily and so often in recent weeks. He meant no insult to Jex. In truth, he was absolutely right about him.

Virda wasn't particularly enthusiastic about academic work herself, but she had a good enough natural aptitude for it and was able to push through her indifference when she bothered to put in the time. With enthusiasm like Berro's, she might've even been impressive, but as it was, she was comfortably average. Jex, on the other hand, wasn't academic at all – never had been and never would be. Apart from his ability in Numbers, he was bordering on hopeless. A full page of plain text had his eyes glazing over in minutes. As soon as he'd had the option of throwing out his more academic subjects in favour of practical foci, he'd done so without hesitation.

The ecolamps in the lecture hall dimmed as Imparter Hebbel – large, ruddy and eager-looking – bustled in and settled behind the podium, fiddling with her slab to link it up with the projector. An excited hush fell over the crowd.

'Right,' said Hebbel, clapping her hands together. 'You all know why we're here, more or less. We have, at various academies around Rheta, collections of centuries-old tech, in particular, storage drives from larger machines and a vast number of portable devices of various sizes. When time and manpower allow, we attempt to refurbish these into working order so we can try accessing any files that might be preserved on them.

'The war, of course, with its catastrophic abuses of marrowcore weaponry, left most of this tech burnt out and beyond repair, with no data salvageable, but every now and then, we find something from a location that was spared this degree of destructive impact. We see the data from these devices surfacing in sociological journals every year, mostly family pictures and the odd semi-corrupted video in which people wearing funny clothes are happily eating things that today we'd only have served to us in our nightmares.' Hebbel shuddered, and a ripple of appreciative laughter spread through the hall. She was an entertaining speaker, and Virda was glad to be there.

'This most recent find, which I am absolutely honoured to have been given by the war-tech salvage team for historical analysis, is significant for us because the subject matter is local. So, while there are several personal images from the individual who took the pictures, there are even more images of Wooden Hill itself, and of the surrounding area. As you're probably aware, there aren't many pre-war images of this region in part because it was a military training base and not very densely populated then. The only locals not employed by the military were the Singers, who weren't enamoured with tech, and left no images in the wake of their annihilation. The area was quite badly poisoned once the bombs started flying to the north and the marrowcore came down in the rivers and groundwater. After the war, the academy building and surrounding forest were recognised as valuable, and so it was one of the first areas reclaimed. The first houses were built in trees as a safeguard against residual marrowcore poisoning at ground level, and of course we've kept the tradition.

'The pictures we've obtained were extracted from a device stored at another academy. The person who took the images must've been here as a visitor, and the device only survived because it wasn't left here.

'Anyway, enough background. I'm sure you're eager to get started, so let's have a look at the first one.'

She tapped her slab screen and a grainy image of trees appeared on the projection. Hebbel cleared her throat.

'Well, I didn't want to show you the best ones first,' she chuckled. 'These are wickerwoods. As you all know, we live in the only region where wickerwoods thrive in such great numbers. They're incredibly valuable trees, for their flexibility and strength that make them, quite literally, the pillars that support our community, for their sap, their leaves, their nuts, their bark, and of course, their blooms… and this was true before the war, too. People weren't living in the wickerwoods then. These trees were fiercely protected as commodities, their products highly valued. There's plenty to go around now, but back then, the gifts of the wickerwoods were available only to the most privileged of Rhetari with the exorbitant income necessary to afford them.

'We suspect our picture-taker was some sort of contractor at the military base. He must've had special access to the forest, anyway. He knew he wasn't just capturing any old trees. It's not a great image, this one, but he took it with purpose.'

Hebbel tapped the slab again. The second image was of three people on an elaborate – and, if Virda was called upon to give her opinion, she'd certainly say *ugly* – softseat. In the centre sat a middle-aged man, balding, wearing the classic, hideous pre-war formalwear: buttons all over the place and stiff, starchy bits with a fiddly neck-ruffle pinned into the apex of an uncomfortable-looking collar. On his left, a woman of about his own age perched, smiling sweetly, wearing a garishly floral-patterned one-piece zippersuit, and on his right was a young boy wearing a bulky synthetic costume resembling a prehistoric shadowcat, his small, sweaty face protruding from a hole inside the animal's gaping mouth.

The hall erupted into laughter, and Hebbel grinned merrily.

'Gods, is that child abuse?' Berro muttered.

'What?' Virda snorted. 'I would've loved that disguise when I was little.'

'If a shadowcat saw a child wearing that, it would disembowel them out of spite.'

'So!' said Hebbel, and the chatter simmered down. 'We have reason to believe that the man in the middle is our intrepid picture-taker. We weren't able to find any data indicating his name, occupation or place of residence, but we've dubbed him Subject Buttons, and I shall henceforth refer to him as such.'

'She's loving this, isn't she?' Virda murmured under the cover of more laughter.

'Oh yes,' said Berro. 'She's almost as entertaining as Undra when she gets going.'

'The next picture is the one that caught the attention of the salvage team and inspired them to get in touch with me,' said Hebbel as a new image filled the projection.

Bare trees beneath a pale grey sky, an open field, patchy with mud, wheeled vehicles parked here and there, people in dark uniforms – coats, caps, boots, marrowcore guns strapped to their backs – marching across the foreground. In the background, the ugly stone finger of the academy building rose from the top of the hill. It had no vines crisscrossing its exterior, and far fewer windows than it had now. In place of the glass observation dome, it bore a segmented metal cap with a large aperture, closed against the elements. Virda wondered if it opened for a long-range scope, or for a missile launcher. Perhaps both.

Hebbel allowed the low, excited chatter to continue for some time, while she herself scrutinised the image on the projector as though she'd never seen it before.

'A lot less hospitable-looking isn't?' she said eventually. 'Notice also the lack of entry tunnels in the hillside. Anyone who has studied the academy architectural records will know that the tunnels we have today were added after the building was reclaimed. Back then, there was a single tunnel leading right out into the forest, but it had partially collapsed by the time of the reclamation, and it was filled in.

'The entire interior was restructured with new levels, rooms and windows, the elevator, and the observation dome. The ammunition storage bunker at the base level was ventilated and subdivided into the dormitories, and of course we have new satellite structures and field units away from the main campus.

'But this is what our beloved academy building was before and during the war. It was one of the many engines of Rhetari destruction.'

A sombre hush fell upon the audience, and they stared at the image in silence for a few moments more before Hebbel tapped the next one into view, prompting a collective intake of breath. It was beautiful, a waterfall tumbling down a stepped cliff into a clear pool, deep blue at its deepest, and brilliant cobalt at the shallow edges. A lush variety of plants in various shapes and colours crowded around the water's edge. In the centre of the pool, creating a ring of ripples, was Subject Buttons, treading water with a wide grin and his arms raised for the camera.

'We think he set up his camera with a timer to get this shot,' said Hebbel. 'Several of the images featuring our subject on this date were taken by him turning the camera on himself to get his face against an interesting backdrop. Clearly this scene was worth a little more effort. The area is currently – and regrettably

– inaccessible because it's in the middle of one of our nearest no-zones, unreclaimed and off limits until further notice. You could get there wearing anti-marrow gear, but it isn't recommended, and the place isn't included in any current studies.

'Subject Buttons was lucky enough to see it before the water was poisoned. The marrowcore, apparently, had a significant toxic impact on this unusual geographic feature, where the cleft created a pocket of humid warmth in an otherwise temperate region. I'm sure an imparter of the red persuasion could tell you more about why this place suffered such an acute level of marrowcore poisoning, but as it's not quite my area, I'm going to carry on…'

A tap on the slab brought another upwelling of excited murmurs. Virda leaned forward, and Berro stiffened slightly beside her.

'Some of you recognise this one,' said Hebbel, gesturing at the projection, which now showed a beautiful filigree glass structure in a sunlit glade, colours refracting in rainbow flares from some of its angles. 'The famous glasshouse of the Singers. It's still around, a manageable distance from the academy, but it's in ruin now, left to crumble after the war. If you've travelled by hovertube at sunset, you've probably seen the ruins reflecting the light on the edge of the forest as the tube passes across the north fields.

'At the time that this picture was taken, the glasshouse was already abandoned, the Singers driven into hiding deeper in the forest by linguistic persecution, but the structure itself was protected as of relic of a so-called primitive culture officially declared to be extinct – even though it wasn't. A shameful stain on our history, a disgrace, and one we must never forget.

'We call it the glasshouse, because the writers of local lore in the immediate aftermath of the war referred to it as such, out of habit more than anything else, I imagine, but, in our more modern and enlightened age, I'd suggest we show respect for the people who built it, and refer to it as they did, as the glass *boat*.'

Virda jerked in her seat, and Berro snapped his head around to stare at her.

'It's not clear from this picture,' Hebbel continued, 'but if you look at the shape of the structure from above, you'll see that it's shaped like a sea vessel, with a pointed front and slightly curved sides. For the Singers, it was more than a gathering place or even a place of worship. It was seen as a vessel of transportation to another plane of existence.'

Virda eased her breath through her nostrils.

'You good?' Berro murmured. 'You look like you just saw a ghost.'

'I'm fine,' said Virda. 'You seemed a little taken aback yourself.'

'I was there the other day,' said Berro. 'For a collection.'

Virda turned to meet Berro's eyes. 'A crosser?'

Berro nodded, and Virda felt something inside of her soften at the haunted look on his face. Hebbel was answering a few questions from students upfront, so they were free to continue talking, but Virda didn't know what to say to comfort Berro. Instead, she asked a question.

'Did you know that people called it a 'boat'?'

'Yes?' said Berro, arching an eyebrow. 'It's not a big secret. It came up in fundamental history, I think.'

Virda flushed. 'I must've missed that lecture. I was a terrible student in fundamentals.'

'Well, you're here now,' said Berro, as if that made up for it. The audience began to chuckle, and Virda turned back to the projection, which now showed a comical and very unflattering close-up of Subject Button's face with some impressive wickerwoods behind him.

Virda wasn't interested anymore. All she wanted to do was get home, tell Jex about the scrap of paper from the commune and what she'd just learned, and then go out into the woods, to the glass boat, and find out if the Singer ruin was the starting point she hoped it was.

CHAPTER 21

'Jex!' Virda pushed open the bedroom door and found him, freshly showered and barely clothed, draped over the bed in a half snooze while lazy instrumental music piped out of his slab on the bedside table.

'Hello,' he said opening one eye. 'Where were you?'

'I went to a lecture. How was flying?'

'Good. Great. Why do you look so chaotic?' He opened both eyes, only to narrow them at her.

Virda smoothed down her hair with her sweaty palms and sat on the edge of the bed, her weight causing Jex's slight figure to tumble into her. 'I need to tell you something,' she said. 'I was going to tell you before, but I didn't know what it meant, and I wanted to figure it out first.'

'Figure what out?'

'I found something. At the commune. In that box Mama Stitch gave me to look at. Remember? It was a note. I think Shani wrote it.'

Jex sat up and turned off the music. He scooted back a little to put space between himself and Virda, and stared at her. 'Shani left a note?'

Virda nodded. 'I didn't know what it meant when I first read it. But I just figured it out. Just now, at the lecture. Here…' She fished the scrap of paper out of her pocket and handed it to Jex.

He stared at it intensely for a long time. 'Directions,' he said. 'To where? What boatwreck?'

'That's what I didn't understand,' said Virda. 'But I was just at a history lecture with Berro and… you know the glass house? The old Singer ruin? Apparently, it's also known as the *glass boat*.'

Jex handed the scrap of paper back to her slowly. 'Why didn't you tell me?'

Virda bit her lip. Why hadn't she? Perhaps, with Jex's help, she'd have figured it out sooner. 'I'm sorry. I wanted to solve the mystery. I didn't want to show you a worthless scrap of paper. I wanted…' The words died in her throat. She'd wanted him to be impressed with her. She'd wanted him to be excited. And instead, she'd managed the opposite. She thought about her secret comspace, and her insides clenched painfully.

'Can we go right now?' said Jex. 'To the *boat*?'

Virda peered out the window, where the sun sank low behind the trees and the shadows gathered. She took a deep breath. 'First thing tomorrow,' she said. 'I'll set an alarm. We can get an early night and then catch the first light.' And perhaps, she thought, Jex would have forgiven her by then.

Jex opened his mouth, and Virda thought he was about to argue, but instead he just nodded and lay back down, turning away from her.

'I'm sorry I didn't tell you about the note,' said Virda.

'Don't worry about it,' he replied.

• • •

Berro sat in the dining hall, gazing into a steaming bowl of frigram broth and dumplings. He moved the dumplings around with his spoon, watching the flecks of green swirl in the liquid. He wasn't hungry, but he needed to eat. Over the course of an afternoon, the weather had turned unseasonably cold, and the broth was pleasantly hot, even if it wasn't settling his uneasy stomach.

Only one other student was taking an early dinner the dining hall, and it was Ryndel. Without even being particularly annoying, she had come to represent annoyance itself, an embodiment of his insecurity, his paranoia. She was, after all, a brilliant student, who had layers to her existence beyond her academic abilities. A multi-faceted individual, effortlessly balancing her ambition with other things. Would she throw up uncontrollably at the sight of a dead crosser? Did she worry about her social status? Did she feel lonely and inadequate and unsure of herself at least once every day? He doubted it.

She was looking at him – Berro felt it as he stared into the swirling green depths of his broth. She was looking at him and most likely thinking about his inadequacies. He shook himself and took a careful mouthful of food. Ryndel didn't know that he was Undra's primary assistant. She didn't know anything. His mind was just spinning stories, trying to create some justification for his feelings of unease. Undra had chosen him. *Him.*

And yet her eyes were still fixed in his direction. He looked up and she looked down and set about cutting the millbean bun in front of her into small pieces. Berro shovelled his dumplings into his mouth as quickly as he could, chewed, swallowed, lifted the bowl to his lips and drained the broth. It burned his tongue, and he didn't care. He deposited the bowl at the cleaning counter and left the dining hall without looking back.

Evening classes were in session, and the mingles were deserted. Berro's footsteps echoed on the wooden floors. He took the elevator up to Undra's office and stood outside the door, wondering if the imparter was in there, and if he should knock to find out, and if Undra would react positively to his presence. He needed to ask questions. Surely there was no harm. It would show enthusiasm, dedication, interest. He'd proven himself stable and capable in his handling of the Hollow Woman. He'd even suffered acute marrowcore poisoning for this project. Surely, by now, he was entitled to a better understanding of what Undra was doing, and how. If Berro used the right words, the right tone of voice, the right facial expressions, surely Undra would tell him everything he wanted to know. *Surely.*

He stood with his hand poised to knock, and heard the elevator hiss open behind him. He turned.

Ryndel.

She stepped out and stopped, eyes locked onto him. 'Berrovan,' she said.

Berro tried on a smile and found that it didn't fit. He lowered his hand. 'Uh… hello,' he said.

'Are you here to see Imparter Undra?'

He could hardly say no to that, his hand having been an inch away from the door only moments before. 'I thought I'd see if he was in.'

Ryndel nodded. 'We need to talk.'

'You and Imparter Undra?'

She huffed. There was a strange anxiety about her. 'No,' she said. 'You and me. We need to talk.'

'Oh…?'

Her dark blue eyes blazed. 'Come with me,' she said, and stepped back into the elevator. Her voice was high, but strong, commanding, serious.

Compelled, he followed her. They stood in silence as she sent the elevator all the way down to Grow Level A.

'Why are we here?' Berro asked as they stepped out into the humid air, wondering why he was taking orders from someone he actively disliked.

'Because nobody else will come here,' she replied, and led him off to a secluded area behind a shelving unit packed full of slimy-looking mushrooms in interlocking punnets. 'Right,' she said, squaring up and pinning him with her bright, hard eyes. 'What is going on with you and Undra?'

Berro suppressed the urge to laugh and said, with more than a little smugness, 'I'm afraid I'm not allowed to say anything about that.'

Ryndel closed her eyes for a moment, and when she opened them, some of the hardness was gone. 'You're his primary assistant, aren't you?'

'As I said, I'm not allowed—'

'Berrovan. Cut the cack. You're his primary assistant. You were chosen, right? Above all others. That's what he told you.'

Berro didn't like the tone of her voice. 'I don't—'

'He told me the same thing.'

The breath rushed out of Berro's lungs. 'What?'

'I applied for the position, just like you did. And I got it. Just like you did. He told me you'd be helping with smaller administrative tasks, but that I was the most important one. He told me to keep it quiet, so you wouldn't be jealous or nosy.'

Berro leaned back against the shelves, felt them shift fractionally, and put his weight back onto his feet, although he didn't feel like he had any feet. The steamy room seemed devoid of breathable air. 'Why?' he managed to say.

'I don't know,' said Ryndel. 'I've been asking myself this question since I started suspecting something was wrong. I wasn't certain until right now. Why can't he just say he needs two people to hammer crystals into trees? I mean—'

'*What?*' Berro's voice went up.

'What?' Ryndel's voice went down. 'Crystals. You don't… you don't do the crystals?'

The crystals. Perfectly symmetrical, purple, pointed, driven into the bark of the trees like bullets.

'You put the crystals into the trees,' said Berro. 'I found two of those crystals. I brought them to Undra thinking he'd be interested, but he wasn't. And they made me… they were like drugs. I didn't realise it was the crystal the first time. I thought I was losing my mind.'

'Oh, cack…' Ryndel's eyes darted back and forth across Berro's face. 'That's why some were missing when I went back to collect them. You touched them? With your skin? Oh, I'm so sorry, that must've been bad.'

Berro nodded, swallowed. 'What are they? What are they for?'

'Berrovan, they're marrowcore. Pure, concentrated, purified marrowcore. I don't know how they work. He won't tell me. Not yet, anyway. I think I need to earn his trust, or something. But… if you don't do the crystals, what do you do?'

Berro felt the bile rising in his throat. He put his hands on his knees. 'I collect the bodies,' he choked.

'Bodies?'

'Dead bodies. Dead crossers.'

Ryndel's mouth dropped open. She seemed, if possible, paler than usual. 'The crystals…'

'Is he triggering the crossings? He told me he was tracking them, trying to figure out what was causing them.'

'He told me he was testing the marrowcore, seeing if he could weaken the boundaries between realities. He has a drone he sends out to scout the forest, to find the next location for me to install the crystals. I've noticed he likes to put them on old Singer sites, for some reason. The dancing stone, the burial ground, the glass boat… He said we were far away from being able to actually manipulate crossings, but—'

'I think that's exactly what he's doing.'

Ryndel stared at Berro, her thin red lips pressed into a straight line. 'Why does he need us?' she said in a small, scared voice.

'I guess he can't be seen wandering around in the forest, hammering restricted substances into the trees.' Berro tried to imagine Undra loading a corpse onto a trailer. 'And collecting the bodies is…' *Difficult. Messy. Heavy work.* Berro looked at his hands – broad, with long, thick fingers – and clenched his fists. His wrists were big, his arms were big. He was big, in general. He had his father's body. Towering, lumbering, dense and muscled, powerful, strong. Anger welled up inside him like lava. His mind was a brilliant jewel, by far his most powerful and impressive asset. Did Undra realise this? Did anyone?

'Thank you for telling me,' he said finally, unclenching his hands. 'I'm going to speak to him.'

'But—'

'Don't worry, I won't mention you.'

Ryndel opened her mouth, but didn't say anything. The colour was high in her cheeks and her eyes were wild with some wordless emotion.

'Goodbye, Ryndel,' Berro said, and headed for the elevator. She didn't follow.

• • •

For several moments after the elevator stopped and its glass panel slid aside, Berro stood staring out, his mind a mess of unanswered questions. So it seemed Undra was triggering the crossings, not tracking them. Bold, controversial – shocking, even – but so what? Why had he lied about it? He must've had his reasons. Berro needed Undra to understand that the subterfuge was unnecessary, that he could be trusted with the truth.

The eleventh floor was deserted – unsurprising, given the hour. He knocked on Undra's office door, wondering if he'd be there or if he'd have left for the field unit. He had sleeping quarters in both places, after all. But the door opened and there he was, wearing his blue uniform, his eyes bright and his hair styled as though it were the middle of the day.

Undra cocked his head to one side. 'Berrovan,' he said, and stepped aside to let him in. 'Is everything all right?'

Berro let him close the door behind them. 'Yes, thank you, Imparter. May I sit?'

Undra nodded, and Berro lowered himself into his usual seat.

'Is there something you'd like to discuss?' Undra sat behind his desk and rested his chin on his fingers. He had that easy smile, a silver-streaked lock of hair falling over one eye.

Berro inhaled deeply and exhaled slowly. 'I'd like you to know that you can trust me,' he said, keeping his voice level, even though his heart pumped frantically. 'I want to know everything there is to know about this project. I'll do whatever I need to do to earn your trust.' He swallowed, and his throat clicked. 'I'm dedicated to this. I'm dedicated to you.' It all sounded stilted and rehearsed, but Berro doubted that such a declaration could ever be cool or casual.

Undra nodded slowly, and anxiety twisted Berro's guts as he waited for the imparter to say something.

'Good,' said Undra. 'That's good. Thank you, Berrovan. I know it must be frustrating, especially for someone with such a curious mind, to be involved in something so momentous without knowing everything about how it works. I appreciate your patience and understanding.' He smiled. 'And your dedication. We'll get into the details soon. As long as you keep up the good work, I can *promise* you that. Now, let me get some coordinates for you.'

'Another crossing?'

'I think so.' Undra stood and slipped into his back room, snapping the door shut behind him, leaving Berro alone in the front office.

Berro dropped his face into his hands. Had he gone too far? Undra was probably pacing the back room, pulling his hair, trying to figure out a way to get him off the project without him kicking up too much of a fuss about it. Maybe he knew, somehow, that Berro knew about Ryndel.

Undra took an extraordinarily long time in the back room – so long that Berro briefly considered opening the door to make sure he wasn't hurt. But no, it was out of bounds. Those were the rules. Undra had practically framed any intrusion into his personal quarters as a Code violation when Berro had signed the contract for the primary assistant position. Berro sat tight, increasingly sick with dread and hating himself. He picked at the gloss on one of his fingernails, chipped it, and then glared at it with furious regret.

Undra emerged moments later. 'Right, here we are,' said the

imparter, placing a small sheet of paper in front of Berro. 'I've been getting anomalous readings from roughly that location. I wouldn't go there now, it's not a good idea in the dark, but if you could investigate first thing in the morning, I'd appreciate it. And I know… I *know* you want me to explain more about these readings to you, Berro, and I will, but it's not quite time for that yet.'

It was the first time Undra had used the short version of his name, but Berro's heart didn't leap as he'd always thought it would. He took the piece of paper with sweaty fingers.

'Thank you, Imparter,' he said.

• • •

Berro arrived at the location just after dawn, following a sleepless night and a dangerously fast mono journey from the academy, and for a minute, he thought it was another false reading. The area was uneven, rocky and scrubby, with small trees struggling to find purchase between the stones. Wan, early morning light illuminated the open space, and Berro couldn't see a body, or any signs of one, nearby.

A shiver of unease ran up the back of his neck. The dry smell of hot sand met his nose, and his eyes caught on a dark, shining patch on the rocks. Blood. A trail of it led into the thicker vegetation beyond the rocky area, and Berro followed it.

It would be another live crosser. It had to be. But this one was hurt. The blood was copious, undoubtedly the result of a serious injury. As Berro advanced slowly but steadily into the shade, he took a mental inventory of the contents of his backpack. He had some medical supplies, but did he have everything he needed to save a life? Did he have the knowledge, or the skill? And what were the odds that this had happened again? Live crossers were so rare as to be almost the stuff of legends, and yet he was certain he was about to meet a second one. Undra's secret process was rewriting the probabilities.

Berro's boot came down onto a thick, straight twig, and it snapped loudly, the sound followed immediately by movement nearby. He turned, sharp, stepped around a mess of undergrowth and there he was, the crosser, alive, crouched and growling like a wild animal.

He was a young boy, probably around the age of twelve or thirteen, and his body was horrifically mutilated. The top left portion of his skull and face was metal – rough, rusty-looking metal – piercing the scabbed and oozing flesh around it. In place of a left eye, he had a spinning bionic orb. A roughly stitched incision curving down his cheek below the false eye had pulled the left side of his top lip into an ugly snarl. Several of his teeth were filed into points and capped with metal attachments. Blood poured down the side of his head from a mangled ear. It was a combination of every worst-case scenario Berro had imagined.

The boy's real eye locked onto Berro's face, and Berro could see the unmade choice strobing behind it.

Run or fight. Run or fight.

The boy pulled his crusty lips back further, baring his terrible teeth.

Fight it is then, thought Berro. But he didn't know how to fight. He raised his hands slowly and said, 'I won't hurt you', in the smoothest, gentlest voice he could muster.

In answer, the boy leapt to his feet and threw himself towards Berro, a bloody shriek tearing its way out of his small, brutalised body. He clawed at Berro with his hands, one of which was hideously butchered and implanted with metal parts. Berro stumbled back and then advanced into the attack, using his size and weight to dominate the child, turning him around and forcing him to the ground. He pinned the boy down with his whole body, straddling his back, and pressing his face into the stony soil to muffle his animal screams. With his other hand he fumbled frantically for his pod. With great difficulty, he managed to locate Undra's comlink and call him.

'It's another live one,' he panted. 'He's out of control. I can't—' Berro cried out in pain. The boy had worked one of his arms free, and he ripped at Berro's leg with his metal fingertips.

Undra's voice, calm and solemn, said, 'Keep him quiet. I'm on my way.'

He ended the call.

'Stop it!' Berro tossed the pod aside and held the boy's arm against the ground. 'I don't—want— to *hurt you*! Just *stop*!'

But the boy didn't stop. He twisted and bucked like a speared beast, growling and wailing through a mouthful of leaves and grit. His legs kicked up, trying to strike Berro from behind. Berro's leg burned where the boy had scratched him.

He cursed under his breath and settled his weight down harder, fighting to keep all four of the boy's limbs pinned to the ground. It was going to take Undra some time to reach them, and Berro worried that he couldn't keep him restrained for that long.

'Please,' said Berro, hopelessly. 'I'm not your enemy. *Please...*'

CHAPTER 22

Hours before dawn, at the very first chime of Virda's pod alert, both she and Jex jumped into action from just below the surface of sleep.

Under normal circumstances, Jex was a slow, slouchy, foot-dragging, bleary-eyed yawner in the mornings, at least until he'd had some tea, but these were not normal circumstances. He was desperately eager to follow Shani's directions, and to Virda's relief, he seemed to have put aside his disappointment in her decision to keep the note from him for so long.

Virda sent a text to Magrin before they left.

: Mag – we've gone for an early climb. See you later. :

Walking as fast as they could without breaking into a run, they reached the academy within twenty minutes and procured a monocraft from the stands at the edge of the field. Jex gripped the controls, and Virda took her position on the board behind him, looping her arms tight around his waist. She cast a glance at the academy building, wondering what Berro would think of their little excursion, before Jex hared off onto the branch paths. All thoughts fled from her mind apart from one that repeated on a loop:

from boatwreck, 20 w, 45 s, snail rock, 4 sw, leaning tree, under root

from boatwreck, 20 w, 45 s, snail rock, 4 sw, leaning tree, under root

from boatwreck…

They'd travelled in silence, Jex pushing the mono at speeds that made casual conversation impossible. It was more than an hour before Jex brought the machine to a stop and Virda stepped from the footboard with stiff legs and wind-wrecked hair. She shook out her aching arms. Jex leaned the mono up against a tree.

The faintest hint of morning light was just beginning to dilute the shadows, but it was still mostly dark and, Virda had to admit, distinctly creepy. They advanced on the glasshouse – the glass-*boat* – a ghostly structure in gloom. The intact planes of its surface seemed to glow with absorbed moonlight, and the broken edges shone like cut gems and polished knives. The way roots, branches and tendrils had coiled around it gave Virda the sense that it didn't belong to them, that if they tried to interfere with it in any way, they'd be swiped aside by the possessive trees crowded against it. These seemed even more alive in the darkness than they did in the daylight, humming and chirruping with invisible life. Disturbed by Jex's clumsy footsteps, a small cluster of glowflies spun out of the undergrowth, and Virda's breath caught as they chased each other into the wreckage of the boat like lost souls, their tiny lights beautiful and strange through the dusty glass.

'I wish I knew more about this place,' said Virda and was shocked by how indecently loud her voice was, even though she'd tried to be quiet. She switched to a whisper. 'I feel like such a cackheaded person for not knowing it was a glass*boat*.'

It didn't look much like a boat, at least not from what she could see in the darkness, but it was ominously beautiful and fascinating in its strangeness. She'd have to return in daylight one day to explore inside it.

'I didn't know that either,' said Jex. 'It's impossible to know everything about everything. Unless you're Berro.'

'It's not even that far from where we live. I don't know why I never thought to—'

'We'll go to a whole lot of a history classes to make up for it, all right?' said Jex. 'Don't worry about that now. We've got a mission.'

'Right,' said Virda, shaking herself. 'So. From boatwreck, twenty west, forty-five south, snail rock, four south-west, leaning tree, under root. I assume the numbers are leaps, not paces, but should we try paces first, just to rule it out?'

Jex nodded. 'Let's rule it out.'

Virda consulted her pod for the direction.

'Right,' she said again. 'Twenty west. We can only approximate. We don't have a lot to go on.' She began to take a series of slightly exaggerated paces, starting at the clearest spot in front of the glass-boat. 'So, this is really inexact but, fine. Now… forty-five south.' She turned on the spot, staring at her pod until she faced in the right direction. She started to pace again, more big deliberate steps that she counted under her breath. '…eleven, twelve, thirteen…'

It was difficult to walk in a straight line with the way blocked by trees of various sizes, and shrubs and rocky outcrops and ditches of shadow, invisible in the darkness. After forty-five slow, awkward paces, Jex activated the lamp on his pod to scour the area. There was nothing remarkable about the place they were standing in, and nothing nearby that could be described as a 'snail rock'. In fact, there were no rocks at all. Virda sighed. 'It's leaps,' she said. 'It's got to be leaps.'

'The sun will be up by the time we get there,' said Jex.

'So be it,' said Virda, and they headed back to the mono in silence.

Twenty leaps west. Forty-five leaps south. With Jex's pod mounted on the front of the mono, they weaved through the forest, dodging obstacles left and right but always pulling back to follow the line they'd marked on the map until, after what felt like an extraordinarily long ride, they arrived at their first destination.

The quickening dawn light brought everything into clearer focus and the sounds of birdsong rose all around them. They'd stopped in a sloped area bisected by a small stream. Clear brown water tumbled over the scree, much of which was covered by moss. Here and there, the odd moist fern unfurled itself into the crisp air. This time, there were plenty of rocks, and so they set about searching for one that resembled a snail. Virda had hoped it would be immediately obvious, but after several minutes of inspecting strikingly unsnail-like rocks, that hope expired.

'What about this one?' said Jex, pointing at a rock that more closely resembled a foot than a snail. Virda glared at him crossly. 'Or that one?' He pointed to another rock.

'Are you going to point at every rock in this whole place?' said Virda. 'None of them look like snails. That one looks like a knife.'

'I was thinking maybe one of those water snails,' said Jex. 'Those pointy ones.'

'It doesn't look like a pointy water snail, Jex. Maybe we're in the wrong place.' Defeated, she flopped down onto a broad flat rock, feeling the deep coldness of it through the fabric of her uniform.

'You're giving up then?'

'No,' she snapped. 'I'm just— Hang on…' She shifted and crouched to inspect an irregularity on the surface she'd just sat on. 'Jex. Jex, look!'

He stumbled over roots and stones in his haste to reach her. She scraped away a tuft of moss to reveal a shape etched deeply into the rock with some thick carving tool. It was a rough spiral with a little rectangle sticking out on one side, complete with two uneven eye stalks.

'Snail rock!' said Jex, and Virda heard – or imagined she heard – a snatch of music, a single, harmonious, triumphant chord in the distance, accompany his declaration.

'This is real,' she said, and discovered that part of her had been desperately hoping it wouldn't be. Shani was in the reformatory. Virda didn't know why, but she was certain that this clue had something to do with it. Jex's bright-eyed enthusiasm for the mission was encouraging, but she had to admit it was more appropriate for a children's treasure hunt. There was danger here, and Virda felt the weight of that now.

'Four leaps south-west of here, we'll find a leaning tree, and under its root—'

'Answers!' said Jex, dramatically. 'Or nothing. Probably nothing. But maybe something.'

'I've got a feeling it's going to be something, Jex, and I'm scared.'

'There's nobody out here,' said Jex. 'And anyway, you know we *have* to do this, just in case it does have something to do with Shani.'

'It definitely has something to do with Shani. I can feel it. I'm just worried about following it in the wrong way. Maybe we should have brought someone powerful and important with us, as insurance.'

'Maybe. Or maybe if we'd told someone powerful and important, they would've quietly murdered us and made it look like an accident. We don't know. It's all unknown. This is as good as any other plan.'

And so they headed off into the unknown, which was not very far away.

They found the leaning tree with no difficulty at all. It was obvious, when contrasted with the perfect uprightness of its compatriots. It appeared to have been knocked askew as a sapling and had compensated by growing a set of powerful reaching roots to keep from falling all the way over. The roots resembled arms grappling for purchase on a cliff edge, and one of them was bent like an elbow, forming a neat, mossy hollow into which a person could easily squeeze.

Virda and Jex paused for a moment and stared at one another, the potential relevance of this discovery held between them like a living thing, an alien, strange but alive, neither of them sure if it was to be feared or embraced. They crept towards the hollow, where they set about scrabbling in the damp, smelly soil, groundworms squirming between their fingers and beetles streaming out of holes and running in panic at this most unexpected of invasions.

Virda's hand closed around a buried object, and she acknowledged a sense of deep inevitability. She'd found the note. She'd spotted the snail. And now she'd discovered the treasure, whatever it was.

It was a sealed pouch containing another note, written in the same hand as the first one.

from here, 48 w, 'no-zone', singer ruin

Together, Virda and Jex read and reread the note in breathless silence. Jex took his pod and plotted a route forty-eight leaps to the west from their current location and, sure enough, the destination point was deep within the boundary of a no-zone near the outskirts of the forest.

'They went into a no-zone?' said Virda, horrified. She wanted Jex to scoff at the idea, to reject this entire adventure as a joke and a waste of time.

But, of course, he didn't.

'We can't go there now,' said Jex. 'Not without protection.'

'Do you think Kini and Shani had protection?'

'They must've,' said Jex. 'They would've lost their minds otherwise.'

'Unless they went in quickly and got out before it affected them too much. But we can't risk that. We don't know.'

Without warning, Jex smashed his fist into the soil.

Virda startled, along with all the beetles remaining in the area.

'Sorry,' said Jex, his face screwed up. 'I thought we were going to find answers.'

'We will,' said Virda. 'I'll think of a way to get some anti-marrow gear from the academy. We'll come back.'

This didn't placate Jex. 'Maybe we should speak to Kini.'

'She won't want to talk about it,' said Virda. 'You know that, Jex. You can't force her to tell you what happened. I'm sure she has her reasons for keeping it to herself. Anyway, Mama Stitch said she's been spending most of her time in Grassy Plains, remember? And you know she never answers her messages. She doesn't want people to reach her.'

They allowed themselves a moment of sombre reflection, and in that moment, they heard a sound – distant, but unmistakable. A scream.

They sat frozen, eyes unblinking, barely daring to breathe. Long seconds passed, and they were almost ready to move or to speak, to confirm that the moment had been real rather than imagined, when it happened again, piercing the morning quiet. It wasn't a scream for help so much as a scream of wild rage.

Coldness seared through Virda. 'We need to go,' she said.

They scrambled back to the mono, Virda stuffing Shani's note into her pocket.

'What do you think—'

'I don't know, Jex, but want nothing to do with it.'

• • •

Berro held onto a desperate hope that his location was remote enough that nobody would be within earshot of the commotion. If anyone happened to be taking a stroll out in this direction, they might stumble upon this violent scene, and what would they think? He was a big, muscular student, in uniform, ruthlessly flattening a youngster into the dirt. The boy might've been half Berro's size, but he possessed four times the ferocity. Berro fought to keep him pinned down, pleading with him even though they couldn't understand each other. There was no way to put a linga onto his forehead when he was thrashing around with such violence, and

Berro wasn't even certain that the boy's spitting and growling was a language.

Berro kept one of his hands on the back of the boy's head, forcing his face into the ground, but he was afraid of suffocating him by accident. He released the pressure slightly every few moments, allowing the boy to send a shriek cutting through the tense stillness of the forest.

It took an age for Undra to arrive, and when he did, Berro felt the relief like a breath of air for a drowning man. The imparter pulled into the clearing on a mono and propped it against a tree. His face was hard, his mouth a thin, straight line.

He crossed the distance in a few strides and pulled out a Code-violating gun from his pocket.

Berro stared at it, uncomprehending.

Undra cocked the weapon and shot the squirming boy in the back of the head, the bullet piercing between Berro's splayed fingers.

The sound sent a distant flock of birds tearing up through the canopy and into the safety of the sky.

Berro pulled his hand back and felt the taut, flailing body beneath him go instantly soft, like a whip after cracking. A profound stillness and silence descended upon the scene.

'You killed him,' said Berro. Blood was spattered all over his uniform. He disentangled himself from the corpse and staggered to his feet, ears ringing.

'Yes, I did,' said Undra, putting the gun into his satchel. 'I had to.'

'Why?' Berro half walked, half stumbled away from the body. 'You— you could've tranquillised him.'

Undra looked at the dead boy, and then at Berro and tilted his head to one side. 'We don't need them alive. They're more trouble.'

It took seconds for Berro's world to fall apart, but he knew, during those seconds, that it had been teetering on the edge of destruction for some time. He didn't feel sick. He didn't even feel shocked. He was hollowed out. The space inside him was cold. 'This is a Code violation,' he said, because he had to say it.

'Is it?' said Undra. 'I do believe the Code was drafted, and I quote: "to serve the best interests of the Rhetari". Would you classify this creature as Rhetari?'

'Creature?' Berro looked at Undra – looked through him. 'Would you have shot Kath if no one else had seen her?'

Undra considered the question. 'No, I don't believe so. She was co-operative and civilised. An inconvenience, yes, but we can learn from her, at least. Her input will add value to the findings.'

Berro looked down at the boy. The blood from the wound in the back of his maimed head seeped into the soil.

'Berrovan, are you up to completing this task with the dedication you professed yesterday evening?'

The words didn't elicit the impact they would have in the past – shame, guilt, desire to please. Instead, Berro was choked by fear. He thought about the moment he'd encountered Virda and Jex on the night that Kath had crossed into his world. Undra hadn't wanted anyone to see her. He'd been disappointed that others knew of her existence. Berro hesitated, unsure of his next move. He needed to buy time, but he didn't know what he'd do with it.

There was nothing more he could do for the boy, so he made a decision.

'Yes, Imparter, absolutely,' he said, standing up straight, his shoulders squared. 'Apologies for my inappropriate comments. This has been a shock for me, but I… I understand. I can do what needs to be done.'

Undra nodded. 'Good,' he said, and his face lit up like a synthetic sunrise.

Berro couldn't keep his eyes on Undra's face. He looked down instead at his own bloody hands.

• • •

Frigid wind gusted over the lake, and Fessi pulled her clothwrap tighter and drew her knees up to her chin. She sat on a grass mat at the edge of the water in the early morning light, idly painting a watersnail on a rough-edged sheet of paper made from leaf mulch. A mug of berry tea sat beside her, coils of steam twisting in the breeze.

Her mother and Kath were inside the house, discussing the upcoming autumn harvest from their vegetable patch around the back. Andish's presence was clear, as always. She radiated calm, her blood moving at a steady pace through her veins, her lungs and heart expanding and contracting without the haste or the hitches of stress or surprise. And then there was Kath, the void. Except she wasn't quite a void anymore. Kath's presence was still a gap in the stuff of the world, but the black hole of nothingness that Fessi had first been introduced to seemed now to be loosely plugged with a gauzy flicker of somethingness.

In breathing, eating and living on Rheta, Kath was beginning to absorb it. The marrow was in her veins and in her flesh, in the tiniest of traces, and Fessi could sense small sparks of feeling – non-specific, rudimentary, but undoubtedly there and undoubtedly a part of the fabric of this world. Contentedness. Curiosity. Affection. Kath had bonded with Andish, and Andish with Kath. Andish cared for Kath like a second daughter, and Kath had found in Andish the closest thing to a mother that she would ever have again, and she was deeply, powerfully grateful for it. Fessi knew this, and she was relieved.

The watersnail took shape, the glistening red of the homemade ink settling into a warm brown as it dried on the paper. The spiral lines soothed her, and Fessi painted them over and over again, deepening the colour for shadows.

The front wall of the lakehouse living room was full of Fessi's paintings. Andish had suggested that Fessi invest in an ecopen and a pad of refined ecopaper, but Fessi preferred to make everything herself. These were skills her father had taught had her. The pressing of the mulch, the straining of the pigments, the cutting of the feathers… they were all as much a part of the process as the painting itself. The completed images usually ended up framed by Andish with smooth lake wood that she whittled some evenings when her hands were restless.

Kath stepped out of the house and shivered in the autumn breeze, curling her toes against the cold, smooth stones of the pathway. 'Fessi,' she called. 'Want to play a game with us? It's nice and warm inside.'

'I'll be right in,' Fessi called back, carefully rolling up her painting and gathering her tools and tea mug. As she stepped onto the stone path, she paused, tingling.

Something was wrong.

It was just too far away to read with any accuracy or understanding, but it was there – a new break in the flow, some distant turmoil, sending out marric ripples, the faintest of which broke against her. She closed her eyes, trying to feel further, sense harder. Just then, without warning, there was a silent snap in the sensory landscape and Fessi dropped her mug with a start. It cracked and clattered across the stones, the dregs of her tea splattering like blood.

The sound of the fallen mug brought Kath back to the threshold. 'Are you okay?' She darted out on her bare feet to gather the broken pieces.

Fessi sensed a flock of birds in the distance moving at unusual speed. She scrubbed her hands over her face. 'I need to speak to Berro.'

CHAPTER 23

Berro watched the blood-tainted water circle the drain of the field unit shower cubicle, the shower Kath had used when she'd lived there after her crossing. What thoughts must she have had as she stood under this narrow jet of hot water, alone in this grim building, in this strange forest, in this unfamiliar world, unsure of who to trust, but with so little choice in the matter.

And now, instead of being used by a living crosser, the shower washed away a dead crosser's blood. Berro scrubbed and scrubbed, but he would never be clean again.

He had sat, numb, staring at the bodybag on the forest floor while Undra wiped the gore from his face and his uniform so he could head back to the field unit without drawing attention to himself. Undra's touch had been deft and gentle, and yet it had sickened him. Holding his face in the right expression had felt like the process of draping strings of lights and ribbons between the trees for a festival: carefully adjusting the slack, winding them around the branches and hooks, working hard to keep it all in balance.

He and Undra had left the scene separately. Acknowledging Berro's state of shock, Undra had taken the corpse with him, leaving Berro, in his still-bloodied state, to race back to the field unit unburdened – at least physically.

The crosser was below his feet now, in the lab, Undra already poring over him. He'd be hearing the rush of the shower overhead and wondering when Berro would join him at the metal table to study his specimen. His victim.

Berro shut off the water and stood, dripping, for a few empty minutes before towelling himself dry and putting on a fresh uniform. The other one was torn, stained, and beyond repair.

As Berro stepped out of the elevator into the lab, Undra looked up at him, smiling softly. 'How are you feeling?' the imparter asked gently.

'I'm fine,' said Berro. 'Much better now that I'm clean.' He kept his eyes on Undra's face, refusing to let them stray to the body on the table behind him.

Undra scrutinised him for a few moments and then sighed. 'Go home, Berrovan,' he said, not unkindly. 'You're trying to prove yourself to me, I understand that, and I appreciate it, but I think you should take the evening off. Get some rest, drink some tea, gather your wits. It's been a stressful day. There's no harm or shame in admitting that. You did well.'

He sounded so concerned, so genuine, and yet Berro was unmoved. He felt no gratitude as he thanked the imparter and took his leave, promising to be available whenever he was needed.

He stepped out of the field unit perimeter gate and set off on foot towards the treehouse, punching a message into his pod as he walked. He had several unread messages from Fessi, but it was Virda he wanted to speak to. He couldn't face the assault of Fessi knowing, sensing, feeling beyond what he wanted to say before he'd even said it, and he'd never needed Virda's tea more than he needed it now. *: Are you home? :*

Virda responded almost immediately. *: yes. tea? :*

: Are you alone? :

: no, jex is here. why? :

: Can you send him away? I need to speak to you alone. :

: fine :

: I'll be there in five minutes. :

• • •

Virda only just managed to pull on one of Jex's loose-fitting sleepsuits before she heard Berro ascending the stairs. He was moving rapidly, and a sense of unease stole into her chest. They all knew Berro preferred spending time with people one on one, but he'd never demanded it like this before, and never with her. He usually chose Fessi as his confidant.

Something bad had happened. Virda knew this to be true as surely as if he'd typed it out into his message. It took effort for her to appear nonchalant as he entered the treehouse, breathless and sweaty, a flurry of leaves rattling over the threshold on a gust of wind behind him.

'Where are Jex and Magrin?' he asked by way of a greeting, snapping the door shut. The treehouse plunged into an insulated quiet that felt nothing like it had in the moments before Berro's arrival.

'Magrin's helping to set up the festival. I told Jex to go climbing. He was a bit hurt.'

Berro nodded and released a breath slowly like a lungful of wickersmoke. He accepted Virda's proffered mug of steaming tea with a quiet 'Thank you.'

'So, are you going to tell me what's going on?' Virda settled on the softseat, curling her legs underneath her and blowing gently on her drink. Her bare feet were cold in the chilly air that had followed Berro into the treehouse. She wriggled them beneath a cushion and settled her gaze on her friend.

Berro took a seat opposite her and then, without any warning, he started to cry.

Virda choked on her tea, almost spilling it on Jex's sleepsuit. Berro never cried. Ever. Except, apparently, he did, and to witness it knocked the wind out of her. 'Berro, what…'

His face crumpled, eyes screwed shut as fat tears coursed down his cheeks. His broad shoulders heaved, and the mug of tea resting on his knee slopped about, forgotten in the violence of his grief.

When finally it ebbed and he came up for air, Berro placed the mug on the low table between them and stared at it, searching for something in the rising coils of fragrant steam.

'Berro,' said Virda. She sat fossilised on the soft seat, gaping at him.

'You were right,' he choked, wrenching his eyes away from the tea. 'About Undra.'

'In what way?'

'You were never convinced by him. You never thought he was brilliant, or even good. How did you know?'

'How did I know what, Berro?'

He ignored the question. 'Am I bad at reading people, Virda? Am I… ignorant?' His voice was strangled.

'Berro, what's going on?'

He drew in a shuddering, broken breath. 'Undra is not who I thought he was. He's a bad person, and I'm— I don't know what to do.'

'You can start by telling me what happened.'

A moment passed. Berro seemed to have regained some control of himself, mentally and physically. He shifted in his seat, straightened his back, and cleared his throat, embarrassed – about his emotional outburst or by what he was about to say, Virda wasn't sure.

'What happened, Berro?'

A beat.

'He killed someone.'

'He what?'

But Berro didn't need to repeat it. Virda was in motion, kicking the cushion away from her feet, slamming her mug down on the table as she leaned forward, one hand grabbing her own hair almost hard enough to rip it right out of her scalp.

Berro's gaze skittered away across the room. He picked up his tea and sipped it.

'Speak!' Virda shouted, and he flinched like she'd struck him in the face. He shrank into himself, deflated, his hugeness suddenly sad and pathetic.

When he spoke again, his normally deep, commanding voice was thin and weak. 'There was another live crosser. Earlier today. A boy this time. A wild boy. Tortured. Probably insane. He screamed and attacked me. I couldn't subdue him. Not without hurting him.'

Virda's pulse raced as she remembered the distant screams in the forest just hours before.

'I didn't know what to do,' said Berro, 'so I called Undra, and he came to help. I thought he would bring some bindings, or maybe a tranquilliser, so we could get him back to the field unit and calm him down. But he brought a gun, Virda. A *gun*. He didn't even hesitate. He didn't give me a chance. He just...'

Berro's voice rose, warbled and morphed into a wretched sob. 'He just shot him, right in the head. My hand was there, right next to where...' Berro splayed his trembling fingers and stared at them like they belonged to someone else. 'Undra shot him. There was blood on me, all over me.'

Virda felt herself sinking into the same swamp of horror that was drowning her friend right in front of her. He was crying again, silently but intensely, his face a saline mess. Virda got to her feet and wobbled over to the kitchen. She returned with a clean rag, which she handed to Berro. She felt light-headed, disconnected from her body as she watched him wipe his face, but she surprised herself with the calm, steady delivery of her next words.

'So. What are we going to do?'

• • •

Fessi was halfway through her first mug of tea – poorly brewed, by Virda's standards – when Jex slouched into the room, kicking the front door shut with the heel of his boot. He grinned at everyone sitting in the common area in the gloom of the late afternoon and snorted. 'Why do you all look so serious?' he said. When none of them smiled or spoke, his grin vanished like wickersmoke in the wind. Fessi sensed his marrow change from languid to energised. It roiled, thickened and focussed as he stepped forward to get a better look at their stony faces. 'What's happened?'

Berro passed a hand over his tired eyes. 'Wait for Magrin,' he said. 'I'm not doing this three times.'

'I don't know anything yet either,' said Fessi, as Jex bristled irritably. 'I've only just got here.' But she did know something. She knew Berro was in crisis. His grief, confusion and rage pulsed around him like a swarm of angry waspiks. She also knew that he'd confided in Virda instead of her for this very reason. He'd wanted a conversation in which he could reveal himself at his own pace rather than being flayed open by her marric sensitivities.

She could feel his guilt, thick and corrosive. It was hurting him.

Moments later, the sound of the elevator grinding its way up to the balcony announced Magrin's arrival. She entered the treehouse cradling a small box against her chest. Fessi sensed the animal inside it, curled up and sleeping. Unlike Jex, Magrin was immediately aware that something was wrong. She placed her box carefully on the kitchen counter and settled herself on the last open seat, her eyes wary and expectant.

'Why isn't Kath here?' she asked. 'She's one of us now, isn't she? We include her in things.'

Virda shook her head. 'Not this. Not yet. It could be traumatic for her.'

Berro took a quick breath. 'Right,' he said. 'So after Virda's message summoning you all here, you're probably wondering—' He choked, and Virda glared at him until he looked up at her, throat convulsing.

'Must I?' she asked, impatience crackling through her. He nodded, and Virda took over, relating what Berro had told her. She glanced at Jex when she reached a part about a screaming boy in the forest. Jex looked pale and scared. Fessi sensed something there, some other painful knowledge shared between them that they weren't intending to divulge to the others. Berro spent the entirety of the narrative staring at the floor, terrified to make eye contact with any of his friends, their horror evident in the stillness of the room.

When it was over, Virda fell silent and let the story steep between them. Fessi's chest felt tight, as though her ribs had been staved in to crush her heart.

What if it had been Kath? It could've been Kath. Had things played out differently in the forest that night, if it had been Undra retrieving the first crosser instead of Berro, would Kath still be alive? She wished Kath were present just then, so she could place a hand on her arm to feel the warmth and the life of her, to be certain that she was all right. The question *What now?* hung in the air, until Fessi decided to answer it.

'You need to go back to him and pretend you're still loyal,' she said. It was anger she felt then – hot, yet calm and purposeful, reinflating her. 'If you go back to him, he'll believe he can trust you, and if he trusts you, he'll tell you everything: what he's doing, why he's doing it. You'll collect the evidence and present it to the council, and you'll get him thrown into the reformatory before he can hurt anyone else.'

'What?' Jex blustered. 'Berro can't go back! Undra's dangerous! Why not just go directly to the council right now?'

Fessi and Virda responded together: 'They won't believe him.'

'Why?' Magrin stared at Berro, tears quivering in her eyelashes.

'It's the word of a student nobody against one of the most respected academics on Rheta,' said Berro. 'And he's running for a seat on the council. It will look like I'm trying to sabotage his chances because of some personal grievance.'

'What are his chances?' asked Jex.

'He'll win,' said Berro. 'No doubt about it.' He turned to Fessi, and she nodded. He was right. You didn't need special senses to know which way the wind was blowing in that regard.

'He's by far the most popular choice at the academy,' she said. 'He's popular with his peers too. Berro's right – he'll win.'

'Caaaack,' said Jex. 'You mean the Wooden Hill representative is going to be a murderer?'

'No,' said Virda. 'We won't let it come to that. I think Fessi's right about what you have to do, Berro. I'm sorry…'

Berro's face clenched.

'We should have some sort of secret signal,' said Jex. 'Like if you're walking with Undra and you think he might be planning to kill you, you could… I don't know. Tug on your earlobe?'

Berro snapped his eyes onto Jex's face. There was no fondness in evidence. 'Seriously, Jex? Tug on my earlobe? Are you planning to follow me around, waiting for the signal? That's stupid. And anyway, he's not going to kill me.'

'How do you know?' said Jex. 'He killed the crosser.'

'I know because, unlike the crosser, I'm Rhetari,' said Berro. 'The Code protects the Rhetari. Undra won't break the Code – at least, not his interpretation of it.'

He lapsed into silence, and the atmosphere congealed. Berro looked ashen, his face creased like he was in pain.

And he was, in a sense. Fessi felt it, sharp and aching inside him. 'Berro,' she murmured. 'It's not your fault. You know that.'

'Why are you friends with me?' he blurted, his fists falling into his lap. 'Why are any of you here?'

Magrin, overwhelmed, pulled her seat alongside Berro's and blubbered into his shoulder, her arms trying but failing to encircle his torso.

'Do you remember how we met?' asked Virda.

'The Darter accident,' said Berro.

'The Darter accident,' Jex echoed, pushing his fingers into his hair where one of his scars was hidden.

Jex had been at the controls, his first ever attempt at driving a four-person Darter, Virda in the seat behind him. He'd been speeding and the vehicle was unbalanced, with no passengers on the left-hand side. He'd lost control and careened into a tree. Virda had been flung from the vehicle unharmed, but Jex had fallen out of the side door and got pinned underneath it. Berro, a fresh student and new to the settlement, had been on his way to the academy, having taken a solo stroll after classes to familiarise himself with the branch paths. He'd heard the overtaxed engine of a speeding hover-vehicle, followed by the crunching impact and Virda's blood-curdling screams as she tried to lift the buckled Darter off her friend. Fessi had heard their account of what had happened only once, but she thought about it so often, that the scene was as vivid in her mind as if she'd witnessed it herself.

'I saved the day with my big arms,' said Berro. 'Lucky you, crashing within earshot of someone built like an ursa.'

'And lucky that he had the wits to contact the medicraft, and to keep Jex stable while we waited, and to comfort and calm us both even though you didn't know us, and the decency not to report Jex for dangerous driving or dismiss us for being stupid and reckless,' said Virda, each cadence rising in volume and pitch. 'And you visited him in the infirmary to see if he was healing, and you asked me if I was doing all right, and I wasn't! Remember that? I wasn't all right at all. And you cared! You sat with me, and you spoke to me, and I thought you were one of the best people I'd ever met. And I still think that, Berro, so stop – *stop* putting yourself down now. I'm *sick* of it!'

The room fell silent, except for the sound of Magrin's sobs, every third one threatening to become a wail. Berro stroked her hair, something Fessi had never seen him do before.

'Magrin,' he said. 'What's in the box?'

She lifted her tear-stained face from his shoulder and sniffed, glancing over at the box on the kitchen counter. 'A scrattin,' she said. 'A baby scrattin. She must've fallen out of her nest. I looked for the nest, but I couldn't find it. She wouldn't survive out there alone.' She sniffed again and wiped her face. 'Want to see her?'

'Yes,' said Berro.

Magrin retrieved the box. She opened it slowly and carefully as everyone gathered around to peer inside, pretending for a moment that they weren't distracting themselves from discussing a murder. The scrattin lay curled up on a handful of dry leaves, her visible eye open and watching them. She swivelled an ear in their direction and twitched her tail.

Magrin made tiny ticking sounds with her tongue and slowly, slowly moved her hand into the box to run one finger along the rodent's smooth, brown head. The scrattin tensed at the first touch, then relaxed again.

'I'm going to call her Pips,' said Magrin.

'Hello, Pips,' said Berro.

He smiled, but it was wobbly and weird-looking.

'I need to speak to Ryndel,' Berro murmured to himself, a stray thought shaking itself loose from his rattled mind.

'Ryndel?' said Magrin. 'I can give you her comlink. She's in the group chat for reds who do grow level maintenance.'

'Thanks,' said Berro. He clicked his tongue at Pips and extended a finger towards her, but pulled it back when she curled herself into a frightened ball of fur. 'I'm so sorry I've dragged you into this.' He seemed, at first, to be addressing the scrattin, but then he looked up at each of his friends in turn.

'You did the right thing, telling us,' said Fessi. 'We'll help you. We just need the proof.'

'Yes,' said Virda. 'Get the proof, and then we'll end him.'

CHAPTER 24

Berro rapped his knuckles three times on the office door. At the sound of footsteps approaching, he stood slightly back and smoothed out his face. The door opened.

Undra's shapely eyebrows climbed his forehead when he saw Berro standing there.

It was the morning after the day in which Berro's life had veered wildly off course almost as violently as a crossing between two realities. His fear was at odds with the dull sense of unreality that told him none of this was true, none of it mattered, he'd wake any moment and carry on with his day, just like any other day. Millbean porridge, lectures, friends – pressure of the academic rather than the existential sort.

'Berrovan,' said Undra. 'I didn't think I'd be seeing you so soon.' He hesitated, but then let Berro inside and closed the door behind them. As Undra took his seat at the desk, Berro did a quick sweep of his own body language to make sure everything was still properly arranged – shoulders back, hands loose, brow soft.

'Why is that Imparter?' Perhaps he shouldn't have said it quite so brightly – he had witnessed a murder, after all. He infused his face with a bit of gravity and turned down the corners of his mouth. 'I thought this might be a good time to get some feedback about the last crosser.'

'I'm glad you came,' said Undra. 'I thought perhaps recent events had been outside the limits of your tolerance, but it seems I underestimated you.' He smiled, but it was a cautious smile.

Berro smiled back. Being underestimated used to hurt. This didn't feel much like an underestimation, though. Having the ability to forgive murder wasn't a stripe of honour he wanted to stitch onto his uniform like the military men in the war.

'If that were to happen again,' said Undra, 'a wild crosser, beyond reasoning, screaming and threatening our safety and the safety of this project… If that were to happen again, and you were properly armed, what would you do?'

'Armed with what, Imparter?' Berro feared this was the wrong question.

'A gun, Berrovan. A lethal weapon.'

An image of Pips the scrattin surfaced in Berro's mind, and he latched onto it. *Smooth fur, tiny paws, sweet little eyes shining.* 'I would shoot the crosser, Imparter,' he said.

'You would shoot to kill.'

'Yes. If it seemed necessary in the context.'

Undra nodded, peaked his fingers, and rested his chin on them, staring at the ceiling with his mouth drawn to one side. He clearly wasn't done asking questions – he was pondering the next one.

Berro willed his gut to stop clenching. It was making it difficult to sit still. His eyes roamed over the items on Undra's desk. The slab, the pod, a pad of ecopaper, an empty tea mug, a pointed glass carving shot with colour, which reflected the light from the overhead lamps in interesting patterns on the desk.

'What are your thoughts about the reformatory and its patients?' Undra asked.

Berro hadn't been expecting this question. Had Undra researched his family history? All those evenings he'd sat at his mother's deathbed, hating her for refusing treatment, and hating the reformatory protesters who'd had the audacity to kick up a fuss about the testing on patients. It was only ever optional. There wouldn't be half as many cures if it weren't for those who opted into the programme in exchange for perks at the reformatory. More than they deserved. More than Undra deserved. He imagined Undra, bound, dragged away, thrown into a small room, opting into some tests and being unlucky with the results. A reaction, perhaps. A rash pocking his handsome face. Something that made his silky hair fall out in chunks. Berro felt uncomfortably warmed by these imaginings.

'Berrovan?'

'It's a necessary institution,' he said. 'I don't care much for the patients. I suppose it's difficult for people who have a loved one in there, but I haven't had that experience myself, so my opinion has never been affected by irrational emotions. Patients need to learn to respect the Code.'

The tiniest of smiles tugged at Undra's lips. 'Yes. You were very outspoken about Code violations yesterday,' said Undra. 'You seemed to think I was a Code-violator, after I dealt with the crosser.'

'I was in shock, Imparter,' said Berro, picking through his words like shards of glass. 'I am strongly against Code violation, but I was misinterpreting the situation. I don't believe that what you did was a violation of the Code. The crosser was not Rhetari, and – and more than that, he'd clearly been twisted into some sort of abomination. You performed a mercy, more than anything else. This, our work, is important. Progress, and the acquisition of knowledge, can't be made without some degree of… mess.'

The smile on Undra's face grew wider. Berro knew he was saying the right things, but he didn't know why they were right. He gambled his position with every syllable.

'Tell me more on your feelings about the reformatory,' said Undra. 'I know you have a history.'

So he *had* done his research. Of course he had. Sarla, if she was still alive, would've been as famous an imparter as Undra was.

'My mother died of a curable disease,' said Berro. He needed to say it, to explain his feelings out loud, in context, even if Undra knew the story. The fact was nobody had ever asked him about it in this way. It had been an unlanced boil for far too long, and he was grateful to Undra in spite of himself. 'She refused treatment because she opposed the way the treatments were tested on patients at the reformatory. She never called them patients. Always *prisoners*.'

'How did that make you feel?' Undra asked.

Smooth fur, tiny paws, sweet little eyes, shining... 'It made me angry,' said Berro. 'They're Code violators. And the testing programme was – *is* optional. People were going on about the Cohera, making accusations of hypocrisy and claiming the tests were Code violations too. "You can't punish Code violations with Code violations!" But why not? And who said it was a punishment? What sort of punishment is optional? My mother was convinced by the protesters. She also said she had a secret source of inside information. I don't know why she listened to these people. I think it might've been a symptom of her illness. She wasn't herself. She got swept up in this propaganda, and she died because of it.'

'You're passionate about this,' said Undra, studying him. 'I'm glad. You're probably wondering why I'm asking you about it.'

Berro had forgotten to wonder about that for a moment, old memories and anger stirred up like sunken debris in a churning lake.

'I'll be honest. I wasn't sure about you after the recent incident, Berrovan. I wasn't sure if you were the one for the job, but this meeting is giving me new confidence in you, and I think you've earned the right to know the truth.'

The truth. *Already*, the truth was being offered to him. Fessi had been right, but even she couldn't have known that her plan would come to fruition so rapidly. The truth. It meant something completely different now. It was no longer a shining treasure, just out of reach. Berro was terrified of it.

Pips, he thought. *Soft little Pips. What a simple, furry life she leads.*

Undra was about to tell him how he triggered the crossings, and with this information would come a greater burden of responsibility and entanglement in the whole affair. Berro wished his hands weren't resting so visibly in his lap. He wished he'd left one of them in his pocket wrapped around his pod, ready to make a recording. He couldn't risk that now.

'I don't track the crossings,' said Undra.

'Excuse me, Imparter?'

'I create the crossings.' Undra said nothing else, waiting for Berro to react.

Berro tried to decide whether he should act surprised or confess that he'd known this since his conversation with Ryndel in the grow room. 'I don't understand,' he said. And it was true – he didn't. Undra had never revealed the process to him, and now was his chance to learn about it.

'It's simple,' said Undra. 'I don't know how to track crossings. Normal crossings happen in an instant, and the catalyst is in another world. I can't know about them before they happen, unless I'm in control of them happening from our side. So I make them happen. To be honest, I thought you would've questioned that from the start.'

'I did, Imparter, I questioned everything, but I trusted—' He stopped himself from saying *you* and toned it down. 'I trusted that you'd tell me more when the time was right.'

Undra nodded. A satisfactory save.

'How do you create the crossings?' Berro was a disembodied voice. He was elsewhere. He was in his dormitory, or at the treehouse. He was tiny and furry, crawling around inside the pen with Pips, looking for wickernuts. Anywhere but here. He considered for a moment seizing the pointed carving on Undra's desk and driving it through the imparter's heart. He'd be thrown into the reformatory for murder, but at least this would be over.

'I've devised a system using clarified marrowcore crystals, remotely activated by Singer tricks,' said Undra. Berro was glad Undra had the decency to look ashamed at this point, his eyes sliding sideways. 'I'll show you the mechanics of it. I owe you that at the very least. I apologise, Berro, for not being honest with you about those crystals. It wasn't the right time, but I regret the way I handled that. I should've given you more information when you brought me the first one. I didn't think you'd find a *second* one.'

Undra rubbed his thumbs against his temples and sighed. He seemed tired. 'I can't influence what happens in the other worlds,' he said. 'It's chance. Sometimes I activate the crystals to make a crack, but nobody falls through it. We've seen that. It needs to coincide with a trauma, as we know. Luckily, there's plenty of trauma in the other realities, and plenty of realities layered on top of one another, so people are bound to fall through sometimes.'

Luckily.

'I'm… amazed, Imparter,' said Berro. 'This is going to change the world.' He wanted Undra to interpret this as a compliment even though it wasn't one, necessarily. To act as an ally without saying anything unambiguously supportive was a difficult line to walk. *Nobody else is listening to you, Berro. You're not even recording this. Say what you have to say.*

Undra nodded thoughtfully, assessing him. 'I've refined the technique as much as I need to. I have enough information now to move onto the next part of the project.'

Berro's stomach dropped, but beneath his fear was curiosity. He couldn't help it. Perhaps the horror of collecting corpses in the forest was over, and he would simply need to obtain a recording or steal the gun or some notes to prove Undra's guilt, without having to worry about any more murders. And then he'd be free. Perhaps, once Undra was locked away and suffering through his re-education at the reformatory, Berro could manage the project himself, ethically, using the information Undra left behind. Perhaps he could pick up Undra's fallen, tarnished mantle and salvage its prestige for himself.

'What is the next part of the project?' he asked.

Undra pressed his fingertips together. His smile was thin and tight as a loop of wire around a neck. 'We've crossed people in,' he said. 'And now we're going to cross people out.'

'Out?'

The words made sense, but their meaning seemed disconnected from reality. Undra, having recently torn aside his mask to reveal his true face was now tearing away yet another mask, and Berro was unmoored, slipping, losing his grip on the situation. 'Why?'

'Well,' said Undra. 'My ultimate goal is to control the process entirely. Incoming and outgoing. I envision us having a catalogue of knowledge of other worlds and being able to visit specific worlds at will. Of course we're a long way from that. First, we need to learn how to trigger outgoing crossings. The destinations will be random at first, and we'll have no way of knowing if the crosser survives the process, but we're just figuring out the basics. If we're going to learn how to control the process, we need a fundamental understanding of how to rupture reality in both directions. Bringing crossers in has been quite easy, but I suspect that pushing them out will be a little more difficult.'

'Who will we cross out?' Berro asked, and immediately thought of Kath. She didn't belong on Rheta. Her birth wasn't registered here. She had no family, no history in their world. She was known only by a small handful of people. If Undra wanted to push someone out of a crack between their world and another, what better candidate than the person who'd recently survived a similar journey in the opposite direction? Berro's gut felt like a chasm of boiling acid and when he swallowed he could taste the acrid fumes of it in his throat. Then he noticed the look on Undra's face, smiling, expectant, ever so slightly patronising. He was waiting for Berro to answer his own question, and the answer was blindingly obvious once the thought of Kath was pushed aside.

Of course Undra wouldn't try to force Kath out of the world or take her away from the people who now cared for her. She'd befriended them, lived with them, grieved and grown with them. She was in the process of integrating. Whatever Undra felt about Kath, he'd never dare to try extricating her from the safety of her new life. He'd meet far too much resistance. No. He needed subjects who existed outside of mainstream Rhetari culture, separated from their loved ones, with a blurred relationship to the Code and Cohera.

He'd asked Berro for his opinions on the reformatory system and he'd been pleased by Berro's responses, and now Berro knew why.

SIX YEARS AGO

RHETARI DISTRO* > *GRASSY PLAINS* > *year 216, month 8, day 17

>>NEWS: REFORMATORY TESTING PROTESTS CONTINUE — Distro Megs

The Grassy Plains local council building has been surrounded by protesters for the past week, as anger mounts over the issue of reformatory testing. The protests were sparked by revelations about reformatory conditions claiming that the well-known opt-in system for medical testing on reformatory patients is not quite as straightforward or voluntary as is widely assumed.

The claim was made by respected researcher and academic Imparter Sarla, who would not divulge her source for fear of their safety. She had written to the distro some weeks ago detailing her claims, but her call for action only drew noteworthy interest when she refused treatment for a recently diagnosed terminal illness in protest of the reformatory conditions. She released the following statement:

'Many of the recent medical innovations we benefit from in the post-war world are obtained through so-called "opt-in" testing on reformatory prisoners. The term "opt-in" is applied to neutralise a broadly unappealing concept, by suggesting that it's entirely voluntary and that prisoners are aware of the risks involved. Both of these assumptions are untrue.

Conditions in the reformatories, contrary to popular belief, are dire by default, and "voluntary" testing is presented as a means for prisoners to achieve live-able conditions. Depriving people of basic rights and then offering these rights in exchange for their participation in dangerous and sometimes fatal medical testing does not make the testing voluntary in the way the broader population of Rheta believes it to be. Prisoners are forced to gamble with their health to receive things as fundamental as a bed to sleep on, clothing to keep themselves warm (often in freezing conditions) and enough food to avoid malnutrition and physical wasting.

In addition to this perversion of justice, the risks of the tests are rarely, if ever, fully understood by the prisoners involved. Tests have been known to result in persistent physical and mental illness, painful injury, permanent scarring and disability, and, in extreme cases, death.

Another level to the controversy is in the process of incarceration itself, which sees Rhetari citizens locked away unjustly for extended periods. Regardless of one's guilt or innocence, incarceration in a reformatory does not constitute the removal of one's status as a Rhetari citizen who should at all times be protected by the Code and the Cohera.

The reformatory system, so removed from the rest of daily life on Rheta, has managed to become a hotbed of Code and Cohera violation. This is unacceptable, and doubly so considering it was established for the very purpose of combatting these sorts of violations. There is no hope of "reform" within a system like this.

Along with a growing number of concerned Rhetari, I am calling for an immediate response from the council. Ultimately, we would like to see the reformatory system dismantled altogether, but in the interests of pragmatism, for now our demands are as follows:

1. *Reformatory testing must be stopped immediately.*
2. *Reformatory conditions must be improved to standards that satisfy both the Code and the Cohera, recognising the status of prisoners as Rhetari citizens.*
3. *Code and Cohera violations by reformatory staff against reformatory prisoners must be dealt with seriously and swiftly.*
4. *The reformatory system must be made entirely transparent, from the moment at which a Rhetari citizen is arrested through to the point of their release.*
5. *The reformatory system must be overhauled to address the wellbeing of prisoners as well as the process by which people are incarcerated. Instead of being one large institution in a remote location, there should be smaller and more localised reformatories to enable contact between prisoners and their friends and families, and to facilitate transparency and accountability.*

As a recognised figure in the Rhetari academic community, I have opted out of treatment for a curable condition in the hope that this protest will be noticed and taken seriously. Until all five of these demands have been met, I will not be accepting treatment that has its origins in reformatory testing. I do not expect to survive this, but my decline and probable death will, at least, serve to draw attention to this unacceptable situation and, at most, speed up the process of change.'

The mounting protest has resulted in widespread use of the word 'prisoner' in reference to patients at the reformatories – a word that was systematically pushed out of common usage in the years following the establishment of the Code and the Cohera. A brief comment on behalf of the council was released yesterday, stating that Imparter Sarla's accusations are unsubstantiated falsehoods and that Rhetari citizens should be encouraged to afford the reformatory patients the respect they deserve by referring to them as such rather than labelling them with an offensive term.

When interviewed outside the local council building, Imparter Ferriar of the Grassy Plains Academy, a long-standing friend and supporter of Sarla, stated that the term 'prisoner' is not an indictment of the people held in the reformatory, but a reference to their status and Rhetari rights, which, despite the assertions of the Rhetari council, are unjustly diminished upon their entry into the reformatory system. In a heated exchange with distro journalists, Ferriar accused the council of 'obfuscation' and 'deliberate derailment of dialogue'.

Counter-protestors have referred to Sarla as 'selfish', citing the life-saving innovations enabled by reformatory testing, and the fact that she threatens to leave behind a partner and a young son. Her partner has declined to comment on the situation. There have been calls from counter-protesters demanding that Sarla be interrogated about her source, with mounting suspicion that she may have had contact with an unreleased and potentially dangerous patient who should be detained. White Peaks reformatory has not reported any missing patients.

CHAPTER 25

Fessi sat silent in the seat beside Magrin, who had her head down and her shoulders curled forward, cradling Pips in one hand and stroking the scrattin nervously from head to tail, head to tail. The weather was turning. Outside the grubby treehouse windows, the forest cringed in the cold, heavy air, bracing itself for unpleasantness. The atmosphere was similar inside. Fessi watched Magrin's fingers flatten the tiny animal's fur. Pips was very still, as though sensing a winged predator circling above. Her whiskers twitched.

'So, he's going to torture prisoners,' said Jex. 'He's going to cross them out of Rheta.'

'Patients, not prisoners,' said Berro. 'Criminal patients.'

Virda bristled and huffed. 'Seriously, Berro? That's what you want to fight about right now? Whose side are you on?'

Berro's marric presence was chaos. The turmoil inside of him was nothing short of agony. His fists tightened, and Fessi sensed his resolve tightening with them.

'It's important,' said Berro. 'I don't agree with what Undra is planning. I don't want him to do it. But none of that means I'm obliged to change my mind about the reformatory.'

'Of course it does!' Virda rose slightly from her seat, and Jex tugged her gently back down by the sleeve of her clothwrap. 'Of course it does. He's going to torture people, and the reformatory is going to let him do it. You know it's true, and you know it proves everything your mother said—'

'Don't talk about my mother.'

'Berro, why are you defending Undra?'

'I'm *NOT!*' Berro roared, and everyone recoiled at the sudden power of his voice.

Magrin let out a small sound and stood, clutching the scrattin to her chest. She excused herself with a statement that was more of a jumbled noise than a coherent sentence and retreated into her bedroom.

Berro winced. 'Undra is dead to me,' he said, quietly. 'He's a sick, twisted, disgusting man, and I want him to rot *in the reformatory.* Where he *deserves* to be. I'm not about to get involved in radical anti-reformatory activism right at the point where I need the reformatory to lock up this cacking murderer—'

Virda shuddered. It was rage and it was grief, and it was reaching a head. 'You want Undra to suffer in the reformatory,' she said. Her voice was dangerous.

'Yes,' Berro replied.

'Because you think that people in the reformatory are people who deserve to suffer.'

Berro opened his mouth, then closed it again.

'Just say it, Berro. Just say what you think. *Say it!*'

'Virda,' whispered Jex. Where Virda was drawing herself together into a sharpened point of anger, Jex was coming apart in the face of disunity.

Berro stared at the floor between his boots, saying nothing. The silence sat heavy, like a dead thing, and every second that passed without Berro speaking, without him trying to explain himself, seemed to inflate Virda a little more. Her mouth was a crooked snarl, and her chest heaved beneath her clothwrap with the effort of holding back a torrent of barbed words.

Fessi sensed the danger building within the silence, so she broke it. 'Berro, please, you have to understand… There are bad people in the reformatory, but not all of them are bad. Not all of them deserve to be there. And do you think anyone would knowingly sign up to be tortured by Undra for his crossing experiment? I wasn't sure before, but if Undra has approval for a project like this, then it really *is* as bad as your mother said. I think Virda is right about this. The opt-in experiments are a violation of the Code and Cohera.'

Berro took a deep breath. When he spoke again, his voice was low, but tight. 'There are people who break the Code in terrible ways, and they must be reformed. That's what the reformatory is for. I want Undra to be put in there. I don't want him to have a wonderful time. I want him to learn a lesson. He thinks he hasn't broken the Code because of a semantic loophole, but he's wrong. Of course he has – he had a lethal weapon, and he took a sentient life, and he needs to be punished for that. The punishment is to be removed from civilised society and forced to confront the facts of his crime. Patients don't have to participate in the tests. Maybe they want to do something meaningful while they're in there. To contribute to the world they damaged with their actions outside. It's their choice. The people they raped and murdered weren't given choices.'

'I literally can't believe what I'm hearing,' said Virda. Blotches of colour stained her face, and her eyes were flinty. 'Who are you? How can you be so smart and so cacking stupid at the same time?'

'I'm not saying that Undra's experiments are justified—'

'Oh, but all the other experiments they've done over the years have been fine? Even though you have no proof of that, and your own mother argued the exact opposite?'

Berro swayed in his seat. His lips trembled, his nails dug into his palms and he blinked and blinked. Fessi wanted to lay a hand on his shoulder, but she couldn't, she wouldn't.

'We don't know...' he began. 'We don't know what they've done in there. Nobody's ever performed Undra's experiments before. It's the first time. It's bad, I agree, but it's the first time. My mother didn't know, she *couldn't* know—'

'It's *not* the first time there's been torture at the reformatory!' Virda roared. 'I know people, Berro! I know people who have lost people.'

Jex's head jerked in Virda's direction, and Fessi sensed a sharp change in the focus of his marrow.

'You know people?' he said. 'Who?'

Virda's face throbbed redder than before. 'I speak to people,' she said. 'There's a comspace.'

'A comspace?' said Jex. 'What kind of comspace?'

'It's…' Virda squirmed. 'It's a comspace for activists. Reformatory activists. I—'

Determined to sever this new tension before it took hold, Fessi interjected.

'Berro,' she said, pretending not to notice the way Virda and Jex were glaring at each other. 'Why won't you consider the possibility that Undra's plans are just another example of something that's been going on for a long time? Why can't you accept that your mother might have been right?'

A terrible broken sound loosed itself from Berro's mouth, and his teeth chattered together. 'She wasn't,' he choked. 'She wasn't right. She was brainwashed by an escaped criminal into believing things that aren't true.'

Virda shook her head, turning away from Jex. 'If she'd been my mother, I would've been so proud—'

'Well, she wasn't your mother!' Berro spat. 'And she chose to die instead of being *my* mother.'

And there it was. The burning core of it, all the layers stripped away to reveal its raw, smouldering ugliness.

Virda wiped the back of her hand along her mouth. 'Are you going to stop Undra or not?' Her anger was front and centre, crackling hot and undeniable, but Fessi sensed the grief behind it. It was too deep, too painful to be borne of an abstract adherence to principles. This was personal. This was about Shani.

'How?' Berro barked. 'How am I going to stop Code-approved

testing by a world-famous imparter? I have no chance of getting evidence against him before he leaves for the reformatory. He's closing up the field unit because we're done with the collections. I don't have access anymore. He cancelled the access codes. If I report him to the council without evidence of the murder, nobody will believe me. And if you're right about these tests being just like all the other tests, then why would they care anyway?'

'So you agree about the tests.'

'No,' said Berro. 'I'm just exposing the inconsistencies in your own argument.'

'He wants you to go with him. You have to go,' said Virda. 'You have to keep pretending to be supportive. You have to stop him killing more people.'

'How? By wrestling him to the ground? He has a gun, Virda. Remember? I thought I was safe before, when I said he wouldn't kill me because I was Rhetari, but reformatory patients are Rhetari too, and if he's willing to risk killing them, then he's willing to risk killing me too. I can't go with him.'

'But you're bigger than him, Berro. You're stronger. You have to—'

'I don't! And I won't! I can't pretend anymore. He'll realise I'm faking it, and he'll kill me.'

'My cousin is in there, Berro! You're the only one—'

'I *can't*, Virda!'

'What would your mother say—'

'*STOP TALKING ABOUT MY MOTHER!*'

'I'll talk about her if I want to!' Virda spat, and Fessi felt the disintegration of Virda's last shred of self-control. 'She deserved better than you!'

The silence that followed was profound, the intrusion of birdsong after several moments somehow embarrassing. Jex had melted away into the softseat, and Fessi sat still and silent, braced against Virda's rage and anguish and the indiscriminate hatred flowing through Berro. His face was impassive as he stood up. He fixed Virda and then the others with a blank look before he turned and crossing the room to the front door in measured steps. He didn't hesitate at the threshold or look back to deliver a final retort. He simply opened the door, stepped out, and closed it gently behind him. They listened to him descending the stairs, the wood groaning under his weight.

He did it carefully and evenly. Mechanically.

Creak. Creak. Creak.

• • •

Virda and Jex sat in silence on the softseat, avoiding each other's eyes. Shortly after Berro's departure, Fessi had cited Kath as her excuse to leave and let herself out, and now they were alone. Rain had begun to fall, and the white noise pressed in around them, intensifying the close, crushing atmosphere Berro had left behind him. Virda expected Jex to start interrogating her about the secret comspace at any moment. She felt sick. Standing, she brushed herself off as though leaves and dirt had settled upon her and went to Magrin's bedroom door. She knocked gently.

'Magrin?' she said, cheek pressed against the wood. 'I wanted to ask you something.'

The door opened slowly. Magrin stood there, puffy-eyed and miserable, the scrattin still cradled in her hands. 'Uh,' she said. She clearly had no desire to speak with Virda just then, and Virda felt terrible, but she had to do this. She *had to*.

'You've taken samples from no-zones before, right?' she asked. 'For your red studies.'

'Ye–es?' Magrin looked perplexed. A couple of birds squeaked in the room behind her, and she stepped forward into the mingle, closing her door slightly.

Virda pressed on. 'So you have access to anti-marrow gear?'

'Yes? Why?'

Behind Virda, Jex shifted in his seat and made a sound like a muffled cough.

'Is it difficult to arrange to use it?' asked Virda. 'Do you have to fill in application forms or ask permission or anything like that?'

'No,' said Magrin. 'If you're doing a subject that needs anti-marrow gear from time to time, they give you the codes for the storage locker. Why are you asking?'

'Can I have the codes?'

Magrin scrunched up her nose. Pips ran up her sleeve, and Virda watched the lump wriggle its way along to settle at Magrin's elbow. Hands now free, Magrin placed them high on her hips. 'Virda, what's going on?'

Virda sighed. 'It's just… there's this tree. Apparently, it's a great one to climb. Ancient. I think it used to have some sacred significance before the war, but it's in the no-zone now, so nobody climbs it anymore. I want to climb it. To take my mind off everything else.'

'I don't think it would be fun to climb in anti-marrow gear,' said Magrin. 'It's not flexible like a uniform.'

'Oh, it's not about the climb,' said Virda. 'It's about the view. That's why I want to go. I want a good view, and I don't want to share it with other climbers. Except Jex, of course. We'd manage in anti-marrow gear, no problem.'

Magrin seemed unconvinced.

'Would you get in trouble if we borrowed some gear with your codes?' asked Jex, and Virda turned to him, relieved to have him helping her. But he didn't meet her eyes.

'Not if they don't find out,' said Magrin.

Jex brought out his brightest, most winning smile, and predictably, Magrin couldn't help but smile back at him. 'I'll grab you a couple of sets later today,' she said.

'You're the best, Mag,' said Virda ignoring the burr of guilt caught up in her chest. The ends justified the means, and she'd tell Magrin everything at a less tumultuous time. Besides, it wasn't all a lie. She did want to take her mind off everything else. Discovering Shani's secret was something important – a good direction to channel her energy right now, rather than succumbing to fear, rage and helplessness over the situation with Berro and Undra.

Magrin retreated into her bedroom and quietly pushed the door closed behind her, leaving Virda alone with Jex once again. She'd hoped that, by helping her with Magrin, Jex had started the process of mending whatever bridge had been damaged between them, but as soon as Magrin was gone, the winning smile fell from his face like a paper mask, and he stared at Virda, his eyebrows raised, lips twisted to one side. He wanted to investigate the no-zone, but that was for Shani. He was angry with her, and it was up to her to make it right.

'What?' Virda said. 'Talk to me.' Shame clutched at her throat.

Jex simply shook his head, then stood abruptly and walked into their bedroom, leaving her to deal with the dirty tea things alone.

• • •

The settlement felt wrong. The marrow moved in fits and starts, sputtering and surging as the rain came down in violent sheets, and Fessi had to rely on her eyes to distinguish between people and trees, between air and soil in the late evening gloom. She almost walked into the back of someone as she made her way up the hill towards the academy.

'So sorry,' she mumbled and stepped aside onto the grass to gather her wits, the rain pounding against her waxed umbrella. Her mind felt clotted and broken, her thoughts and emotions disordered.

'Fessi?'

She looked up to see Magrin heading down the hill, carrying a large black satchel. Instead of an umbrella, she wore a peaked hood and glove attachments with her uniform, which was tucked into rainboots that sealed just below her knees. Under normal circumstances, Fessi would've sensed Magrin's approach and been prepared for it – her stance, her expression all arranged in their friendliest configurations. But not this time. Magrin had caught her unawares.

'Everything good?'

Fessi knew that if she lied, Magrin would not argue with her; she'd be warm and friendly and try to undo whatever was troubling her without pressing her to confess what it was, but she'd still know that there was something wrong. Fessi didn't want to lie to Magrin – not now, not when their group was already so bruised by bad energy.

'No, unfortunately,' she said.

Magrin stepped into the shelter of the umbrella.

'I'm just feeling really unbalanced. Anxious, I suppose. My mind is all over the place.'

'Oh, I know what you mean,' said Magrin, then rolled her eyes a little. 'Well, I don't know *exactly* what you mean. But I've also been feeling quite scrambled since… you know. Do you want to talk about it?'

Fessi smiled. 'No, thank you, Mag. I'm better at thinking things out.'

'All right,' said Magrin. 'I have a suggestion then. Go to the observation dome. I doubt anyone else will be up there tonight, with all these clouds. It's a great place to think. And if you feel like watering the tamatams at grow level B on your way up, you'd be doing me a favour.'

'You know,' said Fessi, 'that sounds perfect.' And for a moment, Magrin's marrow was bright and clear in all its gentleness. 'What are you doing here so late, Mag?'

'I had to label a few samples and pick up some things for Virda and Jex.' Fessi sensed her friend's hand tighten around the strap of the black satchel. There was a barely perceptible curdling of her mood, and then it smoothed once again.

'Well, I'll take your advice. I'll visit the dome.'

'You won't regret it!' said Magrin, smiling. She embraced Fessi in a brief, one-armed hug and then trotted away down the hill, puddles splashing around her boots and the satchel swinging in her hand.

The elevator sighed to a stop on grow level B. Drawn by the elevator's light, the blooms of flowering shrubs in painted pots crowded against the glass tube like curious faces, watching Fessi as she stepped out into the rich-smelling air.

Rows upon rows of plants stood peaceably in the dimness. There were leafy plants, woody plants, thorny plants, plants with reaching roots and curling fronds, shelves packed with seedlings and seeds not yet sprouting. A couple of plants with long, blade-like leaves turned slowly on a set of rotating plates that hummed on the edge of Fessi's hearing.

She found the tamatams without difficulty, sensing their sweetness, the nutritious potential of their berries, green now, but just starting to yellow. A cool calm washed over her as she watered them, their cells swelling appreciatively. When she was done, she placed the beaker back on its shelf and ascended the stairs. The banister was completely tangled in the curling tendrils and soft leaves of a creeper emerging from a trough set alongside it.

There was no one in the observation dome. She wouldn't have relinquished her visit if there had been, but she was glad to be alone. She dragged a large, soft cushion from the stack in the centre of the room and seated herself on it, cross-legged, near the curve of the dome, where she gazed out across the field and the surrounding forest for leaps and leaps into the distance, to where the darkness of the trees merged with the darkness of the sky. Higher up, moonlight filtered through the clouds, infusing them with a subtle glow. For a moment, the clouds parted to reveal a dusting of sleepy stars. Everything was pure and peaceful, and as she felt her mind begin to ease, she made a mental note to thank Magrin for this idea.

Fessi closed her eyes and felt the shape of the room, tracking the currents of the air as it moved up from the grow level below, bringing with it the whiff of humus and particles of plant life. And below the grow level to the study and common area, mostly empty but with some stirrings. The thrumming of a few focussed minds, some tingles of curiosity in one cubicle, a smattering of fretful confusion in another. In a third cubicle, two people close together, definitely not studying. And down to the offices on level 12. Two sleeping imparters, each curled up in their own private backrooms. A few more imparters awake and at work. And down to level 11, where all the imparters were awake but not busy, perhaps sleepy, perhaps winding down at the end of a long day. One of them exuded the extra-slow aura of the tincture-intoxicated, and one of them—

Fessi gasped and tried to reel her mind back in, but it was as if she'd been hit headlong by a speeding mono. For a single note, a solitary flash of time, she was inside a howling vortex of darkness and then she crashed into the curve of the dome and fell sprawling across the floor, several long paces away from the cushion she'd been sitting on only a moment before. She pushed herself up onto her knees, and stared, blinking at the cushion. It was too far away to reach. She hadn't just fallen off it, she'd…

She'd sensed something. Someone.

Undra. He was there, alone in his office, his mind unguarded. Whatever he was doing or reading or thinking had his marrow bristling with a sharp, ice-cold determination and indifference unlike anything Fessi had sensed in another person before. It was so unyielding, so single-minded, corrupting him entirely in the very matter of his bones, the fibres of his muscles, the cells of his living blood, that when her senses had struck upon it without warning, it had triggered something. She'd snapped into a strange nowhere space for a moment and then there'd been a dislocation. A relocation. A teleportation?

Fessi's pulse stabbed in her throat. With clammy hands, she pushed herself up onto unstable feet and wobbled her way back to the cushion. High above the dome, a cloud passed over the moon, and the world grew inky dark beneath the cold stars.

>>comspace/locked/new
>>Berro has requested a comlink
>>Ryndel has accepted the request

Berro– *: Hello, Ryndel. It's Berro. I got your comlink from my friend Magrin. I need to speak to you about the situation. :*

Ryndel– *: Switch to video or send me a timestamped picture of your face. :*

>>One new image. Berro > Ryndel

>>Access image<<

Ryndel– *: You look terrible. :*

Berro– *: Thanks. :*

Ryndel– *: Is this about what I think it's about? :*

Berro– *: Yes. I can confirm he triggered the crossings. Something bad happened after I spoke to you. There's a lot you don't know. I don't mean that in a condescending way. I'm telling you because it's not safe to be involved in the project anymore. He's dangerous. :*

Ryndel– *: I'm not involved anymore. He said it was over and he thanked me for my help. :*

Berro– *: It's not over, he's just moving onto another phase of research. I'm glad you're out. If he changes his mind and tries to get you back in, make an excuse. It's not safe. :*

Ryndel– *: What happened? Tell me what you know. I won't use it against you or anything. :*

Berro– : *I know you won't. I'm not being cryptic for selfish reasons. I'm not sure it's safe to tell you. I just wanted to make sure you got out.* :

Ryndel– : *Are you in danger?* :

Berro– : *Don't worry about me. I'm going to get out too. Thanks for accepting the unsolicited comlink. I know you don't like me much.* :

Ryndel– : *I don't like you, but I do respect you.* :

Berro– : *>>emote: bow//sincere<<* :

Berro– : *I'm sorry for dismissing you before, when you told me about the crystals. I respect you too. We'll speak again.* :

CHAPTER 26

Virda stood at the bedroom window, elbows on the sill, staring out into the forest at the driving rain as she curled the scrap of paper around her finger. She'd always loved the early autumn rain – the lush patter of fat drops on the leaves, the mulchy smell of it – but she wasn't happy about it now. It had been falling relentlessly for two days, and the anti-marrow gear Magrin had procured for them sat folded and unused on the chest of drawers opposite the bed. She had proposed waiting for better weather before they ventured out into the no-zone to investigate Shani's second clue, and Jex had grudgingly agreed with her.

Everything Jex did or said seemed grudging since the fight with Berro. He hadn't mentioned the fight, nor asked her about the secret comspace she'd admitted to using, but Virda could feel his questions and judgements simmering behind his face whenever they were alone together. The way Jex looked at her, the shortness of his words, had been so out of character, so damaging to her happiness and self-esteem, that she couldn't stand it, not least because she knew it was her fault.

She looked down at the paper scrap for the millionth time.

from here, 48 w, 'no-zone', singer ruin

'Come back to bed,' Jex grumbled. 'I'm cold.'

Virda clenched her jaw. She wanted to say, *Yes, you* are *cold! You're being so cold to me!* Instead, she sighed, her breath steaming up the windowpane. Before the rain, autumn had crackled in like a lazy fire, burning the tips of the trees to red and gold, and scorching the blue from the sky. This cold front had rolled through in its wake, dousing the brightness in wet grey, and consuming their waking hours so that the day's activities commenced and concluded in the watery half-light of a sun reluctant to rise and eager to set.

Leaving the paper scrap on the windowsill, Virda got back into bed and leaned against the wall, propping her slab against her knees. Jex kept his distance at first, but once the slow, even breathing of sleep returned to him, he unconsciously wriggled himself close to her, throwing an arm across her lap and burying his face in her hip. Virda blinked against the hot sting of tears. She typed a message.

Virda– *: have you heard anything from Berro? :*

Fessi– *: I invited him to the lakehouse for tea, but he said he wasn't keen on facing the weather. He's catching up on reading instead. :*

Virda– *: i feel terrible for what i said :*

Fessi– *: It was harsh, but he'll be all right, Virda. He needs to sort through things. :*

Virda– *: should I message him? :*

Fessi– *: You could, but it's fine to give him space for a while. :*

Virda– *: i hope so. i'm really anxious about all of it :*

Fessi– *: Me too. :*

A gust of wind drove the rain against the window with rattling spite, and Virda shivered. Jex tightened his arm around her and snuffled, dreaming.

: how's kath? :, she typed, needing a change of topic.

Fessi– *: She's well. More at home by the day. I can hardly remember the lakehouse without her in it. It's like she's always been here. Andish enjoys her company too. :*

Virda– *: i'm glad to hear it :*

Fessi– *: She wants to go to the festival next week. :*

Virda– *: >>emote: surprise<< :*

Fessi– *: We've polished her backstory. She should be able to blend in. :*

Virda– *: let's hope the weather clears up by then :*

Fessi– *: It will. The rain will stop tonight. :*

Virda glanced at the folded anti-marrow gear. If Fessi said the weather would be clear by tomorrow, then the weather would be clear.

'Jex,' she said, gently jiggling his shoulder until he grunted and flopped onto his back, blinking up at her with gummy eyes and a line of drool at the corner of his mouth. 'We're going into the no-zone tomorrow morning.'

'Mmmm, fine,' he mumbled, turning away from her. 'T'mrrow.'

• • •

Virda and Jex stood in a cool, grassy grove at the outskirts of the no-zone. The mono was out of sight beneath a thick chayberry bush with autumn leaves all the colours of a sunrise. They'd changed out of their comfortable, camouflaging green uniforms and into the anti-marrow gear, which was a lurid shade of purple. There was little chance of stealth while wearing it, and they could only hope nobody else was out at the crack of dawn to explore a no-zone so far away from the settlement.

The gear covered each of them from head to toe in a single piece of thick, moulded impermeable fabric, with a double-sealed opening that ran from the base of the spine to the top of the head. Magrin had picked the sizes well – Virda's longer in the leg and wider in the hip than Jex's – but they were uncomfortable despite the good fits. Their heads were sealed inside tight hoods with transparent plates in front of their eyes. At their mouths, noses and ears, filters embedded into the fabric allowed them to hear, speak and breathe, while keeping any potent marrowcore essence at bay.

Virda was glad they weren't climbing the tree she'd invented in her lie to Magrin, and hoped that whatever they were about to do, they wouldn't need the precision and peripheral vision the gear deprived them of.

It was hard to imagine that the forest just beyond this grove, though indistinguishable from the forest around it, was tainted and corrupted by a maddening concentration of marrowcore. A diluted essence would be wafting over them even now as the gentle morning breeze moved the air from the no-zone into the surrounding area.

'Shall we?' Jex's words sounded strange through the filter, tinny and distant like an old pod speaker. He lifted a hand to scratch an itch on his head and, finding this to be impossible through the thickness of the fabric, resorted to smacking himself instead.

'We're not even in the no-zone yet, and you've already started devolving,' said Virda.

Jex ignored her, which stung.

'Let's go,' he said, and they tramped out of the grove, their thick, inflexible bootsoles leaving distinctive prints in the soft, mossy ground. They walked in silence for several minutes.

Jex consulted his pod. 'Well,' he said. 'We're in the no-zone now, apparently. I don't know why, but I thought it would feel different.'

'So did I,' said Virda. 'I read about it – the article described a humming or ringing sound at the edge of your hearing. I can't hear anything like that.'

'Maybe we're not sensitive enough,' said Jex. 'Maybe you need to have Fessi-level sensitivity to pick it up.'

'Or maybe the anti-marrow gear is more advanced these days,' said Virda. 'It was an old account from the first stage of the reclamation.'

'Maybe,' said Jex. 'Coordinates lead this way.'

They followed a stream gushing merrily over the rocks. It disappeared into slippery fissures and reappeared as small, splashy waterfalls that caught and tossed spangles of morning light. The water tumbled down across the rocky ground, gradually descending into a broad, shallow basin. In this area, the trees were quite sparse, but most of those present stood tall and strong, with powerful, ancient roots coiled between the rocks, gripping the hard earth like the fists of giants. One fallen tree lay broken across the stream in the distance. Jex tramped towards it, and Virda picked her way across the rocks and grassy tussocks, following his lead. He walked with a steady, solemn determination that unnerved her. In times of fear, stress or uncertainty, she depended on Jex to keep things light, to clear her head when the storm clouds started to gather, to make her laugh when she took things too seriously – but he wasn't doing that today. Even with the silly-looking, bright-purple gear and the awkward, ungainly movement it caused, he cut an intimidating figure thumping his way over this unfamiliar territory, pod in hand. He was on a mission for truth, and so was she, and if they didn't find what they were looking for, whatever that was, they wouldn't be able to brush it off as an inconsequential failure. There would be emotional repercussions if they failed, and for the first time, Virda questioned her wisdom in tackling this task in the midst of the crisis with Berro. Surely that was more important right now, with higher stakes and closer, clearer danger. Could they really afford to be distracted by a years-old mystery, the truth of which was unlikely to bring them any closer to helping their estranged cousin? Too late now, to be pondering this.

They reached the fallen tree, and Virda wrenched a small, pleasingly straight branch from it, pulling away twigs to fashion a neat and sturdy walking stick. She felt better with her hand gripping a branch, even if she couldn't feel its woody texture through the fabric encasing her hands like wax.

She followed Jex along the trunk of the tree across the stream. It had grown in size and power, joining up with other streams running into the rocky basin. Once they'd cleared the fallen tree and the rocks jutting up around it, they found themselves quite exposed and with a wide view of the landscape beyond. There were almost no trees ahead, the rocks softened by low shrubs and grasses growing thick and lush along the water. The stream was nearly wide enough to be a river now, and it ran smooth and fast, following a wide channel before it vanished over the edge of a cliff into a green gorge. They could hear the distant sound of the water crashing into a pool below and see the fine mist it raised, holding delicate rainbows that trembled in the sunshine.

'The coordinates are at that waterfall,' said Jex.

'At the top?'

'How would I know? We'll have to look around.' His voice was clipped and hard. Virda tried not to let it affect her, tried to stay focussed on the task at hand, but Jex's un-Jex-like behaviour hurt her, and her cheeks burned with emotion inside the clammy hood.

The waterfall's edge was strikingly beautiful. They crouched atop a flat slab of rock and peered over through the fresh haze of the mist into the wet trees below. Autumn didn't seem to have reached this place. The trees were different to those at the settlement: lush and vibrant green, their branches host to myriad glistening ferns and springy mosses, dangling fronds and small pink flowers, their bright mouths open in the sunshine. Between the branches, Virda caught a glimpse of the wide pool at the base of the waterfall. Something stirred in her memory.

'We should go down there,' said Jex, indicating a likely route on their left. The way was rubbly and overgrown but looked almost Rhetari-made in the way it wound between the rocks and plants, never too steep or precarious to hamper their descent. At the bottom, they pushed through the juicy foliage to the edge of the pool. Young trees crowded around the water in among dense bushes and ferns. The water was clear and blue, with ripples radiating from the frothing foot of the waterfall. Small fish darted in and out of the shade cast by large, smooth rocks beneath the surface.

'I've seen this place before,' said Virda.

Jex turned to her.

'Subject Buttons.'

'What?'

'In that history lecture I went to with Berro, the one where I learned about the glass boat. Remember I told you that Hebbel showed us all these pictures from before the war? Taken by Subject Buttons? Well, in one of the pictures, he was in this pool, swimming.'

'Wow, uh. What did Hebbel say about it?'

'I can't remember. Not much. She talked about it being in a no-zone, which is why it wasn't familiar to any of us. I mean, you'd remember finding a place like this in the forest. If it wasn't toxic, there'd be field trips out here. I'd swim myself if I didn't have to wear this stupid gear.'

'Fessi and Magrin would love this,' said Jex. 'So would Disa.'

'I still can't believe how normal it feels. How healthy.'

'I haven't seen anything that looks mutated,' said Jex. 'I mean, I know that depends on all sorts of things and mutations might not look like mutations, but this place is perfect.'

'Thriving.'

Jex attempted to scratch his head again and resorted to the same head-smacking technique as before. 'Well, this is where the coordinates have led us,' he said. 'I don't understand.'

'It's not a Singer ruin. We're missing something.'

'Obviously,' said Jex, unkindly. He'd lulled Virda into a false sense of normality with a neutral tone, and then undercut it without warning. All day he'd seemed just on the edge of angry, his bad mood communicated as much by his lack of frivolity as by his outward coldness, and she'd tolerated it, but this was a step too far.

'Why are you being like this?' Virda snapped. 'You were so eager to find out where the clues were leading. And now you're acting like we're searching for a corpse or something—'

'Well, one of our friends might be a corpse soon enough,' said Jex. 'You commanded him to risk his own life, and the last thing you said to him was that his dead mother deserved better than him.' He said it rapidly and precisely, like he'd been waiting to say it for ages, the words sharpening on his tongue before their delivery. Virda felt like he'd kicked her in the stomach. She'd assumed Jex was just going to let time heal whatever wounds the argument with Berro had opened up. Instead, he'd waited until they were in the middle of nowhere, dressed in anti-marrow gear, and undertaking a potentially dangerous mission, to allow his real feelings to bubble up to the surface. It was not a good time. Virda switched to defence.

'You know I didn't mean—'

'Didn't you?' Jex's voice rose. 'I can guarantee you Berro thought you meant it.'

'Jex, I was angry. I was thinking about Shani in the reformatory. Shani being tortured. I'm going to speak to Berro. You know I will. Why are you doing this now?'

'Because you asked,' he said, and walked away from her, feigning interest in something further along the water's edge.

Virda followed him, heart sore. 'Jex,' she pleaded. 'Don't walk away. Please talk to me.'

'Why?' he said, without turning. 'It's not like you talk to me anymore. We used to be allies, partners, a unit, but now you do things I don't understand, you keep secrets from me, as if you're the centre of everything, as if things matter to you more than they matter to me.'

Virda stiffened and stared at the back of Jex's head. He was right. There was no denying it. She'd kept the note from him, she'd kept the comspace from him. Shani had meant as much to Jex as she did to Virda, and Virda should've included him, immediately, in everything concerning Shani, or at least given him the option of including himself. All her notions of keeping Jex happy and safe through ignorance were revealing themselves as selfish and ill-considered.

With a surge of self-loathing, she realised that some of this had been motivated by jealousy. Jex had his flying, his purpose, his future worked out. She didn't. She *wasn't* a part of everything he was part of, and she'd wanted some things for herself. Unfortunately, she'd picked the wrong things. And these, now, were the consequences. She'd been slowly but surely undermining her most important relationship, and it was no wonder Jex hadn't been sympathetic with her after the argument with Berro. Her guilt about that exchange was enormous – an enemy too great to defeat without Jex as an ally, and she felt horribly alone without his amiable companionship.

She swept her burning eyes across the pristine beauty of this forbidden pool, taking in none of it, until they snagged on a small detail just beside the base of the waterfall. A gap. Right there, above a rock that formed the top step of a natural staircase, slick with strands of watermoss and glistening in the rainbow spray. 'Jex!'

He hesitated, clearly reluctant to abandon his protest, but after a moment he turned back and looked to where she was pointing.

'A cave!' said Virda. 'Behind the waterfall. That could be it. Do you think so?'

Virda detected the hint of a smile in the shape of Jex's eyes, just visible through the spangly reflections on his eye mask. 'I do think so, yes,' he said.

They scrambled up on hands and knees, pushed through the vigorous spray of the waterfall and slipped through the gap into a cold, shady passage beyond.

'This is definitely Rhetari-made,' said Jex, running a hand along one of the rough-hewn walls. Water droplets twinkled all over his gear and dripped from his arm as he raised it. The anti-marrow suits were, mercifully, completely waterproof. Sunlight flickered through the waterfall, but the passage was dark beyond its reach. Virda switched on her podlamp and held it up. The passage was long and descended gently, the end of it out of sight. She looked at Jex and found him looking back at her.

'Jex,' she said. 'Are we fine? I don't want to walk into the unknown without my best.'

'We're not fine,' said Jex. 'Not yet. But we will be. Just because I'm upset with you, doesn't mean I'm not your best.'

Virda wished it was a good time to indulge in a bit of crying. 'I know. It's just… you almost never get cross, so when you do it makes me fall apart. I'm sorry. I messed up with Berro. And with other things. I'll fix it all, I promise. And I know I shouldn't expect you to be on my side every time, even when I don't deserve it.'

'It's all right,' said Jex. 'Don't worry about it now.'

It wasn't a resolution, but it was a start. Virda nodded and packed her feelings away for the moment.

They began their gradual descent into darkness, the sounds of the world outside soon snuffed out into a pressing silence. Just as Virda began to feel like they were being slowly crushed in the immense gullet of an ancient beast, the passage stopped descending and broadened out. The rocky walls ahead gave way to a massive open darkness beyond. Dark, but not entirely. As her eyes adjusted, Virda registered the hint of a silvery light ahead of them.

'Ohhh…' Jex breathed.

It was a vast underground space, a temple, wide enough and high enough to comfortably house any of the trees they'd ever climbed, and taller ones too. It had been roughly but skilfully carved from the rock, and at the very apex of this enormous stone vault, a small hole allowed a trickle of sunlit water to plunge down into the centre of the structure. The sheer staggering height of the drop meant most of the water had scattered into a fine drizzle before it reached the bottom, but some of it was captured by a wide flat bowl, held aloft by a colossal stone figure hewn from the same rock as the temple itself. She was green with moss that grew thick as paint over the top half of her body, her raised arms and the bowl, and became thinner and patchier nearer the stone floor. Her face was simple and roughly carved, gentle and serene, turned up towards the shimmering watery light above her. Her bowl was tilted forward, and a thin stream of water trickled from it into a narrow channel that ran across the floor, terminating at the foot of a great stone slab, which lay beneath a broken arch.

It was the arch that drew their attention. The pieces of it that still stood, as well as those that lay broken on and around the slab, glittered strangely, studded with jewels. Virda and Jex moved forward slowly and fearfully, drawn to the broken arch like moths to a flame. It seemed possible that any sound or sudden movement could bring the temple down around them, or provoke the wrath of the stone woman.

The jewels were dark purple crystals, so dark they were almost black, set into inner edges of the stone that had once formed the arch. Unbroken, it would resemble the upper jaw of a skag, with its terrible inward-facing teeth. Only these teeth weren't terrible – they were beautiful.

'What is this place?' Virda whispered. 'Why is this broken?'

Jex crouched with his masked face close to some crystals on a broken piece resting on the great slab.

'These crystals,' he said, casting his pod torch over them. 'Look. They're all the same, all perfectly spaced. They didn't grow organically out of the stone. Someone made holes and stuck them in.'

'For decoration?'

Virda crouched beside him.

'I don't know. What do you reckon?'

'I can almost feel something,' said Virda. 'Like in that article I was telling you about. Maybe I'm just imagining it but—'

'No,' said Jex. 'I can feel it too. A vibration in my head if I stop speaking. You think it's the crystals?'

'Could be. They're the only thing here I can't identify. They look—'

'Like marrowcore?'

'I think so. I'm not sure.'

'This slab,' said Jex, pacing slowly around it. 'It's like an altar.'

'Imagine how it must've looked with the crystal arch over it. It's something important.'

The water from the woman's bowl pooled around the altar, and the stone floor was slippery. Here and there, the tiny, optimistic fronds of cave ferns rose from the moss, reaching weakly for the wan light above them.

'Jex, the broken edges of these pieces aren't worn like the rest of it. I think it was broken quite recently. I mean relative to the age of this place.'

Jex inspected another chunk of crystal-studded stone lying in the water. 'Do you think…'

Their eyes met across the altar.

'Do I think it got destroyed around the time Shani was taken away?'

Jex stared at the great stone slab. 'What would that mean?' he said, his quiet words distinct in the cavernous silence.

'I have no idea.'

Virda began to take images with her pod, trying to capture the vastness of the temple, its vaulted stone, the towering statue, the altar, the broken arch. Around the edges of the great space were rows and clusters of boulders and large stones worn smooth and glistening with moisture. She could imagine hundreds of people sitting on the stones, facing inward, watching the giant woman pour her water before the altar, watching the altar and the arch, watching… watching what? What was it for? What happened here?

Jex seized a piece of stone and struck it against a fallen section of the arch. The sound echoed angrily around the chamber, and Virda flinched with each strike. As a crystal snapped in half, Jex jumped back and slipped, landing hard on his backside. Virda rushed forward.

'I'm fine,' said Jex, getting gingerly to his feet. 'I thought I saw it flash, like a spark.' He moved forward to retrieve the broken crystal, lifting it into the light for a moment.

'It smells weird,' he said.

Virda could smell it too, a strange chemical tang detectable even through the filters of the anti-marrow gear, as though something was burning. The hairs stood on the back of her neck, and she reached out and curled her gloved fingers around Jex's arm, tugging him gently. 'I think you should put that down, and we should leave. I want to leave.'

'Me too,' said Jex, placing the crystal shard on the altar.

Virda didn't run, but she wanted to. She felt the stone woman's eyes watching their retreat. Something had happened in here – something bad – and Virda was fearful and desperate to know what it was.

CHAPTER 27

A person could fall through a crack between realities, into a different world at the same place and time, but to manipulate the fabric of a single world, to skip across distances without the passing of time, had always been something reserved for the heroes and villains of fictional worlds, imagined by people across the spectrum of realities. At least, that's what Fessi had always thought. Now, she wasn't so sure.

She couldn't stop thinking about the moment that had left her lying stunned on the observation dome floor. The momentary hallucination of chaos. Her body had occupied a particular space, comfortable and heavy on the cushion – and the next moment, she wasn't on the cushion anymore, but sprawled off far to one side, pushed her from the seat. No, not pushed – she hadn't moved at all. She'd been relocated. Her entire physical mass had blinked out of existence in one place and blinked into existence in another.

How had she done it? She asked herself this question again and again until it morphed into a more interesting question: Could she do it again?

It was warm, one of those balmy golden autumn days, the lake still and clear. Fessi slipped from her boat, relaxing as the cool water enveloped her. Everything felt closer underwater, so close she was no longer separate from it, sensing the world around her, but also against her and inside her. On land, her connection with the marrow was akin to stirring a pot of paint – she could see it, smell it, feel the thickness of it – but in the water, it was as though she'd submerged herself in the paint pot and dissolved. She *was* the paint.

Fessi dragged her arms lazily through the water and melted her mind into it. A string of tiny bubbles tickled along her leg and a slick blade of waterweed slid over her foot. She sank deeper, deeper, touching her toes to the stony ground, stirring up a puff of gritty sand, unsettling a tiny crab, sending it scuttling into a hole. She threw her mind in all directions, trying to find something to strike it against while she imagined herself teleporting, just like she had in the dome, and clenched her whole body trying to make it happen again.

But nothing happened.

In her drifting liminal marric wanderings at the observation dome, it had been the shock of encountering Undra's malevolent marrow beneath her that had triggered the jump. She was unlikely to replicate this experience here – nothing in the lake could shock or frighten her.

With a single, powerful kick of both legs, she sent herself soaring up through the clear brown water, breaking the surface with barely a splash and drinking in a deep breath of rich lake air. She floated, watched a few clouds scud across the early afternoon sky and then closed her eyes, the sunshine glowing red through her eyelids. She skimmed her mind across the surface of the lake, like the palm of a hand reaching out from a swift boat. She found a floating leaf, a dandlefly darting above it and a fish circling below, a piece of driftwood, the reeds on the bank and then the grass, the path, the house, and inside the house – *snap*.

The void.

And she was back under the water, deep, her mouth open and the lake rushing into her. Flailing, choking, heart slamming in her chest, Fessi struggled back up to where the sun spangled innocently on the surface. She burst back into daylight some distance from where she'd been floating before, gasping and spluttering, swam gracelessly to the drifting boat and clung to the side of it to catch her breath.

It had happened again. She'd teleported. Her mind had been blissfully mellowed and melted into the marrow of the lake around her, and then her senses had struck against the void of Kath's presence, the contrast of her otherness to the world around her.

Fessi's breathing gradually returned to normal, but she didn't climb into the boat just yet. Instead, she swam to the shallows on the far bank, dipping beneath the water where the surface was just above her head and the ground beneath her feet soft and muddy. Safe.

Her rare connection with the marrow, it seemed, was more than just an ability to read it. Perhaps, if she practised, she'd be able to write it too.

• • •

Late morning on the day of the autumn festival, Berro woke to find himself alone in the alcove. Kem was probably out setting up his stage, tuning his stringboard, practising the songs for his evening performances with Disa. Perhaps Yurek was helping him, or just getting a head start on drinking.

Berro wasn't normally one to sleep in, but he felt gutted, hateful, and bitterly sad, perhaps more so than he'd ever felt before. It must've been worse when his mother died, but time had clotted those wounds, and they'd grown over with scar tissue – imperfect and sometimes uncomfortable, but certainly better than this raw anguish.

It had been days since his argument with Virda, but each day felt worse than the last; the very act of waking each morning tore away a scab, leaving the wound beneath bigger and deeper every time. He wasn't sure what the worst part of it was, her awful opinions about him and his mother, the fact that she hadn't made any attempt to apologise to him, or the possibility that her opinions might hold within them a kernel of terrible truth.

No.

He pressed the heels of his hands into his eyes to stop anything leaking out of them and heard a shifting of sheets above him. 'Ebra?'

'Yes?' she said.

He wasn't alone after all. 'You're going to the festival?' he said, hopefully.

'No,' she replied, sounding offended by the question. 'Of course not.'

'Why not?'

'Because I have reading to catch up on for about five subjects, and the dorm is going to be nice and quiet. And I hate festivals. Are you going?'

She sounded just as eager to be rid of him as he was of her. He was about to remind her that almost an entire level of the academy was dedicated to quiet study, but decided against it. He couldn't deny there was something appealing about reading in bed in a deserted dormitory while wearing your most comfortable clothwrap.

'I don't know,' said Berro, considering it for the first time. He'd assumed he'd be staying in the dorm, hiding away from his friends, but he felt so acutely terrible, unable to calm down or to stop his thoughts from circling and descending upon the awful scenes of the past few weeks, like scavenger birds eager to tear into a corpse.

The decision he made was surprising, even to himself. He'd leave Ebra to her reading. He'd go to the festival.

• • •

After hours in the water, and several successful blink-jumps across short distances, Fessi retrieved the boat and paddled back to the island, her mind swarming with possibilities. She imagined herself dancing beneath the strings of lights at the autumn festival, teleporting around the space to the shock and awe of everyone else in attendance. But no, that wasn't her style. She wasn't even particularly keen to attend the festival at all, but she'd promised Kath she'd take her there. Kath had spent days reading, trying to cram in as much knowledge about the settlement and its people and customs and celebrations and social norms as she could before setting out to experience it all for the first time.

They'd decided Kath would go to the festival posing as a visiting traveller from Mass 1, something that could easily be slotted into her backstory if anyone asked questions and would provide a handy excuse for any confusion or ignorance she might display. Fessi had reassured her that nobody would be asking awkward questions anyway. The festival was an occasion for eating, drinking and dancing, and strangers from other settlements were always joining in.

She found Kath in the lakehouse mingle, with Andish already fussing over her hours before the festival. Andish was thrilled at Kath's willingness to be dressed up, something Fessi had never shown any interest in. Neglected clothwraps and festive enhancements had been hauled out of Andish's personal collection, and Kath was in the process of being pampered and preened from head to toe, her skin and hair rubbed with iridescent powders, her wrists laden with beads, her braids coiled into a pretty bun on top of her head. Within the void of her presence, there was a flicker of detectable emotion. Apprehension. Excitement. Joy. Fessi left them to it.

Later, in the boat on their way across the water, Fessi struggled to keep her eyes off the crosser. Kath wore a smoke grey clothwrap shot through with threads of silver that hugged the comfortable curves of her body but lay in loose folds at the top, leaving her shoulders and upper back exposed to the balmy air. The boots that Andish had laced onto her feet were beaded with tiny shells. Her skin sparkled, her hair shone, her smile was radiant.

Fessi had become adept at managing the affliction of physical attraction, but it was a difficult thing. She knew better than anyone the role that attraction played in muddying clear thoughts and driving poor decision-making. She'd sensed the gnawing ache of longing unfulfilled in others, and rationalised her own longings into non-existence, but still, it was a chore. She envied Berro in his effortless immunity to these things. He could appreciate physical beauty without ever connecting it to anything more, even when others all around him were making those connections constantly, desperately, exhaustingly.

There were and always would be limits to how close Fessi allowed herself to get another person. Just like Andish, her marric sensitivity made intimacy too intimate. She'd always known that her parents had struggled to be together, and if her father hadn't died, Andish most likely would've left him before long, not because she didn't love him, but because loving him and being close to him meant living inside his mind and body, and it was exhausting.

Upon their arrival at the festival, many eyes were drawn immediately to Kath, who slipped eagerly into the bustle of the crowd, face lit up with wonder. Fessi felt Kath's emotions clear and strong now, and it took a moment for her to realise that this was abnormal in its normalness. They were simple, blunt, easy feelings to read in a person – indeed, even one with no marric sensitivity could pick up on them just through physical clues – but Fessi sensed them where once she'd sensed nothing at all. There was no doubt about it – Kath was changing.

'Fessi,' Kath breathed, her fingers curling tightly around Fessi's wrist. 'This is *amazing*!'

A warm breeze carried the thump of dance music between the trees, strings of tiny ecolamps glowed warmly overhead, and between the branches were cords hung with fluttering fabric strips, like colourful moths drawn to the lights. The illuminated area was alive with voices and the excited press of bodies, people laughing and drinking, chatting and trading, dancing and kissing and smoking and eating.

Kath tugged Fessi along, dazzled and bouncing with excitement. 'Can we drink something?' she asked, taking her pod out of her pocket, eager to try her hand at a credit trade, which she'd practised for days.

'Yes,' said Fessi. 'If it's green, it probably has a bit of wickerbloom tincture in it, just so you know.'

'Is that bad?'

'No, it's the same as smoking it, just a bit slower to get going.'

'Those?' said Kath, indicating a roving drinks vendor carrying some transparent cups of dark green liquid on a tray.

Fessi nodded, and Kath swirled over to the vendor beaming brightly, holding up two fingers on one hand and her pod in the other as though she'd done this a hundred times. Fessi watched as the vendor beeped his pod against Kath's, and Kath thanked him with a brief bow, hand to chest, natural as anything, taking two drinks from his tray and turning back to Fessi, fierce with joy.

'Oh, no, I don't really—' Fessi began, but Kath had already thrust one of the drinks into her hand and linked arms with her, drawing her deeper into the crowd.

Kath sipped from her cup, and her face contorted momentarily. 'Gods, why does everything have to be so sour in this place?' she muttered, but she seemed more amused than disgusted.

'You'd probably prefer the treacle fizz,' said Fessi. 'It's golden-brown. Sort of bubbly and sticky. Disgusting.'

'Yeah, I'm getting one of those next.'

Just then, Kath's hand shot into the air, and she waved and grinned. Fessi didn't have to turn around to know that Virda, Jex and Magrin were barrelling towards them.

'Kath, you look blooming!' said Virda. She and Jex wore simple clothwraps, and Fessi knew they'd be climbing trees before the night was over. Magrin had woven some beads and feathers into her braids, and her cheeks glowed with pearly powder. The swirl of excited marrow in the early stages of intoxication was heady. As Fessi was swept into a five-person hug, she wished Berro was with them.

• • •

It was already raucous by the time Berro arrived. Blurred bodies moved around in a haze of wickersmoke, the smell of it tangling with the scents of food and drink and perfume, while music swelled and excited voices filled the night with laughter.

Berro purchased a drink and sipped it as he walked through the golden lamplight and the shadows, wending his aimless way between clusters of intoxicated people. He didn't know where he was going or what he was looking for, only that he'd be avoiding his friends if he spotted them. He wasn't sure he'd made the right decision to come at all. He'd assumed it would be easier to stop fixating on toxic thoughts while surrounded by distractions, like at the solstice field party, but he couldn't shake the oppressive feeling that sat in his chest, a malevolent creature with its claws in his heart.

The field party had been great because he'd been with his friends, and they'd been warm and loving and kind towards him. Now, he was alone, having caused a seismic rift between himself and everyone he loved. The fight had been between him and Virda, but none of the others had rallied to him in the aftermath. Not really. He'd exchanged a few messages with Fessi, but she hadn't said a word about Virda, and Berro suspected Fessi's deepest sympathies did not lie with him. They were avoiding him, just like he was avoiding them, and it hurt.

The music changed and a beautiful voice carried over the other noise, accompanied by the rich tones of a stringboard.

Berro followed the music into the crowd. People made way for him, as they always did, automatically deferring to his towering size and stepping back, and so he moved easily. Kem and Disa were set up on a low platform backing onto a thick stand of trees. The lights fixed at their feet and in the branches above them framed their rustic stage, throwing everything else into warm shadow and drawing the gazes of everyone nearby.

Kem's voice was crystal clear, soulful, uplifting, and Berro drifted towards it. Someone bearing a tray of paper cups full of pale liquid moved through the crowd, distributing the drinks, apparently free of charge. A cup was pushed into Berro's hand. He downed his first drink, tossed the empty cup into a nearby receptacle, and sipped tentatively from the new one. It tasted fresh and sweet and faintly herbal. What was it? Why had he never had it before? He found the cup empty moments later and helped himself to another one when the tray-bearer moved past him again. She didn't seem to notice.

The inhibition that normally kept him standing on the outskirts of the crowd, disguising his massiveness with his back against a barrier, was dissolving rapidly, and soon he stood in the middle of the crowd, head and shoulders above most of them, indifferent to his visibility. Nobody cared. It didn't matter. Why had he ever thought it mattered? He felt warmer and lighter, the nagging tension in his chest beginning to ease. His body moved slightly in time with the beat of the music. Disa, the percussionist in the musical outfit, struck a ball-tipped stick against the side of a wooden drum, and the rhythm synchronised with Berro's heartbeat.

He danced and danced until his third drink was almost empty and then wandered off in search of the person with the tray. He'd probably have to pay credits for the next one. He didn't mind.

• • •

Virda and Jex dashed through the dark, the sounds of the festival echoing and fading behind them. They'd left Magrin, Fessi and Kath drinking and snacking on a log bench with a great view of the stage where Kem and Disa were performing. Virda thought she'd spotted Berro for just a moment, moving away at the edge of the crowd, but perhaps it had been another large person in blue.

Jex sang and skipped, and Virda struggled to keep up with him. They ran until they reached the edge of the settlement, and then they ran a little more. There were no treehouses here. They chose a tree at random, and they climbed.

The forest was a beating heart, the air warm and smooth and alive with swarms of glowflies that curled and stretched like shoals of phosphorescent fish. Virda waved her hand through them, and they scattered and reformed. Jex climbed ahead of her, showering her with bark dust. It tickled her face. She reached one of the footholds where his climbing had scuffed the dry bark away. She could smell it. It smelled like him. Woody, but also new. Like a sapling in turned soil.

Her limbs felt slow and sore, but it was a good pain, the sort of pain you got from holding a mug of hot berry tea against the side of your face on a cold day. A rich burn.

She couldn't see or hear the festival anymore, but she felt it, like a vibration in the air, its power enhanced by the wicker she'd smoked just before the urge to climb had seized her. Perhaps this was how Fessi experienced the world when she used her special senses. The tree pulsed warm against Virda's palms, and it moved to give her the grips she needed, a strong friend offering a hand to pull her up. Infinite hands. Hands clasping hands. Symbiotic. Harmonic.

They reached the canopy, clambered onto a perch, and looked up. The stars were crushed crystals against a velvet clothwrap, the colour of bleeding berries. A sailing star streaked across the sky, and then another one, further away. The full moon was close and bright, the pits and shadows clear to see on its surface. A wisp of cloud drifted in front of it and absorbed its silvery glow.

Jex howled at the moon, and from a great distance his call was returned by an arbawolf. The sound echoed across the undulating greenblack expanse of the canopy that stretched out in all directions, as far as they could see in the moonlight.

Virda lay back against the branches and waited for another sailing star. 'It's weird to think about other worlds,' she said. 'That we're not alone.'

Jex took a while to answer, and when he did, his words were slow and distant. 'We are alone,' he said. 'They don't exist here and now.'

'They do exist here and now. We're just… separated.'

Another pause. 'That's not how I think about it.'

'How do you think about it?'

He lay down next to her. 'I think this is the reality we're in, so it's the only one that matters.'

'I'm sure Kath would disagree.'

'I suppose she would. And Berro, too.'

'I don't want to talk about Berro,' said Virda.

'You're going to have to talk *to* Berro, at some point.'

'He's not ready to talk to me yet. I need to give him time.'

'Will you tell him about the temple?'

The arbawolf howled again, and further away, so far they almost couldn't hear it, another wolf answered the call.

'I suppose I will,' said Virda. 'He told me about the murder. He told me before he told anyone else.'

'This conversation has gone bad,' said Jex. 'I don't want to think about that stuff now. Not tonight.' He nuzzled his face into Virda's hair, his hot breath tingling along her scalp.

Another tiny streak of light flashed across the sky. Virda blinked, and it was gone. 'Sailing star,' she said.

Jex wriggled himself into a more comfortable position, and they gazed up together into the glittering darkness.

• • •

Berro downed most of his fourth drink as he drifted towards the edge of the clearing. The music filled his head, and the lights filled his eyes, and the drinks filled his chest with lazy bubbles. He felt warm and loose and increasingly detached from reality – invisible, almost.

'Berro,' said a voice. He turned and saw Tarov leaning against a tree, smoking a wicker. Languid. Indolent. He was perfectly at ease, the definition of casual, not a tensed muscle in his body. He was someone born and raised at a festival. He had the festival in his blood. He was the festival personified. Tarov belonged there so entirely that Berro felt suddenly conspicuous again by comparison.

'Tarov,' he said.

Tarov offered him a wicker, and against his better judgement, Berro accepted it.

'So,' said Tarov, flicking his flinter into life. 'Two parties in one year?' The dull flame throbbed and threw his cheekbones into dramatic relief for a moment.

Berro didn't bother to respond. He allowed Tarov to light the wicker and then took a tentative draw.

Tarov arched an eyebrow and let smoke curl out of his nostrils.

After a single draw, the wicker was already starting to cloud Berro's head. His hand felt pleasantly heavy as he raised it to his lips, like lifting a warm stone.

He didn't recall ever having a proper conversation with Tarov before. Tarov had only ever been one of Virda and Jex's climber friends, a familiar face around the academy, the student who sometimes took the early shift in the kitchen and leered at Berro while he ate his porridge, the person he'd embarrassed himself in front of at the field party. Tarov smiled then – that appealingly sharp smile, lopsided but working pleasantly on his face. He seemed happy to have someone to smoke with.

Virda always said such horrible things about Tarov. Why? Because he was competitive? *Perhaps he's a better climber than her.* A spark of spite crackled through Berro's mellowness.

Tarov's eyes were the colour of mossy wood. His ears were slightly pointy, to match his brows, teeth, and the cut of his smile. Berro drained the last of his drink and dropped the cup at his feet without thinking, before lifting the wicker to his lips again.

'Amazing,' said Tarov. 'I never thought I'd witness the blameless Berrovan Blue littering at a festival.'

'I'll recycle it later,' said Berro. 'Who said I was blameless?'

'Everybody,' said Tarov. 'You never slip up. You're always in control. It's who you are, isn't it?'

Did Virda and Jex speak about him to the climbers? Was this the sort of impression they gave of him? Or had Tarov been a background appraiser of Berro's academic success? They shared a few classes, certainly, but Berro never took much notice of the greens. Or the reds, for that matter, apart from Ryndel…

'I'm sorry,' he said, unsure of how else to respond. If only Tarov knew how untrue it was. Berro was not blameless, and not in control. But he didn't want to think about that. He swept aside the fuzz of dark thoughts trying to crowd into the front of his mind.

'Don't be.' Tarov's smile formed a dimple in his cheek, and Berro wanted to press his thumb to it. 'Nothing to be ashamed of. Anyway, it looks like you're relaxing. First the dancing, now the wicker.'

Berro covered his face with his hand. 'You saw the dancing? I wish nobody had seen that.'

'Why? You were good.'

'It's Kem's music that's good. Hard not to dance to that.'

'You share an alcove with him, don't you?' said Tarov, blowing a thin stream of smoke from between his lips.

'Yes,' said Berro. He looked down and mashed some leaves under his foot. Then he looked up and their eyes met for an exceptionally long moment. Berro broke the connection first and let his gaze stray over the rest of his smoking partner. *Smoking partner? Was this really happening?* Tarov was tall and lean, obviously strong from climbing, his muscled arms emerging from a plain clothwrap that wasn't fastened very securely, a sliver of his chest and stomach visible between the folds. The melter on his upper arm, which Berro had noticed before, was on full display. It was a sapling, with two branches curling towards one another. He looked up again and found Tarov's gaze still fixed in place.

Rattled, Berro took another draw of the wicker, too deep this time, and set off an explosion of coughing and spluttering that set his face aflame with embarrassment.

Tarov didn't laugh. He only smiled. His face was so warm. Wickerbloom turned time into treacle. Berro saw what was about to happen before it happened. Tarov pushed away from the tree and stepped forward. Berro's heart was a drum, and his lungs required manual operation. Tarov leaned in, tilting his head, a question in his eyes, and Berro turned his face away, an answer. He expected Tarov to smirk then, to step away, shrugging, uninterested in what little Berro was willing to offer him, but he didn't. Instead, he smiled, and the warmth of it rushed through Berro like a gulp of tea. Barely believing what he was doing, Berro raised a hand, heavy and slow, to untwist the knot in Tarov's hair, letting the dark, silky length of it fall over his shoulders.

'Hmm,' said Tarov. 'I thought so.'

He curled his strong fingers around Berro's wrist and guided him into the crowd. The air was thick and fragrant. Music pulsed in everything. They danced.

Kem was still playing. His repertoire was infinite. He had so many words to sing, so many chords to strike on his stringboard, all of them beautiful, perfect, drugging, impossible, stirring up the crowd, stirring up things inside of Berro that he hadn't even known were there. Tarov touched him, one hand hot as a brand against the skin of his arm, the other tangled with Berro's as they moved, and Berro could hardly believe that he'd never done this before, not once in all his years of being alive.

He'd always imagined it would go one of two very different ways. Either he'd suffer immediate revulsion at the touch of an affectionate hand and end the encounter right away, or he'd have all his long-standing hypotheses about himself violently negated and find himself wanton and desperate with suddenly unrepressed lust. Neither of these things happened. He didn't desire more, but he didn't desire less either. He desired exactly what he had in that moment: the hands of an interesting and attractive person on his skin in a way that suggested it might be because of his body, not in spite of it. He ran his fingers over the sapling melter on Tarov's shoulder, and Tarov didn't stop him.

Berro felt dizzy with the sensations and the discovery of so much unexplored territory. All these people existed outside of his own limited friendship group, and he'd barely noticed them before because he'd always been so fixated on the wrong things.

Tarov was focussed and intentional. He smelled like young berries under the tang of smoke. He was the most beautiful person Berro had ever seen, and he couldn't fathom why he hadn't realised this before. The wicker, the drinks, the music, and Tarov's mossy brown eyes drove the lingering horror from his mind, an entire reservoir of dread dissolving into the sights and sounds and chemicals of the festival.

Tarov moved a hand to Berro's lower back, pulling him closer. Berro let him guide them and marvelled in the relief that came from relinquishing control. An unacknowledged tension eased in his jaw and his shoulders, and it felt good, so good, *so good*. He was alive, he was waking from a bad dream, and everything was going to be all right.

And then, for just a moment, the fog cleared enough that he realised Tarov had steered them right up in front of the musicians and he had his lovely greenbrown eyes not on Berro, but on Kem, and there was a look in those eyes that Berro thought he recognised. It was the look of an emotion that defies all logic, that disregards obstacles, that consumes the host. Berro was certain that Tarov felt for Kem what Berro had once felt for Undra, and the thought was a flood of ice-cold lake water poured without ceremony over his head.

He got his hands between them and pushed Tarov away as gently as he could.

In his distracted and inebriated state, Tarov stumbled and nearly fell. Once he found his footing, he stood gaping at Berro.

'Why—?' he began, but Berro shouted over him.

'*What is this?*' Berro felt wounded and betrayed, but there was another feeling too, and it was even worse. Seeing Tarov almost fall over and now standing there looking so small despite his height made Berro feel like an awful brute.

They had Kem's attention. He hadn't missed a beat, but his lyrics were delivered less passionately this verse as he glanced back and forth between them. Tarov lifted his hand in front of him, hoping

Berro would take it and continue to dance as if nothing had happened. Berro felt sick.

'Thanks for the wicker,' he said and pushed his way back through the crowd. His eyes burned with bitter smoke, and his stomach roiled with acid.

He hated Tarov. Virda would been pleased to know it, but he wouldn't tell her, because he hated her too. He hated Kem. He hated his father for giving him these hands, incapable of subtlety. He hated Undra for ruining his life. He hated himself the most.

CHAPTER 28

Imparter Brym talked through a set of equations, highlighting details on the projection and explaining examples in her gentle, melodious voice. On Virda's left, Fessi sat diligently taking notes on her slab, and on her right, Jex slid slowly down until his head rested on the back of his seat. She elbowed him gently in the ribs, and he straightened up with a start and glared at her.

'Why did we even come to this lecture?' he hissed under his breath. 'My head is pounding.'

'We've missed so much of this class lately,' Virda hissed back. 'And I told you to drink more water before you went to bed.'

'I'm not achieving anything by being here. I can't even concentrate.'

Two rows ahead of them, Ryndel whipped around and gave them a filthy glare. Jex cringed apologetically and activated his slab. Virda saw him open a group message, and pulled out her own slab. *: where is berro? :* she typed, before Jex could write any further complaints about his hangover.

Jex– *: how would i know ?? maybe in bed like i should be :*

Virda– *: he doesn't skip lectures when he doesn't have to :*

Jex– : *he's been skipping numbers quite often … so far ahead of everyone else he doesn't need the lectures :*

Virda– : *he only skipped them when he had business with undra. :*

Jex– : *maybe he just hates us :*

Without turning to them or giving any indication that she'd been reading the messages, Fessi entered the chat.

Fessi– : *I saw Berro at the festival last night. I don't think he saw me. He was very drunk. :*

Jex– : *drunk !! i thought the field party was a once-in-a-lifetime incident :*

Virda– : *do you think he's seen undra since we argued with him? :*

Jex– : *he can't avoid the man forever . said he didn't want to go to the refrmtry, but i think undra was expecting him to … sooner or later he will have to tell undra he's not going :*

When they finally filed out of the lecture, Virda looked around the mingle. Berro's next lecture, if she remembered his timetable correctly, was Tech, and that was on the same level as Numbers. In her experience, if Berro wasn't spotted upon the first sweep of an area, then he wasn't there. Nevertheless, she looked again.

'No Berro,' she said. 'Should we be worried?'

'Maybe we just need to give him time,' said Fessi.

'I feel wrong about this whole situation,' said Jex. 'I want to know what he's said to Undra.'

'He'll let us know if anything important happens,' said Virda, as much to convince herself as for the benefit of Jex and Fessi. Fessi seemed to agree.

'He does this, you know,' said Fessi. 'He reaches out when he needs us, but most of the time, he operates alone. He detaches himself so he can focus.'

'I hope he's feeling all right.' Virda didn't feel entirely all right herself, terrified that at any moment Undra would emerge from a doorway, and she'd do something she couldn't control – scream, gasp or perhaps just allow her face to fall into a look of such contempt that it would give her away and set Undra on a warpath. What would he do, if he knew that they knew? Would he kill them? Surely not. Too risky and complicated. But he could ruin their lives in other ways. His murder of the young crosser may have been opportunistic and spontaneous, but Virda thought him fully capable of cold, calculated premeditation.

From Numbers, she and Jex went straight to a mid-morning climbing meet in the forest. Much to Virda's annoyance, all the climbers apart from Kem were late – probably sleeping off their hangovers. Kem gave a muffled greeting through a mouthful of sweet millbean bun, waving at them with the hand that held the rest of it.

'Hey,' said Jex, flopping down onto the ground beside him. Kem offered up the remains of the bun, and Jex helped himself to a chunk, smearing treacle over his fingers. Virda declined the offer with an impatient flick of her head.

'Everything all right?' asked Kem.

'Yes,' said Jex.

'No,' said Virda. 'I've got stuff to do. I can't wait around here for late climbers.'

'Anything interesting?' asked Kem, refusing to rise to Virda's aggressive tone.

'No,' she said. 'I've just got to find Berro.'

'He didn't spend the night with you at the treehouse?'

Virda's skin prickled, hot then cold. 'What? Why? What do you mean?'

'I just wondered where he'd gone, what he was up to, seeing as he wasn't in the dorm last night. Or this morning.'

Virda turned her head sharply and met Jex's wide eyes. 'He wasn't?'

'Uh, no,' said Kem. 'Last time I saw him was at the festival. He uh… I saw him leave.'

Virda blinked.

Kem swallowed the last of the bun and licked his lips thoughtfully. 'Did he maybe go somewhere interesting, for a study?' he said. 'He didn't mention anything.'

Something opened up inside of Virda then, a yawning pit of darkness, and she cast about urgently for ideas, answers, explanations she could plug it with before it swallowed her up.

Kem drew his orange eyebrows together. 'Something wrong?'

A message pinged onto Virda's pod. Jex patted his pocket and extracted his own pod with sticky fingers. It was something in the group chat. When Virda saw that the message was from Berro, she felt a surge of relief as blissful as stepping into a hot shower after a climb in the cold.

The relief was fleeting.

The message contained nothing but a blurry image with a location tag. Jex let out a small, strangled gasp. It took a few dragging moments for Virda to process what she was seeing. Then the world slid sideways.

'Kem,' said Jex. 'Kem – we'll have to climb some other time.'

The picture was of Berro's earlobe, and Berro's manicured fingers, tugging on it.

PART 3

THE ROT

CHAPTER 29

Berro awoke in the passenger seat of a skycraft, staring blankly out the window through half-closed eyes and a fog of confusion. Everything felt heavy and slow, even as his heartbeat kicked up with the onset of fear. He kept his head turned to the left, tilted down, eyes fixed on the low clouds blotting out the landscape below.

Undra was beside him, piloting the vehicle, either unaware of or indifferent to Berro's consciousness. It wasn't a particularly stable consciousness. Every few moments, Berro would forget where he was and then remember with a frisson of shock. He tried to gather the scattered bits of his mind and memories.

He'd left the festival in a state of great intoxication and misery. Someone – *Tarov* – had disappointed him, and he'd been angry with everything and everyone. Not wanting to encounter Kem in the dormitory at any point over the next twelve hours, he'd gone to the silent study area and ended up falling asleep in one of the cubicles, head on his arms. He'd awoken the next morning at the crack of dawn to a message from Undra, asking him to come to the field unit – *: Exciting developments in the project... :* – and Berro, slighted by Tarov, abandoned by his friends, and wracked by a toxic mixture of confused guilt, pride, rage and self-hatred, had decided to go.

The memories rushed back.

A new day. Head pounding, mouth dry, eyelids edged with sharp crusts. Berro felt wretched and lost. He was surprised that Undra wanted to meet him at the field unit, since the imparter had said the field unit wouldn't be needed anymore now that the specimen-collecting part of the crossing project was over.

Berro had gathered himself as best he could at the ablutions, scrubbing his hangover away with scalding water and ungentle hands. He hydrated with grim determination, forcing the liquid down his throat in great gulps until his stomach seized up. He was desperate to feel better, but he wanted to hurt himself at the same time.

He'd arrived at the field unit to find a darter parked outside and the perimeter gate unlocked, meaning he didn't need an access code to get in – useful, since he'd received an automated message telling him the old code had been cancelled. He went in, closed the gate behind him, and parked his mono at the front door.

Hearing Berro's arrival, Undra had opened the door and ushered him in, a broad smile on his face.

The field unit had been stark and stripped inside, holding nothing but the basic furniture, with two mugs of tea and a slab on the desk. All Undra's things – his samples, his papers, his clutter – had been removed.

'Berrovan!' Undra had clapped Berro on the back in an overly friendly manner that made Berro's skin crawl. 'We've had our permissions approved by the reformatory. Not that I thought we wouldn't, but they were very quick about it. Very accommodating.'

Berro had settled himself onto his seat and taken a sip of the tea, trying to decide how to respond to this news.

Undra's smile was too wide. 'So, are you ready to travel? You'd be assisting me as project partner, not as an assistant.' He tilted his head, eyes burning with excitement and expectation.

'Does that mean I'll have access to all the background information about the project?' Berro had asked. 'How and why and to what ends… I'm really very eager to understand all the technical stuff and—'

'Of course!' had been Undra's emphatic reply. 'Of course. It's all here, compiled and ready to transfer to your slab, as soon as you agree to work with me at the reformatory. It's all very confidential, I'm sure you understand.'

Berro had sipped his tea and said nothing, watching Undra's smile falter in the silence. 'Before I agree to anything,' said Berro, 'could you tell me exactly what we'd be doing at the reformatory?'

'Opt-in testing, like I told you before,' said Undra, a trace of impatience thinning his lips. 'Berrovan, I thought you were eager—'

'Oh, I am eager to know everything,' said Berro. 'I just want to understand, in detail, what's expected of me before I commit. What will the nature of the testing be? Will we be assisted or supervised by anyone at the reformatory?' He had paused for the briefest moment, considered the words that were ready to leave his mouth, and then spoke them: 'Will there be suffering?'

He was aware that he'd just stepped far over a line he'd barely come near to before. The only other time he'd asserted himself with Undra was immediately after the shooting of the young crosser, when, in his shock, he'd accused the imparter of a Code violation. He'd made up for that initial challenge, but this second challenge was bigger, in its own way. Berro's face, his tone of voice, the way he reclined slightly in his seat, presented a pure defiance that Undra had never witnessed from him before. Surprisingly, however, Undra had not appeared affected by it.

'There will be suffering, yes,' he said. 'They will suffer, because that's what we need them to do. It's not because we want them to suffer, you understand. Crossing is triggered by trauma, and so trauma needs to be engineered. And I need your help with this. And you're going to help me.'

At about the same moment that Berro had begun to grapple with the implications of Undra's shocking words, he became aware of a strange numbness in his fingertips, a thickness to his tongue, a sense that the shadows in the corners of the room were big and furry, growing, darkening, blurring the edges of his vision.

'I knew you were having second thoughts,' said Undra. 'If you're trying to record my words, you should know that the field units are equipped with marrowcore blockers for confidentiality. Without your access codes, none of your tech is functional. I hoped I was wrong about you but, unfortunately… never mind. You'll have plenty of time to think about it on the flight over. And you'll thank me in the end. You're going to be renowned and respected, Berrovan Blue. You've earned it.'

Renowned and respected.

Renowned.

Respected.

Berrovan Blue.

The words swirled, hollow and meaningless through Berro's fading consciousness as the darkness crept in from all sides and then—

—And now… Berro wasn't sure how long he'd been awake. For a while, there were slow, dreamy lapses in and out of wakefulness, and each time he surfaced, he was more convinced of the reality of his predicament. Despite the fog in his head and the yawning void of lost time that his mind scrabbled to make sense of, he was certain of several things. He was in a high-altitude skycraft. He was alone with Undra. They were heading to the reformatory at White Peaks. These certainties led Berro to the conclusion that Undra had drugged him, bundled him into the darter, and driven him up to the airfield.

He'd never agreed to this, and no degree of intoxication would've been able to elicit his consent. He knew this, because he had decided firmly against accompanying Undra to the reformatory long before their final meeting at the field unit. He'd only agreed to the meeting because it was his last chance to gather information before Undra left for the reformatory. In among his bitter, anger-scrambled thoughts, he'd imagined presenting an audio file to the council and having Undra put away without any help from Virda or the rest of his friends. But he had nothing now. Nothing at all.

There, in the stripped-down field unit, in the wake of a drunken night of disillusionment, Berro had looked right through the man and seen his corruption as clear as warpaint on his face. Something in Undra's eyes – and something in Berro's heart – had shifted dramatically, and there was a sudden, stark clarity between them that Undra must've foreseen, driving him to poison Berro's tea before he'd even arrived. Undra wasn't just a murderer who needed to be brought to justice for a single, terrible crime – he had revealed himself to be a ruthless, malevolent individual, capable of and indeed plotting to commit himself to a career of evil.

Undra would have struggled to move Berro's massive deadweight, but the imparter was nothing if not determined and resourceful. Perhaps the initial transfer of Berro into the darter had been managed while he still had some use of his legs and could be guided, a stumbling and stupid giant, into the waiting vehicle. Tender points throbbed on his upper arms and midsection – over his ribs on the left, in particular – and he imagined Undra hauling him like a sack of squash into the passenger seat of the flying vehicle, bruising him in the process.

Berro let his eyelids hang half open, his gaze unfocussed, his body slack and resting uncomfortably against the hard side of the vollop. As long as Undra assumed he was insensible, he could think in peace and try to work out what sort of danger he was in, and how to get out of it.

Undra wanted help at the reformatory, and he wanted it from Berro specifically, probably because Berro knew all the damning details of the crossing project, and using Berro meant he wouldn't have to risk revealing them to anyone else. Perhaps Undra thought he'd be able to emotionally manipulate him into cooperating, even after drugging him. Berro realised that he was counting on this. If Undra hoped for minimal resistance, then he could use that against him. If, on the other hand, Undra was expecting resistance, Berro could find himself up against a much more dangerous adversary, almost definitely armed and certainly willing to drug him again.

He didn't know what Undra needed him for… or if Undra intended for him to emerge from the project alive. On reflection, Berro guessed not. He'd demonstrated his defiance, and it couldn't be worth the risk to Undra to let him live at the end of all this. Covering up Berro's death wouldn't be difficult for such a respected academic and probably soon-to-be council member. It would be simple, clean and convenient. He'd force Berro to assist him, make him utterly complicit in whatever horrors awaited them at the reformatory, and then finish him off, snuffing out all evidence of his own misdeeds in the process. Undra wasn't aware of how much Berro had told to his friends, but none of that mattered now. They had no evidence, because Berro had failed to obtain any, and Undra's word was worth far more than all of theirs combined.

The last time Berro had been seen in a public place was at the festival, clearly drunk and unhappy. His friends would have to admit that they'd had a falling out and hadn't heard from him in a while. In all likelihood, people would say that Berro simply walked away into the great unknown and put himself out of his misery. They'd never find his body.

With deliberate gracelessness, Berro allowed a guttural groan to spill from his mouth and shifted heavily, flopping in his seat, coming to rest in a different position, mouth drooping, eyes still half-closed, his right hand resting against his left shoulder and his left hand falling against the thigh pocket of his uniform, out of sight of the imparter. Undra reacted momentarily to the sound and movement of his live cargo, but decided it was of no consequence, and continued to fly without speaking. Berro could see him in his peripheral vision now, just enough to know that Undra wasn't looking at him.

He crept his left hand slowly but surely into his pocket, heart tripping with fear as his fingers made contact with the pod. Undra really should've removed it, as a precaution. The imparter wasn't at his best, of late. He was rattled and distracted, and Berro felt heartened by this. With tiny, carefully restricted movements in the shadowy space between his thigh and the door of the vehicle, he activated the pod and navigated to the message window, selecting all social contacts and bringing up the image capture function.

His next move, similarly disguised beneath a groaning shift, was going to be much trickier than the first.

CHAPTER 30

Virda paced the length of the treehouse mingle, polishing a track along the dusty wooden floor. Jex perched on the edge of the kitchen counter, tapping his bare heels on the wood. Fessi stood against the wall, arms folded, head bowed. Kath sat on the softseat beside Magrin, who held Pips tight against her bosom, stroking the scrattin's head with the pad of her thumb.

All of them had been sent the image of Berro pulling on his earlobe, with the out-of-focus interior of a vollop skycraft behind him. The location tag placed Berro's pod within the expanse of ocean north of Mass 2 – above it, Virda hoped. Jex had accessed the academy vehicle database to confirm that a vollop had been checked out of the hangar at the airfield earlier that day.

Occupants withheld.

Destination withheld.

Even without all the information, they knew what they needed to know. Berro and Undra were on their way to the reformatory at White Peaks, and Berro was in danger.

'What do you think happened?' Kath sat with her knees up at her chin and her arms wrapped tight around them. It was her first visit to the treehouse, but the circumstances were too grim and urgent for hospitality. Virda hadn't even made any tea.

'Berro must've given himself away somehow,' said Jex. 'Maybe

Undra said something murderous, and Berro just lost control and started destroying stuff like a deranged ursa.'

'I don't think he'd have to do that much to make Undra suspicious,' said Kath. 'I wasn't sure about Undra, right from the beginning. He's watchful in that really skilful way, like he always knows something you don't know.'

Virda knew exactly what she meant. 'He has that little smile sometimes, doesn't he?' she said. 'As if he predicted something and he's amused by how right he was.'

'Yes!' said Kath. 'That's exactly— You've totally pinned it.'

Virda didn't know quite what she meant by that, but it seemed to indicate strong agreement.

'What are we going to do?' said Magrin in the fearful, tremulous voice she'd had cause to employ so often in recent days.

'We're going to fly to the reformatory and rescue him,' said Jex. When Magrin's mouth opened in horror, he added, 'Not all of us. It wouldn't be wise to fly a full vollop. You'll have to stay behind, Mag. And you too, Kath. I'm sorry.'

Magrin was visibly relieved by this, while Kath simply nodded in grim acceptance of her exclusion.

Fessi lifted her eyes to meet Kath's and smiled at her. 'You'll look after Andish, won't you? Tell her what's happening and keep her from getting worried?'

'Of course,' said Kath. 'I'll do my best. You're leaving right away?'

'I think that would be wise,' said Jex. He lifted his slab from the counter beside him and started tapping at it with clawed fingers. 'I don't have time to clear permission with Pol to use a vollop, so we're going to break some rules. I'll write to explain everything and send the message when we're in the air, or else they might stop us.'

'Do you think you'll be in trouble?' asked Kath.

'Probably.' Jex shrugged. 'But I have a good reputation, and Pol's a reasonable person. Maybe they'll even help us, when we get back.' He didn't specify what sort of help he was referring to, but Virda was struck once again by the seriousness of the situation. The danger Berro faced might very well be of the mortal variety, and they were about to follow him into it.

'We don't have any weapons,' she said, giving voice to a thought she'd meant to keep to herself.

Jex looked up quickly from his slab. 'Weapons? Well, of course we don't have any weapons!'

'Undra does,' said Virda. 'What can we do against a gun?'

'We have numbers on our side, and maybe we can reason with him,' said Jex. 'I mean, what's he going to do? Kill us all and hope nobody notices?'

When no one responded to this, Jex scratched his cheek, and a flicker of worry crossed his face. 'We'll make a plan,' he said. 'We'll have hours in the vollop to work out a strategy. He won't be expecting us. And by the time we're on our way, Pol will know everything. If we go missing, they'll know why.'

This was cold comfort to Virda. She glanced at Fessi, who hadn't spoken in some time, and saw that her eyes were closed, her face smooth and placid. Various pockets of her uniform were distorted by an assortment of items she'd crammed into them, and her fingers traced one of these shapes at her hip. She appeared to be meditating. Sensing Virda's gaze, her eyes fluttered open, and she smiled. She turned to Magrin, who had Pips cupped in her hands, tiny black nose poking out between her fingers.

'Mag, you should go with Kath to the lakehouse. Have a meal there. In fact, you'd be welcome to stay longer while I'm away, if you don't want to be alone.'

Magrin nodded, her top teeth worrying her bottom lip. 'I'll spend the evening,' she said, 'but then I must get back, to feed the creatures.' She glanced anxiously towards her bedroom door and then back to Fessi. 'Please be careful,' she whispered. 'I'm sorry, I don't mean to be pessimistic, I'm just…'

Jex placed his slab on the counter and hopped off. He made his way over to the softseat and flung an arm around Magrin's shoulders, jiggling her gently. 'We'll be fine, Mag,' he said, and he sounded confident about it. But Virda knew how talented Jex was at projecting a carefree, positive demeanour, even in the face of dire circumstances. With a jolt, she recalled him lying in the infirmary after the darter accident, stitched and bandaged, swollen and bruised, smiling through the agony between his doses of painkillers and sedatives.

'I'll pack some things,' she said, getting to her feet, a faint light-headedness taking hold of her as she made her way into the bedroom. She could hardly believe she'd soon be flying in a vollop for the first time in her life, with none of the excitement she'd anticipated for it.

As they hurried along the branch paths, Jex cut a small hole in the chest pocket of his uniform with his portable multitool. He wanted the lens and speaker of his pod exposed. 'Our hands might be occupied,' he reasoned. 'We don't want Undra to know we're recording him.'

'That's a pretty noticeable hole you've hacked into a perfectly good green uniform,' said Virda. Her thoughts churned and buzzed, sharped-edged and itchy in her skull. She'd always depended too heavily on Jex's light-heartedness to diffuse her own anxieties, and he was so serious now. The only small comfort was that she was no longer the cause of his seriousness, and though his face looked grim, he wasn't acting cold.

Fessi was silent, and it was a particular quality of silence that suggested she knew something they didn't, but had chosen not to divulge it.

'What's in your pockets?' Virda asked her, eyeing a curved shape that looked suspiciously like the handle of a tea mug.

'Lucky charms,' said Fessi. She didn't elaborate. Virda thought of Shani's box of trinkets and papers, tucked away somewhere in the commune. Those wooden charms and smooth amber beads. She wished she had a few of them in her own pockets, even though she didn't believe in luck.

They were going to rescue Berro, but they'd also be nearer to Shani, something she was certain Jex was thinking about too, even though neither of them had said it out loud. She had a vision of her cousin rushing towards her across the snow, arms wide in greeting, laughing and smiling. That wouldn't happen. It couldn't happen. They'd have no access to Shani. They'd be closer to her than they'd been since she was taken away, but no closer to getting her back. It was going to hurt.

At the academy, they occupied two monos – Jex on one, Virda and Fessi on the other – and raced to the airfield at full speed. Jex's full speed was considerably faster than Virda's, especially since she had Fessi on the footboard behind her wearing two backpacks, and they fell so far behind that by the time they reached the airfield, Jex had already coasted the vollop out of the hangar and prepped it for take-off. A side door was open and waiting for them, the marrow-core engines already humming.

Abandoning their mono, Virda and Fessi clambered into the skycraft, and Virda slammed the door shut behind them.

'First time in a vollop,' said Fessi, more to herself than to the others.

'Oh, I forgot!' Jex lit up with his usual enthusiasm. 'Two first-timers. Pity the circumstances aren't uh…' He blew out a breath. 'Are you nervous?'

'No,' said Fessi. 'I know you're a good flyer.' She settled herself onto the back seat, and Virda clambered into the front next to Jex.

They looked at each other for a moment. Virda had so many things she wanted to say to him just then, but all she said was, 'Let's go.'

CHAPTER 31

With the picture sent and his pod slipped back into his pocket, Berro focussed on calming himself. He needed to make a decision. Should he pretend to be more intoxicated than he felt to avoid interaction with the imparter for a little longer, or should he speak frankly with Undra and attempt to find out more about what was going to happen?

It was minutes later that Undra clicked his fingers at him and said, 'Berrovan? Berrovan, are you awake?'

Berro twitched in surprise and shifted to face Undra, the movement of his aching muscles unleashing an involuntary groan from his dry throat.

'Good. Don't panic. Do you know where you are? We're nearly there now. Just relax.'

'Vollop,' Berro croaked. 'Why…?'

'We're on our way to the reformatory, remember? For the second phase of the project.' Undra grinned cheerfully. 'We're going to change the world.'

He was giving Berro an opportunity to pretend that everything was good between them. It made sense that he didn't want to fight Berro, perhaps as much as Berro didn't want to fight him. They could play this game now, but it couldn't last. Berro wouldn't manage it, even if it was his only hope of staying alive. At some point in the next few hours, he'd have to reject this peace offering from the man who had drugged and kidnapped him. The man who had killed a child right in front of him.

'I feel... weird,' Berro groaned. 'Am I sick?' An act, perhaps an obvious one, but he needed to know how deeply Undra was committed to playing this game, and what he would admit to. It was like being in a nightmare with some malevolent monster in the shape of a man – the dreamer knows they're in danger, but does the monster know that the dreamer knows, and will pretending not to know give them time to escape?

'No, no, you're not sick,' Undra said. 'I'm afraid that's my doing. I'm sorry, Berrovan. I needed you, you see. I didn't mean to be so heavy-handed with the tincture. I just wanted you to be at ease, so you'd see reason. There wasn't time for us to get there organically. I know things got a bit complicated. I know you're conflicted. But I also know you're the best man for the job, and it's the most important job in the world right now. I want what's best for both of us. For all of us.'

Berro hummed in what he hoped was a contemplative but non-committal way that didn't betray the hateful pounding of his heart against his ribs. He had no love for the reformatory patients, but he had just as little desire to be involved in whatever Undra planned to do with them to create the trauma necessary to cross them into other worlds.

'I made a request that only lifetime patients be eligible for this project,' Undra said, as though reading his mind. 'They were clamouring for it, apparently. For the chance to earn their freedom.'

'Freedom?'

The word rankled, and Berro's thoughts raced through the familiar arguments. The reformatory didn't arbitrarily or unfairly take one's freedom. One lost their freedom because of their own actions, and it couldn't just be given back as a gift. They were patients. They needed to be treated until their freedom wasn't a risk to others. Why was Undra talking about 'freedom' in such a Virda-like manner? He shook his head to clear it. The deep-worn tracks of his long-held beliefs were easy to slip into. It was confusing and difficult to cut new tracks through the fog of drugs and fear. Whatever freedom meant, whatever Undra was implying, he was wrong. This was wrong. It was all wrong.

'They have no hope of freedom in this world,' Undra continued, 'but they might have a shot at freedom in other worlds.'

Berro blinked as the imparter smiled broadly at him, hands flexing on the steering bar. His posture was tight with restrained energy, his face young and open with excitement. He seemed genuine in his belief that what they were doing might benefit the people they did it to. Berro could barely contain his astonishment at Undra's self-assured and unapologetic delusion. How had he not seen it before? It was like a physical presence between them, impermeable, incomprehensible. Of course he wasn't offering the patients their freedom. He was offering them a minuscule chance to arrive alive – but only just – in a strange world and fend for themselves. He was offering them torture and overwhelmingly great odds of death. Berro didn't think they deserved freedom, but they certainly didn't deserve this either.

'What do you want me to do?' Berro asked. Everything still warped and wobbled around him under the lingering influence of the tincture Undra had slipped into his tea, and he couldn't quite wrangle his thoughts into order, or decide on how he meant to play this.

'We'll see,' said Undra. 'I've never conducted experiments like these before, so it's new territory for me too. I just know I'll need assistance – a capable pair of hands, preferably attached to someone with a capable mind, who understands the project and what's at stake.'

'I… I don't know what's at stake. I barely understand…'

'You're in no fit state for me to explain things to you right now.'

'I am!' said Berro, strangled and desperate, and then, with more control, 'I am. Please explain it to me. I want to know how it works. How you triggered the crossings.'

Undra shifted in his seat like a suncat getting comfortable. 'You know how lingas work,' he said. It wasn't a question.

Berro sifted through the inventory of his knowledge, which was difficult to access just then, drugged as he was. Techspec wasn't a field he'd devoted much focus to, but he'd read enough, and he could remember the important things from fundamental classes.

'Intentional tech,' he said, 'crafted to work with our biology, using marrowcore. Biomarric tech.'

Undra clicked his fingers. 'Exactly. Well, not exactly, but close enough. You've seen the crystals. Microtech threaded through a concentrated marrowcore power source. I had all the bits commissioned and assembled separately, with vague explanations about what I was doing. I don't think anyone suspected these little crystals could rip holes in reality.' He laughed brightly. 'It's amazing to me, how disinterested people are. Not you, of course. You always wanted to know everything.'

'I still do,' said Berro. 'So you had these filaments coded to cause explosions—'

'Implosions.'

'—Implosions. And the marrowcore crystals made the implosions rip between reality streams. But what's the trigger? The biology? The intention? How does it work?'

Undra kept his hands fixed responsibly on the steering console and his eyes forward, but his desire to gesticulate was clear. He grinned and wiggled his shoulders like an excited child. 'So this is where it gets interesting,' he said. 'It'll also have to get a bit confessional. I'm sure you'll be smart enough to understand why I couldn't tell you all of this before.'

'All of what?'

'As far as you're aware, there have been twenty-three recorded crossings into Rheta since the phenomenon was recognised for what it is. Right? And they've happened all over Rheta. Even before our study, the concentration of crossings was higher on Mass 2, but every Mass had at least one recorded crossing. Well, the truth is, actually, the number of crossings on Mass 2 is much, much, *much* higher than anywhere else – an order of magnitude higher – it's just that most of those crossings weren't recorded.'

Berro didn't know what to do with this information, so he just sat there, staring at Undra's energetic profile and waiting for him to explain.

'I came to Wooden Hill because of the higher number of recorded crossings in the region. I had a hypothesis about it early on, all based on a very obscure translation of an old Singer text, but no way to test it. I was a fresh imparter in a new post that nobody was taking very seriously at the time. People thought it was interesting, but... an indulgence. Not important to our progress. Hah!' Undra shook his head, catching Berro's eye for a moment.

'The history imparter then was a very elderly, old-fashioned man. His name was Hilbon. I ingratiated myself with him and took the lead in every Singer-related discovery in the region. He wasn't interested in the Singers. Disdainful, if anything. All he cared about was war and pre-war politics, and not even the interesting stuff. He just wanted to shuffle through dusty old papers and be left in peace, so he was very happy for me to do the fieldwork whenever a Singer ruin was discovered by some intrepid explorer. By the time the temple was found, I was an influential figure at the academy, and Hilbon was almost on his deathbed, so it wasn't difficult to keep it a secret. One or two trusted assistants and a very accommodating friend at the council – that was all I needed.'

Berro blinked, waiting for everything to click into place, but the pieces of information just floated, knocking uselessly against each other. 'The temple?'

'A Singer temple,' said Undra. 'I'll tell you about it in detail one day, but all you need to know for now is that it proved my hypothesis correct.'

'What was your hypothesis?'

Undra cleared his throat dramatically. 'My hypothesis was that the Singers weren't just a bunch of linguistic anarchists. They weren't just chanting randomly for the fun of it. Those chants were *intentional.* They didn't have the reliability of coded tech, but combined with marrowcore, they could catalyse results even without any tech involved.'

'What…' Berro shook his head. 'I don't understand.'

'The Singers were triggering crossings, Berro. Their weird religion was all about transcending reality by splitting it open and letting other realities spill in. Everyone thought that was figurative, that they were just hallucinating on wickerbloom and mushrooms and singing about the other worlds, but it was literal. They'd figured out a way to empower their voices with marrowcore, found places in the forest where marrowcore seams deep underground resonated with their songs and let them sense the presence of other streams. The temple was the most potent place of all, and they made it even more potent by building a marrowcore altar. An amazing thing, covered in crystals. In the temple, their singing didn't just give them a sensory connection with other worlds – sometimes it literally ripped holes into those worlds. And sometimes people fell through. Dead, I assume, but it hardly matters either way. They worshipped these crossers and buried them among their own dead at various Singer sites. After the Singers were wiped out in the war, the temple was empty for decades. I was the first imparter to enter it, and I was ready.'

'Ready?'

'I reproduced the sounds. I activated their altar. I triggered crossings, just like the Singers did. Except I didn't have a chorus of practised singers, so I had to use a bit of tech.'

Undra basked in this for a moment. He turned his head to gaze at Berro, as though Berro was his closest friend and ally, and he was awaiting praise for his incredible revelation.

'What happened then?' Berro asked.

'The temple was compromised. The altar had to be destroyed. I'd learned what I needed from it anyway. I wanted to figure out how to replicate the phenomenon outside the temple, without such heavy reliance on marrowcore. I spent years engineering the microtech, getting everything manufactured and prepared. It guessed that Singer sites would be the best places to test my work. I was right. I made a crossing happen in the middle of the forest, miles away from the temple. But I was…' Undra chuckled self-consciously, 'I was too famous by then. I'd made a bit of a name for myself through lectures and articles, and I couldn't risk tramping around dragging a corpse like some sort of mad killer, and I didn't want to open the study up yet. I didn't need an ethics committee getting in the way before I'd even refined the technique, or got near to the ultimate goal of *crossing out*.'

'And that's where I came in.'

'Yes! And I'm grateful, Berro, don't think I'm not grateful. I won't pretend you haven't disappointed me recently, but that doesn't undo my gratitude.'

Berro clenched his teeth together. There was a dull, persistent ringing in his ears. 'Was it all a test?' he asked. 'Sending me out there to fetch those bodies…'

'A test? No, I needed to refine the technique. I had various sets of crystals with slightly different coding to test, and I needed more artefacts for stage two.'

'Artefacts.'

'You see, I have an idea,' said Undra. 'Crossers and things from other worlds have a strange sort of separateness from native Rhetari people and objects. It's something to do with their lack of exposure to our marrow. They don't have any of our marrow in their cells or materials. People with strong marric sensitivities have written about this in studies of crossers and otherworld artefacts. I think, I hope, that we might be able to use these artefacts like homing devices. If we cross someone while they're wearing or holding or just touching something from another world, perhaps that item will increase the likelihood that their destination is the world the object came from originally. Things want to be with other things like them. Cohesion. Like attracts like. It should – it *could* be a force just strong enough to override the randomness of the process, at least some of the time.

'It's going to take a lot of practise, a lot of trial and error, but I want to devise a method of crossing someone along with a disposable artefact and then immediately triggering an inward rupture at the same spot, to bring them back. It probably won't work every time, but I only need it to work once or twice to figure out if my hypothesis is correct. They'd return covered in samples – dirt, mud, pollen, whatever – and then I could test those samples against the artefact I used and see if they're from the same world.' He was so excited, so much like his best self, the Undra who inspired, informed and entertained.

Berro felt the terrible contradiction of it like a wound in his chest. 'But how… how will we—'

'Relax, Berrovan. All in good time. I'd suggest getting a bit more rest while we're in the air. Would you like some water?'

He lifted a drinking bottle from the holder beside his seat and offered it to Berro, who considered asking whether it was drugged. It couldn't be, he reasoned. Surely Undra himself had been using it throughout the journey. Berro was so, so thirsty.

'Thank you,' he croaked, taking the bottle and drinking deeply until the desperate edge of his thirst was soothed. He handed the bottle back to Undra and sagged into his seat, surrendering himself to silence and the inevitable.

He awoke to the sound of Undra humming, and the breathtaking view of a sprawling dead city below them. His muscles had loosened during his dreamless sleep as the last of Undra's drugs worked their way through his kidneys and into his bladder, but now his whole body tightened.

This dead city could only be the ruins of Osgen, the largest no-zone on Mass 2, where no efforts at reclamation had been made. The remains of the city hadn't even been razed as most other cities had. Complicated knots of elevated transport tracks and crumbling high-rise buildings choked by vegetation rose like monsters out of the wild earth as far as the eye could see, and Berro's heart skipped fearfully at the sheer massiveness of it.

How many people had lived here before the war? How many people had died here? It was almost inconceivable to Berro that this alien ex-urban landscape, built on a scale incomparable to any current settlement, had ever been a living, thriving part of Rhetari culture. It was as though Undra had taken his Realities project to unexpected heights and piloted the vollop through a fissure into an entirely different world.

'We're almost there,' said Undra. 'Quite a sight, isn't it? Almost no one ever sees it, apart from reformatory workers and patients on their way in.'

'It's incredible,' Berro breathed. He wished he was sharing this profound experience with someone he didn't want to murder with his bare hands.

'The city centre hasn't been explored since the war, at least not by anyone who actually survived. The marrowcore is so strong there, it starts to work its way through anti-marrow gear – even the industrial-strength suits – and you can't make it out in time on foot. And no vehicles work in there. You don't even need to touch the ground to be affected by it. We're fine up here, obviously, but I've read some astonishing things about Osgen. If they wanted to reclaim it, they'd have to aerial bomb the place with six times more neutraliser per leap than they've used on any other place.'

Berro pressed his face against the window and watched the towering ruins scroll beneath them, lush with evergreen life. Despite its vitality, it still made him think of a giant old-world graveyard – fully clothed corpses in lacquered boxes, buried beneath big carved stones and statues in tumbledown rows upon rows upon rows. How any population at any time could've thought that less barbaric than a clean mulching, he couldn't fathom.

The Osgen city ruins spread like a malignant growth up the lower slopes of the mountains, forming a toxic barrier between the reformatory and the rest of Rheta. Virda would've argued that the lack of reclamation was intended to keep people away from their loved ones – in practical terms, you couldn't visit the reformatory without access to a high-altitude vehicle, unless you were to hike on foot through precarious gaps in the no-zone. But even if the city barrier was intentional, it could just as easily have been a deterrent for murderous reformatory escapees. Berro shuddered.

If I were to escape from this nightmare, how long would I survive on the mountain, or in the poisoned city?

Eventually, the slopes below gave way to sheer faces of rock and treacherous crags, and by the time the vollop made its descent towards a level surface high up among the cold jagged peaks, the city was out of sight.

The reformatory building came into view, gripping the mountainside like a dull crab. It had a defensive ugliness about it. Upon more careful inspection, Berro could see that the structure was cut into a wedge of the rock face. They were approaching what seemed to be the back end of the building, a blank, windowless façade that jutted out of the rock, with a single door. He caught a glimpse of the massive front part of the building, which emerged from the slopes some distance away before the view was obscured by their descent. The thought of the windowless darkness of the section encased by the mountain sent a spike of cold through his body. Did they keep the patients in that section? Surely not. From what he had seen, albeit momentarily, the front section was enormous and had lots of windows. That must be where the patients lived. The back end would be the labs and offices – that's why they were landing there.

Berro sensed tension in Undra as the vollop made its final descent. He supposed the imparter would be wondering whether he'd take the opportunity to throttle him as soon as they were on solid ground and his piloting skills were no longer required. He noticed for the first time the familiar shape of the gun in Undra's hip pocket. A burst of crazed laughter bubbled up inside him, and he disguised it behind a choking cough and covered his face with his hands.

'Are you all right?' Undra asked, eyes fixed on the console.

'Yes,' said Berro. 'I'll be fine.'

'Good.'

Undra was a skilled pilot, unsurprisingly, and the vollop touched down onto the pristine blanket of snow with barely a bump, the engines immediately winding down. The machine sounded relieved to be back on solid ground, but Berro did not feel any relief. He swallowed against a sickly pulse in his throat.

Undra reached into the footwell and pulled out a large, smart-looking backpack. He drew the gun from his pocket, slipped it into the backpack, and slung it over one shoulder before opening the vollop and dismounting gracefully onto the snow.

Berro glanced up at the ominous reformatory door, glaring down at them from the top of a gentle slope he hadn't perceived during the descent. Nobody had emerged from the building to greet them, and everything was silent in the absence of the engine sound – it was a dense silence with a presence, like hands pressed against his ears. He felt suffocated by another rapid upwelling of terror and considered refusing to get out of the vehicle. But what would that achieve? All he had left was his little act of cooperation, which might or might not fool Undra into trusting him again… to what end, Berro couldn't say. And besides, Undra had a gun, and they were on a frozen mountain, so he clambered out of the vollop into the frigid air and, stumbling and shivering, followed Undra up the slope.

'It'll be warmer inside,' said the imparter, when Berro caught up with him. 'You don't need to worry about luggage. I have everything we need.'

Berro couldn't help but wonder if Undra was referring to a large body bag rather than a change of clothes. He stumbled over his own feet, which felt oversized and numb after the vollop ride, and came down hard on his knees in the snow. Undra turned immediately and offered him a hand. Berro looked up at his face and saw the old Undra there, kind and concerned, but he couldn't bring himself to reach out, so he got back up without assistance.

Undra sighed. 'I'm sorry, Berrovan. I know you must be conflicted.'

An understatement, if ever there was one.

'I really need to piss,' said Berro, and Undra's face shuttered, his lips going thin.

He glanced up at the door and then back at Berro. 'You can use the facilities inside, or you can just...' He jerked his head away from the path.

Considering it might be his last chance to experience fresh air and the outdoors before his untimely death, Berro veered off the path and unfastened the front of his uniform. With his back to Undra, he pissed into the pristine snow, gulping in lungsful of frozen air and trying desperately not to cry.

Undra unlocked the outer door of the reformatory with a beep of his pod against an unfamiliar type of marrowcore pad and stood aside to allow Berro entry before he eased the door shut behind them. Berro heard the lock engage and braced himself with a hand against the wall to keep his balance.

The look Undra directed at him was unsettling, and at Berro's involuntary grimace, the membrane of pretence between them ruptured.

'It doesn't have to be a big ugly mess, Berrovan. If you could just put aside your misgivings, take into consideration everything we've achieved together and how much easier this will be if we're allies, *true* allies...'

The sound of footsteps approaching terminated his monologue.

Berro turned and considered their location for the first time. The corridor in which they stood was lit with small, diffuse lamps set at intervals into the ceiling. They cast weak pools of light on the floor, and shadows gathered between them. The entire corridor – ceiling, walls and floor – was painted in a thick, rubbery-looking coat of lifeless pale grey. It was so predictable a choice for the interior of an institution like the reformatory, it seemed absurd to Berro that someone had actually selected it.

A smartly uniformed man with a slab under his arm hurried towards them, ominously illuminated and then thrown into shadow over and over as he passed beneath the lamps.

'Imparter Undra,' he said. 'My apologies for not being present at your arrival. You're earlier than I expected.'

'Good winds over Osgen,' said Undra, abruptly jovial. 'Is everything prepared?'

'Yes, yes, indeed,' said the man, coming to a halt in front of them. 'Everything is ready. You must be the project assistant? Berrovan?' He smiled at Berro, revealing a set of perfectly straight white teeth that looked slightly longer and sharper than they needed to be. 'I'm Facilitator Pegrel.'

Berro nodded and gave a quick bow. 'A pleasure to meet you. Any chance we might have a quick tour before we settle in? I must confess, I've always been curious about the reformatory.'

Undra's head turned sharply towards him – he hadn't been expecting Berro's sure tone or clear voice – but before he could say anything, Pegrel was speaking again, obviously convinced by Berro's false expression of authority. Undra couldn't contradict it now without thoroughly embarrassing Pegrel.

'Of course, of course!' said Pegrel. 'I'd be delighted. I was rather assuming you'd like a tour. In fact, we expected your vollop to land at the front entrance, which is why I'm little a late to greet you. Lots of corridors, you see!' He chuckled. 'This rear section of the building – the grey wing – is mostly unoccupied. We use it for storage, offices, labs, and projects like yours, of course, but the reformatory proper, where all the patients live, is on the other side, as I'm sure you're aware. Right this way. Imparter, would you like to leave your backpack in a saferoom for the tour?'

'Oh, no, thank you,' said Undra, impatiently. 'It's not heavy.'

Pegrel nodded. 'Very well.'

Berro pointedly avoided Undra's eyes as they followed Pegrel back the way he'd come, taking a right turn at the first junction. He'd bought some time, perhaps, but he could feel the imparter's irritation radiating off him like heat.

Berro had no idea what consequences awaited him at the end of any path he might choose to take. He didn't know whether he could trust the man they'd just met. He didn't know if he could survive a physical altercation with Undra and the gun. He didn't know whether resistance or cooperation was the safer, better strategy, either for himself or for the reformatory patients he expected to find at their final destination, once the tour was over and the work began.

He quickly lost track of the turns they took down grey corridors lined with grey doors, as he tried to formulate a plan. He'd made no headway by the time their corridor terminated at a set of doors with the same sort of marrowcore pad he'd seen at the entrance to the building. Pegrel opened the door with his pod and ushered them through.

'Welcome to the Reformatory at White Peaks,' he said.

The part of the building they now stepped into was in the section that protruded from the rocky slopes onto a snow-laden plateau, and this afforded it some natural light through the high windows on one side. The effect wasn't cheering. The light was cold and stark. Berro shivered. Opposite the windows were several large archways leading into wide, empty corridors lined with doors, some of which had little round windows built into them. At a couple of these windows in the nearest corridor, Berro saw faces looking out and averted his eyes.

'These are the, uh,' he gestured, 'sleeping quarters?'

'Yes,' said Pegrel, leading them past the corridors. 'Each patient is afforded their own space, for peace and privacy.'

'Are there any communal rooms?'

'Communal bedrooms? No. We're not in the business of crowding them together like cattle before the Chaos.' Pegrel chuckled.

Berro thought of the dormitories at the academy, and how the students who shared his alcove were part of the fabric of his social life – a social life he wished he hadn't taken for granted. There was nothing oppressive about the dormitory setup. They shared a space quite amiably. Conflicts were rare, but if they did happen, the academy would happily relocate a student to another alcove at their request. With each reformatory patient in their own little room, how often did they get to speak to one another? Berro wanted to walk down one of the corridors and have a peek into the windowed rooms, but this didn't appear to be part of Pegrel's itinerary. Instead, they kept walking until forced to take a left turn into a hallway where several enforcers milled around in black uniforms.

Near to a large, reinforced, and heavily guarded door that Berro guessed was the main entrance Pegrel had been expecting them to arrive at, a woman was on her hands and knees scrubbing the floor. She wore a tatty uniform in a horrible brownish purple shade, the sort of colour that would result from mixing all three academy colours together. Her thin dirty hair hung over her face as she scrubbed and scrubbed with raw, cracked hands. She didn't look up as they passed her, and though Pegrel had exchanged muted greetings with some of the enforces, he didn't comment on her presence. It was as though she didn't exist at all. Could she be Virda and Jex's commune cousin, Shani? No, of course not. She was too old, surely. Perhaps Shani was behind one of those windowed doors.

Berro shuddered and turned to Undra to see if he'd noticed the scrubbing woman, but Undra was looking away towards a set of double doors, one of which was propped open with a stone stopper. There was movement in the vast room beyond and then, quite suddenly, there was sound as well.

Pegrel stopped dead in his tracks as a voice rang out.

'Medical! Medical!'

An enforcer ambled through the open door, obscuring whatever was happening behind him. He acknowledged the facilitator and his two guests standing still in the hallway and said, 'Pegrel,' as though nothing was amiss.

'What's through there?' asked Undra.

'The dining area and kitchens,' said Pegrel, and then, to the enforcer. 'What's going on in there, Devor?'

'Adverse effects. First meal since a test. Don't think his stomach was ready for it. Ah, here's medical.'

Two white-uniformed officials hurried into the hallway, and the enforcer, Devor, stepped aside to let them into the dining area. Berro had just enough time to see a man in purple convulsing on a floor slick with bright blood before Devor kicked the stone stopper aside, and the door swung shut. Berro felt something swing shut inside of himself too.

Pegrel and Undra had continued walking, but Berro stood rooted to the spot.

'What's going to happen to that man?' he asked. From the corner of his eye, he saw the scrubbing woman falter and fall still.

'Oh, he'll be tended to,' said Pegrel. 'Come along.'

Berro followed them out of the hallway and into another corridor, where Pegrel showed them the ablutions as though they were something worth bragging about. They were awful – grey and cold and sharp-cornered, with open bioclosets ranged along one wall and a painfully strong chemical tang in the air.

Undra's lip curled in distaste as he surveyed the scene. 'Very impressive,' he said. 'Forgive my impatience, Pegrel, but I think it's time to get to work.'

Pegrel's smile tightened as Undra turned and began walking back the way they'd come. He attempted to draw the imparter's attention to another door, stammering something about patient work opportunities and how he'd love to show them more, but Undra was already out of the door, Berro following close behind him. He hadn't managed to buy as much time as he'd hoped.

The arrived back in the hallway just in time to witness the two officials in white dragging the bloody man in purple out of the dining hall by his legs. The man's face was grey, and his head lolled to one side, blood drooling along his cheek.

Pegrel stood behind Undra babbling and fidgeting, trying to get his guests to look away from the scene, but to no avail.

'Where are they taking him?' asked Berro.

'To his room,' said Pegrel. 'He'll get— He'll have the medics attend— Oh, for goodness sake, patient, clean that up, would you?' This last order was barked in the direction of the scrubbing woman, who quickly hauled herself to her feet and dragged her bucket towards the fresh bloody smear on the floor.

'My apologies,' said Pegrel, cringing and slightly red-faced. Berro didn't know what impression he'd been hoping to make with this grim tour, even without the scene that had just unfolded, but clearly, he'd failed. 'Shall we go to your lab then?'

'Please,' said Undra, in a voice unaffected by what they'd just witnessed. Berro, meanwhile, couldn't have spoken if he wanted to. His blood pounded in his throat, and his hands trembled so hard he had to hook his thumbs into the hip pockets of his uniform to keep them still. As he followed Pegrel and Undra in the wake of the dying man, Berro fought back the crowding memories of the young crosser in the forest, whose death he could feel again as though the boy was back underneath him, flailing and then dying as the bullet entered his skull. Between these flashing memories, he thought of Virda, her face, her rage, and the fact that she'd been so right, *so right*, about everything. The reformatory was not a good place, and nobody deserved to be detained here. The malevolent wrongness of the place hung in the air like a bad smell, toxic and undeniable.

Berro wanted to be sick, to lie down, to stop remembering, to stop existing at all, but he couldn't. His agitated breath and blood, and his probable proximity to his own death at the hands of his imparter, made him feel more painfully alive than ever before. He considered grabbing Pegrel by the arm and begging him to detain Undra for his crimes, but he knew it would come to nothing. Undra would laugh. Pegrel would offer to find Berro his own purple uniform right away and order the enforcers to shove him into one of the unoccupied rooms. As they passed those corridors again, Berro tried to catch another glimpse of the dying man, hoping for some reassurance that he'd live, but there was no sign of him or of the white-uniformed officials who had dragged him away.

They re-entered the grey wing, and as they wove through the labyrinth of identical windowless corridors, Berro caught his breath, stilled his hands and, with immense effort, regained his composure. When Pegrel opened a grey door, indistinguishable from the doors on either side of it, with a square metal key and ushered them inside, Berro was just able to control his reaction to the sight that greeted them.

The room was painted floor to ceiling in the same institutional pale grey as the rest of the wing and lit by glaring overhead strip lamps that caught brightly on the polished surfaces of the workbenches and cabinets along the walls. In the open centre of the room were two adjustable infirmary beds, each with an unconscious person strapped onto it. A man and a woman. They wore nothing but ill-fitting, single-piece undergarments in a muddy shade of brown.

'Your lucky crossers,' said Pegrel, beaming as though he were introducing Berro and Undra to a couple of his dearest friends. 'Their paperwork is all there on the counter, for reference.'

Berro went immediately to the papers and ruffled through them. 'I would've liked to have spoken to them before they were sedated,' he said, managing to infuse his voice with some authority, and Pegrel gave an apologetic grimace. The man still hadn't figured out the dynamic between the imparter and his assistant, and seemed willing to defer to Berro as an extension of Undra himself.

'We opted for the slow-acting, long-lasting variety of sedative, to suit your specific purposes,' said Pegrel.

'It's not a problem,' said Undra. 'In fact, it's better this way. We don't have to waste more time or get too caught up answering difficult questions.'

'Surely they have the right to ask questions?' said Berro, maintaining his tone in defiance of Undra's thunderous expression.

Pegrel gave Berro a strange look, and his eyes darted to Undra, who was inspecting one of the sedated patients, two fingers pressed to the pulse in the man's neck.

'Thank you, Pegrel,' he said. 'Everything seems to be in order. And we have the wing to ourselves until we're done?'

'There might be some activity in medical, but that's some distance away from these labs, and nobody will come anywhere near here,' said Pegrel, visibly relieved to be answering an easy question. 'Most of the wing is permanently empty anyway. It's an old Osgen military bunker, as you know, from before, and we don't need nearly as much of it as they did—' Quickly gauging Undra's impatience, Pegrel cut himself short and adjusted his uniform unnecessarily. 'We understand the importance and sensitivity of this project, so you won't be interrupted, and all reformatory personnel will stay out of your way unless you need us for anything. You have our comlink.'

Undra nodded. 'It's all very much appreciated. And thank you for the tour. Most elucidating.'

Pegrel's face flushed. It occurred to Berro that whatever power this man held at the reformatory, it didn't prevent him from being starstruck by the presence of Rheta's handsome foremost expert in Realities. The facilitator handed the square key to Undra and gave small, rather pathetic bow. 'I'll leave you to it!' he said and excused himself quickly, allowing the door to lock behind him.

Undra rounded on Berro right away. 'I think we need to get a few things cleared up,' he said. 'I want your help. I want your cooperation. But I don't need it. And I won't tolerate any more of your attempts to sabotage this project.'

'Why did you bring me here?' Berro felt calm now, but disconnected, hollow. 'After you murdered a child right in front of me, after you drugged me, and took me away from the settlement against my will, what did you think my reaction would be? Compliance?'

'I thought your ambition might steer you back onto the right path,' Undra snarled. 'You disappointed me bitterly, but I gave you another chance. I thought you were intelligent enough to make the right decision. I was wrong about that.'

A sense of inevitability had washed the panic away, and Berro felt nothing but a cold, dead surrender. 'No, that's not it,' he said. 'You never thought I was intelligent. You thought I was useful, and as soon as I stopped being useful, you needed to make sure I didn't become dangerous. You couldn't risk me turning against you in a public way. Even though you're important and respected, and you'd be perfectly capable of squashing any allegations I made against you, there'd always be that little stain, that little bit of doubt. I'm a successful student without a single controversy on my record, apart from one episode of marrowcore poisoning that was *entirely* your fault. There would be people at the academy who'd support me, and you know it. Ryndel, my friends, my other imparters. You couldn't risk leaving me behind to reach that conclusion for myself, so you took me with you. You're going to kill me, aren't you?'

'I'll do what I have to do to finish this project!' said Undra, face reddening. 'You might have a flawless record, but your mother certainly didn't, and I think most people would find it rather difficult to believe that you have no sympathies for her points of view. They're not popular opinions, Berrovan. You know that. These people…' he gestured towards the unconscious unfortunates lashed to the beds, 'they did terrible things. I selected them myself. Man on the left? Serial rapist. The woman drowned her own child in a river. They're about to be more useful, more worth the space they take up and the resources they consume than they've ever been before in their miserable lives. Don't deny them this chance at redemption. Make yourself useful, and you're welcome to be a part of it. Get in my way, and I'll get you out of it.'

'So my options are to help you and be complicit in whatever violations you're about to commit, or… to die?'

Undra made a sudden noise of furious exasperation and

slammed his fist down on one of the work benches. 'There will be no Code violations!'

'I never said anything about *Code* violations,' said Berro. 'But there will be those, too, if you kill me.'

'Then don't make me kill you,' said Undra, and Berro felt oddly satisfied to have extracted this nugget of truth from him.

This was how much the project meant to Undra. Despite all his protestations to the contrary, he was, in fact, willing to make the ultimate Code violation – the purposeful killing of a fellow Rhetari citizen – to protect his work. It wasn't surprising, really. The Code that Undra had defended up until that moment clearly had very little ethical framework, and comfortably accommodated the killing of people from other worlds and the drugging and kidnapping of people from his own. What separated that from a true Code violation was a technicality, semantics, an invisible membrane.

The Cohera.

Berro thought of how he had himself, so recently, dismissed the role of the Cohera with confidence and disdain, and his shame now was a block of ice in his gut. His anger at his parents and the role politics had played in the way their story unfolded had set Berro's mind on those tracks he'd never meant to build and hadn't had the strength of character to dismantle once his thoughts and opinions had momentum along them.

Undra reached into his breast pocket and pulled out a small cloth, which he used to dab his damp forehead. Berro was so distracted by his own churning thoughts that he missed the significance of a change in Undra's posture and wasn't prepared to dodge Undra's sudden lunge forward.

The imparter's hand, still clutching the cloth, slapped into Berro's face, and Berro felt something there in Undra's palm, an oversized blister hidden in the folds of the material, just as it ruptured against his skin. His eyes and nose filled with an acrid, blinding moisture and then the pale grey walls were melting and the room shrinking and Berro slid down the face of a polished cabinet and slumped onto the floor at Undra's feet.

The darkness held him, heavy and dense. It swam and parted at intervals, and he could see the room from below, the painfully bright lamps searing down on him, the polished metal struts of the beds, the imparter's legs, moving. Along the edge of a workbench, various items were arranged – bits of cloth and metal and broken tech, twists of dirty paper and scraps of plastic trash. Disposable artefacts. These weren't the sorts of things Undra had on display in the cabinets in his office. These were the things that had been recovered from the trouser pockets of dead crossers and the forgotten depths of their backpacks, worthless apart from their otherworld origin. Imported garbage.

Was that Undra's voice? An incomprehensible murmur… '*Ah! Uuuuhh ah. Uuuuoooa.*' The darkness thickened and closed in on Berro once again.

The next time it opened, Berro was aware of a smell, tangy and bitter and deeply unpleasant. He felt rather than heard the groan leaving his throat. The imparter's feet appeared in front of his face, boots flecked with blood. Undra said something to him, but he could distinguish only two words, '*awake… marrowcore…*' and a sound like a musical chord, three notes in harmony. The air felt electric.

The bloody boots moved away and Berro held onto this flimsy thread of consciousness with all his might. From the corner of his eye, he sensed a sudden movement, heard a fleshy impact and felt the world turn inside out. Was it the darkness returning? No, this was different. The space around him inhaled sharply and then exhaled. There was a loud crash and a metal bed shifted violently. It felt like the room had bulged outwards for a moment before snapping back into shape. The smell of sand, of burning metal, of hot blood filled Berro's nose, and just before he slipped back into the abyss, he heard Undra cry out, 'We did it!'

CHAPTER 32

The air was still and bitterly cold, and Virda's teeth chattered so violently she feared they might shatter in her jaw. Snow lay thick and bright on the ground. It must not have snowed in some time, though, because the footprints leading away from Undra's vollop were clear and defined, as if they'd been pressed into the pristine whiteness only moments ago. There were two sets of prints: one steady and regular, and the other messy and random, with occasional long gouges as though the person had half-dragged themselves forward.

Berro.

At one point, the messy tracks veered off sideways to a patch of yellow snow before joining the other set leading up the hillside to a single dark door in the blank façade of the back end of the reformatory building. The door was unguarded, at least on the outside. Virda tried to imagine Berro and Shani somewhere inside this hostile-looking structure, but the only images she could come up with were too grim to linger on.

'We're just… going to walk in there?' Jex's voice was low and wrong in the yawning silence around them.

'It's probably locked,' said Virda.

'Oh, well, I guess we should just fly home then,' said Jex.

Fessi held out her hand. 'Give me your multitool.'

Jex fished the tool from his pocket and pressed it into Fessi's palm. She climbed the hill in silence, placing her feet within the existing tracks instead of making new prints. Virda and Jex followed her.

When they reached the door, Fessi paused. Her eyes fluttered closed for a moment, and she appeared to be listening with her whole body, not just her ears. The moment passed, and her eyes opened. She gave a single nod and then confronted the marrowcore lock, glaring at it as if she could melt it with her eyes. She put two fingertips onto the pad, even though there was clearly no fingerprint technology involved. Virda caught Jex's eye for a moment, but neither of them said anything. With her other hand, Fessi raised the multitool and, without warning, stabbed it precisely between her fingertips into the pad. The pad shattered into shiny shards that tinkled into the snow and the door unlocked with a soft click. Fessi pushed it open to reveal a dark, empty corridor. Without comment, she slipped Jex's multitool into her breast pocket. She'd stuffed her pockets with 'lucky charms', but apparently had forgotten to pack a multitool. Or perhaps, thought Virda, she'd had known that Jex was carrying one before they'd left the treehouse.

After a last glance at the world behind them – the vast mountain and the endless open sky, the two vehicles, silent and waiting – they stepped inside, and Jex shouldered the door shut behind them.

The silence inside the reformatory building filled their ears with the sound of their own breathing and heartbeats and tentative footsteps as they made their way down the featureless corridor before them. They reached a junction and Virda stared to the left and then to the right and then at Fessi.

'Right,' said Fessi. She took a tinted wax lip balm from one of her pockets, smeared a small spot of it onto the right-hand corner of the wall and led the way.

Grey, windowless doors lined the grey windowless walls along this section of corridor. Everything was silent and still and felt ominously abandoned. Virda could see Jex's tension, the unusually angular cut of the clenched muscles under the pale fluff at his jaw. Sensing her gaze, he glanced at her and grimaced, as if to say, *What are we doing? Why are we here?*

Fessi paused, and they stopped alongside her, searching her face for information. She drew in a deep breath and released it slowly. An odd tremor ran through her, and for a moment she was difficult to look at. 'We're going the right way,' she said. 'They're not far from here. But we're not going to like what we find.'

Virda's stomach turned. 'What are we going to find?'

'I can't see through walls,' said Fessi. 'I don't know what we're going to find.'

Virda opened her mouth to argue, then closed it again. 'Fine,' she said. 'Let's go.'

Fessi nodded curtly, and they continued down the corridor, completely exposed and vulnerable should someone step out from one of the rooms. It didn't seem likely, though. The place was deathly quiet.

Fessi guided them down a corridor to the left, and another to the right, leaving her tinted balm smears on each corner as she went. When they reached their destination, Virda knew it before Fessi confirmed the fact. Something had made the hairs on the back of her neck stand up – a sound? A smell? A change in the air? She didn't know what it was, but she knew that this corridor wasn't abandoned, and that something was happening behind one of the doors.

Fessi identified the door – the third one on the left – and they stood some distance away from it, staring. Virda felt naked and fragile. Her heart beat high in her chest, in her throat, in her face, in her brain, scattering her thoughts. Fessi wrapped a hand around Virda's wrist and pressed it lightly.

'Are we doing something stupid?' Jex whispered.

'We're doing something necessary,' said Fessi.

'But I don't think we're prepared… Are we going to get him out?'

Fessi was no fortune-teller – something she had to remind them of from to time – but Virda was grateful that she humoured Jex now. 'We're going to get him out,' she breathed. 'This entire wing of the building is empty, apart from that room, so I don't think we'll have any other company, at least not immediately. My guess is that Undra's ordered the place cleared for his work. He'd have the authority for that. I'm going to pick that lock as quickly and quietly as I can – shouldn't take more than a second – and then we're going to enter together, all three of us at the same time.'

'And then?' asked Jex.

Virda's throat burned with fear.

'And then… whatever happens, happens.'

• • •

Berro woke, and his situation revealed itself one piece at a time. He lay on something wet. His arms and legs were bound, but he barely had the strength to move them anyway. His vision was smeared and blurry, as though he peered through filthy greenglass, but his sense of smell was sharp and terrible. The chemical tang in the air burned his nostrils and tingled unpleasantly down the back of his throat. His head throbbed. A warm hand took one of his own. He rolled his dry eyeballs down and blinked and blinked until a person came into focus beside him. Imparter Undra, pressing Berro's fingertips against the screen of a slab and then another device…

Thwuck.

Bloodmark. The pain was delayed by several seconds, then it went through him like a warm tide. He turned his head slowly and settled his eyes upon the bed there, and everything became clearer. On the bed lay the man from before, the sedated patient, the serial rapist. He was dead now, there was no doubt about it. His body was mutilated, his face gone. He was no longer bound to the bed but draped over it, the liquid parts of him soaking into the thin mattress and dripping onto the floor.

Berro was strapped onto the other bed, the one that had

previously been occupied by the woman. Where was she? He didn't know if he'd asked the question out loud or if Undra could read his mind, but Undra started speaking then, close to Berro's ear, his breath hot as pain.

'Patient One came back, though a little worse for wear. Patient Two didn't come back, but I know what I did wrong with her. There's a trick to it. It's a matter of balance. With him I went too far – with her, I didn't go far enough. One more attempt. That's all I need.' He squeezed Berro's fingers in a way that felt fatherly. 'We're going to make history, Berrovan.'

'No,' Berro croaked. 'Please.'

'You'll come back!' said Undra. 'I know how to do it now. You'll come back, and you'll be the first Rhetari ever to have left our world and returned to tell everyone about it.'

Berro shook his head, and his brain jangled. 'I won't… consent.'

'Oh, but you already have,' said Undra, raising the slab. His face swam out of focus, and when it came back, he was smiling.

Through it all, Undra was still handsome, bright-eyed, his hair stylishly mussed, his smile knowing. He looked like a clear-thinking, sharp-acting man of the world. A pioneer, a protagonist. His body projected what he wanted the world to think about his mind, and the world believed it.

Berro, meanwhile, thick of limb and heavy of brow, lay strapped to a table like an animal from a flesh-eating world, set for slaughter. To Undra, he was flesh. The brain he'd put such work into polishing was nothing more than an inconvenient organ lodged inside the meat of his body. None of it mattered. He'd be tortured and crossed, just like the patients, and nothing he'd learned, nothing he'd said or done or worked for, would help him now. 'Please,' he said, and then sobbed, not in fear or anger, but grief.

Undra looked almost pitying, just for a moment. He moved out of Berro's view and returned holding a hideous weapon – a metal rod about the length of his forearm, the top half of which was twisted and bristling with short spikes.

An animal noise came out of Berro's throat and he twisted against the straps that held him to the bedframe.

'It has to hurt, Berrovan, I'm sorry,' said Undra. He didn't sound sorry.

Berro thrashed and twisted and turned his head away as Undra gripped his bound wrist, hard as iron, and the rod came down with a sickening thump against the front of his left shoulder. He felt the teeth pierce into his flesh through the fabric of his uniform, felt the hot blood welling out of him as Undra dragged the weapon down, tearing his skin.

He didn't scream. He couldn't. The air wheezed out of his lungs, and his vision swam. His eyes found Undra's face. There was nothing handsome about it now. The man looked distorted and sick, his skin spattered with red so bright it was unreal. Who was he? Had he ever been Imparter Undra?

Everything started to slip and warp, and when the lab door unlocked and swung open and his friends spilled into the room, Berro disregarded the event as an hallucination.

But they were real. They were there. Fessi, Virda, Jex, in the flesh, witnesses to the lowest and probably last moments of his life. He hadn't meant to summon them. He'd only wanted to tell them what had happened to him, to warn them about Undra, but of course they'd come.

Of course.

They were better people than he was, and he'd doomed them, just like he'd doomed himself.

• • •

The floor was a slick of blood. That's what Virda saw first, everywhere, *everywhere*, obscenely thick, bright in places and congealing darkly in others. She could smell it, taste it, meaty and metallic in the closeness of the room. The horror of its colour and quantity delayed her acknowledgement of the three figures before them.

Two lay on the infirmary beds, one of them bloody and broken, as if they'd fallen onto the bed from a great height. The other was Berro, strapped down, his chest and shoulder soaked in blood, with Undra standing beside him.

The imparter gaped at the intruders, his handsome face twisted into an ugly mask of rage and disbelief. In one hand, he gripped a spiked and twisted metal implement clotted with gore. His other hand pulled a small gun from the pocket of his uniform and pressed it to Berro's head.

Jex twisted around and heaved with a choking bark of disgust. Virda and Fessi were motionless.

'What have you done?' said Jex in a crumbly whisper.

'Go,' said Berro, writhing uselessly against his bonds. 'Please…'

'Do as he says,' Undra spat. 'Or I'll kill him.'

'You'll kill him anyway,' said Fessi, each word a glass splinter. She stepped forward, and in an instant, she changed.

Virda couldn't make sense of what she was seeing, or feeling. Fessi was the same person – a slight, dark-haired figure in a blue uniform with pockets full of charms – but at the same time it was like she'd shrugged a massive, hooded cloak from her shoulders to reveal her true self underneath it. She was a cocoon of heat. She was a marrowcore hallucination, a pulsating figure between the trees after a bad wicker. A presence.

Virda stepped away from her, turning to Jex to find that he too was wide-eyed, staring at Fessi rather than the man with the bloodied weapon, pointing a gun at Berro.

Fessi took another step forward. 'Imparter,' she said. 'Put down the weapons.'

Virda dragged her eyes back to Undra.

His face was wild, pupils dilating his irises into non-existence. 'Stop,' he said. 'I will kill you.' He lifted the gun away from Berro and pointed it at Fessi, who took another step forward into a puddle of blood.

'Why haven't you done it already?' she asked. A valid question, but it sounded rhetorical. She knew something. 'You've broken the Code. You have nothing to lose.'

'Who do you think you are, Fessima?' Undra laughed, a crazed, shredding sound like a wound in his throat. 'You think you understand the Code? You don't understand it. You don't have any idea what it means to be Rhetari. The potential we have. The possible futures. There's no opportunity for greatness in this cackpit unless you can understand the way things are and acknowledge that they could be better. There's more for us to do, more for us to know, more for us to *be*.' It sounded like a speech he'd dreamed of delivering in front of an audience of adoring fans. In the wretched stink of this hellish room, it was deranged, pathetic. 'I thought Berrovan understood, but I was wrong. As it happens, he's nothing but a set of big arms.'

'It's you who doesn't understand what it means to be Rhetari,' said Fessi, taking yet another step forward.

Virda's eyes met Jex's, and they tunnelled into each other, thinking of other times and other places. For a sliver of a second Virda could feel his animal warmth, the gentle twitchkick of his foot as he slept, like an arbawolf cub dreaming of scrattins. The room throbbed with the horror of the unreal, everything twisting quickly out of control.

'Fessi, please,' said Berro. He struggled again, prompting Undra to thump him viciously on the head with the butt of the gun before turning it back on Fessi.

Jex screamed as Berro went ominously still. Virda blinked and blinked again, but she couldn't stop Fessi from shimmering, vibrating, flickering in the centre of her vision. *It's the fear*, Virda thought. *It's the panic. It's latent wicker.*

'Stop,' said Undra. 'I said I will kill you, and I mean it.'

'Your interpretation of the Code forbids it.'

'And yet I'm pointing a gun at you. What are you hoping to accomplish here, Fessima?' He sounded almost like his old self – confident, smooth, assured – but then there was the chaotic state of his hair, the blackness of his eyes, the way the blood from his spiked weapon dribbled in crimson rivulets down his bare arm to soak into the rolled-up sleeve of his uniform.

'I want to rescue my friend,' said Fessi. 'And I want justice for the people you've harmed.'

'Justice?' Undra laughed. 'There's another concept you don't understand. I've discovered something that could enrich the lives of every single Rhetari in existence, and you're more concerned about the wellbeing of a few criminals?' His face was a writhing sneer. 'These are people with no regard for civilisation. They would sooner assault you than share their food with you. You're not qualified to stand there, lecturing me about justice. Berrovan spoke so highly of you, but you're as disappointing as he is, unworthy of that blue uniform. Have you forgotten who you're talking to?'

'Not once,' said Fessi. 'Not for a moment.'

She pulsed, and Undra seemed to shrink slightly. 'This is how it is,' he said. 'I'm on the edge of a breakthrough, and you're in my way. Your friend can't leave. He's helping me with my work. You, however, can leave. So do it. Fly back to Wooden Hill and tell everyone what you saw here today. I'm sure they'll thoroughly enjoy the entertainment.'

'And if we don't leave?' said Virda, her anger eclipsing her confusion and fear. Undra's work was more important to him than anything else, and surely that work would be jeopardised if the reformatory staff were to enter this lab and find several dead students, and an imparter armed with a code-violating weapon. No doubt he'd already fabricated some excuse for Berro's sorry state, but there was no way he'd be able to explain away an entire killing spree on reformatory grounds. Even though he'd probably prefer them dead, they'd cause a lot of trouble for him if they died right there in the lab.

Perhaps he was confident that if they ran off and reported him immediately to the authorities, he'd be able to discredit or disappear them later using his power and influence. He didn't look particularly confident just then, his face waxy and beaded with sweat, but it made sense that he'd want them to leave rather than killing them. And this, in Virda's view, gave them leverage – leverage she intended to use.

Undra had not responded to her question. His eyes, and the gun, were still trained on Fessi. Virda took the opportunity to scramble forward. The movement of her own body felt like a remote operation – too much distance between intention and manifestation, her hands made of rubber, her lungs a broken machine, but she had to do something. She had to.

As she reached Berro's side, Undra pointed the gun at her instead.

'Leave him,' he said.

Shaking hard, ignoring Jex's wordless sounds of protest and the threat of Undra's weapon, Virda started to undo to the straps holding Berro to the bed.

Berro's eyelids fluttered open, his breath coming in short bloody bursts.

'I said leave him,' Undra repeated, his voice caustic with loathing. Virda glanced up and realised a moment too late that she'd been wrong. Undra wasn't determined to make them leave. Something had broken inside of him, and he'd moved beyond what was pragmatic for himself and his work. His eyes had gone cold. No matter the consequences, Imparter Undra *was* willing to kill them, and he was going to kill her first. He steadied his hand and aimed the gun at Virda's chest.

Virda considered lifting her hands away from Berro and raising them into the air, or perhaps dropping down behind the bed to hide, but she couldn't move. All she could do was stare down the barrel of the gun while her heart thumped slowly once, twice…

Undra squeezed the trigger.

In that moment, that crackling, infinite moment, Fessi moved like a spark, so fast that she disappeared in Virda's peripheral vision and instantly reappeared on the other side of the bed, directly in front of Undra. The bullet hit her in the centre of her chest, and she melted to her knees, planting her head at Undra's feet.

• • •

Berro's eyes were open just wide enough, and his mind was just clear enough for him to see Fessi fall as Undra reached for the marrowcore needles on the workbench behind him.

Stop him... stop him...

But nobody heard Berro speak, or perhaps his voice hadn't shaped the words at all.

Jex and Virda shouted things that melted and ran into each other before Berro could make sense of them. Virda was trying to get around the bed to reach Fessi. Undra lunged forward with the needles, and none of them were quick enough to stop him. Berro heard the impact of the needles against Fessi's flesh, and the bed jerked as she convulsed against its metal legs.

The silence that followed was sudden and breathless. It smelled of woodsmoke and hot sand and blood.

CHAPTER 33

There was pain, and then there wasn't. Noise upon noise – yelling, crashing, blood thumping, breath sawing in and out of lungs – and then quiet. The bloody scene blurred, and Fessi closed her eyes. She could feel them all. Undra a crackling mass of hatred, lancing out, eating itself and trying to eat the world too. Virda and Jex, flaring hot and bright, wild fear, desperate hope. And Berro, pulsing, flickering, fear and despair giving way to insensibility. The signals scrambled, the colours and textures, smells and tastes crashing into each other and then into her. Undra was upon her. An impact, powerful but painless and then everything, all of them, all the chaos and the hatred and the fear and the love spiralled away into the darkness.

Fessi was weightless, and then moving at such speed that her head snapped back, and her eyes snapped open. She saw droplets of her own blood streaming out behind her in the blackness and a pinprick of light in the distance as it vanished. The instant it was gone, a new light appeared in the same place and with a violent jerk her momentum switched so she was hurtling towards it, the blood she'd left behind her spattering into her face as she blasted back through it. Fessi closed her eyes again.

All of this, she thought, is packed into a moment. It is nothing but a moment, and soon it will be over.

CHAPTER 34

Undra wrenched himself back onto his feet, two pointed, bloodied instruments in one of his white-knuckled hands and the gun in the other. Jex was scrambling to get to Virda, while Virda scrambled to get to where Fessi had been just a moment before, ramming Berro's bed out of the way so hard it almost toppled over. Undra lurched, lifted the gun, hesitated for a second in the chaos, trained the gun on Virda, and missed the moment in which Jex swiped the spiked torture stick from the floor. Virda did not miss this, and she tensed a moment before it connected Undra's outstretched arm with a sickening crunch, flinging the gun out of his hand. Jex dropped the terrible weapon in shock as soon as it made impact.

The imparter roared in pain and turned, slipping, fear showing on his face for the first time. He hurled himself at Jex, and they grappled and hissed like a pair of shadowcats, tumbling across the floor in a flurry of feet and fists. Undra's hand found the spiked weapon, and he dragged it across Jex's face before losing his grip on it again. The imparter made to stand, but he was weakened, and he fell, grunting as his head connected the side of Berro's bed with a terrible clang. Jex dragged himself away, bleeding horribly from a set of deep cuts across his face.

Virda, meanwhile, had retrieved the fallen gun, and she rounded on Undra, pointing it between his eyes. Her body quaked. She felt gelatinous, electrified, dissolving in a pure, white-hot hatred. 'What have you done!' she choked. 'Where is Fessi? Bring her back! Bring her back *right now*!'

Was Fessi dead? She couldn't be. She just couldn't be. Virda refused to give the idea any space in her head. Considering it would make it irreversible and true.

'Or what?' Undra gritted out. 'You'll kill me?' He bared his teeth. His face was a horror, the blood of other people smeared all over it, streaking his hair, while his own blood leaked from the corners of his mouth and stained his teeth red. His chest heaved up and down.

'*WHERE IS SHE?*' Virda screamed. She felt the sick rising inside her, thoughts of Fessi and of Shani blurring together into a powerful raging grief she couldn't contain.

'She gone,' said Undra. 'She's in another world, and you didn't… allow me the testing conditions I needed… to choose a specific one. It was a bit of a… a rushed job.' He had the audacity to laugh, a wet hideous sound. 'She could be in any one of a million… a billion worlds, and nobody… will ever know which one. It doesn't matter anyway,' he said, as though offering some kind consolation. 'She's dead.'

His lips slid back from his bloody teeth into a garish red smile, and revulsion surged through Virda, starting in her stomach and exploding upwards into her head and along her arms, like the breaking of a dam. A scream tore out of her, and her hands contracted into fists, firing the gun.

The bullet hit Undra between the eyes, and he sagged, still smiling, a ragged breath wheezing out of his dead lungs. He slumped hard onto the floor and lay still.

Virda looked away from the man she'd just killed as if he wasn't even there, and never had been. She dropped the gun and rushed back to Berro's body.

It was more than a body. There was still life in there, but only just.

Jex stood, panting from blood loss and shock. Virda looked

at him and he looked back at her, fierce beneath his injuries. He passed no comment on the fate of Imparter Undra.

'We need to get out of here,' said Virda.

'Berro needs a surgeon,' said Jex.

'So do you. We can't trust anyone here. We have to get him to Halin at the academy.'

'Virda,' said Jex. 'That's… far away.'

'I know. But it's what we have to do. I'll patch you both up at the vollop. We just need to go.'

One of Jex's eyes was wide, its pupil a large black void of terror, and the other had swelled almost shut amid the bloody gashes on his face.

'Grab Undra's slab and paperwork,' said Virda. 'We're getting Berro out of here.'

They unstrapped Berro, eased him off the bed, and dragged him from the room, leaving a smear of blood in their wake, edged with fresh droplets from Jex's face. Even if they managed to reach the vollop, they wouldn't be safe with this trail of gore leading right to them. Virda was desperate to get into the air.

She thought again about Shani, and considered that perhaps it was a mercy if Shani was dead. But no, she wasn't – she couldn't be. She was in the building somewhere, and they'd get her out too. Not now, not today, but with the horrors they'd just witnessed, perhaps they could challenge the entire ethical framework of the reformatory and find an argument for her release.

Although there was still no sign of anyone else anywhere in this dark, grey wing of the reformatory building, Virda couldn't shake the urgent sense that they were seconds away from being discovered. What if someone tried to get hold of Undra to check up on him? What if they were expecting an update, or anticipating him at a reformatory staff gathering for a meal break or some such thing? An image bloomed unbidden into Virda's tainted imagination: several Undra-like characters gathered around a gutted corpse on a table, feasting on it.

Shani...

She felt sick. Fear was a cold hand around her throat.

Jex buckled as he struggled to hold Berro's dead weight. Virda urged him on. They turned the corner, following the neat smears of tinted balm Fessi had left on the walls. Virda had thought this unnecessary at the time, but now, with her world in tatters, she knew they would be utterly lost without Fessi's help. It felt like an age since the three of them had crept along the corridor in the other direction, Fessi feeling out the space around and ahead of them, making her marks, guiding them. She alone had been calm and collected. She alone had walked into the chamber of horrors without fear. And now she was gone.

They reached the outer door. Virda shouldered it open and in the sudden shock of cold air, Jex lost his hold on Berro, who fell and flopped over the threshold onto the frozen path.

'We're nearly there, Jex,' Virda soothed. 'Let's go.'

They dragged Berro down the hill to the vollop and placed him on a clean snowdrift alongside it. Jex pressed his own face into the snow and swept it from side to side, cleaning away some of the clotted mess. Shaking with adrenaline, Virda boarded the vollop to retrieve the medikit. She wished she'd practised stitching and cauterising. She wished she'd read the notes more carefully and paid more attention in survival classes.

With trembling hands, Jex ripped away the top of Berro's uniform. Berro was still unconscious, but his chest rose and fell with his shallow breathing. Jex pressed a snow-cold hand against Berro's brow as Virda pulled the thread through the main wound on the skin of his left shoulder, her fingers clumsy with fear. The stitches were untidy, and blood oozed between them, but they would have to do. She opened a tin of antibacterial ointment and smeared three quarters of it over Berro's wounds before binding his shoulder as best as she could with bandages. It was an awkward part of his body to bind, and her efforts weren't good enough. They needed to get him back to Wooden Hill as soon as possible.

Summoning impossible strength, Virda and Jex heaved Berro into the back seat of the vollop. His pod fell from a pocket of his uniform, its screen crushed and dark. Virda tucked it into her own pocket and wondered for a moment if Berro had managed to record any evidence, and whether it would be retrievable.

By the time they had him on the seat, his shoulder bandage was soaked through with blood. Virda set about winding more bandages on top of the others and fastening them in place with stretch clasps, all the while biting back a torrent of frustrated tears.

Jex was bleeding slowly but heavily from the three long, deep cuts running diagonally from his forehead, over his right eye and down his cheek. The eye had swollen completely closed. Having done as much as she could for Berro's shoulder, Virda strapped his prone body into the seat using both seatbelts, then clambered into the front where Jex had slumped himself behind the console. With a fresh sponge from the medikit, she dabbed the blood away from Jex's face – his beautiful, perfect face. Jex didn't flinch. His hand rested on her leg, and she could feel him shaking. She applied the remainder of the ointment, pressing it carefully over his cuts and smoothing it against his skin and then binding his head, winding the bandages around and around his forehead, over his right eye, across his cheek, under his ear, over and over until the bandages ran out and she tucked in the loose end to secure it.

'Jex,' she said. 'You're not fit to fly.'

'What choice do we have?' he replied. 'I have to fly.'

Virda closed the medikit, wrapped an arm gently around his shoulders and squeezed him.

A moment later, it happened. A group of reformatory guards burst through the open doorway at the top of the slope. Two of them were armoured, and armed. There was a sudden cacophony of shouting and pointing, and they began their rapid descent towards the vollop.

Jex flicked switches and turned dials with frantic fingers while Virda wrenched the door of the vollop closed and locked it. She opened her mouth to tell Jex to hurry up, but stopped herself. He knew.

They had mere seconds before the armed guards were upon them, one of them hammering the butt of his weapon against the door. The other one pointed his gun directly at Jex's head, nothing but the smooth glass surface of the vollop window between them.

'Are these windows bullet-proof?' asked Virda. The unarmed reformatory guards gesticulated, shouting, issuing commands into their pods. With the sealed vollop muffling the sound and her heart thumping so loudly, Virda could barely hear them.

'It's built to withstand minor impacts, but I'm not sure about bullets,' said Jex. He finally had the marrowcore engines firing, and the vollop heaved itself clumsily off the ground and hovered a couple of feet in the air. It tilted dangerously to one side and Virda had to stop herself from screaming at Jex as she tumbled across the seat and smacked painfully into the window. Her head rang with the impact. The tilting had had the favourable effect of blasting the engines directly at the guards, who stumbled back, shielding their faces, and cursing.

'Go, go!' Virda shouted, unable to restrain herself any longer.

One of the guards advanced and began grappling with the door handle, smashing his weapon against it to break the lock. Something snapped inside the mechanism, and Virda saw the inside parts moving back and forth as he jiggled it furiously from the outside. Jex was frenetic at the controls, trying to rush the build-up of power. 'Come *on*,' he said through gritted teeth. 'Caaaaaack…'

An ominous crack announced the failure of the door lock, and the guard tried to force it open just as the marrowcore engines reached power and the vollop jumped up with a jolting sideways lurch. The door was open slightly and the guard hung onto the vehicle, bellowing, one armoured foot wedged into the opening, two armoured hands trying to force it wider to allow him entrance.

Virda scrambled over to him and grabbed the first loose object to hand – the medikit case, heavy, with blunt corners. It would do. She swung it as hard as she could against the guard's hands. He lost his grip with one of them and before he could get it back, she swung the case again. It smashed against his other hand, but he held on, roaring commands at the other guards over the scream of the engines. 'Open this door! Bring this vehicle down, right now!'

Jex took the vollop higher. 'Hold on,' he shouted. 'I'm tilting it.'

Virda grabbed onto a seat-back with one hand, the medikit case still grasped in the other. She felt the marrowcore engines moving beneath the vehicle, which tilted suddenly to the left with more force than she'd anticipated. Her hand slipped from the seat, and she was thrown towards the open door. Out of the corner of her eye, she saw Berro's unconscious form slide out from under one of the seatbelts, but the other belt caught under his arm and held him. Virda smashed into the door and felt the hand of the guard grabbing at her.

She still held the medikit. With all the force she could muster she lifted it and threw it against the gap. It slammed into the guard's face, and he screamed and fell and crashed into the snowy ground below.

Virda's face squashed against the glass, and she gazed down at the fallen man, trying to determine whether she had just killed another person. With the snow swirling beneath them, she couldn't see if the man was moving. Jex righted the vollop, sending her sprawling back across the floor, and then ascended at speed, the frigid air screaming in through the open door. Virda dragged herself to it and wrenched it closed, but the lock was in pieces and the door didn't seal, jets of cold air continuing to stream in, burning her tear-stained cheeks. She hoped it would hold.

She had so many things she wanted to say, so many things she needed to yell at the top of her voice, but they caught in her throat, and she eased herself back onto the floor, gasping.

'We did it, Virda,' said Jex. 'We're leaving. We're fine. We'll make it.'

Berro moaned slightly from the backseat. Virda ignored him for a few more moments. She felt molten, like a painful throbbing blob of something with no discernible separate parts. But her lungs kept hauling the air into her and forcing it out again, and eventually she was able to lift herself stiffly from the floor and go to her friend. His shoulder was bleeding again, badly. Sliding out of the seatbelt had torn the bandages away, and his wound looked worse now than before she'd stitched it up.

'Jex, how long until we reach the academy?'

'Three hours at least until we get to the airfield. Then we still have to get from there...'

'We won't make it,' she said quietly, as cold descended upon her.

Just then, Berro's eyelids fluttered, and his eyes opened. They were unfocussed at first, rolling around in their sockets, but then they locked on to Virda's face, and his pupils shrank into sharp points. He coughed and said, in a rough whisper, 'Grassy Plains. Go. Forty...' Another cough. 'Forty-seven north. Two and a half. East. The... the house.'

'Did you hear that?' said Virda.

'Most of it,' said Jex, tapping his map. 'Forty what?'

'Forty-seven,' said Berro. 'Forty-seven.'

From a storage drawer under the seat, Virda pulled out a spare clothwrap and pressed it to Berro's shoulder, the bright blood blooming quickly through the fabric. She placed a hand against his forehead. 'Forty-seven north, two-and-a-half east,' she said. 'We've got it. Your father?'

Berro nodded weakly and squeezed his eyes shut. He was in pain, and there was nothing she could do for him, having thrown the medikit from the vollop, along with the reformatory guard.

'I would love to promise that everything's going to be fine, but I can't,' she said. 'But we're going to try, Berro. We're going to try.'

• • •

The afternoon sky was a vivid cloudless blue just beginning to pink at the horizon. Bitterly cold, but bright. In all directions, the hills undulated in mottled scrubby greens and browns. The snow had receded under the unblinking glare of the sun, but it still clung in the shadowy nooks and between the trees clustered here and there.

Virda surveyed this unfamiliar landscape as it passed beneath her. The rural dwellings were few and far between, the farmed land too sparse to form a patchwork, so each separate shape stood out brightly against the dull colours of the untended land. A bright orange rectangle declared the presence of young snow squash. A rich, jewel-green square announced a frigram bounty, and another nearby, in a shade of reddish brown, boasted a successful millbean crop, harvested over the summer. Most of these farms were near to the vehicle tracks that cut across the region, curving away from the hovertube stations like fine tendrils, each eventually terminating at some small building or patch of farmland. Some homesteads, however, were more isolated, disconnected from these arteries of civilisation, gravitating instead towards other features: a river glittering in the sunshine, a semi-frozen lake, a hill just high enough to start calling itself a mountain, a swathe of thick forest.

It was beautiful, but the beauty of everything hurt so much – a deep ache in Virda's chest. There was no justice in it. Not with Fessi gone and Berro dying and Jex maimed. How could such beauty and such horror exist in the same world at the same time?

A state of defeated calm had enveloped her. She hadn't exchanged a word with Jex for an hour. She hadn't commented on the men she'd killed, or the loss of their friend. She had only looked at Jex from time to time to make sure he was still conscious. His shoulders were rounded and his head sagged on his neck, but his jaw was set and his grip strong, fingers poised and precise over the controls. Berro wasn't conscious, but he still breathed and the bleeding from his shoulder seemed to have slowed. His face was ashen and spent, his lips pale and dry. He looked so much smaller than usual.

'We're nearly there,' said Jex, startling Virda out of her reverie.

'How long?'

'Ten minutes, maybe more. Maybe less.'

'Do you think the landing will be fine?' asked Virda, immediately regretting the question.

'The area around the coordinates looks quite flat. I think it will be fine,' said Jex. 'I'm all right, Virda. And the vollop is all right.'

He smiled at her – a grisly smile – and she smiled back.

'Jex. You know I love you more than anyone.'

'Yes, I know,' said Jex. 'But don't say it like that right now, because then I'll cry and crash the vollop. The end of this story is bad enough as it is.'

He began their descent, and the ground loomed up towards them, the shapes on the hills resolving themselves into discernible rows of squash and millbean shrubs. Trees cast long shadows across the scrubland.

'It must be that house over there,' said Virda, indicating a small hut set back against a low hill, with an elongated strip of planted land at the front and a stand of young trees to one side, tapering off up the slope. Jex selected a nearby area of flat, open ground and brought the vollop down with surprising smoothness. The landing itself was a nasty jolt, followed by a whining silence that pressed in on them close and cold as rising water.

Virda pulled the vollop's broken door open and dashed towards the house a hundred paces away. A large figure had emerged from the doorway. It hesitated and then began to move towards Virda's approaching form. They met among the crops.

'You're Berro's father,' Virda gasped. The resemblance was uncanny. She didn't need him to confirm her assertion, but he did anyway, nodding uncertainly, his eyes scanning her blood-stained uniform and beyond her to the vollop, the dust still settling around it. 'Berro's hurt,' she said, all the intensity rising within her once again. 'He's in the vollop. Please. Please help. Please—'

Before she could finish, Marruvan sprinted away from her towards the vehicle. She sank slowly to her knees in the cold earth. It had been recently turned and was loose and soft. Some unfamiliar beans grew there, in pretty, curved pods. A movement at the house drew her gaze. Another figure stepped outside into the crisp air of the perfectly imperfect early-winter evening.

Virda blinked, stared, blinked again. The figure stood frozen, staring back at her. Virda's mouth dropped open.

'Kini?' she said.

CHAPTER 35

Berro crouched behind a lectern. The lecture hall was full, and everyone shouted down at him out of the darkness, row upon rising row of angry people. He was so ashamed. He put his hands over his head, willing them to stop, but they wouldn't. Individual voices rang clear above the cacophony, shouting, 'Stand, up, Berrovan! Stand up! Shame on you!' And so he stood, the spotlamp dazzling his eyes before swinging around to pan over the faces of his audience. Virda and Jex were there, glowering at him from the highest row. And there was Tarov and Kem and Magrin. Undra sat at the front, frowning in disappointment. Alongside Undra stood Ryndel, arms folded, lips pressed together in a straight red line. In the centre, his mother, shaking her head slowly. And there was Fessi.

Berro clutched at a sudden pain in his chest. The spotlamp moved again, and he saw his father. Unlike everyone else in the room, Marruvan didn't look angry or upset with him. Instead, he looked fearful, and he mouthed something. An instruction. A warning. A plea. He said, 'Berro, keep still', and his voice was as clear as river water, and close, as though he too stood at the lectern. Berro was shaking and sweating, and the room tilted like a ship tossed on a stormy sea.

'Berro,' said Marruvan.

Berro's eyes snapped open, and his father's face was there, right above his own. He gasped and choked, gulping in breath after breath. He was on a bed, Marruvan pressing a cool cloth against his forehead.

'Berro. You're safe. Calm down. You're safe.'

And for a moment, Berro did feel safe. His body throbbed strangely, and a dull discomfort gripped his shoulder, but as his heart slowed and his sweat cooled, he realised he was clean and tingly, with a pleasant sensation in his hands and feet like one might experience after drinking a mug of hot berry tea laced with a calming tincture. He wore an exquisitely soft clothwrap that smelled like fresh air and herbal laundry cleanser. When he rubbed his lips together, he found them slick with a rich balm – the mild antibacterial type his mother had always used. He knew this room with its little window facing the hillside. A potted plant stood on the windowsill, and a wooden box. As a child, he'd taken that box with him wherever he went and used it to carry 'samples'; pebbles, feathers, interesting bits of wood, snail shells, insect casings... Fessi had had one similar, for her sentimental trinkets. He'd contributed something to it. What was it now? A piece of cloth. A piece of blue cloth.

He cast his eyes around the room and brought them back to the face of his father. Marruvan looked so much older than Berro remembered. He tried to recall how long it had been since he'd seen him in the flesh, but he didn't manage to retrieve the memory because his mind snagged instead on recent events, and they crashed over him like a landslide, forcing the breath out of him once again and triggering the pain in his shoulder. *Fessi...*

'Everything went so wrong,' he said to his father. 'One of my friends is dead, and it's my fault.'

Marruvan pulled his chair closer to the bedside. His face was lined with worry, but not with anger or judgement. 'Tell me what happened, Berro,' he said. 'Start at the beginning.'

• • •

In the farmhouse's rustic but spacious washroom, Virda scrubbed the blood, sweat and tears from her aching body with a homemade herbal mix, her mind racing so quickly that it might as well have been completely blank, incapable as it was of settling on a single thought for even a moment. She washed thoroughly but quickly, dried herself with ungentle haste and pulled on one of Kini's clothwraps. It was too short in the legs and arms but fit well enough around the middle. She'd always thought of Kini as being taller than her, but in truth, she'd overtaken her commune cousin in height several years ago.

Virda returned to the front room, her damp hair sticking up from her head at all angles, and was relieved to see that Jex had been expertly tended to, his face and neck wiped clean, his cuts neatly closed with dissolvable adhesive stitches, each wound covered with clear anti-bacterial ointment and transparent bandages. A soft, wet, healing patch was fixed over his injured eye. He cradled a large mug of hot tea in his hands, and Virda could tell from its colour that he'd dissolved at least three treacle nibs into it.

'Feel better?' she asked.

'Much,' he replied, with a weak smile. 'You?'

'Better, yes,' said Virda. 'The shower was necessary. Thanks, Kini.' She flicked her eyes shyly at the older woman. Kini had insisted on Virda washing while Jex was patched up, and Virda had resisted at first, impatient to talk and find out what Kini was doing in Marruvan's farmhouse.

Kini offered Virda some tea, and Virda gratefully accepted it, taking the warm mug in her hands and sinking onto the softseat beside Jex. They sipped in silence for some moments, the only sound that of Berro and Marruvan's low voices coming from the bedroom and the quiet chirping of nightbeetles outside.

The bare bones of their story had been imparted during the process of getting Berro into the house, and now, with an air of grave obligation, Virda and Jex set about detailing the events of the day. Kini sat rigid with horror, and at the end of it, she fetched more tea with the urgency of a surgeon administering a life-saving tincture.

Virda, sensing the build-up of questions she didn't yet want to answer, turned the conversation towards Kini, and Kini, understanding this tactic after years of living with Virda, accepted the diversion. 'Why are you here?' was the first, inevitable question.

The answer, apparently, was not a straightforward one, and Kini considered it for several moments while she fiddled with the string bracelet on her wrist. Though the bracelet was faded, Virda could just make out its three colours woven together. It was the twin of the one she'd found in Shani's box at the commune.

'Marruvan and I…' Kini said. 'We have a relationship. I'm not sure how to define it yet. I've never had to define it before.'

'You don't have to define it now, either,' said Jex. 'It's your business, not ours. It's just… unexpected. Mama Stitch mentioned you'd been visiting someone in Grassy Plains.'

Kini smiled. 'You can always count on Mama to spread the news.'

'How did you meet?' asked Virda.

Kini blushed. 'I uh… I sought him out. It was just after Sarla had died. I'd followed the story closely, of course, what with Shani being in the reformatory and Sarla being the loudest voice of reformatory scepticism. I offered him my condolences, and we became friends. It was only in recent months that I started visiting him. Being a commune parent… it takes a certain type of person, and I don't think that's me. It was getting to the stage where I'd have to start taking on primary parenting roles rather than just assisting, and I didn't feel ready for that, so I started making excuses and getting away as often as I could, and eventually I just stopped going back.'

'Do you think you might end up living with him permanently?' asked Virda.

'Maybe,' Kini said. 'I have my anger, my grief about the reformatory, and so does he, and we've bonded over that, but there's more to it now. He's a good person. I didn't know you were friends with his son.'

'They've been… estranged,' said Virda.

'I know,' said Kini. 'It hurts him. It hurts him a lot. He blames himself, but he doesn't know what he could've done differently. He respected Sarla's decision, you know. He didn't fight her on it. So I think Berro blames him for what happened. Thing is, even if Marruvan hadn't supported Sarla, he couldn't have done anything to stop her. Berro doesn't understand that.'

'Or he does, but he won't admit it, even to himself,' said Jex. 'He's like that sometimes. He needs an explanation for everything, so maybe if he has somebody to blame, then at least he can make sense of how he feels.'

Kini scrutinised Jex for a moment. 'You've grown up, Jexi,' she said. 'Flying a vollop, getting a wound dressed without whining, delivering insightful commentary – I'm impressed. I always thought of you as this little barkermonkey scampering after Virda, getting up to mischief.'

'I'm still a barkermonkey – just a less talented one than Virda,' said Jex. He pulled a face and laughed, then winced as the expression distorted his injuries. 'She's the best climber in Wooden Hill. Literally no competition.'

'Is that so?' Kini turned to Virda with a twinkle of sentimental pride in her eyes.

Virda settled back into the softseat to bring her commune cousin up to date with the Wooden Hill climbing scene – the gatherings, the races, the wicker bounties, the audacity of Tarov – and for a while, everything seemed all right, as though their lives had followed roughly the courses they'd expected when they were younger. Except, of course, they hadn't, and without warning, Kini lifted a hand to shield her face.

Virda fell silent.

'I'm sorry,' said Kini. 'It's just – hearing about all this – I can't stop thinking about Shani. Which is weird, because I had it under control.'

'Kini,' said Jex. 'We found notes – clues that Shani left behind. Directions leading into a no-zone.'

Quite unexpectedly, Kini laughed. 'You found them, did you?

Shani never wrote those notes,' she said. 'I did. After they took her away. I was young, I couldn't tell anyone what we'd found because I was too scared, but I couldn't do nothing, either. I should've guessed you'd find them eventually. Did you get inside the temple?'

'Yes,' said Virda. 'But it didn't answer a whole lot of questions.'

Jex immediately started to list some of these questions, tapping a fingertip for each one. 'What was it for? Why is it a secret? What has it got to do with Shani being taken away? How did you get in there without anti-marrow gear?'

'You don't need anti-marrow gear to get in there,' said Kini. 'It's not really a no-zone.'

'What do you mean it's not really a no-zone?'

'We saw people going in and out with no anti-marrow gear,' said Kini. 'We spied on them for days. They were sneaking around, trying not to be seen, going in and coming out with these big parcels. We followed them right into the so-called no-zone and nothing happened, so we figured they'd somehow had it designated as no-zone just to keep people away. And that got us *really* curious, and we wanted to know what they were hiding. We thought maybe they were mining something precious. They kept going behind this waterfall, and two of the big ones would stand outside on the rocks, keeping guard. So we waited one evening until they left, and then we went behind the waterfall ourselves.' A faraway look misted Kini's eyes. 'I suppose the place was abandoned and the crystals were gone by the time you saw it. It was a bit like a no-zone in there. Definitely too much marrowcore. We saw it in use. We stayed in there overnight and hid in a crevice, and the next day when they came, we watched them.'

'We saw the crystals,' said Virda. 'What do you mean you saw it in use?'

'The arch with the crystals, all pointing at the flat rock right in the centre—'

'The arch was broken,' said Jex.

Kini nodded, as if this didn't surprise her. 'It was a portal,' she said. 'They had some machinery with them. There was a man – I didn't see his face, really. Smaller guy, with a beard. He set up some kind of machine at the far side of the temple. It made a noise. A really stupid noise, actually. I remember Shani and I were trying so hard not to laugh. He'd fiddle with it, and it would blast music, but just for a second, like a broken speaker. And every time, the arch would sort of buzz and wobble. It sounded like the noise was coming out of the arch, but I don't know. The acoustics were weird in there. The sound was a little bit different every time this guy played with the machine. Always loud, though. And then, somehow, I don't know what he did, but I guess he got the sound just right, and it… it activated the arch. The space under the arch split, like lightning, except it wasn't bright. It was more dark than bright, actually. I can't describe it. Cold air blasted through, like he'd opened a crack into a winter place. And a body fell through onto that rock. It took a second, the whole thing. And then it was over, except for this weird, burning smell and the body, just lying there. They bagged the body up and took it away.'

'Crossing,' said Virda softly, and something shifted in her mind, like sundered pieces of heavy stone fitting back together.

Kini looked at them, through them, unseeing, lost to her memories. She was telling the story because she needed to tell it, and the process of telling it had begun. The audience was irrelevant now. 'We waited until long after they'd all left, and then we went over to the arch to look at the crystals. I'd gone back to the crevice to fetch a flashlight, and that's when one of the heavy men returned, and he saw Shani. She was standing on the flat rock, like she'd just come through the portal herself.' Kini's voice was heavy with loss now. She stared at her hands resting in her lap. 'We had a signal,' she said. 'A finger, longways over the lips. And Shani did that, knowing I would see it. And so I stayed hidden the whole time they were tying her hands and taking her away. I thought if I was free that somehow I could rescue her, but…' Kini rubbed her neck. 'You know, I tell myself this story all the time, and I wonder if maybe the real truth is that I was a coward. A secret that big is bound to be protected by powerful people, and I was scared of what they'd do to me if they knew I'd been there too.'

'This portal,' said Jex. 'Do you think Undra knew about it?'

'I have no doubt that Undra knew about it,' said Virda. Something itched at the back of her mind. 'Hang on.' She grabbed her pod from the table with such haste that Jex and Kini both jumped in their seats. Her thoughts were rushing ahead of her, and she couldn't find what she wanted to find nearly fast enough, her fingers flicking wildly back and forth through old comspace logs. 'Here!' she said at last, presenting an image to Kini with a look of triumph on her face. 'Was this the guy? The guy with the machine?'

The image was one that Berro had sent her while he'd been perusing Undra's private collection – a picture of Undra, nearly a decade ago, standing next the preserved body of the Rainbow Woman. He was smiling and bearded, with long hair.

To Virda's immense disappointment, Kini only shrugged. 'Possibly,' she said. 'Like I said, I didn't get a good look at him. We had more interesting things to focus on. But yes, it could've been Undra. It probably was.'

Virda set her jaw and nodded. 'It was him. He is – *was* – the foremost expert of the crossing phenomenon. He must've learned his technique from studying the portal. Maybe he destroyed it by accident, or on purpose, but it didn't matter by then. He knew how to recreate the phenomenon in other places, so he could just carry on doing it, for prestige or profit or whatever it was he wanted. Collecting bodies, studying them, being the only one with any access to the information. And now he's dead.' She stared into space for a long moment, chewing her lips. Then she looked up at Kini, eyes sparkling. 'We're going to get Shani out. We're going to get her out, and we're going to change the world, and everyone will know she did nothing wrong.'

Kini opened her mouth to say something, but Jex spoke first. He was looking at his pod with a small smile on his face. 'Imparter Pol is on their way here,' he said.

'Pol?' said Virda, bewildered by the sudden change of topic.

'Yes. They got my message and decided to follow us. Either to stop us or to help us, I'm not sure. But by the time they were flying, we were leaving the reformatory, so they changed course to Grassy Plains.'

'Who is Imparter Pol?' asked Kini.

'My Vehicles instructor,' said Jex. 'And if everything goes the way I want it to, they're going to help us fix things.'

• • •

Virda, Jex and Kini stood outside the farmhouse, warm light spilling from the open door behind them and throwing their shadows long and lean towards the rows of bean pods. They watched the vollop descend out of the starry sky, moonlight catching its curves as it touched down alongside the one already parked on the grass. Earlier today, these two vehicles had been safely stowed side-by-side at the academy airfield, with no flights scheduled for at least a week, and now here they both were, in a moonlit field in Grassy Plains.

Not one but two figures emerged from the vollop, and Jex fidgeted nervously, straining to identify the person alongside the short one who was obviously Pol. *Reinforcement?* Perhaps, after all this, Pol was about to have them thrown into the reformatory for gross misconduct.

As the light from the farmhouse reached the approaching pair, Virda recognised the taller figure as Surgeon Halin from the academy infirmary.

Whatever Pol had been intending to say to their star student was immediately discarded as they laid eyes upon Jex's battered face. 'Oh, skies!' said Pol. 'We should've come sooner! We had to find another surgeon to fill in at the infirmary, and the logistics for securing a vehicle at short notice, even when you're the imparter—! Of course, that's why you didn't— Oh, skies…'

They all bustled inside, and Virda shut the door behind them, a great weariness washing over her. Marruvan had emerged from the back room, and everyone seemed to be talking at once, bringing each other up to speed on what had happened and why. Halin was quickly dispatched with her medical supplies to give Berro a more thorough examination. Despite his injuries, Jex seemed to be the one in control, leading the narrative, his maturity and confidence boosted by his imparter's presence.

Virda decided to make tea rather than sitting down with the others, allowing their voices to merge into one another and flow around her like the white noise of a vollop engine. As she busied her hands with the pressing and straining of berries, she gazed out the farmhouse window at the silent orb of the moon. When the tea was done, she'd take a walk, clear her head. She'd call Magrin, tell her what she needed to know about Fessi, about Undra, about everything.

Magrin and Kath had been eating with Andish when Fessi had crossed.

Magrin's liquid voice warbled through the pod speaker as she related the incident to Virda. 'She had a spoonful of broth she was lifting up to her mouth, and I noticed her hands were shaking,' said Magrin. 'And then she dropped the spoon and grabbed her chest. I thought she was having a heart failure.'

'She knew?' Virda spoke softly, even though there was no one nearby to overhear their conversation. Night birds called in the trees, and frosty grass crunched beneath her boots. She felt invigorated and despondent in equal measure, the contrary feelings tugging back and forth painfully inside her.

'She knew,' said Magrin. 'We rushed over to her, Kath and me, and she just started sobbing, "Fessi, Fessi, Fessi, oh, she's gone, she's gone…", over and over, like that.'

'And Kath's with her now?'

'Yes. It's a relief, honestly. She seemed to know exactly what to do. She had her own grief, but I could see her packing it up, putting it to one side so she could be there for Andish. Andish sees her as a daughter, and I think she's adopted Andish as her mother, since she's been cut off from her own mother.' There was a pause, broken by a small sob. 'I know how to care for creatures, but when it comes to people who need help, sometimes I'm just a sobbing mess. I'm no use to anyone.'

'Oh, Mag, that's not true,' said Virda. 'We're all different, and that's fine. And Kath is with her, like you said. She's not alone. But you are. I'm worried about you.'

'I'm not alone,' said Magrin. 'I've got all my creatures here, and I'm in touch with you, and with Kath. I just can't wait for everything to be sorted out. I mean as best as it can be, you know. I want some time. I want a quiet day to – to sit and think. About Fessi.' Her voice cracked again, and she made a frustrated sound, losing patience with her own emotions. 'I need everything to stop happening so fast. It's like I'm out of breath. It's like—' She inhaled sharply, and her breath shuddered as she released it.

'We'll be home soon. We've got Pol and Halin and Kini and Marruvan, so it's not just us anymore. We don't have to do this alone. They're going to help us. Things are going to change.'

'I hope you're right,' said Magrin.

A long, reflective silence stretched out between them. They listened to each other breathe. Another bird called across the field, loud enough for Magrin to hear it. 'Sounds like a moontuk,' Magrin murmured. She must've been pacing around the treehouse because Virda could hear her prosthetic foot squeaking against the floorboards.

'I need to get back to Jex,' said Virda. 'He's being so strong, but he had a terrible time, and he got hurt. I need to look after him.'

'Give him a hug from me, and stay well,' said Magrin. 'Oh, and Virda… thank you for calling me.'

'Of course, Mag. We'll see you soon.'

Virda reached a hackerwood tree stump in the middle of an open grassy area. A new branch poked out from the edge of the severed trunk, reaching towards the moonlight like a narrow arm with a leafy hand outstretched. She leaned against the stump and watched a wisp of cloud pass over the pitted face of the moon and imagined someone in another stream of reality looking up at the very same thing.

Fessi… What world are you in?

• • •

Pol's face was hard as they placed Jex's pod onto the table in the centre of the room. Jex had excused himself after handing the pod to his imparter and withdrawn to another room in the farmhouse. Neither he nor Virda had dared to watch what he'd managed to capture on his pod through the hole in his uniform pocket, but if Pol's face was anything to go by, he'd captured enough.

Virda cautiously removed her fingers from her ears.

'Horrific,' said Pol, dragging a hand across their close-cropped hair. 'Horrific.'

'We have to do something, Pol,' said Halin. 'We need to take this to the council immediately. The reformatory is complicit! A student has died!'

Virda flinched as he said it, vigorously reining in her thoughts to stop them drifting back to the chamber of horror, and to what had been lost in there.

Pol turned to Kini, who sat stiff and silent, her fingers digging into her legs like claws. It was one thing to hear a first-hand account of a terrible event, but another thing entirely to hear and see snippets of the event unfolding – the voices and the violence, the movement, the chaos, the fear. 'Kini,' said Pol, their voice gentle. In her frozen state, Kini was more akin to fragile pottery than to stone. 'Would you be willing to testify about the arrest of your sister? The more evidence we can present, the greater the impact will be.'

Kini nodded. 'Yes. Yes, of course.'

Marruvan had been standing to one side, and he stepped forward now and placed his hands on Kini's shoulders. She looked up at him, and he looked down at her, and something passed between them – a shared knowledge, an agreement. A decision. Marruvan cleared his throat. 'There's someone else,' he said.

Everyone stared at him, waiting for him to elaborate.

'He knows a lot about the reformatory,' said Marruvan. 'But he'll need protection. He'll need some guarantees. He's an escapee.'

Halin's eyes bulged. 'An escapee?' she said. 'I haven't heard anything about anyone escaping from the reformatory in years, and even back then, it was always only a rumour. Wasn't it?'

'No,' said Marruvan. 'It wasn't a rumour. He's been in hiding for seven years. His name is Terek.'

'Terek,' said Pol. 'I haven't heard that name.'

'He was incarcerated seventeen years ago, escaped seven years ago and was rescued by my late partner, Sarla.'

There was a pause, a momentary holding of breath.

'The source!' said Pol, gaping at Marruvan. 'I remember reading about it. Sarla always refused to reveal her source. And you've been protecting him ever since?'

'Yes,' said Marruvan. 'Sarla and I helped him construct a new identity. We found him work. We brushed away all the trails leading to him, so to speak. After Sarla died, everyone assumed she'd taken the secret with her, but I knew. Berro never knew. He'll be upset with me, I think, for keeping it from him. He had a lot of anger, and perhaps if he'd known more…' Marruvan shook his head abruptly, as though ridding himself of unwanted thoughts that settled on him like falling ash. 'I'm quite sure if Terek thought there was any chance you could dismantle the reformatory system, he'd be willing to step out of hiding to help you.'

Pol and Halin turned to one another. Halin's lips moved, but she couldn't seem to decide what to say.

Virda sensed the growing energy, the thoughts and ideas turning into strategies and intentions, the cut stones fitting together to form something massive and strong and bold, like a pre-war fortress on a hilltop, primed to withstand an invasion. Unlike poor Berro, Jex's faith in his primary imparter was not misplaced. Pol had responded at once to his distress call, dismissed his indiscretions in context, and was now wholly invested in this fight for justice.

And Pol had not come alone. Halin was a respected and influential figure at the academy and beyond. Together, they were a formidable force. With the added arsenal of Kini's and Terek's testimonies, Undra's slab and notes, Berro's eye-witness account of the reformatory conditions, and Jex's recorded evidence from the lab of horrors, Virda was tentatively optimistic that the events of the previous day would have enough kindling packed around them to set Rheta alight and free Shani from the clutches of the reformatory. She'd always known Shani was innocent, and now she knew Shani could be freed.

A stand of tall, infected trees grew at the heart of their civilisation, and it was time for them to burn.

SEVEN YEARS AGO

year 215, month 1, day 5

Sarla placed a towel, some thermals, a thick cloth wrap and a pair of winter boots outside the shower cubicle. They were Marruvan's spares from the cabin's storage cabinet, and they were too big for Terek, but at least they'd be comfortable and warm. While he showered, she returned to the kitchen to reheat the last of the food. It was hard to believe that the frying of snails and the chopping of snow squash was something that had happened mere hours ago. She had not felt her hunger throughout Terek's narrative, but now it clawed at her, and she ate quickly by the stove, spooning the broth right out of the pot. She'd have to cook again tomorrow.

Terek had been imprisoned for attempted murder. A mistake, he insisted – one he'd never forgiven himself for. He'd been a different man then, entitled and arrogant, using his cartography as an excuse to trespass in restricted no-zones, and when authorities had come to interrogate him, he'd been drunk and ill-advisedly whittling a small figurine of a shadowcat, and he'd slashed one of them in the face with his carving tool. The man had lost an eye, and Terek had lost a decade of his life.

From what Sarla knew, the few people who'd ever been released from the reformatory, usually through the assistance of a well-respected relative on the outside and a great deal of administration, had almost all put their voices towards the anti-reformatory movement, even at the expense of alienation from their Code-abiding families and friends. Whenever possible, the administration relocated them to far-flung towns in rural areas, supposedly for their own safety and post-incarceration rehabilitation 'away from the potential triggers for further Code-violations', but really it was to prevent the dissemination of anti-reformatory rhetoric through their social circles and family ties. If the administration could justify it, Sarla thought, they'd strip the ex-prisoners of their connections to the rhetalink to stop them talking to each other.

The sound of the shower ceased, and soon enough Terek came back into the room wearing the boots and the bottom of half of the thermal set. His face was puckered in pain. He gestured at a terrible wound running down his side, from armpit to hip bone. Sarla gasped.

'Hate to trouble you for more favours, but do you perhaps have any wound dressings?' Terek said through clenched teeth. 'I got so caught up cleaning myself, I seem to have ripped a few of these stitches.'

Sarla nodded, her gorge rising. It wasn't a ragged, accidental-looking rip in his flesh; it was perfectly straight and clean – a surgical cut, the stitches so neatly and evenly spaced, they might've been applied with a machine.

One or two had pulled loose, and the wound seeped watery blood that Terek dabbed quickly with the medicated pad Sarla gave him. He insisted on dressing his own wound, which seemed to be something he'd done many times before. He spread the paste evenly and applied the healing strips adeptly over the tiny blue stitches. Terek must've been a big man once, perhaps almost as big as Marruvan, but now his abdomen was sunken and scarred, dusted with patchy grey hair. Sarla pitied him.

When he had himself patched up, Terek put on the rest of the clothes, then planted himself on the soft seat.

'So now you've seen it,' he said. 'The most recent one, anyway. It's part of what I still have to tell you – that is, if you want to hear the rest.'

Sarla nodded.

'Everybody knows about the opt-in testing, and yes, it exists, but it doesn't work quite the way you think it does. People believe there's a tolerable base-level quality of life at the reformatory, and the opt-in provides unnecessary enhancements to it.

'Before I was incarcerated, I remember my father ranting about it, going on and on about how the patients have access to luxuries that even the Code-abiding Rhetari population doesn't have, and all they need to do is take a few vitamins. He said it was abominable and the

system was broken, and they should be shackled and starved for the things they did, not treated like kings of the war. I do wonder if he still held all those opinions after I was put inside. I wonder if he's still alive… Anyway, I held some of those opinions myself, back then. I imagined the reformatory as a sort of mountain gathering, warm and jovial, with simple, comfortable beds, and wholesome meals served up every day.

'I was fresh out of my academy back then. The idea of not having to cook anything for myself was appealing and seemed like a great perk of being hauled away for reform. I never thought about it much beyond that. I didn't know anyone who had been incarcerated. I didn't even know anyone who knew anyone who had been incarcerated. The reformatory was just an idea. Something semi-real, inconsequential, or maybe sometimes comforting, when I thought of it as a place for keeping dangerous people away from everyone else. I hadn't ever bothered to find out any real information about it. There never was much available on the rhetalink, was there? I understand why, now.

'I'd always figured that if I was detained for something like trespassing, I'd be taken to a local station where they lecture me for a few hours and put some tags onto my rhetalink profile. But then the carving knife incident happened… It was stupid. I was stupid. I'll never stop replaying that stupid scene over and over again.

'On the flight over, the detainers were stone silent. They wouldn't answer any questions. They pretended I wasn't there. I was strapped into the seat with my hands against my sides so I couldn't slap one of them even if I wanted to. I was anxious, but I still had my ignorant ideas about what it would be like inside. I wasn't expecting anything grand, no feather beds or a five-course solstice buffet with herb dressings, but I still had it in my head that it would be reasonable. Of course I was wrong.

'On arrival, I was given a load of paperwork and my purple clothes and bundled into my room for my first night in captivity. There was no bed, just a ragged sleeping pouch on the floor and a bio receptacle in the corner that flushed automatically twice a day. I was shattered,

but against all reason I had hope that reason would prevail, and I'd be out of there soon enough. I'd admit to my Code-violations and be reformed and go back out into the world, humbled.

'The next day, I encountered some of the other patients, and that put an end to my delusions. Wretched, broken people, thin and haggard, dead behind the eyes, rotting away inside that prison. Because that's what it is. Always has been. You go there to be imprisoned, not to be reformed. There were no other fresh arrivals at that time, apart from myself – all the others had been in there for a while. They didn't speak to me, barely acknowledged me. I was only around them at mealtimes, and those were quiet, depressing affairs. I wanted to believe they were inside for crimes worse than my own and that my case was different, but… no. There was no denying that their fate was my fate, unless I fought it with everything I had.

'In my naiveté, I sought out one of the staff and asked if there was any way to get additional bedding for my cell. She'd had this question asked of her before, that much was obvious. She referred me to the lead facilitator, a man by the name of Pegrel.

'Pegrel was – is – the sort of person you're initially thankful for and then you grow to loathe more than anyone else in existence. He greeted me kindly, bowed, offered me a softseat in his office, which, I noted, was not significantly larger than a patient's cell. He listened to what I had to say without a shadow of malice in his face, nodding the whole time, scratching his chin. And then he told me how things work.

'"Terek," he said. "I'm sure I don't have to remind you that this is the reformatory, not your home. It's not going to be as comfortable as what you're used to. All the patients here start off with the same supplies. There are ways and means of getting additional luxuries, but there's a cost. A cost to us and, therefore, a cost to you. Nothing unreasonable, mind, so if it means that much to you, we can always look into the options."

'Options! I was happy to hear that word, and I confirmed that, yes, I would like to investigate them. Pegrel seemed to expect this. His nod came almost before I'd finished saying what I had to say.

'"Very well," he said and started flicking through a list of documents on his slab. He had a fresh face back then. He was – is – barely older than I am. A good-looking man with fine features, the sort that one gravitates towards without meaning to. If I saw him now, I'd run as fast as I could in the opposite direction.

'So he smiles and says, "Ah yes, several options. You're aware of the reformatory opt-in system, I assume? A harmless test in exchange for perks. You can be on your new bedding within two days." It occurred to me to point out that reasonable bedding to ward off hypothermia, physical agony, and sleeplessness couldn't really be considered a perk, but I didn't want to present myself as a problem patient so early on, and I had it in my mind that he simply didn't realise how bad my bedding actually was. I was even a bit ashamed, thinking he considered me some sort of pampered eco-urbanite throwback. So I asked him about the tests, and he gave a bit of a vague response, telling me that there were some little supplement tests and procedures in the queue, and if I'd like to put my name down on the waiting list, I should be lucky enough to get into one of the tests by the next day at the latest.

'He made it sound like something coveted, something I should look forward to, so I put my fingerprint to it and that was that. I was apprehensive, but not fearful. I was thinking about the new bedding more than anything else. By that stage, I was running on about a four-night sleep deficit, and when a member of staff approached me the next morning to say my opt-in had been approved and scheduled for that evening, I was overjoyed, imagining I'd be sleeping warm and sound that very night.

'They were waiting for me at the entrance to the dining hall just before dinner. "No food?" I asked. I was jovial. I remember it clearly. I'll never forget it. "No food," the official said to me. "It interferes with the supplement. We need you on an empty stomach. The kitchen will keep some for you."

'Every patient around me was looking at me like I'd caught some terrible disease. There was this woman. She had grey hair and sunken eyes, and she just stared and stared at me. As I was turning away to

follow the officials, she laid her hand on my arm and that was the moment I first thought something was wrong. They all stood there, watching me walk away, food trays in hand. It was the beginning of something. Some rite of passage. Everything was going to change.

'There was an entire testing wing through this door I'd never been through before. It looked a bit like a military bunker, a maze of corridors with no windows, and part of it was like an infirmary, with doctors and nurses milling around, masked and gloved. I hadn't expected that. They ushered me into this little waiting room, and Pegrel was there with his slab. He had a horrible smile. I sat opposite him, and he gave me a mug of water and told me to drink it because I should be hydrated to get the best results from the supplements. He started telling me some other stuff while I drank the water. It tasted strange, and then I must've blacked out.

'I woke up strapped to a bed in darkened room and... it was like being inside a cocoon of pain. I couldn't distinguish the parts of my body. It was just pain. All of it. There was a blanket over me, I couldn't see anything. My ears rang, and I was nauseous. I threw up, and then I must've started screaming because someone came into the room and did something to my arm, and I was gone again.

'I came to on my new bedding. A thin, lumpy little mattress, and a scratchy pillow. I still had the sleeping pouch, and they'd added a ratty little blanket with holes in it. That was what my pain had purchased. All these assessments I made much later. When I first woke up, I was completely unaware of the new bedding. My head was heavy and foggy. I could feel my pulse everywhere, all over my body. I wasn't in pain anymore, but I couldn't move much. I felt so weak and fragile. The lights were off in my cell, but the light from the corridor outside came through the little frosted window and the gap under the door and burned my eyes. When I gathered the strength to lift my arms and use my hands, I pulled the blanket away from my body and found that my entire torso, from my hips to my armpits, was wrapped in grade 5 marrowcore bandages.

'I never found out what it was they did to me. Pegrel tried to keep

up appearances, tried to maintain his jovial, persona, but it was over, and he knew it. I could see that he recognised his loss of my trust, even through his toothy smiles and tactfully furrowed brow when he heard my complaints.

'"Yes, yes, I'm afraid there were some unexpected reactions to the supplement. Rare indeed, but a known possibility, as you must've noted in the documents you fingerprinted beforehand. It's a good thing we have so many highly trained medical staff watching over each patient test with such dedication and care. Terrible misfortune. I'm glad to see you back on your feet. Enjoying the new bedding, I trust?"

'Oh, he was such a waspik. His words were like wickernut oil, and even though he knew that I knew, he kept up the act to make it impossible to declare open warfare against him. My memories were muddled, and I'd lost a lot of time, so he was able to deflect my questions about why I couldn't remember taking any supplements at all. I remember fingerprinting the documents, giving them the right to do whatever they wanted with me. I wish I'd realised…

'The worst thing is that most reformatory prisoners voluntarily sign up for further testing after their first experience, even if that experience is as bad as mine was, or worse. Why? Well, I got my bedding, didn't I? It was rubbish, but it did help. You get what you're promised, to some meagre extent, and that's what makes the system work. They mangle your mind up and have you believing that it's all fair, that they're upholding their end of a bargain, except it's a bargain you never made. It's a gamble. You put your name down, and maybe you'll end up in the biocloset for three days, cacking yourself into a desiccated husk, or maybe you'll get covered in rash or pustules or tiny holes. Maybe you'll end up with stitched wounds, or bits of your body missing altogether. There's no way to know. The documents you press your finger to are vague, the facts obscured behind carefully crafted nonsense. Everyone reads the documents the second time they're in for a test, but there's nothing truly informative there, and they all fingerprint the slab regardless, because they all need something. They

have no choice but to be dragged off for some form of horrendous torture in exchange for things that free people think of as basic Rhetari rights. Sleep, food, medicine.

'I don't know what they did to me to give me this wound. It wasn't my first, and I didn't expect it to be my last. Some of the earlier scars I got in exchange for meal improvements. I managed to get some vegetables added to my gruel, and another opt-in test got me a bit of real millbean porridge instead of the sawdusty substitute that comes standard. Important improvements, and I paid heavily for them. I was bedridden for over a week with my jaw wired shut after the first one. Pegrel having a private laugh, I suppose, drip-feeding me after I'd just earned myself some proper food. At first I didn't think it was worth it, but months later when I had some strength back and the holes in my gums had healed over, I was grateful every day for those undercooked vegetables.

'There were prisoners who didn't prioritise food improvements through the opt-in system, and they were all skin and bone, wasted away, going about their days in a trance of weakness and indifference. Some chose this path on purpose and even skipped their standard meals. They wanted to die rather than live out their lives in that place, but the reformatory doesn't let you die by choice. They'd drip-feed the faders back to relative health and push them back into their labour designations. Cleaning for the able-bodied, document tagging for the physically weak but mentally sound. The strongest of us had a range of jobs, sometimes outdoors, like building-maintenance, snow-clearing, hauling supplies in from the depot or working in the greenhouse where the decent food is grown.

'That was my favourite job. I took a test just to increase my greenhouse workdays per month. That was during my second winter, when I couldn't stand shovelling snow anymore. I was already starting to see my health as currency by then. I let them subject me to so many tests in the first few years. I bounced back strong at first, but after years of testing, my recoveries grew longer and longer. I'd be put back to work before I'd healed properly, and I had to stop doing it so much.

'It's a scam, you see. They whittle away the privileges you've earned, but slowly enough that you don't notice it happening until one day you think to yourself: you know, I'm still hungry after this meal. I started scrutinising the meal, counting the cubes of vegetable I'd paid for in blood, and sure enough, it was about a cube less every week until the portion just wasn't filling me up anymore and I was hungry all the time. I took it up with Pegrel and, well, you know how it goes by now.

'They break you slowly and skilfully. If you're useful, that is. If you're not useful, if you can't work, if you cause too many problems... People die. They take a test, and they don't make it through and then we get informed through the dining hall bulletin that a patient unfortunately has succumbed to a long-standing illness or, on the rare occasion when there's no way that this explanation would be believable, they say that they "had an extremely rare adverse reaction to a test supplement" and "died for the betterment of the Rhetari, with honour and selflessness". I don't even think that all these tests were opt-in. I have plenty of reason to believe that difficult prisoners and serious liabilities to the system were strong-armed into that infirmary wing and put down.

'I lost a friend that way. The only friend I ever made in that place. She came in a few years after I did. We worked in the greenhouse together. She told me it was the only time she felt any peace, when she was pulling up the vegetables and getting her hands covered in soil. The rest of the time, she fought the system harder than anyone. She got herself into tests and tried to sabotage them. She caused disturbances at mealtimes, throwing food and crushing the bowls. She screamed a lot.

'I tried to warn her. I told her it wasn't worth it; nothing good would come of her disruptions at the reformatory. She couldn't hurt them, I told her, but they could hurt her. She said she knew it, and she didn't care. She wanted them to realise that even though they could have her killed, they couldn't make her submit to them. And it was

true – they couldn't get her to follow the rules of the system, so they ended her. She hadn't even been in there for a year.

'She told me she wasn't going to take any more tests because the last time she tried to upset the infirmary, they just used targeted air tranquillisers on her and she was out cold before she could so much as flip a table. So when it was announced that she had died as the result of an adverse reaction during a voluntary supplement test, I knew the truth of it. They had dragged her in there completely against her will and probably pressed her limp finger against the slab for good measure so all their paperwork would be in order, and then they murdered her. My only friend.

'It was around that time that I started looking for ways out. I wanted to get out so I could tell someone the truth about what happens in there. I wanted to tell someone about my friend, someone who cared. I needed to escape for myself, but also for her.

Her name was Shani.'

CHAPTER 36

Shortly before they were due to return to Wooden Hill with Pol and Halin, Kini took Virda and Jex aside. She led them to the stand of trees at the hill near the house, her face grave and her hands shaking. Virda felt cold, inside and out.

'I need to tell you how I met Marruvan,' said Kini. She glanced at Virda for a moment, then flinched and looked away. 'The truth this time.'

'Kini, what—' Jex began, but Kini silenced him with a raised hand.

'I met Terek before I met Marruvan. I knew of Marruvan, because of Sarla's involvement in anti-reformatory activism. Anyone – *everyone* who had a personal grievance with the reformatory knew Sarla's story. I'd followed it closely. But I never met Marruvan until after Terek contacted me.'

'Why did he do that?' Virda wanted to shake Kini's shoulders and tell her to get to the point, but instead she stood stiff, and dug her nails into the palms of her hands.

'When Terek escaped…' Kini swallowed hard. 'He went into hiding for a while, with Sarla's help, but after Sarla died, he tracked me down. Sent me a letter. He knew about me because Shani told him about me. They met. Inside.'

'Kini,' said Virda, but Kini didn't seem to hear her.

'Shani's dead,' said Kini, and she looked up at Jex and then Virda, her jaw set. 'Shani's dead. She died at the reformatory. Years ago. She's been dead for a long time.'

Virda swayed, and Jex grabbed her arm and they stood like that, silent, a cold wind batting at them.

Kini continued to speak, and her words seemed to come from far away. 'I reached out to Marruvan. Terek knew him, through Sarla, and he introduced us. I wanted to tell him to carry on fighting Sarla's fight. For Sarla and Terek and everyone still trapped in that terrible place, but especially for Shani. I couldn't do it alone. That's how I met him.'

'Why didn't you tell me?' Virda's voice crumbled, dry as dust. 'You were never alone in this. I never stopped fighting for Shani. All these years.'

'You had hope,' Kini said. 'I thought it would be cruel to take that away from you.'

But hope was not all that Virda had lived with. There was also the anger, the frustration, and the aching sadness that had eaten away at her for all these blighted years.

And now she was broken. The loss of Fessi had cracked her into pieces, and the loss of Shani took away her ability to hold those pieces together. They were sharp-edged, scattered around. She feared some were lost forever.

Virda's first days back in Wooden Hill passed in a blur of activity, with emotional peaks and troughs punctuated by bloody flashbacks that tore animal screams from her lungs. Her sleep was fragmented, and her waking hours warped with hallucinations. Jex took her to the infirmary, where Halin administered vastly more powerful drugs than the tranquillisers she'd given her from her travel bag at Marruvan's farmhouse. Berro had stayed behind with his father to recuperate away from the inevitable stress and unwanted attention he'd receive in the dorm at the academy, and sometimes Virda wished she'd stayed there too.

'This is not unexpected,' Halin said. 'You'll be all right. We'll get you through this.'

Jex said the same, and Virda pretended to believe him, though there was no fathomable way she'd ever be able to stop thinking about what she'd done and what had been done to her friends and the fact that her cousin was not only dead but *long* dead, mulched, reabsorbed into the cycle, atomised.

She visited Andish and Kath at the lakehouse only once in the weeks after their return, ostensibly to give her condolences, although she quickly found the situation flipped around, with Andish cradling her as she sobbed and sobbed until she couldn't sob any more. She recovered herself on their softseat with the aid of some extremely strong tea laced with one of Andish's soothing tinctures. Later, they gathered on the edge of the island for a ritual.

Virda, Jex, Magrin, Kath and Andish each lit a small candle for Fessi and sent them out onto the water on little wooden floats. They stood in silence on the bank watching the candles bob along in the breeze like a handful of fallen stars as a dark bird circled silently overhead. Virda began to weep again, and Jex and Magrin had to take her home, supporting her on either side because her legs were unreliable and her mind even more so. They used Magrin's lift to get her into the treehouse.

'You can't simply stop yourself from thinking,' said Halin one afternoon during a therapy session in one of the quiet rooms at the infirmary. Halin wasn't a mind specialist, but she had a bit of general experience in the field and more knowledge of the situation than any other medical practitioner. Virda refused to speak to anyone else. 'Fighting against your own thoughts isn't going to help. You'll just get stuck in a cycle of anxiety and terror. What you need to do is focus on acceptance. Recognise the thoughts for what they are, and try to let them pass through you without tearing you to pieces.'

She practised daily, Jex with her, sitting in the sunshine on the floor beside the bed, breathing in and breathing out and trying to step back, step away, step out of the spinning blades of her memories.

The academy had been notified that Virda, Jex and Berro were on a leave of absence following undisclosed traumatic events. On Virda's insistence, Mama Stitch had not been informed of any of this. Jex sent her an occasional message to tide them over. By their next visit, Virda hoped they'd be able to impart an edited version of events without her breaking down.

'If you need Mama, go to her, but I can't handle her emotions, Jex,' she said. 'I'd use all my energy reassuring her that I'm fine. I just can't do that right now.'

Jex sat cross-legged on the warm floorboards, palms resting on his knees, sunlight catching in the eyelashes of his unpatched eye. He leaned forward and placed a hand on Virda's arm.

She looked up at him. 'Jex, I want to climb.'

'Then let's climb,' he replied.

'But your eye...'

'I'll take it easy,' he said. 'And so will you.'

Tarov, Kem, Gunli and Disa were congregated in their favourite clearing, as if they'd been waiting for Virda and Jex to arrive. They certainly hadn't been waiting, though, as their looks of astonishment made clear.

Kem's jaw dropped, Tarov froze in the middle of tying up his hair, Disa lifted her hand to her mouth, and Gunli hurried over to them, gushing a string of half-formed phrases. 'You're back! You're— Oh, your eye, Jex! Cack, what happened? What did you— Virda? Virda, oh...'

They fell into Gunli's embrace, and the others moved forward slowly, with an almost fearful hesitance.

'We've heard so many rumours,' said Disa. 'I don't know what to believe. I'm so glad to see you both.'

Gunli dabbed Virda's wet cheeks with the sleeve of their green uniform.

'What rumours have you heard?' asked Jex. 'We can't confirm anything. There's a trial in two weeks, and then it will all come out, but—'

'Some people are saying you stole a vehicle and crashed it and that's how Fessi died. But I know that's not true.'

'I wish the part about Fessi dying wasn't true,' said Jex.

'I'm so sorry.' Kem placed his hand on Jex's shoulder. 'I really am. I didn't know her, but she must've been special if she was friends with you two.'

Jex nodded, his eye blinking rapidly.

'I also heard that Imparter Undra's been detained at the reformatory, for some reason,' said Disa. 'Is that true?'

Virda clenched her teeth.

'We can't talk about that,' said Jex. 'I'm sorry.'

'I'm just glad you two are here,' said Disa. 'Your eye, Jex…'

'It'll heal,' he said. 'It's nothing too bad. Virda got it worse than I did.'

Disa looked at Virda, who had Gunli's arm around her back and Gunli's head resting on her shoulder.

'I'll be fine, eventually,' said Virda. 'Mind wounds heal too, you know.'

Kem reached out and squeezed her hand sympathetically. 'We're here if you need to talk. If you need fresh ears.'

Virda nodded. 'Thank you,' she said in a frayed whisper.

Tarov stood a few paces away from the group, watching them with a pained look on his face, his right hand gripping his upper left arm so tightly it was leaving marks on his skin. For the first time at this reunion, he spoke. 'Is Berro going to be all right?'

'Yes,' said Virda. 'He's with his father. He's injured – body and mind – but he's stronger and smarter than any of us. He'll be fine.'

Tarov nodded. 'It's good to have you back in the fold,' he said. 'And maybe I'll stand a chance against Jex now, at least while he has his eye patched up.'

Jex laughed. 'What if I beat you with one eye? You'll be devastated.'

'I'll get over it.' Tarov shrugged.

'Well then,' said Jex, tilting his head towards the trees. 'Shall we?'

They climbed, slow but steady, casual and cathartic, and they all reached the top at roughly the same time, Tarov hanging back to hoist Jex up onto the platform ahead of him, prompting Gunli to cheer and Kem to break into a round of applause. Disa rolled a set of wickers as they made themselves comfortable in the canopy's embrace, and passed Jex the first one she completed.

He held it up to his eye and whistled in admiration. 'You're far too good at this.'

'Wait till you taste it. This is special wicker. Deserves proper rolling.'

Once they each had a wicker to smoke, Tarov reached around and lit them all up with his flinter, and they lay back in a comfortably tangled heap, legs across laps, arms entwined, heads resting on shoulders or stomachs or chests to ward against the frosty chill in the air – colder up there than it was down between the trees. Even as they smoked, their uniforms began to glitter with particles of ice, and the stars winked out between the crisp clouds frozen high in the polished winter sky.

'This is very good wicker,' said Virda. 'It's making my mind quiet.'

'Good,' said Disa. 'Infirmary grade. I can get you some more, or you can just ask Halin. Tell her you tried strain three and it helped. She'll give you more, and better, any form you want it. Tincture, pills, patches, powder, whatever. She's good.'

'She is,' said Virda. 'She'd have my vote for council if I didn't think she was more valuable at the infirmary. I told her that, and I think she agreed. I'm voting for Pol.'

'Me too, obviously,' said Jex.

'You're all good, too, you know that?' said Virda, suddenly sentimental.

'Is that the wicker talking?' Tarov laughed.

'No. Seriously. Having cack stuff happen to you makes you realise how good the good stuff is. I appreciate this. All of this. Even you, Tarov.'

Tarov laughed again. 'Thanks, Virda. I probably don't deserve that.'

She turned to him then, resting her chin on top of Jex's head, the smoke from his wicker swirling in front of her eyes. 'Why do you say that?'

Tarov release a thin stream of smoke straight up into the sky.

'Because I'm not always a good person. I've done stuff I regret.'

'Who hasn't?' said Kem.

Tarov wrinkled his nose. 'I guess. But I'm going to be better, from now on. I've got another chance.'

'Another chance at what?' asked Virda, but Tarov only smiled and dismissed the question with a flick of his wrist. He stretched his arm out and tickled the first head his fingers found, which happened to be Gunli's. Gunli purred loudly. Disa and Kem burst into laughter, and Jex snuggled closer into Virda's chest.

A hush settled over them as they listened to the haunting calls of distant birds settling in for the night and the clear, crystalline trill of the first nocturnal insects waking up. After a few peaceful minutes, Virda realised Jex was asleep in her arms. She took the smouldering wicker from his fingers, pinched it out, and pocketed the remains for later.

For the first time in a long while, Virda felt at peace. All the things she'd been so anxious and obsessed about in recent years seemed totally irrelevant now. She was alive, and so was Jex. They had time to figure out the details, and she was grateful for this, even with the pain of loss and injury. She resolved to call Mama Stitch the next morning and tell her everything, through snot and tears if necessary. Mama, like everyone else in her life, would be there for her.

She stroked her fingers through Jex's messy blond hair, cupped his cold cheek with her hand, and pressed her lips to his forehead.

>>comspace/locked/reformatory reformation collective
>>2 reformer(s) in comspace
>>reformer treescrat has entered

Burnitdown– *: >>emote: surprise<< :*

Burnitdown– *: do my eyes deceive me? scratty??? :*

Treescrat– *: it's been ages, i know. so much has happened. don't even know where to start. i'm not allowed to say a lot. the council is involved and i'm code-bound for now :*

Cackfoot– *: wow. gods. is this about that student death at wooden hill? i couldn't make sense of the report. i was worried it might be you, because you were silent for so long, but burnitdown talked me around :*

Treescrat– *: the student was my friend. she died at the reformatory :*

Cackfoot– *: what? :*

Burnitdown– *: >>emote: blink//bewildered<< :*

Treescrat– *: we went to the reformatory to get someone out and things got cacked up. i shouldn't even be saying this :*

Burnitdown– *: wait a second, you WENT TO THE REFORMATORY? did you see your cousin? did you get her out? :*

Treescrat– *: we didn't go there for my cousin. my cousin is dead :*

Cackfoot– *: i'm so sorry. you're making no sense, scrats. are you all right? :*

Treescrat– *: i'm all right. or i will be. i know this confusing, but you'll understand soon. keep an eye on the distro. there's going to be a trial at the council* *headquarters on mass 1. if everything goes to plan, it will be the first step in ending the reformatory :*

Cackfoot– *: really? :*

Burnitdown– *: are you actually scratty? you're scaring me :*

Treescrat– *: yes, it's me. my real name is virda. i'm a post-fundamentals green student at the wooden hill academy. that'll mean something when the news comes out. i don't think they're going to keep our identities a secret, and i figured you should know it's me :*

Cackfoot– *: what happened, scrats? :*

Treescrat– *: i can't tell you right now, i'm sorry. you'll find out. i wanted to ask – do either of you have contact with justicenow since he left the comspace? :*

Cackfoot– *: no, but i could find him. is it important? :*

Treescrat– *: it's important. if you make contact with him, tell him what i told you. tell him my name and to get in touch with me if he wants to help. he can contact a couple of the imparters at the academy – pol or halin. they're helping us :*

Burnitdown– *: helping you? oh gods, this is making me anxious. why do you need justicenow? :*

Treescrat– *: those letters he got. they're evidence of reformatory malpractice. we need that evidence :*

Cackfoot– *: scrats, can we help too? :*

Treescrat– *: find justicenow. that will help. i won't be in the comspace for a while, but i want you to know: there's hope. not for my cousin, not for justice's brother, and everything's a total cackpit, but there's hope. you'll see :*

CHAPTER 37

Berro sat in the farmhouse mingle with his father, Kini and Imparter Pol, who had been dispatched along with two other experienced skycraft pilots to retrieve the academy vollops from their various points of abandonment on Mass 2. Pol had flown first to the reformatory, where one pilot had been dropped off fetch the machine Undra had used, and then to the farmhouse for the one that had been commandeered by Virda, Jex and Fessi. Repairs had been required on that vehicle before it was properly flight-worthy, but within a few hours, the pilot had it in the air and was on his way back to Wooden Hill while Pol sipped tea and chatted to Marruvan about growing fresh produce which, apparently, was something they dabbled in at a vegetable patch behind the academy's skycraft hangar. It wasn't a social situation Berro had ever imagined before, but nothing in his whole life at that moment was how he'd imagined it. The presence of the Vehicles instructor in his father's farmhouse was just another odd detail in a shattered, confusing picture that he was struggling to reconcile with reality.

Through the fog of his grief and confusion, Berro took an instant liking to Pol, and even wondered if he should take a few courses with them, when – if – life ever started to make sense again. He wasn't sure he'd enjoy flying, and he wouldn't want to steal Jex's thunder anyway, but perhaps he could sharpen his hover-vehicle skills. He'd been casting around idly for a new academic focus, and every idea seemed to have so much potential. He imagined himself driving the hovertube across the vastness of Mass 2 and seeing a glorious cross-section of the sights speeding by – how peaceful, practical, purposeful such a job would be, getting people from one place another, for work, for travel, to visit friends and family, in sickness and in health. There was no prestige in it, but he was surprisingly unconcerned by that.

Marruvan squeezed Berro's uninjured shoulder and gave him the sort of fatherly smile that caused an ache in his chest. 'It's been good having you here, Berro, even under these terrible circumstances.'

Berro nodded, not trusting his voice to work. His eyes felt hot.

'You'll visit again, won't you?' said Kini, as though he'd just dropped by for a friendly catch-up.

'I will,' he rasped. 'And I'll see you both at the trial.'

'I'm proud of you, Berro—' Marruvan began, but Berro shook his head sharply and turned his face away as the heat in his eyes went liquid. Marruvan squeezed his shoulder again, and said nothing.

Once he was seated in Pol's vollop, with the engines powering up beneath him, Berro allowed the tears to fall. He watched his father and Kini standing in front of the farmhouse, waving at him, until they were specks in the distance, until the farmhouse itself was a speck and then a recent memory that felt immediately like a dream.

Pol cleared their throat. 'We don't know each other well, Berrovan, but I know your friend Jex, and I've been getting to know Virda through all of this, and they have nothing but praise for you. I can tell you're a good student with a bright future ahead of you. You'll get through this. You need to be kind to yourself.'

Berro wiped his face and smiled into his lap. 'Thank you, Imparter.'

Pol nodded curtly, and they spent the rest of the flight in comfortable silence.

Their arrival back in Wooden Hill was met by a small welcoming party at the airfield. Virda was conspicuous by her absence, and Fessi… Berro screwed his eyes shut for a moment and took a few measured breaths before he stepped out of the vollop to face everyone. Jex and Magrin were there, along with Kem, Ebra and Yurek. A couple of the other climbers – Gunli and Tarov – had come along too. Berro's face pulsed with embarrassment as his eyes met Tarov's and he remembered the night of the festival, but Tarov just smiled like he cared, like he was genuinely pleased to see him.

Jex's face looked a lot better than it had the last time Berro had seen him, but it was still a shocking sight, and his eye remained hidden beneath a patch. They embraced for a long time. Berro's guilt – made worse by the absences – was a raw pain in his chest, but he couldn't succumb to it, tempered as it was by a storm of desperate love for every familiar face present. Emotions tugged him in opposite directions, and he thought he might come apart and drift away like wickerwood seed fluff on the wind.

'It's good to see you,' he said, achingly aware of the inadequacy of his words.

'It's good to see you too,' said Jex, his one visible eye big and blue and warm. 'We're heading to the common area for dinner. Disa's made some special stew she wants us to try. Nothing intoxicating, don't worry.'

'Does it have moss in it?'

Jex, Gunli and Tarov all laughed and said 'probably' in perfect unison before erupting into laughter once again.

Berro allowed himself to be thoroughly fussed over by Magrin, whom he was quite surprised to see out of the treehouse for a gathering with multiple people she didn't know, given her strong preference for staying inside and avoiding such situations. 'Virda would've been here,' Magrin said. 'She asked us to send you her love, and to say she'll see you soon. She just needs to be alone sometimes, and today she wasn't the best. You don't need to worry.

We're taking good care of her. She's missed you, though. You'll visit soon, won't you?'

'Of course,' said Berro, hugging her. 'Of course I will.'

They made their way to the academy with half of them – including Jex and Berro with their respective injuries – crammed into Pol's six-person darter, and the others sharing a few academy monos. Pol dropped them off at edge of the forest and administered serious shoulder-pats to Jex and Berro before driving off along the branch paths, leaving the young people to their merriment.

Because that's what it was, despite everything. There was a strange, energetic, almost celebratory feeling in the air, at least for Berro, and he suspected Jex felt it too. Every time he caught Jex's eye, they shared a meaningful smile – sad-eyed, but hopeful. Grieving, but grateful.

When they entered the common area on level 13 of the academy, they were met by a delicious smell and the friendly face of Disa, who greeted Berro warmly, hugged Jex for ages, and then attached herself to Kem's hip in a way that made Berro certain he'd be asking Kem for details in the dorm later. Disa had pulled several tables together and surrounded them with chairs from all over the room, and ten bowls of stew were dished up and steaming. Berro's mouth watered.

There was one seat empty after everyone had sat down, its bowl unclaimed, and Disa looked across the table at Jex. 'She's not coming then?'

Jex shook his head. 'Not this time. But she sends her love.' He exchanged a look with Magrin, and Berro was relieved that it was a warm look, not a foreboding one. Virda would be fine. If Jex and Magrin both believed it, then he would too.

Berro opened his mouth, and the words *What about Kath?* dangled off the tip of his tongue before he pulled them back in and pressed his lips together. He'd have to visit her and find out. He was glad she was with Andish, and that Andish was with her. His mind lurched towards the epicentre of his grief for a moment, but he resisted it and forced himself to stay rooted in the moment.

The stew was rich and delicious, packed full of vegetables and flavours he couldn't identify but didn't care to. He finished his serving before anyone else, and Tarov, who was seated beside him, reached for the extra bowl and slid it in front of him.

'Keep going,' he said. 'No sense wasting it.'

Berro looked around to see if anyone else had their eye on the spare food.

'Just eat it, Berro,' said Tarov. 'Nobody minds. You need it.'

He didn't specify why he thought Berro needed it, but Berro sensed no malice in the assertion. It wasn't a slight about his size – it was friendly concern for his wellbeing.

'Thanks. And I wanted to say sorry—'

'You don't need to do that.'

'I want to,' said Berro. 'There were things going on before that night. It's no excuse. I treated you badly for no reason, and I regret it. You were kind to me. I enjoyed...'

'So did I,' said Tarov. 'Can we try again?'

'Try what?'

Tarov shrugged. 'Smoking a wicker together somewhere and talking?'

Berro thought of the way Tarov's hands had felt on his skin. With his cheeks burning, he stared into the depths of his fresh bowl of stew and stirred it thoughtfully, tracking the glistening vesicles of rich grease through the red-brown liquid. Would Tarov still be interested in spending time with him once Berro's involvement with Undra became common knowledge?

'I don't have much to offer,' Berro said. 'I don't want to disappoint you, but I'm not—'

'You're interesting,' said Tarov. 'I'd like to get to know you. I don't have any expectations beyond a smoke and a chat.'

'I don't really like smoking.'

'A chat, then.'

Berro couldn't help smiling into his stew, and when he looked up, he found Tarov smiling too. It didn't look like a smile of pity, either.

'I can chat,' said Berro.

'Jex and Virda trained you well?'

'They have.'

'How about tomorrow? Midday? A stroll along the stream or something?'

'Sure,' Berro said. 'Tomorrow.'

• • •

Sleep wouldn't come that night. Berro lay in his bunk, listening to the gentle ambience of the dormitory alcove, his thoughts roaming here and there, but on a short leash. He thought about his father and Kini, about Tarov, about the blushing grin Kem had given him in the elevator when he'd asked if there was anything new going on between him and Disa. He thought about Kath in the lakehouse with Andish, and the leash pulled tight and painful.

His pod, which he'd placed beside his pillow in violation of his own healthy sleeping rules, lit up unexpectedly. It was a message from Virda.

: are you awake? :

: I am. How did you know? :

: i just guessed. i'm sorry i wasn't there this evening :

: I don't mind, Virda. I understand. How are you? :

There was a long pause, and Berro wondered if it was a question he should've avoided.

: i'm fine. but i want to talk to you about everything. i've talked to halin in therapy, and to jex sometimes, but there's nothing else for us to say to each other. jex doesn't carry burdens like we do :

: You can talk to me anytime, Virda. I would like that. :

: can i talk to you right now? :

: Text or voice? I can leave the dorm if you'd like. :

: voice, please, if it's not too much trouble. i'm on the balcony :

: Give me three minutes. :

Berro slipped out of bed, threw a robe over his clothwrap, jammed his feet into his boots and scooped up his pod and slab before slipping out of the dormitory and into the elevator. He sent the elevator to Grow Level A without really thinking about it, and when he stepped out into its close and fragrant darkness, he knew he'd made the right choice. There was nobody in there at this time of night, and he was comforted by the warm, slightly moist atmosphere with its pleasantly earthy scent.

He settled himself on a damp plastic chair behind a long table of fungi terrariums and linked with Virda on his slab. Her face filled the screen, a golden orb floating in the darkness, illuminated by light from the treehouse kitchen window. He could hear the hush of the wind in the trees and the gentle creaking of the treehouse behind her.

'Aren't you cold?' he asked by way of a greeting.

'A bit,' said Virda, 'but I like it. Makes me feel awake. I've got a thermal clothwrap on, don't worry. Where the hells are you?'

'Grow level A.'

Virda chuckled, and it was the best sound Berro had ever heard. 'Sure, why not, I guess,' she said. 'Look, I'm sorry for getting you out of bed.'

'I was awake. It's not a problem, Virda. I'll do anything for you. And not just because I owe you my life. Which I do. You're one of my closest friends. In fact...' He stopped himself from saying his next words out loud, but the way Virda's face clenched made him suspect she'd understood him anyway. *In fact, now that Fessi's gone, you* are *my closest friend.*

Virda took a deep breath that sounded meditative, like something Halin had instructed her to do to keep herself calm. 'Berro,' she said. 'I tried to explain, at your father's house, but everything was so chaotic there, we never really got a chance to talk properly. What happened at the reformatory… Maybe you didn't see what I saw, what Jex saw. I tried to describe it to Halin, and she humoured me, but I don't think she understood. I need you to understand. Fessi did something impossible. I know I didn't imagine it. With everything that happened afterwards, I couldn't think about it. But Berro, she moved. She jumped. She disappeared and reappeared in a different place. I saw it, Berro. I—'

'I saw it too,' Berro said, allowing himself to return to that room of horrors for the first time since he'd been broken there. He remembered the feeling of his blood pumping out of his shoulder and his head swimming, the sounds and sensations warping and blending around him. He remembered seeing the shape that was Fessi blink out of existence at the corner of his eye and materialise some distance away as the bullet struck. 'I saw her move. I thought I'd hallucinated. Everything was a nightmare, I was bleeding.'

'She moved, Berro. She definitely moved. And the way she did it, the way she planned and managed the whole rescue, all calm and Fessi-like, but even more than usual, it was like she knew something we didn't know. Like she knew it was going to happen. And she knew she could do *that*. I know this sounds like a desperate, crazy thing to say, but what if she survived? What if she's still alive?'

Virda's eyes glistened wide and hopeful on the screen, waiting for Berro to say something.

'We'll never know, Virda,' he said. 'We don't know where she went. We don't—'

'I *know* that, Berro! But do you think it's possible?'

'It's possible,' Berro conceded.

'I mean.' Virda rubbed her hand across her hair, messing it up. 'Kath, survived, didn't she? It's possible to survive a crossing.'

Berro didn't need to remind Virda that Kath hadn't been shot or stabbed with a set of marrowcore needles prior to her crossing.

Virda sighed. 'Would you think I was deluded and pathetic if I carried on with the rest of my life believing that Fessi was alive somewhere?'

'No,' said Berro. 'I wouldn't. And would you think poorly of me if I believed the opposite? If I grieve her, will that hurt you?'

Virda shook her head. She seemed about to say something, but then shook her head again and stared off into the darkness beyond her own screen.

'Virda,' said Berro. 'When I woke up in the vollop with Undra and sent that you all picture, I thought I was going to die. I just wanted you to know that Undra was responsible, that it wasn't your fault, and I hadn't left you out of choice. I never thought it would lead to everything that happened. I didn't mean to summon you. I was so angry with myself, for leaving things on a sour note. It was so stupid, all of it. And you were right, about me, my mother, the reformatory, everything. I'm so sorry.'

'Yes, I was right,' Virda said, 'but some of the stuff I said, and the way I said it… I'm sorry too, Berro.'

'I think it's time to put all this apologising behind us.'

'Maybe,' said Virda. 'It's just that… I'm happy to be alive, but I don't feel like I deserve it.'

'Why wouldn't you deserve it?'

'I killed two people, Berro.'

'No, you didn't,' said Berro with such conviction that Virda snapped her mouth shut and blinked at him.

'I'm going for a walk with Tarov tomorrow,' Berro continued, before she could say anything else. 'He wants to *chat*.'

Virda wiggled her eyebrows, and Berro gave a sharp burst of laughter that felt so good, so liberating. He breathed in the smell of soil and mushrooms, and the tension leeched out of his shoulders.

'Did you really have to start something with the most annoying person in our climbing group?' Virda groaned, but she smiled as she said it. 'He's so full of himself.'

'Is he really that bad?'

'No. He's not that bad. And I'm sure he'll improve if he spends time with you.'

'I'm quite full of myself too, as you know,' said Berro. 'At least I was, before. It's something I'm working on. I'm trying to be better.'

'It's all we can do, isn't it? Try?'

Berro wished he could wrap his arms around Virda and give her a long, strong hug. He loved her, and the immensity of the feeling was almost too much. 'Thank you,' he said.

She didn't ask him what he was thanking her for. She simply smiled and said, 'Any time.'

CHAPTER 38

SPRING

The garden surrounding the council building was lush and pristine, a vigorous yet orderly and soothing beauty. Berro sat on the wide steps that fanned out from the building, gazing at the garden, tracing its lines, shapes and symmetry with lazy eyes. The sun pulsed in a cloudless sky, and all the flowers were open wide, drinking in the light. A fountain burbled in the centre of the view, sunlight twinkling through the droplets that plinked into its shimmering pool.

Unlike his friends, Berro had not worn his academy colours. Instead, he wore a specially cut clothwrap that left his bandaged shoulder and upper arm exposed and held the arm in a soft sling. His wounds had healed considerably, but the arm remained weak, and the pain persisted. Virda sat beside Berro, quiet and calm. Her hair had been cut, shorter than she normally had it, and neater. Jex, who sat on her other side, had made an attempt to neaten his own hair, but bits of it had escaped his dutiful ministrations and poked up in all directions. The vicious cuts across his face had mostly healed now, and both his eyes were open, but the scars were still a raw, livid pink-red that stood out shockingly against his pale skin.

Berro watched a brightly coloured bird flit around a cluster of tubular, blue-speckled flowers, its wings moving so fast they were a glinting blur. Nearby stood a tall trellis alive with vibrant blooms that hummed with the enthusiasm of insects. Ryndel loitered there, inspecting the plants. Her red hair and uniform matched the flowers, and a couple of buzzing pollinators circled her head, perhaps confused by the colour. With practised delicacy, she took one of the creeper's tendrils between two fingers and unfurled it, putting her sharp blue eyes close to the plant to inspect it in detail. Even here, on this important and emotional day, she was dedicated to the pursuit of knowledge.

As Berro watched Ryndel, a bright beacon in the tropical Mass 1 sunshine, he felt a kinship with her. He recalled the fact of their old animosity but was incapable of summoning even the faintest trace of its essence. He was, after all, grateful to her for being there, for agreeing to share her part of their terrible story. They had perhaps more in common than anyone present, having both been close to Undra, and both, at some point, deceived by him.

With every voice of truth, the picture became clearer, more undeniable, strengthening their case for meaningful reform, and though the solidarity couldn't fill the void in Berro's chest at the loss of Fessi, it was something to hold onto, and he held onto it.

Another voice that had joined their cause was that of Amar, a stout, middle-aged man of nervous disposition who had contacted Virda in the weeks preceding the trial. Virda refused to explain the context of this event, who the man was, how she knew him or why she kept referring to him as *Justice*, but Berro had decided not to dig. He was bone tired, sore and grieving; he had enough on his mind without taking on new mysteries to solve.

Amar was with them now at the council headquarters, bearing evidence of his own against the reformatory. He sat in the shade of a sweet-smelling tree on a small filigree metal bench, reading something on his slab. Berro sensed a deep sadness in him, but also a freshly kindled flame of determination, and hoped that this stranger too could find some resolution to whatever trauma the reformatory had stamped onto his life.

On the bench beside Amar sat another man, grey and weathered, with a steely, resolute look about him. When Marruvan had introduced him, Berro had taken the name – *Terek* – like an ice lance through the chest. This was the man whose name and face he hadn't known but at whose feet he'd laid a large portion of the blame for his mother's death. He knew now that this was wrong. Terek, *the source*, had not radicalised his mother into her act of martyrdom, he'd simply told her his story, and she'd made her choices accordingly. Terek had lost more to the system than Berro, and Berro knew they needed to talk once the trial was over. This man had been in his mother's confidence at a time when Berro had been fighting her. He knew things about Sarla that Berro wanted to know. He was, apparently, a not insignificant part of Marruvan's life too, and if Berro wanted to re-establish a relationship with his father, acceptance of Terek would be part of that.

Beyond the fountain, two figures emerged from behind a meticulously trimmed hedge, ambling slowly, deep in conversation. One of them was Marruvan, a large man by any standards, but smaller than Berro's memories of him, and indeed smaller than Berro himself. Marruvan paused alongside something that caught his eye and exchanged quiet words with the other, smaller figure. Kini. She reminded Berro of his mother in some ways – something in the stiffness of her posture, the hardness of her eyes, her slightly detached and distant nature. He knew very little about his father's relationship with this woman, but he was glad she'd been there, keeping him company while Berro had kept his distance – while he'd figured out who he was.

And so, who was he? Who was Berro? He was not Berrovan Blue. There was no colour that could define him. No focus subject. No specific skill or interest. No status. No special access to important secrets. He'd learned the secrets he'd been desperate to know, but they weren't secrets anymore. The officials in the council building who'd been poring over Undra's research probably knew more now than he did. But what did it matter? He wasn't his knowledge. He wasn't his achievements or even his relationships. He was bits and pieces of all these things and more, put together, broken apart and put together again in a different way.

And what did that make him? Berro. That's all. He didn't know what that meant yet, but he wasn't worried about it. He just was. He had been, and he was, and he would continue to be, until he wasn't anymore. Berro.

A message pinged onto his pod, and he opened it, enjoying the smile it put on his face.

: hello B. hope everything goes well today. thinking of you and looking forward to you getting back. tell virda and jex i say hello and when virda asks why i didn't message her directly, tell her i like you more than i like her and she just has to cope with that. >>emote: grin//sly<< be well. Tarov :

Virda placed a hand on Berro's knee, and he turned to her, still smiling.

'Are you ready?' she asked.

'I think so,' he said, putting his pod back into his pocket. 'Tarov says hello.'

'Oh, he needs a man in the middle, does he? Couldn't possibly message me himself.' She shook her head. 'Send Tarov our regards and tell him not to get too arrogant about being the fastest climber in the settlement because we'll be back soon to put him in his place.'

'I'll tell him.'

Marruvan and Kini had nearly reached them now, and Ryndel, Terek, and Amar fell into step behind them, a motley procession across the verdant expanse of the grass. Berro could hear their voices, but not their words. Marruvan said something, and Kini laughed. Jex got to his feet and brushed his backside as though he'd been sitting in the forest and there might be dirt and twigs all over him. Force of habit – the stairs were pristine.

Berro looked up at the open doors of the council building. Pol and Halin had just emerged from inside, blinking into the brightness. A new council pin shone at the collar of Pol's green uniform, and Berro smiled. Another council official stood to one side of the door, exchanging words with Halin, who turned and caught Berro's eye. Berro nodded and placed his hand on top of Virda's. Her face was a picture of fragility and resilience, fear, hope, and love.

'I'm ready,' Berro said.

EPILOGUE

SOME WEEKS EARLIER

'Good afternoon. Could I speak with Mrs Sibanda-Katz, please?'

'Speaking.'

'Hello, ma'am. This is in connection with the missing persons case.'

'Oh god, is she—'

'I'm afraid we haven't found your daughter, but we have been informed of a Jane Doe in possession of your daughter's driver's license.'

'Excuse me?'

'An unidentified young woman. She was found in Norge. Shot and stabbed, we believe. No witnesses, no suspects, yet. She's in ICU, unconscious, but in a stable condition and likely to make a full recovery. She might be able to help us find out what happened to Kathleen.'

'In *Norge*? That's— And you're sure she's not my daughter? The Jane Doe?'

'Yes ma'am. No resemblance. Similar age. Perhaps a friend of hers?'

'Okay. All right. Okay...'

A few moments of crackling silence.

'Ma'am?'

'Yes. Sorry. I'm here. This is a lot to take in. If I book a flight to Norge, can I see the girl when she wakes? I'd very much like to speak with her.'

ACKNOWLEDGEMENTS

Overcoming my fear of finishing things has always been a challenge, and in this case I couldn't have done it without the editorial and emotional support of my friend Tallulah Lucy. The book would have been a lot less coherent without her help, but more than that – it wouldn't have existed at all. Tallulah, thank you.

Thank you also to the wonderful writers who gave me beta feedback on an earlier, even messier draft of this story – Xan van Rooyen, Masha du Toit, Cristy Zinn – to Cat Hellisen for giving it a much-needed line edit, to Nerine Dorman for the brilliant proofreading, to Kelly Waller for the eagle-eyed final readthrough, to Lindsay van Blerk for the beautiful cover illustration and to Namkwan Cho for the wonderful typeset and cover design. Your time and skills are so very much appreciated.

Finally, thank you to Luc for putting up with my bottomless self-doubt and always believing that I could finish something, to my parents for supporting me even in my most embarrassing moments, and to AJ, for putting everything into perspective.

ABOUT THE AUTHOR

Laurie Janey was born and raised in Cape Town, South Africa, where she completed an MA in Creative Writing at UCT before moving to London to pursue a career in publishing. After working as an editor of non-fiction, she went freelance as a proofreader (casually writing and illustrating on the side) and never looked back. She lives in South West London with her husband Luc and baby AJ.

You can find out more about Laurie and sign up for her occasional newsletter at www.lauriejaney.com

Printed in Great Britain
by Amazon